Rosa Nouchette Carey

Mary

A Novel

Rosa Nouchette Carey

Mary
A Novel

ISBN/EAN: 9783337002138

Printed in Europe, USA, Canada, Australia, Japan

Cover: Foto ©Andreas Hilbeck / pixelio.de

More available books at **www.hansebooks.com**

MARY ST. JOHN .

A Novel

BY

ROSA NOUCHETTE CAREY

AUTHOR OF 'NELLIE'S MEMORIES,' 'WOOED AND MARRIED,' 'QUEENIE'S WHIM,'
ETC.

A NEW EDITION

LONDON
RICHARD BENTLEY & SON, NEW BURLINGTON ST.
Publishers in Ordinary to Her Majesty the Queen
1892

CONTENTS

CONTENTS

CONTENTS

CONTENTS

MARY ST. JOHN

CHAPTER I

DOLLIE'S BIRTHDAY

ALL her life long Dorothy Maynard remembered a certain bright windy day in September.

She was crossing Kensington Gardens; it was late in the afternoon, just verging upon evening; a certain blush and redness seemed over everything, a golden ripple and stir made up of sparkles, of the distant gleam of water, of waving tree-tops, and the sunshine playing with golden splashes on innumerable leaves.

She had been walking vaguely in a green mist; by and by the quiet and the shade and the flicker were all behind her; she had tripped across the road, under the shadow of the great bronze and marble monument, into a Babel and confusion of life.

What a busy world it was! how bright! how well dressed! True, the great London flow of fashion had long ago ebbed away; the great ones of the earth—the upper ten thousand had betaken themselves to other regions,—to Scotland and the Continent, or to seclusion in princely country-seats.

The houses wore a desolate and dismantled look; yet still the carriages rolled on; a fresh wind blew down Exhibition Road; the dust whirled under the horses' feet; there were plenty of children and sunshine,—for neither are ever wanting on God's earth; and a certain sweet wholesomeness of fresh air and open spaces.

Dollie went briskly on, walking with erect head and clear girlish eyes that saw everything; more than one person turned round to look at the slim figure in the gray gown and the broad-brimmed hat,—a certain lightness and grace of carriage allured them, but no special beauty tempted them to look again. It was one of Dorothy's quaint fancies to speak of herself as plain—as undeniably and unredeemably so. Probably she half believed what she said; and, indeed, the small glass that hung in her bedroom made sad havoc of her youthful charms.

Many months afterwards she saw herself reflected full length in a gorgeous mirror; she was tripping downstairs, humming a little tune and thinking of nothing, when all at once she paused a little bewildered. At an angle of the staircase she came upon a girl—a slim creature in a green gown, with puckered sleeves, with some red and yellow dahlias in her hand—a girl with soft yellow hair and a pale face; it was quite half a minute before Dollie recognised her own high cheek-bones and rather small blue eyes. When she did so she dropped a low mocking curtsey to her image.

'You are not so bad after all, Mistress Dollie,' she said, with a knowing little nod of the head; 'no one in their senses could call you pretty, but you are decidedly uncommon-looking; the old glass in Abercrombie Road made you a positive fright, but you are not the scarecrow I thought you.' And Dollie gathered up her long dress, dropping one of her dahlias as she did so. It was worn as a trophy in a certain button-hole all the evening, to Dollie's secret discomposure.

She was carrying a few late roses now,—for flowers were as dear to her soul as jewels are to some high-born beauties,—and every now and then she touched them lightly and caressingly with her little gloved hand. A fellow-student at the School of Art had given them to her, and the roses and the sunshine, and the freshness of the September wind had excited her spirits to more than their usual buoyancy.

'I am sure something is going to happen,' she said to herself; for, in common with most girls, she loved dearly to indulge in a daydream. 'I am eighteen to-day. One cannot go to sleep all one's life, or go dreaming on like a stagnant old mill-stream. Look at all those faces, and every one with their own story. I have not begun to live mine yet, and never shall as long as we live in that stupid out-of-the-way place,—just mother and I and no one else.' And Dorothy's sunny mood changed, and she gave a little shrug of discontent as she hastened on.

She had left South Kensington with its great squares and houses behind her, and was now threading the labyrinth of roads that lie between Kensington and Earlscourt. By and by the traffic ceased; she had turned aside out of the main thoroughfare, and was making her way swiftly down a dull secluded-looking road, suburban in aspect, and somewhat meagre as to gentility.

A road that had no individuality of its own, and seemed to lead vaguely to nowhere, which bore a general aspect of sameness, a little tempered and toned down by age. The houses were not modern; one could say so much for them —they had too much old-fashioned primness for that.

Some of them had seen better days; a few of them had tried the embellishments of a coat of paint, or a Virginian creeper; some had narrow little bay-windows and green verandahs. On the whole, they were meek, unpretending houses, befitting the meek, unpretending lives that were lived in them, 'not one of them with a story worth reading,' as Dorothy thought scornfully; for she had what is common among young people—a certain haughty intolerance of her belongings, and could be hardly made to understand that her neighbours were of the same flesh and blood as herself.

'Trevilian Terrace, Abercrombie Road,—who with a grain of sense or an ounce of imagination would consent to drag out existence in such a place?' grumbled Dorothy to herself for the nineteen-hundredth time, as she pushed open a green gate, and a moment afterwards found herself in a dark, narrow little hall.

But, as though by way of contrast, the dark little lobby opened on a small room full of evening sunshine—a room so green and bowery, with its one window so framed with Virginian creeper and the gray-blue clusters of the Wisteria, that the very canaries singing so lustily in their gilded cage could have imagined themselves back in their native woods. And sitting working busily in the midst of the sunlight was a quiet little woman in black, who raised her head and said, 'Well, Dollie,' in a voice that was very quiet and pleasant.

Dorothy and her mother were not much alike. Mrs. Maynard was a little woman, with a trim, rather youthful, figure, and reddish hair still untinged with gray.

The brown eyes had a clear, gentle look in them; but the lines of the face were sharp and somewhat worn, and a certain droop of the head and figure gave a stamp of unconscious weariness that was slightly pathetic.

'Well, Dollie, my dear,' she said again, as she folded up her work with a nervous haste that was at times habitual to her. Dollie had merely nodded in a brisk, off-hand manner, and had thrown herself into a low basket-work chair. In a moment the broad-brimmed hat and the gray cape were on the floor beside her; the roses were falling on her lap one by one.

Mrs. Maynard carried them away, while Dollie stretched her lazy arms over her head, with a sort of unfledged grace and weariness. She was too much used to her mother's waiting upon her to notice it; she knew the cape would be folded and the long gloves smoothed out, without any exertion of her own. What was the use of mothers if they were not to wait on 'Dollies,' and when Dollie was the widow's mite too—the one small treasure that remained to her out of the waste and loss of her life.

So Dollie lay with her fair head buried in the green cushions, and the canaries sang, and Mrs. Maynard quietly arranged the roses. The trim little maid brought in tea, wheeling the round table quite close to Dollie into the sunlight, and then her tongue suddenly unloosed as Mrs. Maynard knew it would, and her girlish talk quite rippled and overflowed, like a little brook when its toy dam had been destroyed.

And how Dollie could talk! and about such trifles too! Few girls, coming in from a day's work or a country walk, could find such fruitful matter for conversation, and serve it up smilingly at the family meal, as Dollie could day after day.

She talked so picturesquely, too, of the flowers and the sunshine; of the crowds in Exhibition Road; of the crippled boy in his wheeled chair, under the trees in Kensington Gardens; of the one-legged crossing-sweeper, who always said, 'Bless your sweet face, my lady,' which brought him in a harvest of Dollie's pennies; of her work at the School of Art, with all sorts of little quizzing remarks on her companions; and whatever she said, however trivial and foolish, Dollie knew her voice was like music to her mother's ears.

'You are very happy, my dear, to-night,' with a little sigh.

'Happy—well, yes, I suppose so,' returned Dollie nonchalantly; 'it is no good being miserable because it is one's birthday. I did think as I walked along that it would be nice to be like other girls, and have quantities of presents and nice dresses, and to go out to balls; we live in such a sober, middle-aged fashion, seeing no one but the curate and the doctor and a few old ladies. For my part,' continued Dollie, with charming frankness, 'I am sick of old ladies; and old gentlemen are almost as bad— not quite, perhaps, because they say nice things, which the old ladies certainly do not say.'

'Do you hate Mrs. Trelawney, Dollie?'

'Old Mrs. Trelawney! she is an old dear, and I love her; she is a jewel among the old ladies. When I meet her waddling down the road, with her fat spaniel behind her, I think she is a perfect angel,—only angels are not short in their breathing, but I am pretty sure she is as good as gold.'

'Miss Lamartine is as good as gold too.'

Dollie pursed up her lips, and shook her head vehemently.

'Ah, but she is; just look at her devotion to her bedridden father!'

'That may be, but she is an old maid; and one cannot have anything in common with old maids.'

'For shame, Dollie! you may be one yourself some day.'

'What! an old maid? a hundred years hence, perhaps; but of course,' a little discontentedly, 'I cannot expect anything else, living in a place like this. Do you think any one could marry old Mr. Frier, or that sandy-haired, washed-out Mr. O'Brien?—an Evangelical Irishman, too.'

'Then if your fate is to be like hers, you ought not to say such hard things of Miss Lamartine.'

'What hard things?' and Dollie opened her eyes. 'I only said she was an old maid! poor misguided woman! why does she not turn up her thin hair, and wear a cap and a plain black gown, and make herself look well dressed and comfortable? When I am an old maid I mean to take to caps; and I shall not expect young girls to come and make a fuss over me; I shall visit at the children's hospital—the poor little things will be glad enough to see me; and I will have birds—dozens of them; not the typical cat—not even a tabby kitten; and I will pick out a few nice old gentlemen of my acquaintance—no snuff-taker available—who will come and talk politics to me once or twice a week.'

'My dear,' remonstrated her mother, 'are you not talking a little wildly?'

'Wildly? well, perhaps I am, but did you not begin the subject, madre mia? and when you know I detest Miss Lamartine. Oh dear, this restlessness! I wonder if it be very wicked, or if it be only natural to have one's nature working up like yeast, and to be always fermenting with a sort of inward excitement; if only something would happen; but nothing ever does happen.'

'Do not be too sure of anything in this world, my dear;' and Mrs. Maynard's lip trembled a little. 'It is my Dollie's birthday, just the day for a pleasant surprise; and then one ought never to be too sure of anything.'

Dollie's blue eyes were opened wide enough now. 'Do you mean that you have a pleasant surprise for me, mother?' and then she laughed a little scornfully over her own words; for her quiet, protected life held no mysteries in it, and she was somewhat incredulous of change. Changes were good; they were better than most things in life, but none would ever come to her.

'That is for you to decide,' returned her mother quietly. 'Here is a letter that I have lately received, and on which I must ask your opinion; whether it be pleasant or not you must own that at least it is a surprise. You remember that I have spoken to you before of my aunt, Mrs. Reid?'

Dollie nodded assent; her curiosity was too impatient to allow of any pause for answer; her hands quite trembled with excitement as they unfolded the thin foreign paper.

Of course she knew all about Mrs. Reid; there were no secrets, no possible mysteries between her mother and her. Dollie knew all about her mother's former life, and had often contrasted it somewhat discontentedly with her own.

Mrs. Maynard had been the only child of wealthy parents; all sorts of wonderful things had happened to her in her girlhood; its record read like a glittering fairy story to our Dollie, a sort of impromptu Arabian Nights Entertainment; she had gone with her parents everywhere—to Venice, to Rome, and once to Constantinople; the villa on Lake Maggiore, the Châlet at Lucerne, the woodman's hut in the Black Forest, where the belated travellers had remained for a night, were as well known to her as Cinderella's Glass Slipper or the Castle of Bluebeard were to other children.

Another person had formed part of the household in those days, — a fair-haired girl, her father's only sister, whom Mrs. Maynard called Aunt Isabel. She had drawn certain sketches of her that were very alluring in Dollie's eyes. She would think with pleasure of the bright young aunt who told stories and sang wonderful old ballads, who came dancing into the nursery in the summer twilight to show her pretty ball-dresses and trinkets to the wondering child.

Then had come a change; a certain shadow had fallen on the house; there had been disagreements—loud, angry voices that seemed to sound everywhere—Aunt Isabel had gone away weeping, saying that she was ill-used by her only brother, and would never forgive him. By and by they told the child that Aunt Isabel would never come back. She had married a very rich man—a certain Mr. Reid, whom nobody liked or respected; and after that they said no more. And so the thread of her mother's story ran on; to the petted childhood succeeded a happier girlhood, and while still very young she had been wooed and won by Richard Maynard, a young officer in the 4th Dragoons. All had gone smoothly at first; he had nothing but his pay, but Mrs. Maynard's parents were rich. But before the brief honeymoon was over the first blow fell. Her father's property was invested mostly in mining shares; these were found to be insecure; the vein of iron-ore had suddenly ceased to yield; in the general panic that ensued it was found that the shareholders were liable for immense sums, and when Margaret Maynard returned home it was to find that her father was virtually ruined.

Even this could have been borne if it had not led to separation from his only child. It had been Mr. Tilney's intention to assist his son-in-law to exchange into a regiment that was not likely to see active service; it was with this proviso that he had given him his daughter. All this was now altered. Captain Maynard's regiment was at once ordered to Southampton, *en route* for India, and poor Margaret had to take leave of her broken-hearted parents, and follow her young husband across the seas.

True, she loved him with her whole heart and soul, but she was scarcely more than a girl; and this sundering of all her home ties was a very bitter ordeal. But, alas! this was only the beginning of troubles.

Sad indeed was the record of those Indian summers; every year seemed to bring her new trials and losses. First the news of her parents' death—one after another—followed her. Then came still heavier troubles : two boys and one girl had been born to them beside Dollie, but one by one they had been snatched away, and before many years were over Major Maynard had succumbed to jungle fever on one of his toilsome marches; and the broken-hearted widow, clasping her little daughter to her bosom, fled panic-stricken from the land of graves, as she always called it, and came back to England sad and solitary, to begin life over again—this time not for her own but for Dollie's sake.

And so the years passed on, and but for her child her life would have been absolutely joyless. She had been a woman much given to idolatry — to that interior and engrossing idolatry which lies at the heart of some women. It was not that she was without the consolations of religion, but that the living objects of her love engrossed her so completely.

While her husband lived, her children had been less to her—not that they had not been dear to her, for she was of all mothers most tender and full of care ; but her husband had been the lord and master of her life, the possessor of her very inmost and secret soul, from whom she had no reservation and hardly a separate thought.

When he died her heart had turned to stone. She told herself that no woman was ever more completely widowed than she, that henceforth no joy of life was possible to her.

But Dollie had altered this ; the child became first an interest, then an occupation, and presently an absorbing passion ; the old habit of worship and idolatry revived. She ceased to look so mournfully at the wrecks of her former life ; she must smile and try to forget sometimes for Dollie's sake ; she must not blight her youth with sadness. And so for her child's sake Mrs. Maynard lived down her great sorrow, and a certain golden haze — closely approximate to sunshine — stole into her sorely-tried life.

CHAPTER II

THE BUDGET OPENED

MRS. MAYNARD looked at her daughter rather sadly, as Dollie, with flushed face and trembling fingers, read the letter. How long and closely written it seemed to be! Had it fallen from the stars she could hardly have been more surprised. Could anything really be about to happen?

'My dear Margaret,' it began; and that in itself was a marvel to Dollie, who had never heard her mother called by her Christian name—

MY DEAR MARGARET—I wonder if you have any recollection of the Aunt Isabel who used to play with you in the old nursery in Portman Square? or whether I shall have to recall myself to your memory? You were such a little creature then, and I only a grown-up, wayward child.

I will say nothing of the circumstances that led to such complete separation; girls are sometimes self-willed, and it may be that I was in the wrong. But if your mother had been more judicious and less intolerant in her judgment, she might have healed instead of widening the breach that caused me to throw off my brother's protection and leave his house.

Ah well! I was with them when they died, and all was understood between us then; but I never knew why it was that when the news of their death reached you, my letters were not sent with it. I think, had our correspondence commenced then, that we should never have lost sight so completely of one another.

From that day to this I have never succeeded in tracing you to your present address. The merest chance—a casual encounter with an old neighbour of yours—has led to the discovery of your whereabouts. True, I read the announcement of your husband's death in the papers, but I could gain no intelligence of your movements, until

I learned quite recently that you were living with your daughter in a secluded part of Kensington.

You would doubtless have heard of me, but since my husband's death I have quitted Crome Park,—the property Mr. Reid bought soon after our marriage,—and have lived abroad. My bad health, and other circumstances with which I will not trouble you, has led me to adopt a wandering life. Many people have attributed my avoidance of my native country to pure caprice, and I am loath to disturb the conjecture. The opinions of the world—my world—have long been nought to me. Two years ago my health improved, and I grew weary of travelling and of foreign watering-places, and as an old chateau in the neighbourhood of Lesponts took my fancy, I purchased it, and settled down with a distant connection of my husband, Charlotte Morell, who acts as my companion.

Some of my husband's relatives have visited me from time to time ; one of these—Mary St. John—has promised to pay me a long visit this autumn.

I am telling you all this that you may know how I am circumstanced—a lonely woman growing old, and indebted for stray visits of charity to distant connections.

And now to the point and gist of my long letter. Can you, my dear and unknown niece, be induced to leave your quiet English home and visit me in my Flemish chateau ? You shall not be parted from your daughter ; bring her with you, and she will be a companion to Mary St. John.

I could plead many arguments in my favour, but I will say no more until I hear your views on the matter, and will only subscribe myself your long-lost aunt,   ISABEL REID.

'Mother!' broke from Dollie's impetuous lips as she laid down the letter—two bright spots of colour were in her cheeks; her eyes shone with eagerness; 'mother! how shall you answer this letter?'

'I have answered it,' returned the widow gently. 'Forgive me, my dear,' as an incredulous exclamation burst from her daughter; 'forgive me if I kept this matter to myself for some days; it troubled me greatly, and I could not talk about it—not even to my child. When I had made up my mind I wrote a long letter to Mrs. Reid.'

'You answered it, and never told me one word about it!' and the tones of Dollie's voice, injured and a little shrill, brought a flush to the mother's face. For a moment she felt like a culprit before her child. Never since her

Dollie had emerged from childhood had that simple heart kept anything to itself.

'Hush, my dear! Indeed you must listen to me a moment. I thought it better to keep my own counsel in this. You could not help me. For this once I knew we must be content to differ.'

'To differ, mother! What do you mean?'

'Does the word displease you? Indeed, it is a true word. How could you put yourself in my place—a young thing like you, with all life before you?' and then she paused. How could she bring herself to tell her child that the change—that Dollie was already anticipating with such joyful eagerness—was absolutely impossible to her; that she had so grown into the narrowed grooves of her present quiet life that any emergence from thence was like death to her; that to sit beside a strange hearth and fit her words and purposes to the will of others, would be so galling to her crushed spirit, that she could not bring herself to undergo it? As she had lain awake pondering over the matter during more than one sleepless night, she had told herself bitterly that no shadowy ghost revisiting the haunts of men would feel more absolutely unfit for human duties and the usages of society than she would feel if she stirred out of the niche into which she had almost grown. And yet if she said such things to her child, would Dollie understand her—Dollie, whose pulses were already beating high with excitement, while her own were so faint and sluggish?

'If I were to talk until midnight you would not comprehend me,' she said, with a quiet hopelessness which came with a sort of shock to Dollie. 'You are young, and I am getting old—old, and tired, and weak—and I cannot bring myself to do things now. You cannot understand me, and that is all I have to say—that I am tired, and cannot do things any longer.'

'Mother, why will you make me so unhappy by talking so? You are not old. You have not a gray hair—not a single one. You are as young and sweet and pretty as ever.' And Dollie was now on her knees caressing the widow's thin hands, and laying them against her warm young face. 'You shall not talk against yourself to me; my mother will never be old.'

'Have you a charm against time, Dollie?' she asked, with a faint smile; but her voice was very sad. 'No, my dear, no; you are young, and these things are possible to you. I wish I could have done it for your sake; but I am obliged to confess that it would be too hard for me. Do not let us talk about it any more. You shall read what my answer was in Mrs. Reid's second letter.' And then Dollie read it.

I have been ill again, my dear Margaret (it began), and I fear that in consequence my letter must be brief. I shall not attempt to shake your resolution—greatly as it has disappointed me—or to persuade you that such change as I would offer you might do you good. Your letter speaks for itself, and I am too well acquainted with trouble to be surprised at what you tell me. I mean to be very patient, and to let you get used to the idea; and perhaps next spring, if I be living then, you may feel more equal to the exertion. No, I will not seek to persuade you—not yet. I will even praise you, and tell you how good it is of you to spare your child to me for a little. Indeed, my dear Margaret, I will do all in my power to make her visit pleasant to her. I have told you that Miss St. John is coming to me next month. I have not yet made her acquaintance, but from all accounts I think she must be charming. If so she will be a nice companion for Dorothy. Last year her brother Maurice paid me a visit. He is a truly excellent man, but in some respects I thought him weak. Our Church views differed, and on the whole, we scarcely agreed. Unfortunately I took the strongest aversion to his wife. She struck me as ambitious and designing. I am rather prone to strong likes and dislikes; and I have never asked them to repeat their visit.

I trust Miss St. John will be more to my taste. They are my husband's nearest connections, and I am anxious to do my duty by them. But I must break off here now, as a recurrence of my old pain is numbing my fingers. I will write again in a day or two and let you know all particulars.

And then somewhat abruptly the letter ended.

'Is that all, mother?'

'No; I had another note this morning. You will see from that how generous and thoughtful my aunt seems to be for your comfort. Well,' as Dollie let it fall on her mother's lap with a little gesture of astonishment, 'will not these arrangements please you?'

'Please me! I suppose so. But I am so bewildered that you should have settled all this with a stranger, and never even told me!' And indeed there was much room for bewilderment in the girl's mind.

Mrs. Reid's third letter was very business-like and a little peremptory. She informed her niece somewhat curtly that she intended to provide for the girl's journey, and enclosed a ten-pound note for any incidental expenses. She excused herself for choosing a somewhat circuitous route for the traveller, but without giving any reason for such choice; but added that all necessary arrangements had been made, and everything settled with the St. Johns; and that she wished Mrs. Maynard to make their acquaintance without delay, and introduce the girls to each other. The date fixed for the visit was surprisingly near, and the letter ended with a renewed assurance that Dorothy should be made heartily welcome by herself and Charlotte Morell. It was a kind letter in spite of its peremptoriness; but Dorothy felt a little afraid of the writer, and though her cheeks still glowed with excitement, she looked a little thoughtful.

'Well, Dollie, my dear,' said her mother, with an evident effort at cheerfulness, 'are you not going to praise me too? Do you not think I am good to spare you?'

'Do you mean that I am to go and leave you alone?' asked the girl slowly.

'Yes, dear; that is exactly what I do mean. I cannot go myself, but I must not bind my child down to my quiet life. It is not good for you. It is not right. Young things like you need change and movement. My Dollie must not be unlike other girls. She must see the world.'

'But to leave you all alone! No, mother darling, it is not possible.'

'It will only be for two months,' pleaded Mrs. Maynard. 'Mrs. Reid does not ask you for longer. You will write to me. And I shall be very busy; and I shall be looking forward to your return, and to all the news you will bring me. Think of all the advantages such a change offers.

And then I cannot help feeling as though we owe some little duty to Mrs. Reid.'

'Do you really mean what you say, mother—that you wish me to go?'

'Yes, indeed, my child, I really wish it;' and Mrs. Maynard's voice, though it trembled a little, still preserved its cheerfulness. Had she not nerved herself to the sacrifice? Had she not vowed to herself with many tears that. Dollie should never know what this first parting with her treasure would cost her—her child who had never been absent from her for a single night? No wonder the prospect of those two months was strangely dreary to the poor mother. 'For your sake,' she continued more firmly, 'I do indeed wish it; and I think—I cannot help thinking—that Mrs. Reid has some sort of claim upon us.'

'If it were a duty, and if it were not for leaving you—oh, mother, how delicious it would be,' exclaimed the girl with a little burst, 'to see strange cities and strange things. Not to get up every morning, and do just the same things all day long—trudge up and down Exhibition Road in the dust and sunshine, and come home and see Susan and the tea-things——'

'And me,' put in her mother softly, which interruption made Dollie suddenly fall on her neck, with many protestations and kisses.

'Then it is settled, and to-morrow we will go and introduce ourselves to the St. Johns. And now, if you will call Susan, we will have prayers, and go to bed. No, indeed, Dollie; it is growing late, and I will not talk about it any more to-night.' And somewhat awed by this unusual firmness on the part of that tender mother, Dollie reluctantly submitted to silence.

CHAPTER III

It was somewhat late in the afternoon of the following day when Mrs. Maynard and her daughter set out to pay their intended visit to the St. Johns.

Dorothy, for the first time in her life, was almost dumb with astonishment at her mother's unwonted activity and decision of manner; the little nervous flurry that character-ised the widow's usual movements was for once laid aside. 'To-morrow we will go and call on the St. Johns,' she had said, in a quiet, business-like way, as though calling on strangers was a thing habitual to her; and yet Dollie knew that her mother had a morbid dread of new acquaintances.

They seemed to have changed characters all of a sudden. Dollie seemed a little shy of the whole business, and had turned decidedly prim. In the first place the address dis-pleased her—The Rev. Maurice St. John, 23 Lime Street, Whitechapel. Her girlish pride took alarm immediately.

'Who ever heard of such a place?' she grumbled. 'Mother, how can they be gentlefolks, and live in such a dreadful neighbourhood?' And Dollie drew her dainty raiment more closely round her, as they threaded their way somewhat dubiously through the hot, unsavoury streets.

'The clergy cannot always choose very desirable resi-dences,' returned Mrs. Maynard quietly; 'and the vicar told me yesterday that he knew Mr. St. John slightly, that he was a young, hard-working man, who had applied many years ago for a curacy at the East End, because he had an enthusiasm for mission work. Unfortunately he fell in

love, and married on rather a small income; and from
what Mr. Roberts told me, I fancy he is a little overworked, and that he ought to exchange his work for a
country curacy, for the sake of his wife and family.'

'Poor creatures!' observed Dollie pathetically; and
now indeed Trevilian Terrace, Abercrombie Road, blossomed in her memory as a sort of earthly paradise, as she
glanced round her at the slipshod squalor and dirt that
seemed to encompass their footsteps.

They had left the main road, with its butcher's shops
and noise, and rough-voiced crowd, behind them, and were
now in a quieter neighbourhood. The houses were tall
and shabby; smartly-dressed Jewesses—for it was Saturday
—congregated in small groups round some of the open
windows; black-eyed children, with unwashed faces, and
bright bead necklaces showed their marked physiognomy
at every corner; ragged, barefooted children played in the
gutter; miserable women, with thin-faced babies, glided in
and out the courts and alleys; oaths, dirt, and the shrill
voices of children were everywhere. No wonder Dollie
shrank closer to her mother with a little gesture of disgust.

'Madre! it is impossible; no lady could live here.'

'Not in this street; but, my dear, just think what I
have just told you—an enthusiastic man full of love for his
kind, and needing work. Look around you; do you see
no scope for mission work here?'

'I know I should like to wash those children's faces,
and give them something to eat. Are there two worlds I
wonder—one in Kensington and one in Whitechapel?
Why must some people be always cold and hungry? there
seems to me so little justice in this sort of thing!' broke
in the young heretic, for the Dollies of this world would
have everything bright and sunshiny.

'I am afraid these things are too high for our compre-
hension,' returned her mother with a sigh. 'As long as
the world lasts there will be pain; we must take life as it
is, not as it looks to us. Wherever one walks there are
always patches and bare feet shining in the sunlight. Perhaps these contrasts are to teach us something.' But

Dollie turned away rather impatiently from this gentle
moralising.

'Yes, yes, that is all very well; but one wants to know
the meaning of things; why those poor babies are born,
when there is no room for them; why they live to grow up
to find their happiness in the gutters, to wear rags, to
thieve, perhaps to do worse. Mother,' continued the girl
solemnly and yet with a little excitement, 'look at that
poor, weazen-faced baby that tawdry-looking woman is
carrying; who knows, if it lives, that it may not grow up
to be a housebreaker or a murderer, and yet it looks as
innocent as an angel now.'

'A terrible thought, Dollie; but it strikes me we are
getting a little out of our depth; women feel too much ever
to become good philosophers. Look what a quiet, respectable street we are entering; there is the sugar bakery at the
corner; from the description Mr. Roberts gave me, I am
sure it must be Lime Street; some of the houses look quite
trim and comfortable.'

'We have not yet got rid of the Jewesses,' returned
Dollie in a quizzing voice.

'No, but they seem of a better sort; we passed some
lovely faces just now. In this sort of neighbourhood I
fancy one must be thankful for small mercies; for clean
pavements and washed doorsteps, and bright knockers, for
example. Yes, this is twenty-three, and really the house
looks large and comfortable.' But Dollie, who was put out
with her walk, only gave one of her dissenting shrugs; not
even the clean steps and the bright windows and the
glories of a brass knocker could elicit the faintest commendation.

'If there is one thing I detest more than another, it is
a shabby-genteel house,' she said a little sulkily, before the
door was opened.

Mrs. St. John was at home, and would be with them
directly, but Miss St. John was at the schools, was the
answer to their inquiries in unmistakable brogue. But as
Biddy was clean and good-tempered-looking, Mrs. Maynard
found nothing amiss in the coarse bib-apron; only Dollie

. groaned in spirit as she muttered, 'Maid of all work!' to herself, and followed her mother reluctantly upstairs.

They passed the open doors of two light, airy-looking rooms, in one of which some children were at play; the room they entered was evidently the drawing-room, or at least the best room of the family.

It was a pleasant, old-fashioned room, with brown wainscotted walls, and three narrow windows, with wooden window-seats. On one of them a girl was sitting, or rather crouching in a heap, reading. A bird sang in the sunshine; some flowers in a green stand bloomed gaily; in spite of the worn carpet, almost denuded of its pattern, and the faded, washed-out chintz, there was a homely air of comfort that attracted them. Evidently Mrs. St. John was a good manager.

'My dear, are you one of Mrs. St. John's children?' asked Mrs. Maynard, advancing with a kind smile to the window-seat. The girl uncurled herself somewhat awkwardly, and looked at the intruders with frightened eyes.

'Yes, I am the eldest—Lettice. I hope Biddy has told mamma. I—I will go for her,' becoming conscious all at once of her shabby frock and rough hair, as she caught sight of Dollie's fresh and trim appearance.

'No, do not trouble yourself; your mother will be here directly, and we are in no hurry. How old are you, and what is that book you are reading?' and Dollie, who had recovered from her brief ill-humour, and was determined to make herself agreeable, smiled at her in such a fascinating manner that Lettice was quite dazzled.

'I am thirteen, at least nearly thirteen, and I am reading father's *Paradise Lost*. I don't think Satan ought to be quite so interesting, do you?' looking up in Dollie's face with large dark eyes, full of intelligence. But Dollie, who was much bewildered by this unexpected question, was spared all answer, for a voice said somewhat sharply, 'Hush, Lettice,' and turning round, they saw that Mrs. St. John had entered the room.

Dollie afterwards confessed to her mother that the first sight of Mrs. St. John almost took away her breath. An

exotic in a garret would not have been a greater contrast
than this grand-looking woman, set off so strangely and
yet so intensely by the shabby background and homely
accessories round her.

'An Esther, or a Judith in a nineteenth-century print
dress all the worse for washing,' as Dollie quaintly
described her afterwards, and somehow the simile was not
inapt.

For, in Dollie's opinion, there was something suppressed
and tragic in Mrs. St. John's appearance, although to most
people she would only have seemed a grave handsome-
looking woman of rather an unusual type of beauty.

She was very tall; but she carried her height with a grace
that was simply perfect, and the pose of the head and neck
was magnificent. Mrs. Maynard thought her proud and a
little chilling; but to Dollie the pale face and dark eyes
were full of unspoken eloquence. And then her voice,—
in spite of its sharp thinness,—how it seemed to change
and vibrate and soften! Very few voices, Dollie thought,
held so much in them. She was quite angry when Mrs.
Maynard called her a little abrupt.

'We have been looking for you all the afternoon, Mary
and I; and now Mary has gone out with my husband.
They are at the schools,' explained Mrs. St. John in her
harsh, vibrating voice, which, nevertheless, held such
musical chords to Dollie's ear; 'they will not be long, and
you shall have some tea; and when you are rested they
will be back, and Mary and your daughter can have their
chat,' she went on with a perfectly well-bred suavity which
rather extinguished poor Mrs. Maynard. If Mrs. St. John
were a duchess she could not be more urbane and con-
descending.

'I ought to say a word about our intrusion first,' began
Mrs. Maynard mildly; but the younger woman interrupted
her at once.

'Pray, do not mention such a word. Mrs. Reid's
introduction is sufficient. We have been expecting you,
but Mary's conscience would not be satisfied, and she was
full of excuses. My sister-in-law is one of those painfully

conscientious people who pile up duties until molehills become mountains; she is my husband's right hand in the parish; she has quite taken my place, for when one has a house full of children, outside business must be curtailed.'

'Have you—are there many children?' asked Dollie rather shyly, for she saw her mother was somewhat suppressed by Mrs. St. John's serene flow of words.

'Yes, we have five girls,' and here there was an unmistakable sigh; 'five little girls—rather unfortunate for a poor curate who has to make his way in the world.' But though Mrs. St. John affected a light smile as she spoke, her visitor's practised ear caught the weary dissatisfied tone.

And being a woman of keen penetration she noticed something else, that as her mother spoke, an expression of pain crossed Lettice's face, as though the words troubled her. She looked up eagerly, as though she would say something, and then thought better of it, and buried herself in her book again. Her awkward stoop attracted Mrs. St. John's sharp eyes.

'You have your book in your lap again, Lettice; there, put it down, and tell Biddy to bring us some tea, and then stay with the children and amuse them. No, leave the book with me for the present,' as the child hesitated. 'She is such a bookworm that we are obliged to watch her closely, or her whole time would be spent in reading,' she observed apologetically, as Lettice withdrew looking abashed and uncomfortable.

'I am sure she is very clever,' returned Mrs. Maynard, whose maternal heart yearned over all children. She was somewhat attracted by the child's appearance; it was strange that the mother and daughter should be such contrasts. Lettice was certainly very awkward and uncouth-looking; the long legs had outgrown the shabby frock; but the thin, pale face—though it was very plain—was redeemed from positive ugliness by the bright intelligence of expression. 'She looks clever, and good too,' she continued hesitatingly.

'Yes, Lettice is a good girl,' returned Mrs. St. John, somewhat carelessly; 'she needs to be clever, for she has no beauty, poor thing!' and Mrs. Maynard perceived that poor Lettice's want of attractiveness was very galling to the mother.

'It is an awkward age. I recollect when Dollie was all legs and arms,' she observed, smiling.

'I do not think your daughter could ever have been awkward,' returned Mrs. St. John, looking at Dollie with momentary interest. 'Lettice has more angularity than most children of her age, and then she grows so fast! She resembles her father in face; none of my children take after me but little Bee the youngest. They are all tall and thin. But I should like you to see Bee;' and her manner became more animated. 'But here is your tea, and I hear my husband and Mary coming in.' And the next moment Mr. St. John and his sister entered the room.

No two people could have been less alike; it was difficult to imagine that they were brother and sister. If the children took after their father, no wonder poor Mrs. St. John had reason to sigh over their want of beauty.

Mr. St. John was a plain—a very plain man. He was very tall, and his thinness made him appear more so; and his gait was awkward, degenerating into a sort of stoop, perhaps with weakness. He had a pale, long face like Lettice's, and his nose was large and somewhat too prominent, and his fair hair and the poorness of his colouring gave him a sickly, washed-out look. Nevertheless his voice was pleasant, and when he spoke his ugliness became a thing of no moment.

His sister was darker and stouter, and had a healthy sunburnt look. She was not without some comeliness; but though she had beautiful gray eyes, she was short-sighted like her brother, and carried eyeglasses. Dollie said afterwards to her mother: 'Miss St. John is not at all handsome, and no one would dream of calling her pretty; but I never liked a face so much in my life; it is such a dear face!'

'Well, wife!' was Mr. St. John's first words, after he and his sister had exchanged cordial greetings with their visitors—greetings that somehow warmed and set them at their ease in a moment; 'where are Lettice and the children?' and his eyes moved anxiously round the room until they fell on the worn copy of Milton, and then they lit up well pleased: 'What! has my little Eve been at her stolen fruit again?'

'Lettice is with the children. You are so tired, Maurice, and so are our visitors,' pleaded his wife; but as she spoke a change seemed to pass over her; her voice and even her features softened as though by magic; hard, cold, and egotistical as Mrs. St. John might seem to others, she loved her husband dearly.

This love had been the ruin of her life and his, so she told herself in those morbid wild moods of hers; and yet if her life could have been given to her again she could not have done otherwise.

He was her fate, and she could not choose but love him; his goodness, his saintliness, his unselfishness—qualities all so opposed and contrasted to her own—had won her love. Had she ever been able to resist him? She had loved gaiety; she had been courted and caressed, and had planned great things for herself. The purple and fine linen of this world had been dear to her. It was in her ambitious self-seeking nature to sell herself to the highest bidder. To be rich, to have plenty of loaves and fishes, and to rejoice in unlimited influence over others; these were the secret desires of her heart, the planned purposes of her life. But Maurice came and wedded her to him and poverty, and she had been conquered yet rebellious ever since.

She could not choose but love him, but this love had cost them both dear. In her inmost thoughts she was never false to him; and yet there were times when she loathed her very life—when the yoke of her existence was so bitter to her that she could have stretched out her hands to her husband and prayed him to kill her rather than subject her to such misery.

For she loved the worker, but had no sympathy with the work.

And herein lay her grievance.

It was not enough that they were poor,—she knew that when she married him; it was not enough that she worked hard, rising early, and taking rest late, that he and his children might be well clothed and comfortable; but he was ever reproaching her in his loving way for her lack of interest in all that made up his life.

While Maurice loved his kind with a passionate love, that had led him, well educated and delicately nurtured as he was, to find scope for his wide energies in a neglected East-end parish, Janet merely tolerated her life. She was clever; she had good health; she had plenty of energy; if the work had pleased her she would have been his invaluable helpmate,—whatever she did was done better than by most people; but she set herself silently against the work; in her inmost soul she hated it; it was not worthy of her husband; it was ignoble drudgery,—nay more, it was killing him.

The dirt, the squalor, the vice of their surroundings caused her positive agony. Was Maurice, with all his talents, his influence, his vast energy, to throw away his life and hers—nay more, his children's—in working among the wretched courts and alleys of an East-end parish; were those sermons, whose eloquence might have roused thousands, to be silenced by an envious superior, or else spoken to almost empty walls; was his precious health to be ruined by hours of ministration spent in noisome haunts, while she trembled and wept for his safety at home, and yet he would not listen to her?

'You do not sympathise with my work, and yet you love me, Janet,' he had said once to her very sadly, when he was more than usually weary and cast down, and for once the sight of her great beauty failed to gladden him. 'A wife should enter into all her husband's interests; is it not so, my dear?' drawing her closer to him as he spoke; for he was ever lover-like and fond in his ways.

'Mary is coming to live with us, and she will be able

to help you more,' she replied evasively, not drawing herself away, for such caresses were dear to her; but he remembered afterwards that she had failed to answer him fully, and her silence and want of response had saddened him still more.

And yet what could she have told him?—that she hated his work, and hated it chiefly for his sake; that it was her rival, defrauding her of his time and thoughts; that whereas her heart belonged solely to him and his children and Mary, his was shared with every Jew-baby who danced with glee in its mother's arms at the sight of him—women, children, animals, everything helpless and weak and suffering, seeming to find room and to spare in that great heart of his.

His very children threatened to become her rivals too. The poor little girls, whose sex was such a disappointment to Janet, who had ardently desired boys, were perfect joys and treasures of beauty in their father's eyes.

He had his way now, as she knew he would; for Maurice was pre-eminently master in his own house; and they came up presently—four tall lank children, with pale thin faces and fair hair like their father's. There they were scrambling over him with their shabby frocks and long legs—all but the youngest, little Bee, who sat dimpling and laughing, a perfect little rosebud of a child, on her mother's lap. They all, however, had sweet voices, which, in Mrs. Maynard's opinion, went far to reconcile her to their plainness, as she sat watching the family group with interest.

'There they all are, Mrs. Maynard,' announced Maurice proudly; 'my five fingers I call them—my little helpers and workers—Lettice and Hatty, Rosie, May, and Beatrice, whom we call Bee, our busy Bee, who gathers honey out of every flower, bless her dear little heart!' and he clapped his hands at the flushed, beautiful child.

Janet kissed her passionately. 'My beauty bright—mother's own dear beauty,' she whispered, as she picked out a dainty little cake for her darling.

May, who was second youngest, and who was an uninteresting-looking little girl with pale blue eyes, looked on enviously and seemed almost inclined to cry, until Bee benevolently invited her to the first bite.

'No, Baby, the cake is yours; May will have her tea presently,' interposed the mother jealously.

'No, no; let Bee share it with her sister,' remonstrated Maurice. 'That is right, my little love; another and another taste for poor May. Nothing is so sweet as when it is shared with others; remember that, children.' And, spurred on to unusual generosity by her father's praise, Bee shut her eyes tightly and gave her last mouthful to May.

'May I not give her another, Maurice?' whispered Janet, much touched by this magnanimity on the part of her darling.

'Certainly not. What, bribe virtue! offer a reward to benevolence! Come to me, Baby; father can tell you a pretty story that is nicer than all the cakes in existence;' and then he gathered his little daughter to him and covered her face and dimpled neck with kisses.

Mrs. Maynard's reserve and quietness quite expanded into friendliness before half an hour was over—Mrs. St. John she admired but disliked; Mr. St. John she could almost love.

Meanwhile the girls in a distant window-seat were making giant strides towards intimacy.

'I am sure we shall get on well together—it will not be my fault if we do not. I am determined to be particularly and persistently friendly. Your mother calls you Dollie; is your name Dorothy? What a pretty old-fashioned name! Do you know, I am very seldom Miss St. John, or even Mary, though my sister-in-law calls me so sometimes. Most people call me Aunt Mary—it——'

'Aunt Mary!'

'Yes; it began with the children of course. I am always Aunt Mary to them; and then Maurice fell into the habit, and afterwards Janet, and then other people took to it too. It has got into a sort of pet name at last.'

'I am sure you would never be Aunt Mary to me.'

'Wait and see; it will come quite naturally soon.   I do
not mean you to be Miss Maynard when we get abroad;
they will be all strangers there, and we must fraternise.'

'Will it not be delightful?' broke in Dollie rapturously;
'seeing all those strange places, I mean.'

'Indeed it will,' responded Miss St. John heartily.   'I
have been looking forward to my holiday with the greatest
pleasure, only I wish Maurice and Janet and the children
could come too.   Do you think my brother is looking very
thin?' she continued anxiously.   'I mean, does he strike
you as seeming very delicate?   Janet is always alarming
me with all sorts of dreadful suggestions; she says he is
overworked, losing flesh and appetite, and that the air of
these confined streets is killing him by inches.'

'Mr. St. John does not certainly look very robust; but
then you see I am not a good judge.'

'Strangers sometimes see things more clearly than
relatives,' returned Mary thoughtfully; 'and then one is
always so anxious over those one loves, and certainly
Maurice is not the man to spare himself.'

'Have you always lived here?' questioned Dollie a little
abruptly; she was less interested in discussing Mr. St. John's
health than in watching his sister; there was something so
bright and harmonious in her expression.

'No, I lived with the aunt who brought me up until she
died, about eighteen months ago; and then Maurice and
Janet invited me here.   It was such a lovely little village in
Dorsetshire where Aunt Emma lived, and her cottage was
such a quaint black-timbered little place, quite smothered
in roses!'

'What an awful change for you to come here!' ejaculated
Dollie, with a solemnity that made the other laugh.   'I
do not think I could exist for a month in such a place; it
must be so terribly trying always to have that sort of
spectacle before one's eyes,' pointing to a group of ragged
children playing before the house.   Miss St. John put up
her eyeglasses and inspected them.

'They are some of my scholars at the ragged schools;
yes, one does have one's heart wrung very often, one is so

sorry for the poor little creatures.   If you could only see some of the homes that Maurice and I visit ! '

' I should not like the work,' confessed Dollie honestly.

' No, I daresay not ; one must have a vocation for it. Maurice sometimes declares that I am cut out for a sister of charity, but I tell him he is wrong.   I have too great a horror of rule and routine.   I like my work to be stamped with my own individuality, and to do it in my own way.'

' And you can be happy here ! ' with a gesture of surprise and pity.

' Yes, I can be happy even in Whitechapel,' returned Miss St. John, much amused ; ' I think a good deal of work and a little love suffices for the lives of most women.   I miss my roses ; but then there are the children. and Maurice —and Janet too, of course,' with a little laugh over the omission ; but she said it with a change of tone that did not escape Dollie.

CHAPTER IV

IN THE SCHOOLROOM

'WHAT a charming family the St. Johns are!' were Dollie's first words when she found herself alone again with her mother; and, in spite of her habitual tendency to reserve her opinion of people Mrs. Maynard cordially endorsed her daughter's criticism.

The visit had been an entire success. Before they parted Miss St. John had promised to come over to Kensington in the ensuing week and spend a long day with her new acquaintances. This passed off so satisfactorily that it was quite a matter of regret when her brother made his appearance in the evening to escort her home.

But he brought a message from his wife. The distance was too great for constant intercourse, but Mrs. St. John hoped Mrs. Maynard would allow her daughter to spend a night with them; her sister-in-law had so few friends, and this would give them all the greatest pleasure.

Mrs. Maynard hesitated and looked dubious, but a glance at Dollie's eager face seemed to change her opinion, and with a slight effort that only Dollie noticed, the invitation was accepted.

'How good of you to spare me, mother!' exclaimed Dollie gratefully, when their visitors had gone.

'I saw you wanted to go, Dollie,' was her mother's answer. She did not like to damp the girl's pleasure with a hint of her own dulness, and yet she was counting up the days as a miser does his gold—only a fortnight more and Dollie would be gone.

Dollie was far too enthusiastic about her new friends to spoil her enjoyment with these sort of thoughts; when the day came she set off in the highest spirits, carrying her little bag. Mrs. Maynard had some shopping to do in St. Paul's Churchyard, and insisted on accompanying her daughter to the very corner of Lime Street. When they parted Dollie waved her hand and went on gaily, she had no idea that her mother was standing at the corner watching her.

'What a slim graceful figure she has, and how well she holds herself!' thought the poor mother fondly. 'There is no one like my Dollie, and yet I suppose few people would call her pretty; God bless her sweet face!' But perfectly unaware of all this admiration Dollie marched on straight and briskly, swinging her little bag.

Biddy received her full of smiles. She had the same bib-apron, and her arms were bare; nevertheless Dollie did not object to her so strongly as on the first occasion. 'Miss Mary was out, but the Missis was in the dining-room; would the young lady walk in?' and Biddy took charge of her bag hospitably. The dining-room lay at the rear of the house—a long dull room with a shabby green wainscot, and two windows looking out on a small back yard.

The prospect was not enlivening: to the left were the blackened walls and many windows of the sugar bakehouse; a dead wall closed the vista in front; a rugged ivy clung to the brickwork, and at its foot was a little flower border, full of nasturtiums and fuchsias, which went by the name of the children's garden.

The afternoon's sunshine flooded the room, bringing the shabby leather and faded hangings somewhat too prominently into relief. Mrs. St. John, who was sitting busily working at some childish garment, with Bee playing on the carpet at her feet, rose and welcomed her guest with evident cordiality.

She looked a little worn and haggard in the sunlight, but Dollie thought her handsomer than ever; her brown hair had ruddy gleams in it, and the shabby black dress seemed to fall round her in folds of antique simplicity. 'I never saw beauty like hers, never,' Dollie said after-

wards to her mother; 'and yet somehow it seems so
wasted.'

'Yes, she is very handsome,' was Mrs. Maynard's reply,
'but in my opinion her good looks are marred by that
dissatisfied, almost unhappy, expression; a very much plainer
face would please me better;' and Dollie half owned her
mother was right.

'Mary is down at the schools as usual, but she bade
me give you her love, and say she will not be long,' began
Mrs. St. John, taking up her work again, when Dollie had
kissed Bee and had seated herself. She was stitching
with the air of a woman who had not a moment to lose,
and Dollie felt a little oppressed. The idea of a tête-à-tête
with Mrs. St. John was rather formidable. She was
willing to admire her from a distance, but to sit opposite
to her and try to cudgel her brains for suitable topics
for conversation was too much for her youthful shyness.

'Where are the children and Lettice?' she stammered;
'may I go to them? I have brought them some pears
and some roses; and for you too if you would like them.'

'Thank you; they are beautiful; and Mr. St. John is so
passionately fond of flowers,'—and there was a quick gleam
of pleasure in her dark eyes. She thought Dollie looked
very fresh and dainty, sitting there in the sunlight. The
gray gown, and the yellow hair, and the great crimson
roses, made up quite a pretty picture. She was touched,
too, by the girl's thoughtfulness; and then the flowers would
please Maurice.

'They are all in the next room learning their lessons.
They have no governess; we could not afford such a
luxury, but their father and I teach them. Lettice is
almost entirely his pupil; she is quite a good Latin
scholar for her age. I suppose it will be useful to her
some day. We mean to bring them up to be independent,
poor things!'

'I always think it a pity that girls should be so helpless.
I mean to be an artist myself,' said Dollie, who was a
fair copyist, but had not a grain of real artistic talent in
her composition. She was working hard for hours daily

at the School of Art, and there was a small room at the
top of the house in Abercrombie Road that was dignified
by the name of Dollie's studio.

It was a mean little place enough, with an easel and
a few plaster casts, and two or three unfinished sketches
of rather mongrel-looking dogs; for Dollie had struck out
an entirely fresh line, and had aspired lately to be an
animal painter—a miniature Landseer or Rosa Bonheur.
She had already drawn the costermonger's donkey—a
correct likeness, only rather stiff; and the Newfoundland
Leo from next door had been bribed with frequent bones
to more than one sitting.　The sullen bear - like head
was said to be a complete success by every one but
Leo's master, though Mrs. Maynard secretly regretted
this new and surprising ambition on her daughter's part.

'Yes, it is very like, Dollie; and yet there seems
something wanting,' Mrs. Maynard would say, cocking
her head on one side like a critical sparrow, after the
manner of inexperienced admirers, and trying hard to
warm into enthusiasm over the donkey's stiff wooden legs;
'ought there not to be a little more muscle and curve
in that foreleg, my dear? and I do not think—I am not
sure—that the left hind-leg is quite as it should be.'

'If you are going to laugh at my donkey I shall turn
him round to the wall,' answered the young artist pettishly,
suiting her action to her words; 'it is so difficult to please
people who do not understand.　Susan said the costermonger quite exclaimed when he saw it.'

'And what did he say, my dear?' asked her mother
rather feebly, for this irritability of genius crushed her.

'Well, it was rather vulgar, of course :—" Blest, if that
ain't Jemmy's thunderin' old self, and no mistake !"　Susan
said those were his very words, and that he hoped the
young lady would finish her beautiful picture; and then
he asked for some beer.'

'Of course he could see it was a donkey !' returned
Mrs. Maynard, rather indignant about the beer; but
though she meant nothing by the remark Dollie thought
it very cutting.　'This is a donkey,' she wrote underneath

in very big black letters, and then she tore the paper in
pieces.   It was some time before Mrs. Maynard was
invited again into her daughter's studio.   Mrs. St. John
knew nothing about the donkey and the mongrel-looking
dog, so she listened to Dollie's announcement with perfect
good faith.   If she failed to enlarge on the subject it
was because her mind naturally centred on her own
interests and on her children.

'They have no beauty, poor things! and so we must
bring them up to be useful,' she said, laying down her
work with a sigh.   Those four plain-faced little girls were
very dear to the proud handsome mother, and then
she snatched up her little Bee and covered her with
kisses.

The children were learning their lessons in a large
bare-looking room on the ground-floor, opposite the dining-
room, that was sometimes called the schoolroom, and
sometimes father's study; in appearance it was a shabby
compound of both.

There was a large round table in the middle covered
with an inky cloth; a handsome bureau and writing-table
stood in opposite corners; a small bookcase of choice
theological books faced one filled with childish schoolbooks;
a linnet chirped in a small green cage; there were wire
blinds, and some pots of homely musk in the windows.
A street crier was vending cheap fish in the distance.
The children, in their holland pinafores, and with rough
flaxen heads, were huddled together rather closely at the
table.   The youngest, May, was crying; Lettice was
crouched up as usual with her elbows on the table.   They
all looked up a little scared as their mother swept into
the room followed by Miss Maynard.   In Dollie's eyes
the whole group had a somewhat forlorn appearance.

'What is this?   May, leave off crying directly and tell
me.'   Mrs. St. John spoke rather severely-—she was
evidently a rigid disciplinarian; but Lettice interposed
somewhat eagerly.

'It is nothing, mamma; please do not ask her.   May
will be all right directly.'

'But I want an answer, Lettice;' and Mrs. St. John's voice took its harshest chords.

'May was naughty and would not learn her lessons,' interposed Rosie; 'and when Lettie scolded her, she got the ruler and thumped Lettie, and she had a headache and it made it worse. Knocks aren't good for headaches,' added Rosie with a wise air.

'But May was so sorry, mamma, and she gave me such lots of kisses to make the place well,' broke in Lettice. 'You need not make the worst of it, Rosie; there is no good in doing that. Hatty knows that May is sorry.'

'Yes, but she was very naughty,' repeated Rosie, who was given to harp on one idea.

'It is always so when I leave you in charge of the children, Lettice,' was the severe reply. 'Let me look at your forehead,'—pushing back the rough hair with fingers that were not over-gentle. 'May, how could you be so excessively naughty?' as a large black bruise came to light, and Lettice in spite of her stoicism winced at her mother's touch. 'Fetch me the arnica, Hatty, and some cold water; she has had a dreadful knock.'

'I did not mean it, and the ruler was so hard,' sobbed the little culprit, 'and Lettie said she would forgive me.'

'But I have not forgiven you for hurting your sister,' returned her mother dryly. 'Go up into the nursery, May, and stay there by yourself. Miss Maynard has brought some pears for good children, but I could not think of giving you your share. I shall tell your father when he comes in. I do not know what he will say when he hears that in spite of your promise you have given way to your temper again.'

'Oh, mamma, please do not tell father,' pleaded Lettice, when May had withdrawn from the room with a fresh burst of sobs. 'Poor May is really sorry; she kissed me ever so many times, and telling father will be her worst punishment.'

'How can I bathe your head if you do not keep still?' returned her mother in rather a severe voice. 'If your head still aches you had better put away your books, and lie down on the sofa a little. Hatty, clear away Lettice's books, and make the table tidy.'

'And you will not tell father,' repeated Lettice, leaning her aching head gratefully against her mother's arm.

'I shall do as I have said,' replied Mrs. St. John coldly, and she drew herself a little away. 'I daresay the fault was yours as much as May's; I gave you the charge of the children's lessons, and of course you had got to your Latin again—there, I will not hear another word.' And poor Lettice with tears in her eyes was obliged to be silent.

'Do let me stay with them, and help them to finish their lessons,' interposed Dollie, as Mrs. St. John prepared to leave the room; 'I am so fond of teaching, and I never have any practice;' and her hostess assented somewhat ungraciously,—to tell the truth, she wanted Dollie's society for herself, for a visitor was a rare treat in that homely household.

The children looked a little shy and frightened when they found themselves alone with a stranger—Lettice was wiping furtive tears away in her sofa corner, and Hatty and Rosie were fidgeting on their seats. 'Now let me do something for somebody,' began Dollie in her bright, chirping voice; but at that moment the door opened, and a brown hat and then a laughing face were thrust into the room.

'Aunt Mary—Oh, dear Aunt Mary, do come here!' exclaimed Lettice joyfully, sitting up and dashing away her tears.

'Let me speak to my visitor first. How do you do, Miss Maynard? I have been detained at the schools, but I hope Janet and the children have been good to you. Now, my pet, what do these tears mean, and what makes you look so pale?' and Miss St. John placed herself on the floor by the sofa, and tossed off her shady hat.

'Oh, Aunt Mary, such a dreadful thing has happened,' began Lettice with a sort of gasp. 'May has been in a temper again, and mamma means to tell father' (Dollie discovered the children generally called Mrs. St. John mamma, but the father always remained father). 'I begged

her over and over again not to do so—didn't I, Hatty?—
but she said May must be well punished.'

'Humph!' ejaculated Aunt Mary; 'somebody else is
punished too, I can see.   Let me hear all about it, Lettie.'
And Lettice began her dismal recital.

Such a jumble of childish facts and feelings! Lettice
had to do her Latin translation for father—only mamma
never would understand that she was not doing it for pleasure,
and that it was so difficult it made her head ache ; and then
Hatty could not do her sums, and she cried over them
for fear mamma should be angry; and May shook the
table, and spoilt her ciphering-book with such a great blot
of ink! and then Hatty was cross and pushed May ; and
after that nothing was right.   'We were all wrong together,
I believe,' groaned the poor little pupil-governess, 'and the
worst of it all is, mamma believes that my carelessness is at
the bottom of it.'

'My dear Lettice,' began Aunt Mary solemnly, 'once
upon a time a very wise man said, "Give a dog a bad name
and hang him;"' and then she flashed a bright look of fun
across at Dollie.   'Oh dear, the wisdom of those ancients!
Hark! is not that your father's footstep, children?   I have
a wonderful idea ; suppose we tell him ourselves—so much
depends on the way of telling.   Maurice, come here.
Lettice and I have something we want you to know.'   And
Mr. St. John, shaking hands heartily with his guest, came
hastily across to the sofa.

The result was like sunshine after a storm.   Mr. St.
John stroked Lettice's hair, without speaking, and then
stooped over and kissed her, and five minutes afterwards his
long legs were striding upstairs.

At tea-time he made his appearance leading May by the
hand.   Her hair was nicely brushed, and all traces of tears
had disappeared from her face, which was dimpling with
smiles.   'Now run round the table and kiss your mother,'
whispered her father, and May obeyed.

Mrs. St. John took the kiss very coldly, but though she
looked displeased, she made no remark ; she was strict
with her children, and it was hard to say whether the little

girls most feared or loved her—all but Lettice, who adored her mother.

Her husband's leniency was opposed to her sense of justice. When she punished, it was for due cause, and any remittance of such punishment was impossible to her. But she was a woman given to bear her own grievances silently, and not for worlds would she hint before the children that she thought their father was wrong. From her he should always have wifely subservience and honour.

But Maurice, looking across the table with his honest eyes, saw from his wife's face that she was displeased, and at once made overtures for conciliation.

'You look tired, Janet,' he said tenderly; 'these troublesome children have put you out; eh, May?'—laying in her plate the luscious portion of a pear peeled by his own hand. May did not look at her mother for permission, but ate the forbidden dainty as fast as she could.

'I am not specially tired, Maurice,' returned his wife, her voice as usual softening at his lightest word.

'All the same you look as though some fresh air would do you good. We have service in the schoolroom to-night; supposing you put on your bonnet, and come with me; you have not walked with me for weeks.'

'Shall you be alone?' asked Janet in a tone of suppressed eagerness. No happiness on earth seemed so great to her as a quiet stroll through the deserted streets, leaning on her husband's arm or close to him, touching him and listening to his low-toned talk. In the moonlight, or underneath the wintry starlight, her heart had enjoyed such deep quiet communing with his, that the dim narrow streets had been forgotten, and it might have been that they two were walking in paradise.

'Shall you be alone, Maurice?' she asked; and her eyes began to shine with pleasure.

'Well, young Inman will be here presently, and as he is going to sea shortly, I think we ought to ask him to accompany us—there is so much depending on a lad's last impressions.'

'Well, no, thank you. I think I must stop at home to-

night and put the children to bed; Biddy is busy, and
Aunt Mary has her visitor; indeed I would rather not to-
night,' as Mary and her husband seemed disposed to argue
the matter; and her tone was so decided that Maurice said
no more.

That he was disappointed was evident from the grave
way in which he turned and addressed himself to his guest;
and the moment the meal was over, he shut himself up in
his study. Young Inman joined him there, and after a time
the two went out—the boy talking earnestly and Maurice
listening. As they passed the house he looked up and saw
his wife watching him, and lifted his felt hat with rather a
sweet sad smile.

'You might have come with me,' it seemed to say to
her; 'you have sent me out to my work as usual, weary
and discouraged, when your presence would have cheered
me.'

'Come, children, it is bedtime,' said the mother sharply;
'bid Miss Maynard good-night.' And as they trooped past
her like a little flock of frightened sheep, Dollie in her
heart felt very sorry for them; they seemed such good
obedient children in every one's but the mother's eyes.

'I wish Janet would have let me do it as usual,' said
Mary thoughtfully, as she took up her work. 'She makes
such a grave matter of the whole business, and when
I am there it seems only like a game of romps;' and
she listened somewhat anxiously to the childish footsteps
overhead.

'I have forgotten my thimble,' said Dollie, when half an
hour had passed, and they still sat chattering and looking
down idly on the street below; the window was open, but
a lamp was burning softly on the middle table.

'Let me fetch it,' returned her friend.

'No, thank you, I shall find it more quickly myself,' and
she ran nimbly upstairs. In reaching the chamber allotted
to her she had to pass the children's room; the door was
opened, and Dollie ventured to peep in. Mrs. St. John
was sitting with Bee in her lap, trying to soothe her to
sleep with some childish hymn. Rosie, who had been

found guilty of some trifling misdemeanour, was sobbing
heavily on her pillow, and Lettice was leaning on her elbow
trying to comfort her.

The sight of Bee in her little night-dress, with her bare
rosy feet and bright tangle of curls, as she joined drowsily
in her mother's hymn, was too irresistible to a child-lover
like Dollie, and in another moment she had made her
entrance boldly.

'There's a home for little children,' sang Janet in her
deep voice, 'above the bright blue sky.' 'Hush, Baby,
don't sing, you must go to sleep.

> 'No home on earth is like it,
> Nor can with it compare,
> For every one is happy,
> Nor can be happier there.'

'Do naughty gells go there, mother?' asked Bee, rousing
up a little.

'Naughty girls? of course not; hush, you must not
interrupt mother;' and Janet resumed her crooning song.

> 'There's a crown for little children
> Above the bright blue sky.'

But Baby was not to be silenced.

''Oo won't have no 'eavens or no crowns,' cried Bee,
pointing her finger with fiendish delight at Rosie, who was
still sobbing drearily; 'no, no, 'eavens, or 'omes, or crowns
—will she, mother?' and Bee fell to counting her toes with
a satisfied air.

'Yes, Rosie will go to heaven, if she leaves off crying, and is a good girl,' returned Janet, whose maternal
heart yearned a little to dry Rosie's tears; and Rosie's
shoulders ceased heaving quite so violently under the bed-
clothes. 'Dear me, Miss Maynard, is that you standing
in the dark? you will think my children are always crying.'

'Never mind, 'Osie, don't kye any more, and Bee will
love you, and give you lots of 'omes,' and Bee put out her
chubby arm and patted the bed-clothes with friendly magnanimity, and Janet, kissing both her and Rosie softly, put
her darling back in her crib.

CHAPTER V

THE LION D'OR

THE ensuing weeks passed over quickly, and the day came when Dollie stood on the edge of a new world ; and indeed this phrase savoured of little exaggeration in Dollie's case, who had seldom from her infancy slept out of the little white bed that stood in the corner of her mother's room. The bed would be vacant now for many a long week, the widow sadly thought, as she lay counting the hours during the whole of the dreary night before Dollie's departure. The room would feel strangely empty when she woke in the moonlight, and saw no golden hair shed over the pillow. What youthful innocent dreams had come to the girl as she lay smiling in her sleep? Good health, a fine digestion, and an easy-going conscience had made life pleasant enough to Dollie. Would it ever come to her to feel the pains and penalties of less fortunate mortals, to experience the temptations and conflicts, the pitiless storms and terrors of life? 'Ah, God forbid!' thought the poor mother fondly ; she had opened her arms wide with maternal self-sacrifice, and her child had escaped from them into the wide unknown world ; and so to her darling the battle of life had begun.

Dollie herself had no such misgivings ; she was a little sobered, perhaps a trifle saddened, at the thought of this first long parting from her mother, but the youthful Eve was too strong in her ; the desire for knowledge, for excitement, for new faces, and new scenes, was too passionately inherent in her nature to be quenched by mere affectionate considerations ; a sort of intoxication, a vague dreaminess, half inexplicable, and wholly delicious, seemed to throb and dilate within her, as they drove through the dark autumnal streets to the wharf.

Mrs. Reid's plans for her protégées were a little misty and involved, and had changed more than once; at the last moment they were bidden to take the lengthy route by Basseville. 'It will be a twelve-hours' voyage,' she wrote, 'but to such young travellers this will not matter. Miss Morell has some important business to transact for me in Basseville, and she will meet our young friends, and will, I hope, make a few hours' sojourn in the place pleasant to them; she will then escort them to Lesponts; after all, this seems the best plan to me;' and in this the girls cordially acquiesced.

The drive from Kensington was a long one, but to Dollie everything was delightful; she liked driving through the dark streets holding her mother's hand, and looking up at the lighted windows. By and by they came to a piece out of fairy-land. Could the Arabian Nights' Entertainments furnish anything more wonderful and enchanting than the Thames Embankment, with its marvellous illumination, its soft moving lights, and the dark river flashing in the distance? Dollie squeezed her mother's hand, and gasped out little sentences of delight and rapturous admiration. Was this London, busy matter-of-fact London? Had some enchanter waved his wand and lit up those mystic lamps, and touched those soft distances? 'Beautiful! oh, mother, how beautiful it all is!' cried Dollie.

She gave quite a sigh of regret when all the glitter faded into darkness again; by and by came crowded thoroughfares, then narrow streets. All at once they stopped; a door opened in a wall; there was a short man with a lantern, who guided them down a dark mysterious path; another man popped his head out of a little window and asked their names; there was a drawbridge; a group of men surrounded it; an expanse of black water, and a bridge over which people were looking. 'This is our wharf, and there is Mr. St. John waiting to help you on the boat. Make haste, Dollie,' said her mother; and Dollie moved forward in a dream.

'I thought we were in some one's backyard; and you call this a great London wharf!' exclaimed Dollie, turning critical in her excitement.

'But look what a nice, clean little vessel it is,' rejoined Miss St. John cheerfully, walking up to meet them. 'Maurice and I have been all over it—there is such a delightful weather-beaten old captain in a fur cap—and, do you know, we are the only lady passengers. The cabin is small, but delightfully cosy, though it does smell rather of oil; but you must come and see it for yourself;' and Dollie obeyed, nothing loath.

She was in the humour to be pleased with everything. The cabin was a little close; but then they had already made up their minds to stay on deck. They all stood in a group watching the sailors idly. There were some flat-bottomed barges drawn up by the vessels; some men were flinging horns into the hold. The air was filled with sharp sounds—some miserable-looking Italians—men, women, and children—were shivering on a heap of jute bags. They looked up at the sound of Dollie's laugh. One of the men had a hurdy-gurdy, and grinned back at her with glistening white teeth; a brown-faced baby began to cry, and was hushed with a dry crust.

'Poor things! they are going to France with their summer earnings,' said Mr. St. John compassionately. Before he left he had said a few words to them in tolerable Italian.

'Si senor; yes, yes, we leave England, and go back farther south. Yes, the winter is cold, and one must get warm and not starve;' and the man showed his white teeth still more, and ground at his hurdy-gurdy.

'We must go ashore; come, Mrs. Maynard, let me take care of you.'

'Good-bye, Miss Maynard; good-bye, Aunt Mary; we shall miss you dreadfully.'

'Is it time to go?' whispered Dollie; her arms were round her mother's neck. She had last words, a thousand fond charges, to give. 'Take care of yourself, do take care of yourself, darling mother, and don't fret.'

Mrs. Maynard said very little in reply. When Mr. St. John called to her again, she put her girl's arms away from her. 'God bless you, my dear!' she said; and then she climbed slowly on shore.

Dollie could see her for a long time waving a white hand in the distance. 'Poor mother, I wish she could have come too!' sighed Dollie; and she felt very sad for a long time.

But Miss St. John's cheerfulness soon roused her. When they came into the open sea, Mary fetched a rug, and covered up herself and Dollie. How she talked and laughed!—the man at the wheel heard her singing snatches of songs in the starlight. Towards dawn, as they grew drowsy and chilly, they crept down into the cabin, and fell fast asleep in their youthful weariness.

Dollie, who was unaccustomed to vigils, slept the longest. It was nearly noon when Miss St. John woke her.

'Come, come, you lazy girl; we are just entering the harbour, and it is such a pretty sight!—it is Sunday morning too, and such a bright sunshiny morning!' cried Mary cheerfully.

Was it Sunday morning, and could her mother really be at church without her? Dollie thought, with fresh wonder, as she climbed up the companion-ladder, and stood on deck.

How strange and foreign it all looked! They were steaming up to an unknown land between great wooden piers and vessels of every size. Everything seemed painted in blues and reds—blue blouses seemed everywhere; figures with red and yellow épaulettes, in blue trousers striped with red; groups of women—bonnes—and fishwives with white caps and gold earrings, strolled down by the water.

Dollie thought it all very odd and picturesque. The bright sunshine shone on the quay; little white low cabarets and estaminets, with jalousies and brightly-painted names, came in sight. Then came more blouses—a soft tone of blue seemed everywhere; the movement, the light, the colouring, the brown faces, the shrill foreign tones, filled Dollie with ecstasy.

'These must be the ladies whom I am expecting,' exclaimed a shrill voice, and a little blue-eyed woman, scarcely as youthful of aspect as of dress, came running up to the bewildered girls, holding out a pair of small gloved hands.

'Which is Miss St. John? I cannot tell, not I. One of you must be Miss St. John, and one Miss Maynard. Of course you know who I am. I am Charlotte Morell, Mrs. Reid's step-niece,' began the little woman volubly, holding a hand of each. 'Are you very tired? Has the voyage been very disagreeable? have you experienced the "mal de mer?" I always say "mal de mer," the English word is so unpleasant. No—ah well! you look as fresh as roses. Now we must follow Pierre to the douane; have you anything to declare?' and without waiting for an answer, their new acquaintance led them rapidly to a sort of shed or outhouse, where she was soon engaged in a good-natured wrangling with a group of gesticulating men.

She came back to them by and by, flushed and smiling, and handed them their bags.

'Pierre is so stupid! I told ma Tante I could manage better without him; this delay is very disagreeable; don't you think so? but it is over now. After all, it was a mere matter of form; one man peeps, and then hands you your bag with a "Merci, madame." These contraventions—these regulations, I mean—are very barbarous, they belong to the dark ages. Now we shall soon be at the hotel, and then you can rest yourselves. I have ordered coffee and pistolets in your bedroom, as table d'hôte will not be ready for hours. We are going to spend all to-morrow at Basseville, as I have not half finished les affaires de ma Tante. Shall you be bored? do the arrangements please you? tell me frankly, both of you.' And Miss Morell paused, perhaps for want of breath, and the opportunity was seized eagerly by Mary, who, by right of priority of age, generally acted as spokeswoman. She assured Miss Morell that they were perfectly satisfied with the arrangements, and were quite sure of amusing themselves.

'That is right. I do love people who are agreeable and make the best of everything. You are so different to some visitors we entertained lately;' and Miss Morell broke into a series of breathless anecdotes relating to some person or persons unknown.

The girls did not listen much; they exchanged glances of amusement as their unconscious companion trotted on between them, airing her little graces of conversation for their benefit. On the whole, they were not prepared to dislike her; though her volubility might prove a source of weariness. There was something innocent and good-natured in her very silliness.

Charlotte Morell was one of that numerous class of women who refuse to grow old gracefully, who cling to youth with a fond pertinacity, that is at once sad and useless.

She had been very pretty and young and artless once, and she was bent on retaining these charms now; only somehow the prettiness was faded, and the artlessness a mistake.

Her figure was still charming, rounded, with soft out-lines, though other women often grow angular or stout at forty; and the blue eyes and dimples were still there, and Charlotte's dimples had always been so admired.

And so Miss Morell still smiled a good deal, and still opened her eyes in the old effective manner, and decked her little person in youthful fineries, in wonderful gowns, that scarcely matched the sharp, faded cheeks.

'If she would only wear a black silk dress, and a little lace cap—her hair is so thin—she would look quite a pretty woman still,' Dollie said that very evening, when she was left alone with her friend. Miss Morell had joined them at table d'hôte in an elaborate toilette. Her little hands sparkled with hoops of rubies and emeralds and diamonds. The golden tinge had faded out of her hair; it looked colourless in the gas-light. When Charlotte waved her hands, as she did continually, with all sorts of little Frenchified shrugs, the gems seemed to blaze with quite a mimic fire; the delicate wrists were weighted with massive fetters. Charlotte had a perfect passion for jewels; a great deal of her slender income was spent in adding to her trinkets. In vain Mrs. Reid argued and scolded. Charlotte was a butterfly by nature, and would paint her wings.

'The wonder was,' Dollie said, 'how any sensible person could live with her.' But in this she afterwards owned herself a little severe. In spite of her fripperies and her gew-gaws, her want of reticence and her unconscious mischief-making, Charlotte was a good little soul in her way.

She had loved once, as most women do in their lives, and had been true to her lover after she had lost him. 'He was in the charge at Balaklava, my dear, and was the handsomest, the bravest, and best officer in the whole of the British army,' Charlotte would say, in an odd little choked voice, when she recounted this unfortunate episode in her life. All her friends knew about it. From time to time, when she could secure a new listener, Charlotte would repeat the whole story, crying softly over it all the time. The pain and the loss had been very great at one time, no doubt, but it could not be denied that Miss Morell contrived to extract a great deal of enjoyment out of the recital of her miseries.

It was a sure passport to sympathy, an unfailing source of interest; but after a time people grew tired of the never-ending story. Perhaps they had had their own love troubles, and had endured them more stoically, and were ready to blame such excessive want of reticence. After all, if Captain Hervey had lived, he might have grown weary of his sweetheart: Charlotte's blue eyes and china bloom could hardly have satisfied a sensible man when he found out her giddiness and want of ballast; and if so, better a dead lover than a dying love or an ill-matched marriage.

Both the girls were somewhat relieved when they turned at last into the courtyard of the Lion d'Or, and two smiling French chamber-maids ushered them into a great, airy front room, with two windows looking down on the narrow street.

Dollie uttered a little cry of ecstasy; she had never slept in such a gorgeous room before. There were four crimson velvet armchairs; a mirror, with a gilded clock; a round table stood in the middle of the room; there was a shining wardrobe, and a cheval-glass, wherein Dollie's slim figure was reflected; two tent beds, with sweeping white draperies, were on opposite sides of the door; the windows looked on a café. As Dollie glanced out, a garçon, with a white napkin under his arm, appeared on a balcony opposite.

Two priests in long shovel-hats went down the street; a fair-haired bonne, with white streamers floating over her shoulders, passed with two little boys in frilled trousers; and then a soldier, with red épaulettes and a fiercely curling moustache, went into the café.

When table d'hôte was over, and Miss Morell had betaken herself to her room, to write some important letters, as she told them, Dollie and her friend ensconced themselves cosily at the open window. The windows of the café were blazing with lights now; dark figures crossed and recrossed before them; in the dusky streets below there were still groups and knots of people; some of them went in to the épicier in front.

'Poor little mother! she has just returned from evening church, and is sitting down to her solitary supper,' sighed Dollie; and then she glanced round her at the gleaming mirrors, and the lofty room, and the great festoons of sweeping draperies, and a pleasant sense of contrast came over her.

'Yes, indeed,' echoed Mary, with another sigh; 'and Janet is putting the children to bed now, and singing to Bee. How I wish I could transport them all here! how Janet and Lettice would enjoy this place!'

Mary wished it still more on the following afternoon when they were sitting on the low sandhills at Lisse.

All the morning, while Miss Morell had been engaged with 'les affaires de ma Tante,' as she repeated more than once, the girls had wandered about the quaint little town. Its brightness and cleanliness impressed them favourably; without being beautiful or picturesque, it had a certain

homely pleasantness of its own, like a plain face with a
smile on it.

They looked at the park—a somewhat shabby affair—
with a lime walk and a small round pond, like a large basin,
where some children were sailing a small boat, while their
bonne sat and knitted a gray stocking under the trees.
Then they went into the cathedral, with its tower opposite
and the road dividing it. It was very dark and still; two
or three women knelt before the tawdry little altars; that
of Notre Dame des Lourdes was covered with small votive
offerings. Dollie looked on impressed and wondering, as
an old market-woman, with a brown, shrivelled face and
great copper earrings, laid aside her basket and knelt devoutly on the pavement. 'How her poor old bones must
ache!' thought Dollie compassionately. It was strange to
go out of the coolness and the darkness again into the
sunny crowded streets.

After déjeuner, Charlotte proposed they should take the
train and go down to Lisse. It was only a ten-minutes'
journey, she said, and it would be so cool and pleasant on
the seashore.

It was an odd lonely little place, the girls thought; the
casino, with its green jalousies, was closed for the season,
and so were les bains. There were very few signs of
habitation; some soldiers were shooting among the sandhills. When they were finished, some boys came climbing
up among the bushes and rank grass, hunting for bullets.

The yellow sands stretched out into the far distance;
a gray-blue sea rippled slowly and softly on the shore;
myriads of faintly-tinted shells—yellow and pink and cream-
coloured—lay under their feet; there were dark patches of
seaweed on the sandhills; and coarse lilac flowers, with a
strange, sickly smell; everywhere, far as eye could reach,
was rank vegetation, mounds of yellow sands, and the
smooth, waveless sea.

'Now let us rest,' exclaimed Miss Morell, when the girls
were weary of collecting shells. Aunt Mary had already
stored up a goodly heap of the fairy treasures for the future
delight of May and Hatty and Rosie; and Dorothy had

generously contributed to the stock. A soft wind blew
freshly over their faces; the water rippled on with faint
splashings on the sand; a purple shadow lay in the distance. It was an afternoon for vague dreams and musings;
but Miss Morell thought otherwise.

'Do let us rest and have a chat,' she said, unfastening
her smart little hat with its red poppies. 'I have been so
busy all the morning that I have not had time to ask you
a question. Do you know, I have been comparing you two
together all the afternoon, and I cannot make out which of
you will please "ma Tante" the most.'

'Is Mrs. Reid really your aunt?' asked Mary, who had
her own doubts on the subject.

Charlotte looked a little confused. 'Not exactly. Mr.
Reid's sister married a Mr. Morell, a widower, and I was
his daughter.'

'Then you were not even related to her,' began Mary
in a matter-of-fact way; but Charlotte interrupted her rather
pettishly.

'Dear me, how very accurate you seem to be, Miss St.
John! When one lives with a person one does not care
to be formal. "Mrs. Reid" was too stiff, so I call her
"ma Tante," or "auntie," sometimes, as a sort of pet
name; you are very English, you two. I was going to
propose that we should drop all formality; it is so absurd
among women; no one calls me anything but Charlotte;
and it is so embarrassing to say Miss Maynard and Miss
St. John every minute.'

'With all my heart!' exclaimed Mary heartily, who saw
she had somehow hurt their companion's feelings. 'Come,
Dollie, shall we make a bargain?' and Dollie smiled assent.

'All the same, I am very curious to know what impression you will make on our chatelaine,' continued Miss
Morell, who had a knack of bringing up the same subject
again; 'so much depends in this case on first impressions.'

'Why in this case, and not in every case?' asked Dollie
innocently.

'Humph!' observed Charlotte, affecting a more
mysterious and reserved manner. 'I do not think I am

4

quite at liberty to divulge what I mean, but all the same you will find my hint useful. You know my cousins the Lyndhursts, of course,' turning to Mary rather abruptly.

To Dollie's surprise, she flushed up a little as she answered, 'Oh yes, she knew them; they often came to Lime Street, but she had not seen them lately. Maurice liked them, and so did Janet—but were they really Charlotte's cousins ?' she observed, a little timidly, perhaps for fear of another rebuff.

Charlotte laughed rather affectedly. 'Ahem! ma Tante's belongings are somewhat involved. You. are only a second cousin of Mr. Reid's, I believe, or cousin once removed—I never can understand how it is. Well, Grey and his brother stand in much the same relation ; we are very distantly related, but they always call me Cousin Charlotte—Bertie especially. Do you know they are coming to Lesponts the end of this week?' and again Dollie noticed that Mary gave a slight start.

'No, I did not know it. I told you that I have not seen them lately,' she answered in a low voice.

'Yes, Grey has been ill from over-study, and needs a change, and Bertie's pupil has gone abroad with his parents; so they are coming down together; it will make your visit more lively, will it not?'

'But who are they? I have never heard of them,' asked Dollie curiously. Mary was sorting her shells, and made no attempt at enlightening her ; but Charlotte was more ready with an answer.

'Well, as I ˙ said, they were distant connections of Mr. Reid, and you must know that ma Tante has been hunting up all his belongings for the last two or three years ; ever since poor Walter—but I forgot, I will not touch on that now. Well, the Lyndhursts were invited, and we made their acquaintance. Bertie was my favourite, but I think ma Tante had a secret preference for Grey ; not that she took greatly to either of them. I think poor Walter—I mean, she seems to prefer girls now.' And then Charlotte came to a full stop suddenly, but neither Mary nor Dollie seemed to observe her confusion.

'Are they young?' inquired Dollie, it must be confessed with a great deal of interest; she had never known any young man intimately, and she thought Bertie especially sounded nice.

'Perhaps Bertie, or Cuthbert, as he is called sometimes, may be two- or three-and-twenty; his brother is three years older. The worst of it is they are very poor, and have rather a struggling life of it; they have both been to the university, but that was before they lost their father. Grey is reading for the Bar, and has pupils; he is very hard-working and clever, and will get on in time, I daresay. But Bertie is not doing so well; he has a tutorship somewhere in Warwickshire, but one can't help feeling that is not much.'

'But it will lead to something,' observed Mary softly. 'Maurice says he is full of capability.'

'Yes, but he is lacking in application or perseverance—at least so Mrs. Reid says; she is a very acute observer of human nature. But, now, it is growing late, and we must be *en route* for the Lion d'Or, or we shall lose table d'hôte;' and Charlotte, who had a keen appreciation of the good things of this life, hurried her reluctant companions from their nest in the sandhills, and led the way rapidly to the station.

CHAPTER VI

IT was quite late on the afternoon of the following day when Miss Morell announced that ' les affaires de ma Tante ' were at last settled, and that she had ordered the fiacre to take them to the station. It was already dusk when they left Basseville ; and before long a complete obscurity veiled the unlovely Flemish landscape from their eyes—the monotonous flats of low-lying lands, with their dykes and windmills and rows of pollards. A general sleepiness and want of animation pervaded everything ; the train steamed on in melancholy slowness, as though time in Flanders were of no object. Every now and then they stopped at clean, deserted-looking stations. Once two sisters of charity got in. Their large robust figures and coarse Flemish faces reminded Dorothy of a Dutch picture she had once seen.

It was nearly nine before they found themselves in the large rambling station at Lesponts—' much too late to see anything,' as Dollie observed regretfully. A few dark quiet streets, without a single foot-passenger, were soon passed, and then they turned into a long avenue. The night-air blew rather coldly in at the open window, fanning Dollie's eager face somewhat roughly. The dead leaves whirled under the horse's feet ; some iron gates stood wide open ; Dollie caught sight of a gravelled courtyard planted thickly with shrubs, and a high irregular house with a peaked red roof and yellow walls, over which the moon was shining ; then the door opened, and in another moment they were all standing in a large dimly-lighted hall, with black and white tesselated pavement, a close stove and swinging lamp, with oak benches and cabinets. A staircase of slippery oak led to another still more dimly-lighted hall or lobby.

Two good-natured stolid-looking girls came out to receive them. Miss Morell spoke rapidly to one of them in an undertone; and then she passed her arm through Mary's, and beckoned to Dorothy to follow.

'Ursula says ma Tante has had a bad day, and has not yet left her apartment. Come, I will show you to your rooms, and Romany shall bring you some coffee and help you to unpack. Romany speaks English, and so does Ursula. In fact, we pride ourselves on being an English household, and having English comforts. For example, you can have tea instead of coffee, and fancy yourself back in the land of fogs and roast-beef again. Look, there are your rooms quite at the end of this corridor. They open into each other, which will be company for you when the wind howls round the chateau. Come, do you find your new quarters satisfactory?' finished Charlotte, in her airy, breathless way.

'They are charming,' responded the girls warmly. And indeed both the rooms had a cheerful, comfortable aspect, with their dark, waxed floors and squares of gay-coloured carpet, their white tent-beds, heaped with snowy pillows, French windows with narrow festoons of pink and white drapery; while a small crimson couch and round table, with a vase of flowers, stood before each close stove.

One of the stoves had been opened, and a snug little fire burned in the grate; a coffee equipage stood on the little round table, and Romany had drawn up two inviting armchairs; the tall candles yielded a soft light; a black bearskin rug lay before the stove; the dark purple china and gleam of silver made a bright spot of colour in the room. Dollie's face dimpled with satisfaction as she surveyed the little preparations for their comfort. 'How Janet would delight in all this luxury!' sighed Mary, who never seemed to enjoy any pleasure perfectly unless she could share it with others. 'She used to describe this sort of thing to me. The Chateau de St. Aubert was a sort of earthly paradise to poor Janet.'

'Why do you always sigh when you speak of Mrs. St. John?' asked Dollie, a little curiously. She was leaning back luxuriously among the red cushions of her chair; her little feet rested on the black rug; both the girls were in their dark travelling dresses; Dollie's slim graceful figure and fair hair showed to advantage in it. Mary was stouter, and had no special grace of outline; but she was fresh-looking, and had a thoroughly English look.

'Hush!' interrupted Mary cautiously, 'I thought I heard footsteps in the next room. One must be careful in a strange place.'

'Nonsense, it is only Romany unpacking our clothes,' returned lazy Dollie. 'When I am at home my mother does all those things for me. It must be a dreadful thing to have to wait on oneself, as you do, Mary.'

Mary laughed in an amused manner, but she did not answer; and in another moment a light tap was heard at the door, and Mary's cheerful 'Come in' was answered by the noiseless entry of a tall gray-haired woman.

Dollie rose to her feet in a startled way, but Mary only smiled again, and did not seem in the least disturbed by the abrupt entrance of their hostess.

'Good evening, my dears,' said Mrs. Reid, kissing the girls lightly on either cheek, and pressing their hands kindly. 'I thought it better to introduce myself in this way. Let me look at you both, and see if I can guess your names; this must be Dorothy, I think, from her mother's description. And, yes'—turning to Mary, and scrutinising the bright face rather closely—'this must be the Aunt Mary who is every one's right hand, and who never thinks of herself. You see I am no mean physiognomist, and I am annotating Maurice, who is surely a good authority.'

'I am not so sure of that; brothers are often partial,' protested Mary, with an honest blush. 'Are you so certain of your identification, Mrs. Reid? Suppose, after all, I am Dorothy Maynard.'

'No, no, here is the veritable widow's mite—Margaret's one ewe-lamb,' replied Mrs. Reid, with a sad smile; and

again she put her hand kindly on the girl's shoulder.
'She was good to spare you to me for a little, though I
wish she could have come herself too.   Ah well, one
understands all that sort of thing—the sympathies do not
narrow with age, thank God for that! You are both very
welcome, my dears.   It was kind of you to come to me;
it is long since I have seen two such happy young faces
in my home.'

'I think it is good of you to have us. You must not
thank us for coming,' broke out Dollie in her impulsive
fashion, and then she became suddenly shy.   Mrs. Reid
only answered with one of her faint smiles, and stood
warming her thin hands by the fire, and looking at them
both with a scrutinising gravity which somehow made
Dollie feel uncomfortable.   Mary did not seem to notice
it.   She only drew another armchair closer to the stove,
and motioned to her hostess to seat herself.

'Do not let me disturb you; you looked so comfortable,
and you were chatting so busily, that I did not like
interrupting you.   Well, if you will let me share your
fireside for a few minutes—but I must not keep Charlotte
waiting;' and then she sank into the chair somewhat
wearily, and lapsed into thoughtfulness.

Dollie returned her scrutiny with interest; unconsciously
she had formed in her own mind a fancied ideal of the
young Aunt Isabel whom her mother had described.
She would find her old and changed, of course, but still
beautiful; those sort of lovely Madonna faces never grow
plain.

The reality was a sort of shock to the girl's young
enthusiasm.   Keener eyes would still have traced the
remains of great beauty in the still fine features; but
Dollie's inexperience only noticed the sickly aged look
and gray hair.

'Aunt Reid is the most singular-looking person,' wrote
Dollie the next day to her mother; 'I am sure you would
not recognise her in the least; and her peculiar style of
dress adds to the singularity of her appearance.   Charlotte
says she never varies it either winter or summer; she

always wears the same black clinging sort of dress, morning and evening, with some sort of black lace scarf draped oddly round her neck—not a scrap of white anywhere, not an ornament except her wedding ring, and yet she is so rich ! Fancy all that blackness, with no relief but her pale face and silvery-gray hair. Mary and I say we have never seen such hair before, so thick and rich and silvery ! '

'You are quite right ; Mrs. Reid has certainly been very lovely, and is still almost beautiful,' wrote Mary at the same time to her brother Maurice. 'There is a picture of the Mater Dolorosa in the churchwarden's room at St. Sauveur's, erroneously ascribed to Jan van Eyck, which reminds me most irresistibly of her face, and yet the features are not at all the same.

'One sees at a glance that she has been a great sufferer. The eyes have a hollowed melancholy look about them ; now and then they have a wild, almost startled, expression. Perhaps her mouth is a little too thin and stern, but on the whole she looks gentle. Dollie seems in great awe of her, and seems to wonder that I do not share it. After what Charlotte has told us, I can feel nothing but interest and profound pity. What a tongue that little person has ! '

A strange conversation was lingering in both the girls' minds as they wrote. Mrs. Reid had sat with them about half an hour, but the talk had been disconnected. Now and then she dropped some kindly word, or questioned them about some home interest ; but she was evidently a reserved woman, and silence was perhaps habitual to her. By and by she rose somewhat abruptly, and left them without any special leave-taking. They were discussing her after her departure with a good deal of interest, when Miss Morell suddenly interrupted them. Her appearance was a little startling. She wore a crimson peignoir, trimmed with a quantity of cream lace ; her fair hair hung in thin pale-coloured tresses over her shoulders, and she had an ivory brush in her hand.

'It is so cold, and ma Tante's conversation has been so dreary, that I am nearly petrified,' exclaimed Charlotte, with one of her little shrugs. 'How cosy you look, girls, and not a bit tired or sleepy. I am not a lethargic person myself,' she continued with her usual frankness. 'I generally sit up half the night reading. Perhaps I shall shock you—but I have a weakness for French novels, and ma Tante detests them, so I generally enjoy them in the retirement of my room.'

'What a pity!' observed Mary in her downright way. 'French novels are considered such unwholesome reading.'

'For children, perhaps; but I am not one of your goody-goody people. I like my little indulgences and relishes, my sauce piquante, and highly-flavoured dishes. Good people and good books are apt to be triste—what you call heavy; they are altogether ennuyé; look at ma Tante, for example; she is admirable, but her Puritan tendencies weary me to death.'

'We were talking of Mrs. Reid when you came in,' observed Mary. 'Dollie seems half afraid of her; she was as quiet as a mouse all the time she was with us, and answered as demurely as a schoolgirl; did you not, Dollie?'

'She took the most notice of you,' pouted Dollie; 'she paid you a compliment directly.'

'Did she, indeed?' asked Charlotte seriously. 'I have said all along that so much depends on first impressions; of course, both you girls have equal chances, and then you came together, but still if she took to Mary——' and here she stopped, for both girls were regarding her with the utmost astonishment.

'Chances of what? Why are you so mysterious?' broke out Dollie wrathfully. She was a quick-tempered little person, and these constant hints ruffled her. 'Why should she not be pleased with us both? we are her invited guests, and she asked us for her own pleasure. If she likes Mary best I should not quarrel with her; she is worth ever so much more than I,' continued Dollie in her contradictory fashion; for, as in all youthful alliances, she was ready to swear by her friend.

'Tut, tut,' responded Charlotte, 'every one is willing

to feather his own nest, and I do not believe that you are
so ready to give everything to Mary; of course, both of
you knew why she sent for you. Maurice's visit last year
was a failure; she could not get on with him or his wife
either. Maurice was too priestly for her, their Church
views differed; and Janet first toadied and then contra-
dicted her. Your sister-in-law is a difficult woman, Mary.'

Mary coloured, but did not answer—the conversation
was evidently displeasing to her; but Dollie's curiosity
was strongly roused.

'Do you mean that Mrs. Reid had any special intention
in sending for us—beyond giving us the pleasure, I mean?'

'Do you think it right to ask Charlotte such a question?'
remonstrated her friend gravely. A sudden light had
dawned on her; she was anxious to silence Dollie.

'Be quiet, Aunt Mary,' returned the girl pettishly.
'Charlotte's mysteries are unendurable, and I intend to
have my question answered. Come, Charlotte, be a good
soul and tell us.'

Evidently Miss Morell was dying to impart information.
She gave Dollie a knowing look, coughed slightly, hesitated,
and played with her ivory brush.

'I did not think you were so simple, my dear. Mary
knows, of course; just look at her.'

Mary's steady brown eyes met hers. 'I know nothing,
and have heard nothing. If I guess anything it is from
your manner.'

'Well, there is no harm in that,' replied Charlotte in
her sprightly way. 'Every one knows that I am disin-
terested; if ma Tante were to die to-morrow, I know
exactly what I have to expect—a comfortable maintenance
and nothing else. She has been perfectly frank with me,
and I with her. "Not a farthing more would I leave you,
Charlotte," she once said to me; "no, not if I had the
riches of Crœsus; you are such a thoughtless, irresponsible
sort of person. I hold my money in trust, and it shall
never go into hands that will squander or use it rashly."'

'Well?' interrupted Dollie breathlessly. Mary had
turned her face to the fire, and sat motionless.

'Well, little simpleton, there are heaps of money, and
no one to inherit it all; and now you know why I am
anxious for you both to make good impressions.'

Dollie gave a little gasp of astonishment. Evidently
she was unprepared for this. Charlotte's information quite
took her breath away. At her exclamation Mary faced
round upon them both; her cheeks were burning.

'Charlotte, do you think it was right or honourable
to tell us this? Is it kind? Kind to us or to Mrs. Reid?
Do you think it will put us at our ease, or make our stay
here happier, to know that our visit is fraught with such
immense importance?'

Charlotte opened her blue eyes rather widely.

'Dear me, what a very earnest, downright sort of
person you are, Mary. Any one else would have been
grateful for such a hint; but you are as bad as Grey;
there is no understanding you. What difference will it
make to your visit, I should like to know?'

'A great difference,' was the steady answer. 'How are
we to be natural, our own selves, if we are always weighing
our words and actions, and suiting them to please people?
If you told all this to Janet, no wonder she failed so miserably. Maurice is a man; it would act on him differently.
He has a mind large enough to rise above such things.'

'He never would hear me out,' was the somewhat sullen
rejoinder; for Charlotte was vexed at the manner in which
her confidence was received, and from that night Dollie
was her favourite. 'Grey was just as bad. He told me
almost roughly to hold my tongue, and not put a parcel of
lies or rubbish, I forget which, in Bertie's head; but Grey
is very wrongheaded about things. He will have it that it
is a shame that Walter is disinherited.'

'Walter! who is Walter?' exclaimed Dollie; while even
Mary seemed suddenly interested.

For a moment Charlotte looked frightened; her manner
changed, and became less flippant.

'Dear me! do you mean that you never heard of poor
Walter? I thought every one knew that sad story. I
never allude to it if I can help, because it is so very painful,

and I do not like dwelling on painful things;' and Charlotte's eyes became a little misty. 'It seems so very dreadful that a mother should be alienated from her only son.'

'Her son!' exclaimed both the girls in awe-stricken
tones.

Miss Morell nodded.

'Her only son—her only child, I should say, for she
never had another. Poor Walter, he was much to blame,
but I think his father was to blame too. Ma pauvre
Tante! she had enough to suffer between father and son.'

'Was not Mr. Reid good to her?' asked Dollie, with a
vague recollection of Aunt Isabel's wilfulness. 'She would
marry him, you know.'

'Yes, against the wishes of all who knew him. I have
heard about that,' replied Charlotte, with another shrug.
'There is a fate in these things, I believe. Why, she was
beautiful, beautiful, and he old enough to be her father;
and though rolling in riches a perfect miser; and with such
a temper! My dears, there must be a fate in these
things.'

'I suppose he was fond of her,' observed Dollie. She
shivered a little at the dreary interest of this recital. It
was late, and the wind was blowing in a gusty manner
round the chateau. Charlotte's mysterious voice made her
nervous.

'He was fond of her! Of course, ma chère, when men
are old and women are young and beautiful, cela va sans
dire; but he had a dismal, contracted nature, and he made
her life miserable. She was generous, and open-hearted,
and incautious. Yes, that is the word—incautious—and
perhaps injudicious; and he made her suffer a martyrdom
when she displeased him. Poor soul! how she loathed
her life and riches! And then there was the boy for him
to mismanage and ruin.'

'Ruin!'

'Well, is it not ruin when a father first spoils a child
and then goads him by contradiction and restraint into
madness? I verily believe there was a touch of madness
in both father and son. From a mere baby she never had

any control over him—his father took care of that.   When
he died she had only lost one tyrant.

'By some strange freak,' continued Charlotte,—'she
says it was a tardy repentance,—Mr. Reid left her in absolute possession of his money.   Railway speculation had
enriched him.   Crome Park was only theirs by purchase,
and he had no landed possessions.   Walter had already
begun his course of hopeless prodigality.   In my presence
I have heard his father call him a spendthrift, gambler, and
drunkard, and he vowed never to leave him a penny.'

'Was it true?'

'It was more than true,' replied Charlotte mournfully.
'His career at Oxford was shameful.   No restraint, no
influence, no prayers, no entreaties on his mother's part
seemed to have any weight with him.   It seemed as
though he were bent on ruining himself and every one
belonging to him.

'While quite young he ran away with an actress—a
woman old enough to be his mother, who induced the
unhappy boy to marry her—a step he has since repented,
for she treats him shamefully.

'After this sad marriage ma Tante lost all hope of
reclaiming him.   He had already robbed her almost before
her face most ruthlessly, and to escape his ceaseless im-
portunities and persecutions she left Crome Park and
began to live abroad.   She had made him a handsome
allowance, which, she vowed over and over again, is all
that he has to expect from her, living or dead; but this is
always squandered either by himself or the wretched
woman he calls his wife.   No money is safe in their hands;
at times they are almost reduced to beggary.

'Over and over again,' continued Charlotte, in a breathless whisper, 'has he sought her out, and cajoled and
threatened her until she has been weak enough to listen to
him.   Since we have been here he has not succeeded in
tracing us.   Every time she sees him I think it will be
her death.   Last time even he seemed terrified by her
agony.'

'Oh, this is dreadful!' broke in Dollie, with a shudder.

'Please do not tell us any more, Charlotte. Poor thing, poor thing! Her only child, too. Do mothers ever out-live their love, I wonder?' questioned the girl, with two great tears running down her cheeks.

'I do not know,' replied Miss Morell quietly; her flightiness had passed for the time; she spoke quite simply and with real feeling. 'Unless anything happens we never speak of him; and then she is always ill, and one is too frightened to notice much. I think she loves him still from something I once saw.'

'What was that?'

Miss Morell looked at Mary and hesitated.

'Perhaps I ought not to mention it. You English people—living in England, I mean—have such odd notions of honour! and yet it can do no one harm.

'It was only a drawer,' she went on, 'that I once opened accidentally in her wardrobe when she sent me for some-thing. The key was in it. There they all were—little piles of baby-linen with rose leaves strewn over them; a rattle and blue shoes; and in one corner a boy's straw hat brown with the sun, and with a torn edge; and two or three dog's-eared lesson-books beside it. Somehow, when I saw it all,' continued Charlotte artlessly, 'I knew that ma Tante had not ceased to love poor Walter.'

Dollie's eyes were still wet when Miss Morell had finished, but the other girl had again averted her face, and still sat silent; and a few minutes afterwards Charlotte rose, with an exclamation at the lateness of the hour.

When she had gone, Mary got up from her seat, and touched Dollie lightly on the shoulder.

'Good-night, Dollie, my dear; you must put all this out of your mind and try to sleep. Charlotte has made you look quite pale.'

'Are you sleepy, Aunt Mary?'

'No, indeed. I was never more awake in my life. Hush! we will not talk any more. I want to be by myself and think over it all. She was very wrong to tell us—very wrong indeed. But the mischief has been done now, and cannot be undone.'

'I did not know you could look so stern; Charlotte was quite in awe of you,' grumbled Dollie, who was over-excited and not disposed to solitary banishment. But Mary, who had a will of her own, though she seldom exercised it, would hear of no relenting.

'Poor little innocent Dollie! I hope it will do her no harm,' thought Mary, as she quietly closed the door and sat down again by the fire; and long after Dollie was asleep, she sat there still listening to the soughing of the wind in the avenue, and watching the dying flame with a sadder face than Mary St. John often wore.

CHAPTER VII

A NUN'S GRAVE

WHEN Dollie peeped through her muslin blinds the next morning, she uttered a little cry of dismay and disappointment; the wind had ceased, but a steady downpour of rain was saturating everything; shining pools lay in the courtyard, the red and yellow leaves in the avenue lay in rotting heaps, the very trees looked dismal with their soaking branches. Mary found her disconsolate and a little homesick, and almost regretful of the green parlour in Abercrombie Road.

'It is an ill wind that blows no one any good,' said practical Aunt Mary; 'now we shall write our letters and cheer the good folk at home, instead of gadding about sight-seeing;' and Dollie owned herself much struck by this sensible view of the case.

An English breakfast was laid out in a quaint little salle-à-manger, where Charlotte in a wonderfully braided morning dress was ready to receive them.

The rooms in the chateau were all quaint and a little foreign-looking, with their waxed floors, squares of brilliant carpets, and close stoves; the girls thought the drawing-room magnificent, though it certainly looked a little cold and comfortless. The Louis Quatorze furniture was white and gold, but it was all hidden away under holland coverings; even the pictures and mirrors were veiled in yellow gauze, the great gilt candelabra and clock shone through the misty folds. Romany with feather brush was dusting the great cupboard of china. The floor was marked out in odd patterns, and on the walls were painted cupids and wreaths of roses.

'Ma Tante and I think this room too big and gaudy for use when we are alone,' explained Miss Morell, when she showed the rooms to her visitors. 'When our gentlemen come we will have the covers off, and you two shall play on the grand piano. It wants a big fire and dozens of wax candles to make such a huge barrack of a room habitable; now it is as cold as a grave, and how the rain drips on the balustrades outside!' And Charlotte, with a little shiver, hurried her visitors away.

'This is the morning-room, where we generally sit, unless ma Tante remains in her dressing-room,' she continued, opening another door. 'We call it le salon Anglais, because we have some of the furniture from Crome Park; look, there is an English fireplace here too, and there are some of ma Tante's favourite pictures.'

'It is a dear little room!' exclaimed Dollie enthusiastically.

The Persian carpet, snowy rug, and soft crimson couches gave an air of comfort; some choice books in handsome bindings were in the carved bookcase; one or two sunny landscapes hung on the wall; a beautiful Parian group and some Sèvres figures were on the mantelpiece; the tables were strewn with work and books. A glass door opened on a stone terrace, with ornamental urns and vases; two or three steps led down to the garden. The girls had a glimpse of wide green alleys and a lawn that looked as trim as a bowling-green. On the rug were two Persian kittens, and a large solemn poodle, who got up and looked at them, and then turned round three times.

'Shake hands with my friends, Mark Antony,' remonstrated Miss Morell very gravely, and Mark Antony marched up to them and gave a tasselled paw to each.

'Now for la cuisine and les affaires!' exclaimed Charlotte jauntily, shaking the chatelaine that hung by her side. 'In the Chateau de St. Aubert le ménage is quite simple. I am housekeeper, butler—je ne sais quoi—and am kept trotting about half the morning. Amuse yourselves, mes

5

amies ; ma Tante has passed a suffering night, and sleeps—
so Justine tells me.   Oh, this provoking rain, but perhaps
it will clear up towards evening.'   And so saying, Charlotte
tripped off, with Mark Antony strutting beside her.

Mary gave an odd little laugh when they were left
alone.

> ' From morning to night it was Charlotte's delight
>   To chat and talk without stopping.

Do you recollect the old nursery rhyme, Dollie ?   What an
important, made-up, affected, yet perfectly original little
person she is ! but under the wrappings there is plenty of
the real article, I fancy.'

' She is so young, you see,' returned Dollie, playing with
the kittens, and trying to be fiercely satirical.   ' She asked
me to call her Char or Lottie this morning—she even
hinted some one had once called her Lottchen.   I wonder
if some one were a " he," Mary.   Heaven send us wisdom
when we are getting old !—and she must be dreadfully old,
ever so much over forty ; ' and both the girls laughed again,
and then sat down in earnest to their letter-writing.

It was a strange solitary day ; Charlotte did not come
near them again until luncheon, when she chattered to
them unceasingly of ma Tante's suffering, and of the attaque
aux nerfs under which she had laboured all day.   ' There
was no leaving her for a moment ; Justine was a martyr, and
was quite weary with her ministrations ; but she had administered a tisane—a sort of composing draught—and in
the evening all would be well.   ' But it is triste, and on
your first day too !   I am quite au désespoir to think how
dull you must be.'

Both the girls assured her that they were perfectly content with their work and books ; but Charlotte was not to be
convinced, and with the good - natured idea of amusing
them, she carried them off to her own room after luncheon,
and exhibited to them her hoard of trinkets and fineries,
which were tolerably numerous, and sufficiently pretty to
excite Dollie's admiration.   Mary tried hard to seem interested, but she soon wearied of this unexciting occupation ;

she was tired, too, with her last night's vigil; the drip-drip of the rain-drops on the window-sill blended drowsily with Charlotte's soft monotone; she was fast asleep in the big armchair long before the trinkets were locked in their cases again.

'Never mind; she is tired, poor darling! we will not wake her,' said Charlotte, not at all offended at this discovery. 'Come nearer to the window, and I will tell you all about it, dear Dollie. Oh, the droll little name! Yes, it was at the charge of Balaklava that my Percival lost his life. Percival Hervey—is it not a divine name? I always thought Charlotte Hervey would have sounded so well. But it was not to be.' The handkerchief was in requisition, and Charlotte's blue eyes were dried again and again as she poured her sad little tale into Dollie's sympathising ear.

'Poor thing! I will never laugh at her again,' said Dollie afterwards—for what girl does not grow tender over even an antiquated love story? Charlotte's faded little romance, with its shreds and snippets of sentiment, stood her in good stead, and invested her with a good deal of interest in Dollie's eyes. 'Poor little woman! I daresay she was very nice and pretty when Captain Hervey loved her; but Heaven send us wisdom when we are growing old!' repeated Dollie for the second time that day—waxing epigrammatic in her earnestness, to which ejaculation Mary vouchsafed an 'Amen.'

They had stolen out of the chateau, and were walking briskly down the avenue, when Dollie gave vent to her little outburst.

When Mary had wakened up, heartily ashamed, from her stolen nap, she found the room quite empty and dark, but in another moment Dollie tripped in, in her little straw hat and with a mischievous look on her face.

'Do wake up, Aunt Mary. I believe we shall all go to sleep in this enchanted castle. The rain has stopped, and Charlotte has gone away to relieve Justine, and a run I must and will have;' and Mary consented very willingly, though she somewhat spoilt the fun by insisting on leaving a message with Romany. They had turned to the right

on coming out of the chateau, and were quite unaware that
they were leaving Lesponts behind them, and were walking
down the wide leafy avenue. The rain had indeed ceased;
and a faint watery moon rose soon after sunset; the air
exhumed moisture, and the rank smell of decaying vegetation ascended from the wet earth and heaps of saturated
leaves; the roads had a forlorn aspect and seemed to
stretch away into nothingness; before they had gone far they
were stopped by the walls of the cemetery, and in another
minute were threading the grass-bordered paths.

It would soon be the time for closing, and they hurried
on, not a little moved by the strangeness and vast emptiness of the place—only a gigantic crucifix with its lone
figure kept watch and ward over the quiet dead. The little
chapel was empty; the mourners who had knelt there had
gone home; many of the little iron crosses were decked
with wreaths of yellow and white immortelles, crowns, and
chaplets, and odd devices in black and white bead-work,
with scrolls and all sorts of quaint fancies, lay on the grassy
mounds; down one side-path were convent graves, each
with its little iron cross,— Sister Marie Thérèse, Sister
Veronica,—just the simple name and age, nothing more.
As the girls wandered on in the glimmering dusk, it seemed
to them as though gray shadowy nuns might have glided
out of their quiet resting-places and followed them.

' I have had enough of this; fancy choosing this for our
first walk!' exclaimed Dollie with a shiver. 'Where is the
church of the Redemptorist, I wonder, and who was this
Sister Veronica who died aged twenty? Could she have
been a girl like us, Mary, with real flesh and blood, with a
heart to feel and to enjoy? Perhaps somebody,' continued
Dollie in an awe-struck voice, 'one of those Flemish priests
we saw, persuaded her that she had a vocation, and then
she went in, and the convent rules, and the monotony,
and the awful stillness killed her—aged twenty, poor Sister
Veronica! yes, she must have died of it.'

'Nonsense, Dollie; the place is making you nervous;
let us go back to the chateau.' But the girl was not to be
silenced.

'I will tell you all about it. Charlotte and I were talking about it at Lisse, only you did not hear; sometimes you will not listen, you know.

'There is a church here, and they call it the church of Le Redemptorist; there is a convent attached to it, and people go to Benediction to hear the nuns sing; Charlotte has promised to take us.'

'Well?'

'No one ever sees the nuns; they sing in a gallery behind a lattice; they are called the red nuns because their habit is red, in recollection of our Lord's passion; they are strictly enclosed, and have a chapel of their own; they never come down in the church; and Charlotte says she will show me the little square hole near the altar through which the priest administers the Blessed Sacrament, and where he hears their confessions. People here say—the Roman Catholics, I mean—that they have a vocation and lead beautiful contemplative lives, that they have lovely grounds, and are very happy; but how do we know? Charlotte says they never do needlework, that their time is spent in devotion and meditation.'

'Perhaps Charlotte exaggerates.'

'No, indeed; she was quite right when she said so many of them died young; they say so much singing kills them; but they are wrong, it is the life; yes, that is what it is, the life, or rather the want of everything that goes to make up life,' finished Dollie, with a little thrill of solemnity in her voice. 'Look there, Mary—Sister Veronica aged twenty!'

'Poor thing!' ejaculated Mary, much impressed by Dollie's dismal recital.

'You see, as Charlotte says, girls have a great deal of religious excitement sometimes. They are dreamy and visionary; it is all white lilies and paradise; they want to do great things, to devote themselves and their whole lives to some grand purpose; they think they can pray life so peacefully away, that they love God so much, and that the world is so wicked, so full of temptation, and then they have a vocation.'

'Yes, but, Dollie, wait a moment; they do have it, you know.'

'What! a vocation?'

'Of course; some women are veritable Sisters of Charity; look at some of our Church of England sister-hoods.'

'Never mind them,' returned Dollie rather pettishly. 'We are too young to argue such wide questions. What different sorts of people it takes to make up a world! I am thinking now of Sister Veronica aged twenty.'

'Alas, poor soul! but she sleeps, and sleeps well.'

'There is another,' interrupted her friend eagerly,— 'Sister Ursula aged twenty-three, and Sister Monica aged twenty-six; even Sister Mary Thèrese is only thirty-one. Think how young and how weary they must have been! Perhaps, when it was too late, they found out their mis-take; they could not go on singing behind lattices for ever; and as earth is not heaven, they may have grown tired with so many prayers; perhaps their heads ached, and they grew weak, and at last their hearts broke under it with the disappointment and the deadness of all things; and so they died. Singing would not kill them!' cried Dollie, with a little outburst of contempt and grief as they left the cemetery.

'You have quite prevented me from ever wishing to visit the church of the Redemptorist,' was Mary's re-joinder; 'nothing would ever induce me to enter the place now.' And she kept her resolution, and waited for a whole dark hour outside in the gloomy street, when Dollie and her companions went one evening.

When Benediction was over, Dollie came out to her with flushed cheeks and hot eyes, as though she had been crying. 'The singing was not sweet at all,' she said; 'it was harsh and rough, and sounded like men's voices, and yet it went through and through one. Somehow I felt,' whis-pered Dollie, squeezing Mary's arm in the darkness; 'I felt as though those poor creatures were singing their own dirge, it was so dull and so despairing!' And after that Dollie never revisited the church of the Redemptorist.

It was quite dark—moonlight, in fact—when the peaked
roof of the chateau came in view.   To their surprise, the
gates were opened and the outer door stood ajar.   ' I hope
they have not been looking for us,' said Mary, as she
pushed it open ; and then she uttered a soft little cry : ' I
thought you were not coming until next week,' she said
quite breathlessly.   Dollie, who had followed her, stood
by confounded ; the dim oil lamp hardly lit up the obscurity,
and at first she could see nothing, not even the faint stir-
ring of a figure stretched on one of the oaken benches in
the corner of the hall, until a sleepy voice answered : ' All
right ; I am sorry I startled you ; ' and a long form slowly
unfolded itself, developing into the figure of a tall young
man in a brown tweed shooting-coat, who came forward
rather languidly, and shook hands with Mary.

' No one expected you.   Charlotte said you were coming next week.   Dollie, this is an old friend of ours, Mr.
Cuthbert Lyndhurst ; this is Miss Maynard, Bertie,' stammered Mary, who seemed still rather taken aback at this
sudden apparition.

' You must not blame us,' responded the so-called
Bertie, ' if Charlotte chose to confuse our dates ; it is bad
enough as it is, to know we are putting the whole household into a fuss and fever ; Charlotte would have gone on
explaining for ever, only Grey carried her off to see to our
rooms.   Somebody said you were out, and nobody knew
where ; so I lay down and had a nap.'

' Of course,' answered Mary, laughing ; ' when did you
ever fail to take a nap under any circumstances ?   Directly
I saw something moving in the corner I knew it would be
you or Mark Antony.'

' That is too bad,' returned Bertie ; but his eyes
twinkled.   ' I never professed to be a downright wide-
awake person like you, Aunt Mary.   How funny that you
and I should meet in this out-of-the-way place ; isn't there
a fire, or a light somewhere, where I can have a good look
at you ?   Why, it is months since we saw each other—
three or four at least, Mary.'

' Yes, quite that,' she answered quietly, as she led the

way to the morning-room, which was quite a picture of comfort, with its soft, gleaming lamps and wide circle of firelight. The usual trio of Mark Antony and the kittens, who went by the name of Castor and Pollux, occupied the centre of the rug, which was instantly shared by Mary, while Bertie propped himself up against the wooden mantelpiece, looking down on the girls.

CHAPTER VIII

CONCERNING AN ADONIS

WHEN Dollie came to know more of Cuthbert Lyndhurst, she became aware of two singular idiosyncrasies : first, that in spite of his great height and powerful muscular develop-ment he was much given to prop himself against all walls or chimney-pieces with which he came in contact, as though his frame were weak and needed support; and secondly, that every one called him Bertie.

People did it generally by mistake at first, but though they apologised they invariably did it again; whereas his brother, save to a few favoured intimates, was always Mr. Lyndhurst. Bertie said he liked it; it saved no end of trouble, and put things on a pleasant footing.

In appearance he was a tall, fine-looking young fellow, as handsome as an Adonis; and he had all manner of Adonis-like attributes; he had a healthy freshness of colour-ing, and in certain moods he had a way of rumpling his fair hair till it stood round his head like a halo; his eyes were gray and clear, and there was an expression of affec-tion in them when people pleased him, that was very win-ning; but the beauty of his mouth was beyond everything, and some had gone so far as to resent bitterly the light, silky moustache that almost hid it.

It was always a woman who made these sort of speeches; but even men petted Bertie, and said all manner of kind things to him, though they sometimes shook their heads, and lamented over a certain lack of energy—a tendency to stand aside and look on with amused eyes at the battle of life; but his best friends, and Mary among them, were always fiercely indignant at such head-shakings and innuendoes.

What if Bertie were not specially clever? Was cleverness the alpha and omega of life? Was not an honest, kind-hearted young fellow worth something in this matter-of-fact age of ours—one, too, who was as beautiful as Adonis? Energy was a good thing, and it might be well to be sufficiently anxious as to a proper quantity of loaves and fishes for the day's consumption, and to have some notion of the limits and settlements of bills, but there was no need to be always studying one's multiplication table; if Bertie were not a shining light in the eyes of hard-hearted dons and college dignitaries, no one could say that he was without a certain illumination of his own.

If his virtues were somewhat negative, might it not be set down to the score of his youth? If he had not yet acquired the art of making money, and was a little helpless on the subject of the future, he was yet free from any stains in the memory of the past—no clogging debts hung round his neck and impeded his movement; no ungenerous or dishonest act fettered his conscience.

'You have plenty of latent power, if you choose to exercise it,' his brother said to him once, when his wrath had been excited by some heedlessness or want of judgment; 'but the mischief is, you never take the trouble to think seriously about anything.' And his brother was right; Bertie was always going to sleep over something.

He was propped up now against the carved mantelpiece, looking down on the girls; he had given Dollie already one of his swift, half-veiled glances, which saw everything and seemed to see nothing; and had made up his mind about her in a moment.

'A nice little thing,' was his inward comment, for he was much given to ruminate over his ideas in an idle, feckless fashion; 'not pretty, but with a sort of winsome way that a fellow might think very fetching, but in his opinion not half such a good sort as Mary, who was such a restful, comfortable person that one might do worse than

——' but here Bertie pulled himself up, with his hair very much rumpled.

'Well, how are all the Jew babies and the ragged schools, and all the unwashed and barefooted pets?' asked Bertie, with an odd twinkle. 'And what do Lettice and all the little Jewesses do without Aunt Mary?' for a friendship of long standing had placed the Lyndhurst brothers on almost a cousinly footing in the household at Lime Street, and even Grey was called there by his Christian name.

Mary shook her head rather gravely. 'I am afraid Maurice will miss me. Janet made me quite wretched the evening before I came away by hinting that he would be ill from over-work long before I came home. Do you know'—looking up in his face and speaking quite earnestly—'I felt as though I were doing something quite selfish in coming away for such a long holiday.'

'Of course you did! every one can understand that. Don't you know those uncomfortable persons, Miss Maynard, who are always wanting to be martyrs—who pile up their own agony like faggots round a stake? I don't like to betray confidence, or else I could let you into a secret. Miss St. John intends one day to be canonised, and so does her brother.'

'For shame! Do not listen to him, Dollie. He says sad things sometimes.'

'I shall say sadder things by and by, if the maternal St. John does not put her shoulder to the wheel, and leave off saying disagreeable things.'

'Hush! I will not have you abuse my sister-in-law. I am always so sorry for Janet; she is such a sadly misplaced woman. Do you not remember what Grey once said about putting a square thing in a round hole? I never think of Janet without remembering that.'

Bertie made a grimace. 'Mrs. St. John was never a favourite of mine—you know that of old; she is such a terribly handsome woman that one is compelled to admire her in spite of oneself. Do you know her, Miss Maynard?'

Dollie pursed up her lips and owned to the knowledge, but in such a way that Bertie was encouraged to pursue

his merciless criticism in spite of Mary's reproving
glances.

'She is so awfully clever; she seems to draw out all
that a fellow knows in the first few minutes, and then she
has a sort of disapproving Minerva-like wisdom that pro-
vokes one dreadfully.   She is always lauding you two to
the skies, and saying there is no one like Mr. St. John, and
yet she throws cold water on his dearest projects.   I don't
call that wifely submission and sympathy, and all that sort
of thing that you women are so fond of talking about; do
you, Miss Maynard?' finished Bertie, who was determined
to secure Dollie's acquiescence.

'Bertie! what makes you attack poor Janet so to-night?
and when we have not met for ever so long!' put in Mary,
with a touch of pathos.   'You need not be so severe on
her because she says hard things of you; that is contrary
to the gospel, and is all malice and uncharitableness.
There is no love lost between you two—every one knows
that.'

'Why did she begrudge you your holiday?' grumbled
Bertie.

'Oh, oh! that is it,' returned Mary, with a pleased
smile.   'I could not make out why you were so bitter.
She does not begrudge me my holiday, sir.   She was quite
pleased about it, and told me how thankful she was I
was to have such a treat.   She is always saying nice things
to me; she would give everything she possessed to those
she loved; she would work her fingers to the bone for us
all and never complain; but she is so wrapped up in
Maurice that she is blind to other things; and she is
always making herself wretched about him.'

'Then she ought not to plague him so about his work.'

'Ah! that is another thing;' and Mary's bright face
changed, and she sighed.   'That is why I said she was a
misplaced woman.   She is like you, Bertie; she does not
like dirt and squalor and misery.   It makes her hard and
wretched living in such a place; she cannot understand
Maurice's way of looking at things; she thinks other men,
stronger in body and with less intellect, could do his work.

She is ambitious for him, and frets because he has no ambition for himself.'

'I can understand that,' observed Dollie in a low voice. She was much interested by the conversation; but Bertie shrugged his shoulders, and said with a sleepy inflection of voice—

'Pax! pax! you are getting beyond me, Aunt Mary;' and Mary, with infinite tact, changed the subject; and after discussing the journey and other more matter-of-fact topics, the girls bethought themselves of the time, and hurried away to prepare for dinner.

At an angle of the staircase Dollie had another encounter. She came face to face with a dark slight young man, who half stopped, hesitated, and finally passed her with a muttered 'Good-evening.'

Half an hour later, the introduction was made in Charlotte's usual fussy manner. Dollie thought Mr. Grey Lyndhurst a great contrast to his brother, and was not very favourably impressed at first.

He was shorter, with dark complexion and hair, and his skin was decidedly sallow. His features, too, were plain, though a pair of honest gray eyes and a general expression of good sense and intelligence redeemed it from insignificance. People who knew him well were apt to speak highly in his praise; Grey's quiet tongue and clever brains were worth all Bertie's social charms, in the opinion of many who were acquainted with both the brothers.

Dollie only discovered on that first evening that he was gentlemanly and quiet, and that he had a pleasant voice and manner of expressing himself; but then girls of eighteen are not very nice observers of human nature, and are rather given to admire an Adonis.

Dollie formed no exception to this rule. She thought Mr. Cuthbert Lyndhurst the handsomest young man that she had ever seen, and was almost inclined to envy Mary the free and easy terms on which she seemed to be with him. She thought it must be pleasant to call him Bertie, and to be scolded and petted by him in that brotherly way.

Were his manners quite brotherly, after all? Dollie puzzled her little head a good deal over this question during the next few days. He certainly looked very affectionately at Mary; but then Bertie's eyes always were affectionate. It might be by accident rather than design that he was generally to be found loitering by Mary's side, while Dollie, by no choice of her own, was left to his brother. Dollie did not know much about lovers except in theory; but she had her own maidenly opinion on the subject, and she thought there was nothing especially lover-like in Bertie's sleepy good-humoured manners.

The doubt lay rather with Mary herself. Even on this first evening, she seemed a changed creature in Dollie's eyes; she was always bright, being one of those happy beings who make their own sunshine, but now she was absolutely beaming; her gentle fun quite overflowed, and touched everything. If she were quiet at all it was with Mr. Lyndhurst, towards whom she seemed more reserved; but to Bertie she talked of everything and anything that came into her head, as though she were quite sure of his sympathy in all that concerned her.

Dollie did say one word when they went up to bed together that night. 'What a pleasant addition to our party! I like both the Lyndhursts so much—but how very intimate you seem with Mr. Bertie!'

'He and I are such old friends, you see,' returned Mary, with a quick blush. 'Grey is quieter than his brother, but he is very nice too.' And Dollie, with quick instinct, understood that she was to say no more.

The girls had a short interview with their hostess the next morning, but it was very brief. The sun was shining, and the young men were waiting for them in the courtyard outside, for they had promised to show them all the sights of Lesponts; but just as Dollie was fastening her long gloves and chattering to Mary, Charlotte came to fetch them to Mrs. Reid's dressing-room.

It was a large, sunny apartment, looking over the courtyard, with a pleasant view of the avenue stretching away towards the cemetery, and furnished in quite the

English fashion, with comfortable chintz couches and arm-chairs.

Mrs. Reid smiled and held out her hands to them as they entered, but she did not rise; she was lying back in a great cushioned chair, looking very feeble and worn.

She wore a gray dressing-gown, with a soft gray Shetland shawl drawn closely round her, as though for warmth; and with her white face and gray hair, and the sad neutral tints of her garments she looked like a gray shadow of a woman. Dollie uttered a ·shocked exclamation, but Mary stepped forward and accosted her cheerfully; but none the less did her practised eye—used. to many a sick and dying bed— read the stern truth before them; Mrs. Reid was more than a suffering woman—she was not long for this world. She received them with soft flitting smiles, but her voice was very low and weak. ' Sit there, my dear,' she said, beckon-ing Dollie to the large square footstool at her feet. ' Have you written to your mother, my child? That is right,' as Dollie nodded; ' never forget her—never let her complain of the least shadow of neglect; there is no love like a mother's love; every other affection has an element of selfishness in it; but a mother gives and asks for nothing again.' And as the girls hardly knew how to answer her, there was a few minutes' silence.

By and by she spoke again, but this time to Mary; but she still held Dollie's hand and patted it occasionally. ' So the Lyndhursts are here, Charlotte tells me; she made a week's mistake in her reckoning, and nothing was ready for them. My poor little housekeeper was inclined to cry over it, not having very wise brains of her own. But for Grey's cool head and powers of quiet management, I doubt whether either she or Romany would have been quite equal to the emergency.'

Mary laughed and said something about a wholesale invasion of the chateau.

' No! we have plenty of room; the chateau would hold half a dozen more; it is'only Charlotte's way of putting herself and every one else in a bustle. I can just fancy her

fretting and fuming, with Romany and Ursula looking open-
eyed and stolid behind her, and then Grey coming in, and
putting them all to rights with a word or two. I suppose
Bertie was having a nap somewhere.'

' Now, Mrs. Reid, I call that too bad,' protested Mary.

' Why, is it not Grey who says he is always falling asleep
somewhere or other? I have not much opinion of young
men in general, but I must say I think Grey is worth his
salt.'

' Do you mean to imply the contrary of Bertie? '

' Humph ! I don't think he will set the world on fire,'
was the dry rejoinder. 'Take my advice, my dears, and
judge a man by his deeds and not by his looks ; it is a safe
rule and a wise one.'

' Bertie has done nothing wrong,' began Mary somewhat imprudently ; but Mrs. Reid stopped her with even a
graver look than usual.

' A little bird once told me that somebody who considered herself a very wise person was a warm partisan of
Cuthbert Lyndhurst's, and never allowed any one to say a
word in his dispraise ; is it not so, my dear? ' But Mary
drew herself up and looked displeased ; she thought her
hostess was taking a strange liberty, and before Dorothy
too.

' I am a warm partisan of all my old friends,' she said
rather stiffly, and with an emphasis on the one word old ;
and then she looked down and fidgeted with her eyeglasses. Mrs. Reid watched her, and an expression of pain
crossed her face.

' Forgive me, my dear ; I did not mean to offend you ;
we sick people think ourselves privileged to say anything.
Your sister-in-law was talking to me about him one day. I
remember so well her telling me that she had a far higher
opinion of Grey than his brother—it was the only subject
on which we seemed to agree.'

' I have the highest opinion of both of them, that is all,'
responded Mary in a low voice ; and then, with more
difficulty, she went on : ' If Janet has been talking to you,
of course I understand how it is ; she and Bertie have

never . been friends—they do not understand each other. When he comes to our house there is always some trouble in keeping the peace; he says such tiresome things, just to provoke her, but it is only his fun.'

'She said nothing about all that; she only hinted that he was purposeless, and let himself drift on somehow. Do not misunderstand me, my dear,' she continued in a lighter tone; 'I do not wish to speak against Bertie, but I have always regarded age as a sort of finger-post to youth— to give right directions, and close up dangerous ways. It is hard—indeed it is, Mary—to live out our own bitter experiences,—to gain wisdom through suffering,—and then to stand by and watch others making just the same mistakes, taking the same terrible roads, and refusing to hear if you call ever so loudly to them to stop.'

'Would you have us walk blindfolded through the days of our youth, and give our hands to be guided?' replied Mary, a little warmly; and then at the sight of the gray worn face before her, she suddenly softened and became her own sweet self again.

'Dear Mrs. Reid, I did not mean to speak so impatiently. I always fire up when my friends are attacked; it is a foolish habit, and Janet is always scolding me for it, but I do like to think the best of people; no one is without fault, we are all so terribly human,' finished Mary, quite humbly.

'Yes, indeed,' sighed Mrs. Reid, and her eyes rested tenderly for a moment on Mary's earnest face; 'well, I have said my say, I will not tease you with any more unpalatable advice; you and I will be good friends, I know, for I love a bold, generous spirit. Now I must not keep you any longer, for I hear impatient footsteps in the courtyard outside; perhaps you will each come and sit with me a little in my dressing-room this evening—come separately, that I may learn to know you better;' and then she smiled at them kindly, and bade them go.

'What an age you have kept us!' grumbled Bertie, whom they found marching up and down disconsolately in the courtyard; Grey was leaning over the gate, and made no

6

remark. 'Does it always take you just an hour and a half to put on that hat?'

'We were with Mrs. Reid; she wanted to see us. I am sorry we kept you waiting, Bertie,' replied Mary a little gravely; and then they went out into the avenue.

CHAPTER IX

THE October sunshine was flooding the avenue with yellow glory as the four young people sallied out of the gates of the chateau, and walked on briskly with much crunching of dead leaves under their feet. Mary's fit of gravity did not long continue. Many a heavy Flemish countenance lighted up at the sight of the bright young faces. Every now and then there were soft ripples of laughter and bursts of innocent merriment, of gay badinage, with odd little breaks of silence.

Dollie talked less than Mary. She was rather shy of her companion, who proved himself a somewhat grave cicerone. But if her words were few, her small blue eyes sparkled with delight, and a little rosy flush tinged the ordinarily pale face very becomingly.

Was it not a dream this strange wandering through an unknown city? Dollie pinched herself more than once to prove that she was awake. If she lived a hundred years would she ever forget this wonderful day?—never, never! and then she started and blushed as she found Grey standing beside her, watching her with quiet amused eyes.

'If we were in England we should have a crowd gathered round us to know what you see on those opposite roofs,' he said, with a certain dry emphasis that represented fun to him—half quizzing and half serious.

'Oh, do stand still a moment; we cannot hurry through this. Where are the others going? I never saw anything half so beautiful,' cried Dollie breathlessly.

They were crossing the Grande Place when Dollie

uttered her little protest. The vast square lay before them looking empty and sleepy in the sunshine; the green benches before the *café* were unoccupied; two or three women in their long black Flemish cloaks stumped slowly across the rough uneven stones; a huge mastiff, harnessed to a baker's cart, came stumbling round the corner;.two priests, with black garments and shovel-hats, walked slowly past Dollie and her companion.

How still and beautiful it looked with the sunlight shimmering on the peaked Spanish roofs and quaint jutting outlines of the buildings. Before them were the façades of les Halles, and in the centre the Tourdes Halles or belfry, with its massive square towers and corner turrets surmounted by a lofty octagon.

'How grand! how exquisite!' cried Dollie; and as she spoke the sweet tones of the carillon floated across the Place. She strove vainly to listen as Mr. Lyndhurst gravely pointed out to her one or two quaint mediæval buildings to which some sort of historic interest was attached. There was 'the Lion de Flandre, now a shop, but which tradition asserted that Charles II once occupied in his exile; and the Crænenburg, now a tavern, where the German King Maximilian, the "last of the knights," was kept in durance vile for twelve days on account of his refusal to cede the guardianship of his son Philip, heir to the crown of the Netherlands, to the king of France.'

Dollie was considered an intelligent listener, but on the present occasion she turned a somewhat deaf ear to her companion's historic details. She wanted to be sure that she was not dreaming, as her eyes roved over the deserted Place. She was peopling it in her own way from the past —figures with peaked Spanish beards in slashed doublets and ruffs, stout old Flemish burghers, and dark thin-faced weavers, crossed and recrossed the vast emptiness, keeping measure with the clanging carillon.

Gentle dames with palfry and hawk and hounds rode noiselessly across the sunshiny square, among them Maximilian's young bride Mary.

'What interests you so much?' asked Mr. Lyndhurst,

somewhat weary of this prolonged silence, and astonished at the girl's spellbound attitude and dreamy eyes. Dollie waved a little gloved hand and broke into a wild couplet by way of answer.

'There they are,' she cried—

'All the foresters of Flanders,—mighty Baldwin, Bras de Fer, Lyderick du Bucq and Cressy, Philip, Guy de Dampierre.'

'Longfellow. Ah, yes. Very aptly quoted. Bertie is always spouting that. But, Miss Maynard, are you not afraid that we shall lose them altogether?' and then Dollie felt herself a little rebuked, and consented to hurry on.

What a bewildering phantasmagoria that morning seemed to be! How bright and endless, with its vivid series of pictures! Now they were threading narrow grass-grown streets, with dark gloomy buildings on either side. Then came a shining piece of canal. Here barges were moored; swans with arched necks and rustling plumage glided past. Quaint peaked cream-coloured houses, with red roofs, bordered the canals. From one of them Dollie averted her eyes with sick feelings of loathing. Mr. Lyndhurst had told her that it had been the Spanish torture-house. Merciful heavens! could such things be? Alas! what scenes of horror and bloodshed had been enacted there! Now the sun shone, and the swans plumed themselves in the dark water, and all looked peaceful as an autumn day. And Dollie gave a little shiver of relief and hurried on. They saw the Hotel de Ville and the Palais de Justice; and the girls were shown the magnificent chimney-place, said to be carved by a prisoner of the name of Halsman. Then they passed over the Place adjoining the Place de Bourg, prettily planted with horse-chestnuts, and adorned with a statue of Jan van Eyck; and after that they went to the cathedral.

The girls were very silent when the great doors closed on them. The young men stood and whispered apart as they watched them. Dollie, indeed, gave one suppressed exclamation as she caught sight of the magnificent interior, with its rich tone of colour and fine proportions. Through the closed gates of the choir they could see the marble

monuments and the ancient Gothic choir stalls.   The walls
were covered with dark paintings; a faint perfume of
incense steeped the air ; kneeling figures were everywhere ;
the chapels round the choir had each its silent worshipper.
Dollie strayed into one and sat down.   There was a painting by Van Oost the elder representing the infant Saviour
in the workshop of Nazareth.   A weather-beaten man in a
shabby blouse, with a grizzled head, came into the chapel
and crossed himself devoutly, and knelt down before
the picture.   Dollie watched him with wide open eyes ;
her thoughts were terribly confused.   She thought of the
closed churches in England, with their few services and
scanty number of worshippers, and the chill, empty feeling
that pervaded them on week-days.

Here there were warmth, life, and perpetual movement ;
noiseless figures passed and repassed through the great
door perpetually.   Everywhere, in each dark corner, in
each dim chapel, was some silent cloaked form.   What
reverence, what abstraction !   How one ought to envy
them, thought Dollie.   Every one bringing in his or her
burden and laying it down in the Holy of Holies, and
then passing out refreshed and strengthened into the world
again—' Every one for himself and God for us all,' thought
Dollie, with a sudden effusion of feeling.

Mr. Lyndhurst found her looking thoughtful and a little
weary, and said a word or two of excuse.

' I feel as though we have neglected you, Miss Maynard.'

' Not at all.   Why should you say that ?   I think it is
good to be here,' replied the girl softly.   She spoke very
simply, but she looked at him with eyes so full of wonder
and veneration that the young man felt himself silenced,
and drew back until she joined him of her own accord, and
suffered him to take her home.

This day, so glorious in Dollie's memory, was the pre-
cursor of many others.   Every morning the four young
people, sometimes under Charlotte's chaperonage, sometimes by themselves, wandered of their own sweet will
through every nook of the quaint old city.

They visited the Hospital of St. John, and saw Hans

Memling's great work, the shrine of St. Ursula. Indeed, before many weeks were over the girls grew quite eloquent over the merits and demerits of the old Flemish painters— the splendid groupings of John and Hubert van Eyck; the freedom and grace with which Memling treated his figures of small proportions; the comparative merits of the two Van Oosts, Kerckhove, Erregouts, Marc Duvenedo and Jesse Aerschout; and the works of Gheerardt, David, and Pourbus, studied patiently in the Académie des Beaux Arts.

The Béguinage and the Hospital of St. John especially delighted them; the long airy wards of the latter, with their single aisle, and the rows of neat curtained beds on either side, the mediæval aspect of the ancient building, interested them greatly; but their visits to the different churches pleased them most.

It may be doubted whether the young men showed this enthusiasm, though they good-humouredly bore the infliction. They would keep guard outside, while the girls hurried on in the twilight to hear vespers and benediction. Mary, who was more orthodox, would sometimes hesitate and be tempted to linger outside, but Dollie in her impetuous way would hear of no compromise.

'What does it matter? We cannot understand their droning. We can say our own prayers and think our own thoughts quite comfortably. I like to see all those worshippers, and to smell the incense. Such strange thoughts come to me as I kneel in that dark old nave,—there is the darkness, and the people are kneeling in the midst of it, and beyond, through the open gates, are the light and the truth. I cannot tell you quite what I mean, but it makes me better, and I like to be there,' finished Dollie, with a little confusion of logic; and though Mary shook her head, and wondered what Maurice would say, she let herself be persuaded. Notre Dame was their favourite church. There was a copy of Van Dyck's Crucifixion that especially attracted them. When Dollie was missing, they always knew where they would find her. She would fetch a wooden chair for herself, and place herself near the picture. It

hung in the old chapel of the Host, just over the altar.
In a black marble niche there stood a life-size marble group
of the Divine Child in His mother's arms.   The figures
were of exquisite beauty.   Dollie learned that the work
was ascribed to Michael Angelo.   Mr. Lyndhurst told her
the composition was undoubtedly his, though the execution
was probably entrusted to one of his pupils.   How Dollie
delighted in that group ! the lovely features of the Madonna
and the Holy Babe, the softly-rounded outlines, the elaborate finish, riveted her with feelings of intense satisfaction.   She wrote whole pages of description to her mother.
The widow, sitting by her lonely fireside, smiled faintly
over those girlish rhapsodies.   How happy she was ! how
full of life and strength and energy !   Mrs. Maynard thought
nothing about those hours in the dim old churches which
Mary feared might be so perilous to her young faith.   Did she
not know her child ?   Was she not good and trustworthy,
sweet, and sound to the heart's core ? thought the simple
woman, with an entire fidelity to her one living treasure.
Those letters of Dollie's were her mother's chief consolations.

The young men were tolerably patient, but they had
their revenge sometimes, and would carry off the girls for
long breezy walks on the ramparts, or down the roads
bordering the canals.

There was a spot that they especially loved to haunt
called Laeken-water.   Standing on the bridge, they looked
down on a little piece of landscape that reminded them of
a choice Dutch painting.

The water lay still and clear beneath them.   In the
distance was a rustic bridge, a church, and some quaintly-
peaked houses.   The sun shone brightly on the red roofs.
There were trees coming low down to the water.   Some
swans were gliding from under the bridge.   Mary and
Bertie went down one day to feed them, while Dollie got
out her sketch-book, and put in a few hasty outlines.

'I must send this to my mother,' she said ; and Mr.
Lyndhurst leaned against the bridge and watched her
busy fingers.   The sunbeams had got into Dollie's fair

hair; it looked soft and golden under her little brown hat. She had no idea as she sketched in the quaint Spanish gables that she was herself a pretty picture.

Dollie's pencil moved, but her tongue was silent. She was wondering what they were saying to each other down there below the bridge. The swans had long ago sailed slowly up the stream; but Mary stood still looking down upon the water, and Bertie was making holes in the wet sandy margin with his stick.

It was now ten days since the brothers had arrived at the chateau, but as yet Dollie's opinions were unaltered with regard to them. She still thought Bertie the hand-somest and the pleasantest young man that she had ever met, and she was still somewhat in awe of his brother.

It was more a negative than a positive awe. Grey's reticence, his gravity, and the weight of his opinions when he chose to unbend and express them, invested him with a certain superiority in her mind. Careless Dollie found herself measuring her words and talking somewhat primly when he entered into conversation with her.

At other times, when they were all together for ex-ample, her girlish spirits would find vent for themselves; and the flood of nonsense, of contradiction, and daring assertion would flow forth. At such times he was always an indulgent listener; he never called her to order, or put her down as he did Bertie, neither did he dryly interpose his opinion as he would often do with Mary; on the con-trary, he seemed ready to draw her out on all occasions, probably to judge for himself what substrata of sense and reality lay at the bottom of the flightiness. Dollie had not a notion that she was being weighed in the balance,—the mere idea would have made her furious. She thought Mr. Lyndhurst very kind and very attentive to all her little wants and wishes; she even told her mother so in her letters, speaking frankly both of him and Bertie. 'I like them both; they are so pleasant and agreeable, but Mr. Bertie is far more amusing. I am always afraid Mr. Lyndhurst thinks me affected and girlish; he does not say so, of course, but he has a way sometimes of curling his

lip that makes me feel very small. I have a notion that I
keep a set of company manners expressly for him, only
sometimes I forget, and am Dollie again.'

Dollie got more used to him by and by, and learned to
judge his mannerisms more truly when they were alone
together, as they often were in their walks. He would be
very gentle with her, bringing himself to her level, and
trying in a quiet way to find out her tastes and opinions.

On the present occasion he had brought himself with
some little effort—for Grey was an essentially shy, reserved
man—to speak about his brother and himself. Dollie
listened to him politely, and tried to show a proper amount
of interest; but presently she had taken out her sketch-
book, and a silence had fallen between them. It was not
that she was ungrateful, but she was very young, and a
grave conversation was not always to her taste. At such
times she would have a hankering after Bertie's fun.

But she had yet to learn that Grey was one who was
accustomed to have his own way. He had brought himself
with some difficulty to speak of his own circumstances and
manner of life, and he did not intend to be repulsed or
silenced until silence was pleasing to him. He was patient
by nature, but withal firm, and, as some people said, a trifle
hard; but the hardness was shown chiefly to himself. To
those whom he liked he could be wonderfully gentle, effac-
ing himself for their sakes, and subordinating his own tastes
and wishes to theirs.

He watched Dollie's slender fingers for some time, and
then resumed the subject as though he were unconscious
of any break.

'Blenheim Square is rather a dreary place; and, for the
matter of that, Teddiford Place is worse.'

'I have never seen either of them,' replied Dollie rather
absently, putting in a willow that hung near the bridge. 'The
dreariest place I know is Trevilian Terrace, Abercrombie
Road—the abomination of desolation, that is what I call it.'

'Is that the place where your mother lives? it lies somewhere between Kensington and Earlscourt, does it not?'
asked Grey with a shade of eagerness; and as Dollie

nodded, he went on, 'I should think it was highly prefer-
able to Teddiford Place; you see it leads out of Blenheim
Square. Blenheim Square is only one of a whole chain of
squares, each with a separate dulness and dreariness of its
own. Many of the houses are large and handsome, and
are inhabited by rich city magnates, who have not yet
moved westward; but Teddiford Place is a shade lower in
the scale. The houses are good, but they are mostly let
in lodgings; there are not more than a dozen houses in
the whole of Teddiford Place.'

'Why do you live there if it be so dull?' asked Dollie
with divided interest, for the willow was claiming her
attention.

'My poverty and not my will consents to dulness,' he
returned with a laugh; 'but I do not mean to go back
to Teddiford Square. I have taken chambers—it sounds
grand till you see them, Miss Maynard'—('If I ever do,'
thought Dollie, with secret contradiction)—'they are near
Gray's Inn. My bedroom is the size of a good-sized trunk,
and my sitting-room will hold about three people comfortably; but what does it matter when one is too hard at work
to notice anything?' finished Mr. Lyndhurst with an attempt
at lightness.

'Charlotte says that you have nearly killed yourself with
over-work,' said Dollie gravely, raising her eyes from the
sketch; 'do you not think it wrong to play with your health
in that fashion?' she continued, forgetting her fear of the
young barrister in her feminine delight at administering a
lecture. 'You were on the brink of brain fever, Mr. Bertie
says.'

'Well, so I was,' he returned, pleased at this manifestation of interest in his concerns; 'at least so they all said;
and so I am here to vegetate and rest a while—why, I have
not opened a book for three weeks! You see a briefless
barrister has hard uphill work before him. I am poor now,
but I am not enamoured of poverty. I must get my feet
on the first rung of the social ladder; but till the climbing
begins, one has to be satisfied with a pittance; that is the
real state of the case, Miss Maynard.'

'We are poor too, mother and I; but I am not satisfied with my pittance,' returned Dollie carelessly. 'I should like to be rich, very rich—to have all the pleasures of life open to me, to travel, to see pictures, to wear grand dresses and jewels. I am worldly-minded enough to care for all kinds of indulgences; rich people have much the best of it in every way,' and then she coloured and stopped abruptly. Grey thought her sensitiveness had taken alarm; but in reality a sudden remembrance of Charlotte's talk crossed her mind, and she hastily changed the subject.

Meanwhile, a very different conversation was taking place under the bridge, where Mary was arguing her point with an eagerness and persistence that was foreign to her usual placid nature, while Bertie had some difficulty in defending himself.

'You know that I am right—that every one who knows you says the same thing,' she continued, when she had concluded her lecture with its various points—Bertie's lack of energy, his indifference to things in general and himself in particular, his lamentable lack of ambition, and other heinous crimes. 'You cannot say I am wrong, when every one whose opinion is worth anything agrees with me.'

'So everybody is to be my Mentor,' said Bertie sulkily; for with all his sweet temper he could be sullen on occasions.

'The wisdom of the many must be right,' she answered playfully, for she had no wish to anger him; 'surely Maurice is a respectable authority, and so is your brother.'

'Oh, we all know your opinion of Grey,' answered Bertie, pulling his fair moustache in an annoyed way. Mary could have laughed outright at his boyish irritation and jealousy, but she was never wanting in tact, so she replied soothingly—

'I think very highly of Grey, but I daresay I could find plenty of faults in him if I were to take the trouble to discover them. Now do not be cross, Bertie, because I am such a true friend that I am more anxious for your future welfare than for your present happiness; come, say something pleasant to me after all the trouble I have been taking.' But Bertie was not to be mollified so easily; he had had his lecture, and it had disagreed with him; in fact, certain words that Mary had uttered pricked him most uncomfortably in his conscience, and Bertie hated to be made uncomfortable.

'If you think me such a thriftless good-for-nothing fellow, I wonder you have anything to do with me,' he grumbled, for his pride was up for once in his life. 'You used not to be so hard upon me, Mary; if you are going to give me up in this way, you had better tell me so at once, before I make a downright fool of myself.'

'I never give up my friends as long as I can keep them; don't talk such nonsense, sir,' she replied lightly; but her voice was very soft, and she put her hand gently on his arm as she spoke. Dollie saw the action, and wondered at the little demonstration. Bertie was for ever making these sort of speeches to her, and she was for ever parrying them; but as yet no word of love had been spoken between them.

'I shall believe the world is coming to an end when you do give me up,' Bertie returned very slowly and seriously; and then as she looked in his face and smiled, the matter seemed understood between them, and Bertie's brow cleared.

'We will go back to them now,' said Mary cheerfully; 'look, there is Dollie waving her sketch-book.' It seemed quite natural that they should climb up together hand in hand. No special word of love had been spoken between them; no promise had been given or received; yet Bertie in his heart was sure of Mary's love, and Mary knew that she would never be the wife of any other man if Bertie were to be untrue to her.

CHAPTER X

A RETROSPECT AND A DREAM

THE days passed happily away in the old chateau. Charlotte, who scarcely knew her quiet home under its present altered aspect, was in a state of fussy excitement from morning to night. She was for ever planning some fresh surprise to please her young guests; every morning there were long mysterious confabulations with Romany, Ursula, or Justine; she tripped along the dim corridors, jingling her keys, and humming little snatches of song, looking quite fresh and young in her smart braided dresses. 'Where are you going, Cousin Charlotte?' Bertie would say sometimes, pursuing her in his teasing way. 'What a charming gown! I suppose that is Madame Elise's handiwork;' for the mischievous fellow knew how to get a rise out of her, as he called it.

Charlotte shook her head at him with a simpering smile—

'Of course not, you foolish boy; why, Madame Elise would empty my poor little purse in no time,' she answered in her airy way. 'Justine made this; oh, she is excellent —a treasure of treasures; she knows that I like "une toilette très habillée." Oh, she is a good creature; ma Tante undervalues her.'

'But what do you call this stuff?' persisted Bertie, with a serious countenance; 'it reminds me of a dress Lady Emily Howard wore last winter.' Now Lady Emily Howard was the mother of Bertie's pupil.

'You don't say so!' exclaimed Charlotte, with sparkling

eyes. 'I must tell Justine that. Of course Lady Emily
has charming toilettes. I suppose you cannot tell me if
her corsage were cut exactly like mine?'

'Oh dear, yes; I should say there was not a hair-
breadth's difference—not the eighth of a fraction of an
inch,' returned Bertie, who had not the faintest conception
what a corsage meant, and who was perfectly aware that
Lady Emily was a stout blonde who always wore black.
'You are as alike as two peas.'

'Dear, dear!' exclaimed Charlotte, who was quite
delighted with this fib; 'how very extraordinary! thank you
so much for telling me, Bertie.'

'And you will be sure to have gâteau for dinner; I am
so tired of compote!' exclaimed Bertie in a coaxing voice.

'Yes, yes,' she nodded, and trotted off well pleased, to
hunt through her stock of preserves; of course there would
be gâteau, and marrons glacés too, for dessert. Bertie
was a veritable schoolboy in his love for sweet things, and
Charlotte took care that this should be gratified. ' "As
like as two peas!" I must tell Justine that,' she said to
herself as she unlocked the great presses in her storeroom.

Sometimes when they had an hour to spare, the girls
would follow her about. Dollie fell in love with the old
Flemish kitchen when she first saw it. The sun was
streaming through the low windows and in at the open
door; the red brick floor, the great oaken benches and
presses, the brass stew-pans and kettles ranged round the
walls, old Kâtchen stumping across the floor in her sabots,
with a long wooden ladle in her hand. 'What a picture it
would make,' thought Dollie.

Kâtchen was quite a character. She was a weather-
beaten Flemish peasant, with a square, stolid face, cheeks
like winter apples, and a skin wrinkled and brown as
parchment.

She spoke English volubly—scolding in a high shrill
key when anything put her out, and arranging her sentences
in a curious confusion, without regard to either person or
tense.

Charlotte was greatly in awe of her, and always spoke
to her in a half-apologetic, half-coaxing manner.

'Now look you, Meess,' Kâtchen would say, hobbling
up to them with her ladle outstretched and pointed
towards them; 'un vol-au-vent ou des petits pâtés, that say
you—bien—va-là—me—am I a pâtissier? can I mind my
pot-au-feu, go to market, make kickshaws, and all at the
same hour of the day? Kâtchen, have you been at the
poissonnerie? have you les poulets? Va l what take you
me for? Am I of all work? can I fly comme le poulet?
can I swim down the canal comme les canards? Bien,
thou shalt mind thyself, Kâtchen Deyster. No English
meess shall put on thee, and drive thee like a lame cow.'

'My good Kâtchen, what has put you out?' Charlotte
would say almost humbly; 'is it the vol-au-vent that
displeases you? Why, that is your chef d'œuvre, my
excellent Kâtchen,—that and your bouilli and your salads.'

'Hein, I am worth my salt,' returned Kâtchen grimly;
'they know me au marché. Jacques Dullaert, he trembles
and turns his back when he me sees. Jacques, dost thou
still sell stale fish? that say I to Jacques when I pass him.
He has not the spirit of a calf to shake his stupid head
even. Va, for cet Jacques-là;' and Kâtchen snapped her
fingers in scornful remembrance of Jacques's treachery.

Dollie took a great interest in the little old woman in
spite of her shrill tones; she used to steal into the great
kitchen sometimes, and seat herself on the low window-sill,
in company with the black cat; she watched the com-
pounding of sundry foreign dishes with great interest, and
soon mastered the mysteries of the potato-salad and the
pot-au-feu; she even accompanied Kâtchen to market.
The Grande Place on those occasions was always her
favourite resort; the vast space under the belfry, the entire
square, was filled with covered stalls; crowds of Flemish
peasants in their long cloth cloaks, with handsome crosses
and pendants and earrings—often of great value and
handed down as heirlooms from generation to generation—
presided over their wares. Dollie used to pace down the
long narrow aisles between the stalls speculating on the

busy faces round her. Once Kâtchen stopped to exchange greeting with an old peasant woman at the corner of the market; she had a yellow puckered-up face, and mumbled out her jargon in a toothless manner. Nevertheless two brilliant earrings set in silver dangled below her withered cheeks, and a great cross hung over her black cloak. 'Marie sells good butter and eggs, but she cheats like an old fox,' said Kâtchen shrewdly, as they left the stall.

Both the girls loved this busy scene. Bertie would join them sometimes, and purchase all sorts of incongruous articles; he brought home once a pair of yellow sabots, a nutmeg-grater, and a handful of nails and old iron; another day he returned laden with plaster images of St. Joseph and the Holy Family, a boy carrying some green flower-pots and a copper kettle followed him. 'I got them for a few cêntimes, and it was such fun driving the bargain,' he said, when Charlotte took him to task for bringing home a pack of rubbish.

The holland covers had all disappeared from the great salon, the red velvet chairs and couches, with their white and gilded woodwork, were exposed in all their magnificence; the huge black stove was opened; in the evening a bright fire burned cheerily; wax candles were lighted in the gilt sconces; the grand piano always stood open.

Mrs. Reid remained in the seclusion of her dressing-room for some days, but both the girls were frequently admitted. Dollie generally had the hour before dinner allotted for her visit. She would come in from her walk, and go upstairs without waiting to take off her hat. Mrs. Reid always welcomed her kindly. Dollie would take the footstool at her feet, and give her a *résumé* of the day's doings, the pictures they had seen, the walks they had taken, and sometimes even the conversations that had taken place.

Mrs. Reid used to enjoy the girl's graphic descriptions. Dollie had a happy knack of making the most of a thing; she would touch up her sketch, putting in all sorts of graceful finishes. They had been down by the English convent, and had wandered ever so far. ' It was all sandy

7

and flat, with nothing but the canal and a windmill or two, but the sunset was lovely, and glorified everything; the sky was all red and glowing, and there was a fresh wind blowing in our faces; we seemed walking straight on as though we could not help it, right into the sunset—up, up, into the heart of the brightness; and then Mary and Charlotte said that we must come back, and we turned round, and then we were on the earth again, and it looked cold and shadowy and gray.'

'That is what we are always doing, turning our back on the brightness,' observed Mrs. Reid softly, as she stroked the pretty fair head that leant against her.   She and Dollie were becoming fast friends.   Later in the evening Mary would come up and have her turn.

It was curious to watch Mrs. Reid's different reception of the two girls.   When Dollie's bright little face appeared, Mrs. Reid would lay down her knitting, and beckon the girl to the footstool at her feet; there would be plenty of kind quiet caresses; but with Mary there would be no stroking of hair, no footstools or attitudes of humility.

'Well, Mary,' she would say, holding out her hand with a smile of welcome; and Mary would stoop over the easy-chair and kiss her cheek, and then she would draw up her seat cosily to the fire, and take out her work.

They had long quiet talks, chiefly on grave subjects. Mrs. Reid used to question her about her work at the East-end of London, the family life at Lime Street, the characters and training of the five little girls who were so dear to Aunt Mary's heart.   She used to consult Mary about her own pensioners.   Somehow she seemed to have an intuitive perception that the girl was reliable and wise beyond her years. Mary had sundry little glimpses into the strange Anglo-Flemish life that the elder woman led.   In a quiet unobtrusive way she did a large amount of good—little secret acts of benevolence, generous contributions to the needy foreigners among whom she lived, were always being traced to the Lady Bountiful of the chateau; and she spoke freely of such matters to her young friend.

'I am not like that large-hearted Shunamite.   I do not

dwell among my own people,' she once said rather mournfully, 'but I think I owe something to the poor folk round me. You must not think that I lose sight of the people at home. Mr. Champneys, our old vicar, has always acted as my almoner at Crome.'

'I think Maurice knows him. He must be very old now—nearly eighty.'

'Seventy-eight on his last birthday. He wrote rather a doleful letter the other day, dear old man! and complained that he was getting very feeble and unfit for his work. He even hinted that he thought of leaving his parish under the care of some conscientious man, and going down into Devonshire to be near his daughter. Poor Mrs. Champneys is a sad invalid, and he thought a year or two's residence in a warmer climate would be beneficial to her. She is his second wife, and is about twenty years younger than the vicar.'

'Do you mean that he is really going to have a curate in charge? I wonder—oh, I wonder—if Maurice could be induced to apply for the curacy,' exclaimed Mary, and then she stopped and clasped her hands; the sudden thought seemed too much for her.

'I thought you told me that his heart was so much in his work,' asked Mrs. Reid, in some surprise. .

'Yes, but he is overworked. Janet says so, and I know she is right. He will not spare himself; and he is not strong, and in winter he gets a cough which he cannot shake off. If we could get him into the country it would be so good for him and the children. They are delicate little creatures, and Janet says it is so bad for them having no garden to play in, and no fresh air to breathe—all narrow streets and chimneys. It is breaking her heart for them all to live in such a place.' And Mary's earnestness was so great that the tears rose to her eyes. The burden of her sister-in-law's complaints lay heavy on her heart; perhaps now there might be a way of lightening the load.

'But, my dear, the living is a very small one. The rectory is certainly very roomy and comfortable, but Mr. Champneys could not afford to give his curate-in-charge more than £200 a year. Your brother could not live on that.'

'That is what Mr. Denoon gives him now, and he lets him live in one of his houses. They say few curates have as much, but Maurice does the work of two. I do not know what is to become of them all if Maurice does not soon get a living. They are drawing out all the capital of Janet's little fortune, and have only a few hundreds left; and the children are growing up and need education,' went on Mary sorrowfully, too much absorbed with the sadness of her subject to remember to whom she was speaking; afterwards when she recollected it in the quiet of her own room, her cheek turned crimson, and she was ready to cry with mortification and vexation.

'She will think that I am asking her to help Maurice and to give us money,' she said, when in the bitterness of her heart she carried her tale to Dollie; and though Dollie comforted her with a great many kind words, the remembrance of her thoughtlessness gave Mary many a secret stab.

Mrs. Reid did not seem surprised at her young friend's statement; she had heard it all before from Janet herself.

'I think it is wrong for any man to over-task his strength as Maurice is doing,' she replied seriously. 'I spoke to him very plainly when he was here; but he did not take my advice in good part; even excellent people like Maurice can be self-willed and put themselves in the wrong sometimes;' but Mrs. Reid did not add that she had made offers of help, unknown to Janet, and that she had been much angered by Maurice's cool and somewhat curt refusal to accept her gifts.

'What right have we to her money? how was I to bring myself to take such sums at her hand?' he had said with a storminess quite unusual to him, as he detailed the interview afterwards to his wife. Perhaps the manner of tendering the gift had offended his notions of independence; but any way he had told himself that the thing was impossible.

'And you refused her bounty! Have you forgotten your wife and your little ones? Oh, Maurice, Maurice,

how could you be so mad, so ungrateful?' And Janet's
pale face flamed and quivered with the passion of her
excitement; never before had she spoken to him so
reproachfully.

'Hush, my dear! hush, Janet! can you not trust your
husband?' he replied tenderly. 'Can I do what I feel to
be wrong because of my wife and children?'

'Why do you reproach me?' he said afterwards, when
there had been silence between them, which, with all her
courage, she had not dared to break. 'You knew when
you married me that I was a poor man, and that your life
would be a hard one. Do you regret it? Is it harder than
you can bear, Janet? If so, look me in the face and tell
me so, dear wife, and though it breaks my heart to hear it,
I will allow that your complaint is just.' But as he took
her in his arms, and she heard the falter in his voice, she
could not tell him the bitterness that seemed to saturate
and poison her very life. Had she not endured already,
and would she not endure, if strength were given her, to
the very end for his sake?

'Your love will always make me happy. I desire
nothing for myself. Is it not enough that I am your
wife?' she murmured, leaning against him, but not showing him her face. 'It is only your good and the children's.
I have never thought of myself.' And in her soreness and
humility Janet spoke the truth—she coveted the money
not for herself but for him.

'I know all about it, my poor darling,' returned Maurice
rather sadly, stroking the beautiful face as though it were a
child's. Why was it that they loved each other so, and yet
that she so often failed to give him comfort? Was it that
in the long years of their union he had learned at last to
read her aright, that in spite of her many virtues the
ambition and worldliness of her character were becoming
known to him? Might it not be that those keen eyes had
discovered under the silence, the seeming submission, the
quiet laying down of her will to his,—the secret rebellion,
the differing opinion, the dumb protest of an active domi-
nant nature? Was she satisfied? would he ever be able to

satisfy her as long as they two, united in heart but with different purposes and aims, journeyed through the rugged ways of life?

Sometimes when he was weary, a secret terror would cross his soul. What if he were to grow weak, and were to succumb to her influence? what if she were to tempt him in some bitter straitened hour, when his body was feeble and his mind dry and arid, tempt him away from his work, from the place where Providence had led him? what if she should hold out to him their poverty and the needs of the poor babes that she had brought into the world, and he should listen to her,—he who had always exalted his priestly office so high above other work, who had always refused to listen to the wife of his bosom, unless her voice accorded with the dictates of his own conscience?

This fear was upon him now, when her weary head was resting on the pillow, and comforted by his tenderness she had slept; he had stood looking down at her for a moment, tracing the unbent lines, the tired droop of the mouth, the furrows that were beginning to mark the smooth white brow.

'My Janet, my poor tired Janet! if I could only rest you and make you happy!' he whispered, shading the lamp with his hand, while the slow moisture gathered in his eyes; and then, as was his custom when his heart was heavy for her and for himself, he went away and poured out the depth of his loving and wounded soul, until he felt that his prayer was heard, and that something of his old peace had returned to him.

Mary knew nothing about this little episode that had occurred during the last days of their visit. Maurice's confidence was sacred, and his wife respected it; she was, therefore, a little surprised and disappointed at what she considered Mrs. Reid's want of sympathy. 'Because she does not like Janet she seems to have lost all interest in them both,' she said to herself.

It was therefore a relief when Mrs. Reid quitted the subject. Her next speech took Mary by surprise. 'Do you know that I parted with Crome once? Has Maurice told you?' she asked somewhat abruptly.

'Crome Park! your beautiful place in ——shire?'

'Yes; the house my husband purchased when we were first married. How proud I used to be of it in those days!' and an expression of pain crossed her pale face. 'It was many years ago; circumstances of which I cannot speak determined me to sell it; it would have broken my heart to part with it if it had not been broken before.' Here she sighed heavily, and went on in a hard, fixed voice, as though she were going through a task: 'It was purchased, this grand old place of ours, by a wealthy American who had taken a fancy to it; he died very unexpectedly about two years ago, and then a great hankering came over me, and I got it again into my own hands.'

'Do you mean that you re-bought it?' asked Mary, wondering not a little over this sudden confidence.

'No, his heirs were willing for me to do so, but the time was not yet come for that. I took it on leasehold, with the intention that hereafter some of those belonging to me might purchase it in the years to come. I had parted with it once, knowing that I should never see it again, and not caring then who should come after me; but now the longing to possess it has been too strong for me, and I have given in to it.'

'Do you mean never to come back to it?' asked Mary, moved to strong sympathy by the weary, pathetic voice. Mrs. Reid shook her head, and a strange expression passed over her face.

'I do not know. I have a great wish to die under my own roof; living or dead, I mean to cross the threshold, which I first crossed as a bride. Do you know, Mary, that in my dreams I am always at Crome? night after night, night after night, always there, never here.'

'Dear Mrs. Reid, I should think that must be a comfort to you.'

'Sometimes, not always; ah, there is pain even in that. Last night I was crossing the great hall between the marble pillars; I could see the anteroom plainly with its large mullioned window opening on the park, the grass running up to the very window-sill, so that one seemed to walk through the rooms straight into the greenness. I had a child in my arms—what child I know not.' Here her voice sank into a whisper. 'I seemed always afraid of dropping it; it was a little creature, but my arms were weak and had no power; all my strength would not let me hold it; the drops of agony stood on my forehead. I thought I tried to call out for some one to come and take the child, but I could not speak; and then it fell and rolled away from me, out among the daisies, lost in long waving grass; but I could see its dumb look of reproach as it fell, and feel the touch· of the baby hand trying to grasp my fingers.'

'Dear friend, you are ill; you must not excite yourself like this,' exclaimed Mary, rising from her seat in some alarm. Mrs. Reid's face had become an ashen-gray, her hands were cold and shaking; it was an inexpressible relief that Charlotte that moment entered the room.

'What has kept you so long? You must be tiring ma Tante,' she said, bustling up to them in her usual fussy way; but on catching sight of her aunt's face she stopped, and her manner changed.

'What is it, auntie dear?' she said, kneeling down and chafing the cold hands between her own. 'What has Mary been doing? We will banish her if she has been naughty.'

'No, no; it was the baby. I could not hold my own baby,' returned the poor woman in the same strained voice. 'Last night, you know,—I told you, Charlotte,—the little white baby.'

'Leave her to me,' said Charlotte quickly. 'She has been over-exciting herself; and want of sleep sometimes makes her like this; it is nothing, just a brief wandering.'

'Oh, let me stay; surely I can do something to help you,' cried poor Mary, feeling dreadfully frightened.

'No, no,' repeated Charlotte, stamping her foot with

impatience.   'I tell you that I understand these moods, and shall quiet her best alone; do go, there's a good girl.' And Mary reluctantly obeyed, but turning round before she closed the door, she saw Charlotte tenderly lay the gray head against her breast and hush her like a child.

CHAPTER XI

THAT scene haunted Mary for days afterwards; she could not bring herself to retail it to Dollie; something in their conversation had touched a too sensitive chord, and the poor tortured heart had given way for a time.

'She is asleep now. I have given her a composing draught, and Justine will sit by her for an hour or two,' Charlotte said, when she came into Mary's room to wish her good-night. Charlotte's eyelids were red; she looked softened and subdued.

'Is she often like this?' asked Mary in a whisper; for Dollie's door was ajar, and that little person might interrupt them at any moment.

'No, not often,' returned Charlotte reluctantly. She evidently wanted to slip away without a word, but Mary's anxiety was too great. 'It is only sometimes—when the pain has been very bad, and she has had a great many sleepless nights; then if she gets talking of the past, she is liable to be suddenly excited. If I had been there, I should have known and hushed her directly.'

'It was a dream she was telling me,' began Mary; but Charlotte interrupted her rather hastily.

'Oh, she is always dreaming. It was Walter, of course —Walter as a baby. It is always the same thing. Sometimes she is stringing daisy chains with him; sometimes she is pelting him with roses, or picking up apples in the orchard; sometimes he is wading through great pools with his bare rosy feet, and she is gathering coloured seaweed for him. It is always Walter as a child—when she was a young mother and he was her idol. Ma pauvre Tante!' finished Charlotte with a heavy sigh, as she hurried away. Somehow Mary never liked the little woman so well.

Mary was dreading a summons to the dressing-room the next evening; but to her infinite surprise they found, on returning from their walk, that Mrs. Reid had ensconced herself in the great crimson fauteuil in the drawing-room, with her shaded lamp and her knitting beside her. Charlotte was warming herself on the rug, in company with Mark Antony, and chattering breathlessly.

Dollie rushed up to her aunt with an exclamation of delight, and Grey followed her somewhat gravely; but Bertie looked rather taken aback at the sudden apparition. In the secrecy of his heart he could have willingly dispensed with his hostess's company. He hung back behind the others, looking a little shy and sheepish for once in his life; and his greeting when it came was of the briefest.

It was evident that he was no favourite, and that he knew it.

Mrs. Reid was far more gracious in her reception of his brother. She inquired about his health, questioned him as to his prospects, and showed some amount of interest in his answers; but she was a little distant in her behaviour to both the young men. Grey's penetration had long perceived this, and it made him stiff and constrained in her presence. It was some time before the little party thawed into its usual sociability; but Bertie's shyness and Grey's hauteur could not long hold out under the infectious influence of Dollie's merriment.

Dollie was very shrewd in her way, and she soon felt the repressive atmosphere. 'The young men bore her, and she bores them in return,' she said to herself. 'Our evenings will be spoiled if Mary and I do not exert ourselves, and wake them all up;' and so she set to work at once.

She came down presently in her quaint green dress with the puckered sleeves, looking very sweet and piquant, Grey thought, as he watched her flitting about the room. She

stopped and made him a sweeping curtsey once, waving her
arms and smiling in a bewitching way.

'May it please your highness to tell us why you look as
grave as a judge to-night?' said wicked Dollie, braving
even the formidable Mr. Lyndhurst in her new crusade.
'Mr. Bertie, Mary and I are going to sing; you may turn
over the leaves if you like—if you will promise not to spoil
our duet with your carelessness.'

'Let me turn over,' exclaimed Grey, putting his brother
aside very unceremoniously, and coming forward eagerly.

Dollie pouted just a little, but she did not dare to
refuse him. She never quite enjoyed singing if Mr. Lyndhurst stood beside her; she had a notion that he thought
little of her execution; she would get confused and lose
her place, and then break off scolding and laughing.

But to-night she must wake them all up; it would not
do to be thinking of herself. There was Bertie sulking and
pulling his moustache on the big settee, and wishing that
Mrs. Reid and her knitting were anywhere else, and that
Grey had not taken his place. 'Confound the fellow!
what does he mean by putting me aside like that? Grey is
no lady's man!' fumed Bertie; and then he grinned mischievously when Grey forgot about turning over altogether,
but just stood bolt upright in his place—listening to the
little bird in the green plumage trilling out her fresh clear
notes beside him.

Dollie frowned at him, but sang straight on. When she
had finished, she took her old accustomed footstool at Mrs.
Reid's feet, and the others grouped round her.

How could even sulky Bertie keep aloof, when her
girlish laughter chimed in every now and then, so softly,
yet so mirthfully? when Mary looked at him with such
wistful eyes, and kept the place vacant beside her? Of
course he slipped into the circle, and in time became his
old bright self again.

'Thank you all for a pleasant evening,' said Mrs. Reid
quite cheerfully, when she bade them all good-night. 'Give
me a kiss, you little yellow-haired witch!'

Dollie clapped her hands, and danced up to her own

room. 'If I am a witch, I shall bewitch you all,' she said gaily. 'If you have not done so already,' was Grey's unexpected answer, as he lighted her candle. As she looked at him, she saw there was a little flush on his face, and his eyes looked bright and dark.

'Why! he is not so plain after all,' she said to herself; and somehow the little compliment did not slip out of her mind. Mary had told her that Grey never paid compliments; that he could not make a pretty speech to save his life; and he had made one to her! she remembered that.

Things soon flowed on more smoothly; the young men soon became accustomed to their hostess's presence. Grey took to reading aloud in the evening; he had excellent taste and a clear sonorous voice. Sometimes the book was laid aside, and a brisk discussion was carried on between him and Mrs. Reid. The girls were astonished at the stores of knowledge displayed on these occasions. Mrs. Reid had excellent reasoning powers, and a retentive memory. Grey did not always have the best of the argument; he was shrewd rather than clever, and could better retail other men's wisdom than originate his own.

He was capable, discursive, and went to work in a cut-and-dried manner. He could not always adapt himself to the vagaries of genius; and would have cleared away the rubbish from the ruins of the past, before he deigned to explore their beauties.

Most people respected Grey; but any one gifted with enthusiasm was apt to find him a little too heavy and matter-of-fact for their taste—all of which he knew, and was much given in consequence to assume a certain taciturnity and reserve that was hardly natural.

Dollie sat like a little bright-eyed mouse on these occasions, and never ventured to open her lips. She thought Mr. Lyndhurst remarkably clever—how much of Grey's eloquence, I wonder, was inspired by the sight of the little fair head bent down over the trifling piece of fancy-work. He used to cast furtive glances in that direction. Sometimes Dollie looked up and caught them; she was puzzled .

but still unconscious; a sense of being watched presented itself somewhat vaguely to her imagination; but she was young, and Grey was so very quiet, and the time was not yet come!

One afternoon the girls went out alone; for once their escort was lacking. Bertie had gone down the canal in a barge, and was not expected back until late in the evening; and Grey had one of the bad headaches to which he had been subject of late, and had been ordered off by Charlotte to the couch in the morning-room.

He pulled such a long face when he found Mrs. Reid was to be his only companion, that Dollie's kind heart was quite moved, and she hinted shyly to Mary that one of them might offer to stop and read to him.

'But the other could not go out alone, and Charlotte is too busy to come with us,' remonstrated Mary; 'besides, our staying would look rather strange,' at which matter-of-fact remark Dollie first looked angry and blushed, and then tossed her head and declared that nothing could be farther from her wishes than to stay indoors this lovely afternoon—that she only wanted to be kind and practise her Christianity, and that Mary was a goose to say such things—strange, indeed! and she went off in a little heat and flurry.

Dollie's brief ill-humour soon vanished, and they passed a charming afternoon in their own fashion, dividing it pretty equally between the Béguinage, the Eglise de Jérusalem, and the Church of St. Jacques; and then, as ill-luck would have it, Dollie took it into her silly little head that they must go to the cathedral on their way home.

Now they had been walking about for three hours, and Mary was tired,—though she would not have owned it for worlds,—and it was growing dark, and they were alone, and the proprieties of the chateau would be offended, and most likely Grey would be coming out to look for them, all of which she gently hinted in her sensible manner; but Dollie was deaf to reason, and would not be coerced.

Let him look for them if he liked; it would do his head

good—better than lying in that stuffy room; if Mary were disagreeable she might go home by herself; but why spoil a delightful afternoon by this sudden fit of prudery? 'You are cut out for an old maid, Mary; I am sure you will be one,' cried Dollie in her teasing way; she had a fancy that Mary would find this speech provoking.

'I shall be what Providence ordains, I suppose,' returned Mary equably; but her colour rose a little; perhaps the thrust hurt her, for she said no more; and Dollie had her way—poor Dollie! how bitterly she rued that piece of wilfulness afterwards!

Vespers were just over when they went into the cathedral; the warm fragrance of incense still lingered in the air. Dolly went gliding from one dim chapel to another, till just behind the choir she paused, where the seven red lamps swung before the tiny altar; and then she sat down and fell into an odd jumble of devotion. She had an idea that she was meditating in the orthodox way—till she began thinking of her mother, poor child, and grew a little wistful and dewy. She was wondering how she looked, and if she were dull, and whether the rooms in Abercrombie Road would seem very small and shabby when she got back, when, all of a sudden, the harsh creaking of a chair near her made her start—for she had thought herself alone in her snug corner.

She started still more when she found herself suddenly accosted. The chapels were dark and gloomy—no one was passing, Mary was somewhere in the nave, where there were lights and people. Poor little Dollie felt sadly frightened by the tall shabby man, who seemed to rise so abruptly out of the ground.

'Pardon me if I startle you, mademoiselle,' said a voice in excellent French, 'that I make bold to address you,—but I am in a little difficulty.'

'I have nothing for you—not even a cêntime,—I have forgotten my purse; please go away,' said Dollie, feeling rather like the rabbit in the boa-constrictor's cage—longing to get up and make her escape, but paralysed by the bold eager eyes.

'Pardon me, mademoiselle, it is not alms that I require;' and there was an angry flush on the man's face. Dollie looked at him again, and this time her dislike increased. She remembered him now; he was in the little chapel at St. Jacques when they had looked at the tomb of Ferry de Gros, and Mary had seemed anxious to avoid him—'An ill-looking man,' she had whispered as they hurried out,— could it be that he had followed them here?

She had made a mistake in treating him as a beggar; he was shabby, it was true, with a threadbare sort of respectability, but he had the accent of a gentleman; his face might almost be called handsome, but for its dissipated look, but its dark, lowering look of anger at her words nearly frightened Dollie out of her wits. She began edging slowly away from him, but he followed her, hat in hand.

'Arretez, chère demoiselle,' he said beseechingly; 'it is only an address I want. I am a stranger here, and they say the good lady of the chateau is benevolent to all who need her bounty. I will not trouble you, mademoiselle; I will tell my own story to the lady herself; her name is Reid—is it not so?'—with a keen searching look at trembling Dollie. 'She is the lady of the chateau, n'est ce pas?—or is it another name?'

'No, it is Reid; but what do you want with her? She is an invalid—she cannot see you,' replied Dollie, plucking up a little spirit when it was too late.

'An invalid! and her name Reid!—bon!—le chateau de St. Aubert, n'est ce pas?' Dollie nodded, by way of getting rid of him, and to her great relief her Frankenstein suddenly made her a low mocking bow and turned on his heel.

Dollie drew a long breath, and then nearly ran into the arms of a gentleman coming round the choir, and drew herself up with a stiff little apology, and saw Mr. Lynd-hurst's grave face.

'I knew I should find you here, Miss Maynard. What, imprudence!' he began; 'how very wrong! I hardly thought Mary capable of such impropriety.' But this little lecture was frustrated by downright astonishment, for there

was Dollie, panting and breathless and clinging to his arm
—actually clinging to him—Grey Lyndhurst.

'Oh, don't scold—don't say anything disagreeable,' half
sobbed Dollie. 'I have had such a fright! A horrid man
has been talking to me; and it was so dark and lonely, and
I had such a dreadful fear that he would murder me,
perhaps for my gold chain, and—and——' and here Dollie
poured out her story into Mr. Lyndhurst's ear.

He seemed nearly as shocked as Dollie herself. 'What
imprudence, those two young girls wandering about Lesponts
at this hour of the evening!' he muttered to himself; but
he did not reiterate his scolding. On the contrary, he was
very kind to the poor little thing—soothing and laughing at
her by turns, and acting in quite a surprising way, for he
said 'you foolish child' once; and then coloured up in the
darkness at the idea of taking such a liberty; but Dollie
never noticed it; she was too glad of his protection, and
when they found Mary, who had been having a semi-doze
in her chair, they all three went happily home.

Bertie had not arrived, and they sat down to dinner
without him. Nothing was said about Dollie's fright in
the cathedral; Mrs. Reid had lectured them in a quiet way
for their late wandering. She had felt nervous about them,
and so had Charlotte; and then Grey had volunteered to
go out and look for them.

Dollie hung down her head and looked very foolish over
the well-merited rebuke, but Mary said bluntly that they
had been very thoughtless, and that they would never stay
out so late again. And then Grey struck in in a good-
humoured way, and the opportunity was lost. A different
topic occupied them at dinner. A Flemish lady, with
whom Charlotte was very intimate, had met with an accident, and her husband had sent round to the chateau
begging her assistance.

Charlotte had been down to the Rue d'Equerre once
already, and she announced her intention of going again
after dinner to sit with the invalid.

'Poor Madame Dubarry!' she said; 'she is in a sad
state of suffering, and her husband is old and deaf, and no

manner of use.   I shall take Romany, and be back before
you retire, ma Tante.'

'To-morrow will do; surely you need not go down to
the Rue d'Equerre to-night,' remonstrated Mrs. Reid.   But
it was no use; Charlotte was bent on having her way.   She
must see her dear Hortense before she slept.

Mary would look after 'la Tante.'   They would all do
excellently well, but her presence was imperatively needed
in the sickroom, as Fanchette had 'les nerfs,' and was of
little use.

Mrs. Reid smiled; she knew well of old that it was no
good reasoning with Charlotte when she had once made up
her mind.   'Come back quickly,' she said cheerfully, as Charlotte gaily waved her adieux.   'That is a good little creature,'
she said, as she took up her knitting; 'her faults are all
on the surface.   She is giddy and frivolous, and will never
make her mark in the world, but at the bottom there is the
woman's heart.'

'She seems very devoted to you,' returned Mary.

'Yes, she is very good to me, and I find her very useful; but we are an ill-assorted pair.   Charlotte has no
mind; she never opens a book,—never does anything but
trot about the house and chatter.   The jingle of her keys
is her only music; a new fashion in dress her chief relaxa-
tion; she is so perfectly brainless, yet so amiable, that I
find myself talking to her as a child.'

'She is very young for her age.'

'Yes, poor Charlotte! and yet in spite of all her clinging to youth, the wrinkles and gray hair must come one
day.   Now, Dollie, my dear, we are ready for some of my
favourite songs; and to-night Grey must turn over for you,
while Mary shows me the new stitch for my couvre-pied.'

Dollie rose from her footstool rather reluctantly.   It was
hard to leave the warm circle of firelight, and go away into
the dim distance with only Mr. Lyndhurst.   It was one
thing to enjoy his protection in the cathedral, but quite
another to have him leaning against the piano, watching
her and finding fault with her songs.

So she showed her gratitude for past favours by present

pettishness. Nothing was right; the lights, or the music stool, or the book rest; the songs he selected were old as the hills, and she was tired to death of singing them. Grey was obliged to take his pleasure sadly, with a good many rebuffs; he smiled to himself a little under his moustache, for he was amused at her childishness. He had no idea that Dollie was finding the evening slow without Bertie's lazy fun, and that she was venting her ill-humour on his brother.

'Was that the hall-door?' asked Mrs. Reid presently, as a cold draught penetrated through the salon. 'I suppose Bertie has come back; it cannot be Charlotte yet. Go, my dear,' she continued, addressing Mary; 'ask Justine or Ursula to see that some food is prepared for him in the salle-à-manger.'

Mary obeyed, nothing loath; for what can be dearer to a woman than to minister to the man she secretly loves? Such ministry forms a part of the sacrament of love. She hurried out full of her mission, and with her eyes already shining with welcome, and stopped disappointed, to find Justine in angry altercation with a shabby-looking man, who had just stepped past her into the hall.

'Mademoiselle, help me to exclude this ill-conditioned person,' cried Justine in a frightened voice. 'It was Monsieur Bertie, I said to myself, when I threw open the hall-door. Stop, monsieur; you shall not go any farther. Madame is in that salon, and no one is suffered to intrude on her; she is ill. Oh! the monster—the rude person,' as the intruder pushed unceremoniously past her and Mary, and marched straight to the door of the salon.

'Pardonne,' he returned, looking round at them with a gleaming smile, half triumphant and half malicious. 'Madame knows me, and I know madame. There is no need of your polite introduction,' and he turned the handle and walked in.

Dollie was singing, but the notes died away in her throat as she looked towards the opening door in expectation of Bertie's tall figure. ' Oh, the man! the man!' she gasped, and clutched Grey's arm again in her sudden terror.

'That dreadful man, and oh, look, look,' pointing towards
Mrs. Reid's chair.

Grey disengaged himself though with difficulty, and
hurried forward.   They might well look ; even the intruder
paused for a moment, paralysed by the sight of the rigid
figure in the fauteuil.

Mrs. Reid was sitting bolt upright, grasping the two
sides of her chair ; her face was drawn and gray ; her eyes
fixed in sudden horror ; the gray hair, the gleaming eyes,
the terribly-constrained attitude, made up a sad spectacle.

'Walter !' was hissed rather than spoken through the
pallid lips.   'This my son Walter !'

'Well, it is long since we met, mother ; it seems hard
for a mother and a son to be so long parted, does it not?'
returned the intruder, advancing a little into the room.
He spoke with a bold flippancy, but his manner was ill-
assured and uneasy.   'I have been looking for you some
time, but I could never discover where you had hidden
yourself until by good luck I hit on this young lady in the
cathedral,' nodding his head at Dollie, 'and she, like a
good little soul, set me on your track.'

No answer ; only the same fixed stare, as of one who
sees an apparition ; only at the sound of his voice a sort of
convulsive trembling passes over the rigid frame.

'Let me speak,' cries Dollie, pushing past them, and
kneeling down at Mrs. Reid's feet.   Mary had already
drawn one of the cold hands into hers, and was chafing it
tenderly.   'It was all my fault.   I was frightened, and how
could I know this dreadful man was your son.   Send him
away, some one,' continued the excited girl, facing round
on them ; 'nobody wants him, not even his poor mother.
Turn him out of the house, Mr. Lyndhurst ; he knows he
has no business here.'

'I think you had better go,' returned Grey sternly.
'There is no knowing what mischief may happen if you
stand there any longer ; go out of the hall-door, and I will
come out and speak to you presently.'

'Thank you, sir, and you too, my young lady,' replied
the man sneeringly, 'but there is no need of your interfer-

ence here.   You will not get me to leave this house until I
have done my business, and as for turning me out, you
had better try,' with a withering look at Grey's slight
figure; 'you might find some little difficulty in doing so;'
and he squared his shoulders, and planted his feet more
firmly on the rug.

'Oh for Bertie's thews and sinews!' sighed Grey to
himself; 'he would be a match for him.   If you are a
man, look at that poor face, and go,' he said more mildly;
for by any means they must get rid of him.

'Look here, mother,' said Walter coaxingly, quite
ignoring Grey and the others, and advancing a few steps
nearer; only she tore her hand from Mary's and waved
him away, still looking at him with the same awful stare in
her eyes.

'What! will you not let me come a little nearer?   Is that
the way to receive the prodigal son?   No fatted calves!
nothing of that kind here;' and then he looked at them
half sulkily, half abashed, and a fit of coughing stopped
him.

He did not look much like a repentant prodigal, this
miserable Walter Reid, standing there with his dark lowering face, on which were stamped the traces of many evil
passions.   Grey noticed with something like pity that the
large frame was gaunt and wasted; the face had once been
beautiful with a young man's beauty, but now it was
pinched and haggard, and almost bloodless; the very
sound of his cough was ominous, and when he wiped his
lips, Grey noticed a faint red tinge on his handkerchief.

'Come, mother,' he said again when the paroxysm had
passed.   'You might come round a little now, for I am
pretty nearly done for; you may take my oath of that;
you might say a word or two to a poor fellow who is
cursedly down on his luck.'

'Speak to him and tell him to go,' whispered Mary.
'Dear Mrs. Reid, we are all round you; we will not let
any one harm you; tell him to go; he will mind you.'

Then she essayed to speak.   'That my boy—my boy
Walter!' she said, pointing to the shabby, disreputable

figure before her; 'that my son—my only son!' and then before they could reach her, she threw up her arms wildly, and before Mary could spring forward, she had fallen on the rug, and lay with her gray hairs grovelling at the feet of her wretched son.

When Bertie returned later on, he found empty rooms and a disordered household; every one was flying about; no one had time to attend to him.

Dollie came down to him by and by with pale cheeks and swollen eyes, and her pretty hair all in confusion. Bertie was poking the fire rather stormily; the sparks were flying out here and there; he was tired and hungry, and no one seemed to remember the fact. Something had happened, but none of the servants seemed to know what it was all about. Grey had gone for the doctor; Ursula to fetch Charlotte. Justine was with her mistress.

'Mary sent me down to you; she heard your step; she cannot leave Mrs. Reid,' said Dollie very demurely. 'Oh, how cold the room is! the fire is getting low, and the salle-à-manger is worse; it was like a vault when I crossed it just now. Mary says you must be cold and hungry; she wants me to ask Kâtchen to get you something to eat.'

'Dear Mary! she never forgets any one,' thought Bertie gratefully; then aloud, 'Let us go to Kâtchen by all means; it will be warmer there, and you can tell me everything by and by.'

'Kâtchen has the catarrh, so she says, and has gone off to bed; but I daresay I shall find you something. Sit by the stove and warm yourself, while I go into the larder; there are the remains of a chicken, I know, and some gâteau.'

The kitchen looked bright and cheerful; the stove was open, and the firelight played on the yellow walls and red brick floor; the brass stew-pans gleamed like polished mirrors; long bunches of sweet-smelling herbs dangled from the old rafters.

Bertie coiled himself up on an oaken bench beside the fire, and watched Dollie, well pleased, as she flitted to and

fro. She had covered the tray with a snow-white napkin.
She had found cheese-cakes, some stewed pears, last of all
she had the chocolate pot in her hands. 'Mary says I am
to make you comfortable,' she said shyly, when at last the
little feast was ready, and Bertie prepared to do justice
to it.

'This is nectar and ambrosia! You might be Hebe
catering for the old Olympic deities!' cried Bertie, as she
placed the foaming beverage beside him. 'Now, sit down
beside me, Hebe, and tell me about everything,' went on
Bertie cordially, doing his best to be grateful, and not wish
in his heart that it were Mary and not Dollie beside him.

Dollie was very glad to obey him; it was rather a
pleasant novelty in her existence to be called Hebe, and to
have to minister to such an Adonis. 'Mary told me to
make him comfortable,' she said, fortifying herself with a
sense of duty, as Bertie, after his manner, looked at her
with clear affectionate eyes. It was a long story, and he
had quite finished his repast before she had ended it.

'Poor soul!' muttered Bertie compassionately, for he was
very soft-hearted, 'it must have been some sort of fit, or
perhaps a stroke of paralysis.'

'We have not heard the doctor's report yet,' returned
Dollie with a shudder. 'Your brother says it was a fit, and
that she has had them before; Charlotte told him so. Was
it not a pity Charlotte was away? Poor Mary was so
frightened! but she did all she could for the poor thing.'

'And that wretched man—what became of him?' asked
Bertie.

'That is the strangest part of all,' returned Dollie.
'When he saw what had happened, he gave a sort of groan,
and began to shake all over; when they had carried her to
her room, he let Mr. Lyndhurst lead him by the arm; he
made no resistance when your brother opened the outer
door. I think he must have gone out with him, for I heard
voices in the courtyard.'

'It is a horrible affair,' muttered Bertie. 'He is down
on her track like a bloodhound whenever he is out of
pocket. Poor creature! one must forgive her all her

cutting little speeches after this ;' and then they were both silent.

'What are you two doing?' said Grey, suddenly appearing at the door, and regarding the scene before him with un-mixed astonishment. There was the supper tray, the fragrant smell of hot chocolate ; Bertie stretching himself before the fire, and Dollie in her green dress, with a napkin pinned over it to keep it clean, standing by the stove looking at him. 'Do you know it is past eleven, and that Mary is asking for you,' went on Grey in a slightly constrained voice.

'How is Mrs. Reid ? Is Charlotte come home ?' questioned both eagerly.

'Yes ; and the doctor has just left. It was a fit, as I said, but she is a little better now. Mary and Charlotte mean to watch her to-night. Mary would like to speak to you for a moment in your own room,' he continued, address-ing Dollie ; and the shade on his countenance deepened, as he closed the door after her, and sat down opposite his brother.

For Bertie had said, 'Good-night, Hebe,' in a loud, cheerful voice, and Dollie had waved her hand to him and had run out of the room without noticing Grey.

CHAPTER XII

MARY was standing by the stove, looking sad and thoughtful, as Dollie entered. She raised her head at the sound
of the hasty footsteps. 'How long you have been, dear
Dollie!' she said wearily; 'I could not have waited much
longer, and I wanted to say good-night before I went in to
Charlotte, and to hear all you have to tell me;' and Mary's
pale cheeks flushed a little, her eyes looked expectant.

'Oh, there is nothing to tell,' replied Dollie carelessly,
stretching her white arms over her head with an utter
abandon of fatigue. She was tired and excited with all the
miserable events of the day, and the remembrance of the
last hour stirred her with a curious thrill of pleasure. She
had done as she was bidden to do; but there was no reason
why Mary should catechise her quite so closely. 'There
is nothing to tell; I made him comfortable, and he is
warmed and fed to his heart's content. So you need not
keep Charlotte waiting,' finished Dollie, who was in one of
her contradictory moods.

'But how did he take it? He must have been so
shocked and sorry,' persisted Mary patiently but wistfully.
She had hoped Bertie would have sent her some message,
some little word to cheer her during her long vigil. Could
it be that her name had not been mentioned between them?

'He had his supper before he let me speak, and that
gave him strength to support it,' replied Dollie half mischievously and half crossly. Mary had no right to question
her like this; if Bertie and she were engaged, she could

hardly have taken more upon herself. 'Of course he was sorry, but it did not spoil his appetite. I never saw him enjoy his food more,' continued naughty Dollie, who was well aware that poor Bertie had not tasted food for seven or eight hours.

Mary sighed, but she was too gentle to retaliate. 'Good-night, dear,' she said mildly; 'I did not mean to trouble you; thank you for taking care of him so nicely. I daresay you are very tired.' And then she kissed her and left the room. Dollie's conscience smote her at the kind kiss and words. Poor Mary! she need not have disappointed her; if she had chosen she could have remembered all sorts of nice little things to have told her; but it was too late to call her back now, and Dollie went to bed, ashamed and discomfited, as though she had done some mean thing, and with a chill feeling of incipient jealousy at her heart, though not for worlds would Dollie have pleaded guilty to such a feeling. But comfort came to Mary nevertheless; for Bertie was lingering outside the door, to waylay her on her passage across the corridor.

He had his chamber candlestick in his hand, for he had made his fatigue an excuse for bidding his brother a hasty good-night; and as he stood there with his fair hair rumpled and standing in a sort of wild halo round his head, and the flame of the candle casting golden gleams over it, he looked like some great glorified angel to Mary's dazzled eyes.

'Oh, Bertie, were you waiting for me?' she exclaimed, and her eyes began to shine with pleasure. If only Dollie could have seen them then!

'Well, I wanted to say good-night. Thank you for sending down Miss Maynard to look after me. She was such a clever neat-handed sort of Phillis to cater for a fellow; but I would rather have had you, you know,' blurted out Bertie, moved to demonstrativeness by something he saw in Mary's face.

'Oh, Bertie!' she said, looking rosy and almost pretty; for though every one loved Mary's face, it depended solely on its expression for beauty.

'Well, of course I would! As though you did not know that! as though I should not prefer talking to you

than to a dozen Miss Maynards! Not but what she is a
nice little thing though,' put in Bertie, with a vivid remembrance of Hebe with the chocolate-pot in her hand. 'And
so you are going to sit up all night. Poor Aunt Mary!
how tired you will be!' and Bertie's voice softened into
tenderness.

'Oh, I do not mind. I am used to night-nursing,' returned Mary, feeling suddenly brisk and rested. This was
what she wanted—a few kind words from Bertie to think
over in the night. 'Don't you recollect the weeks and
months I had with poor Aunt Emma? I have served my
apprenticeship. Charlotte has no idea what a first-rate
nurse I am,' she went on cheerfully.

'Every one knows how awfully good you are,' was the
reply. 'There is not another person in the whole world
fit to hold this candle to you,' continued Bertie, rumpling
his hair still more, between sleepiness and a desire to say
something specially strong and loverlike. Perhaps its
strength somewhat embarrassed Mary, for though she
laughed and blushed, she held out her hand rather quickly,
saying that she must not keep Charlotte waiting any longer.
If her fingers tingled somewhat from his warm pressure,
she did not complain.

'I wonder how many years it will be before I shall dare
to say that I love her,' thought Bertie rather ruefully as he
turned away. 'Eighty pounds a year is not much to offer
a girl, and Mary has not even that; but if I were to keep
her waiting a dozen years, she would not have anything
to say to any other fellow. I'll stake my life on that;'
and a glow came over the young man's face as he thought
how, in the years to come, he would win his bonnie Mary!

Mary had need of some cordial to strengthen her for her
work; for a long terrible night of watching was before her.
The attack had been followed by utter collapse and
exhaustion, and a corpse-like figure, gray in hue and with
closed sunken eyes, lay stretched among the pillows. Mary
took her place beside it, while Charlotte, shivering and crying to herself, withdrew to the armchair beside the stove.

Mary smiled a little at the somewhat incongruous figure

heaped up in the cosy chair. Charlotte wore a pink robe
de chambre, adorned with all sorts of delicate puffings and
finishes. She had tied a lace handkerchief over her hair,
and had a large green fan in her hand, which she fluttered
incessantly. She had brought in a whole array of silver-
topped bottles of essences; before the night was over, all
sorts of different perfumes steeped the atmosphere. Mary
detected lavender water, eau de cologne, attar of rose, and
wood violet. There was even once a subtle fragrance,
somewhat spicy like sandal-wood, against which Mary's
olfactory nerves secretly protested. Charlotte had recourse to them between her brief nodding naps. 'I am
not asleep, but I keep my eyes shut on account of the
light,' she said now and then in a loud whisper, startling
Mary in her open-eyed reverie.

Poor Mary! In spite of her secret fund of happiness,
the night was very long and oppressive. It was weary
work sitting there, watching that still figure in its death-like
lethargy. It was almost a relief when, towards morning,
there were indications of reviving life—low mutterings and
restless movements of the arms, the lifting of the heavy
eyelids, and the vacant, prolonged stare at the opposite
wall. The faint cold gleam of morning was just penetrating
through the unclosed window, before Mary could see that
she was recognised; but even then the eyes were still
dilated and restless; memory and thought were still help-
lessly confused.

'Another bad dream,' she muttered, as Mary applied a
restorative, and then gently laid her down and covered her
over, smoothing the soft silvery hair that strayed so wildly
over the pillow; then the covering was thrown aside, and
the cold hand clutched Mary's.

'Who is that in the armchair?' she whispered. 'Charlotte, oh poor Charlotte! we will not wake her; she is not
as young as she used to be, and she needs rest, poor little
woman! You stay beside me, my dear; I like your face,
I like your face,' she went on drowsily; but Charlotte,
hearing her name, sprang up, knocking against the fireirons,
and disturbed her.

'Here I am, auntie; I was not asleep. I had only got my eyes shut; ask Mary;' and Charlotte winked and blinked her blue eyes, and tried hard not to yawn and not to look as she felt—a very washed-out, weary little person, with all sorts of lines and puckers showing in her tired face—not as young as she used to be, indeed!

'Hush!' remonstrated Mary, for her hand was still tightly grasped, and she saw a grayer tint on Mrs. Reid's face. 'The noise has frightened her,' she whispered; 'and you know Dr. Arnaud says perfect quiet is the only chance. There is no one here; it is only Charlotte and I,' she continued soothingly, for Mrs. Reid had begun to look wild again.

'Another of them, and another of them,—how many more bad dreams?' she went on again, with a low mutter and indistinctness, sometimes waking into coherence. 'Mary, look here. I can trust you, Mary. I have watched you both; and though she is a dear child, I know who will be the better woman by and by, only you must not spoil everything by having him. I will not have it, I tell you; it is feeble—monstrous nonsense—a girl's dream—a delusion—promise me, promise me, Mary.'

'Dear Mrs. Reid, what am I to promise you?' but Mary thrilled a little under the cold touch, the vague mysterious words. What could she mean? What was the oppressed brain tracking now? Could she be thinking of Bertie? But even as she doubted and wondered the mood changed.

'Early morning, fine and windy, and Marmaduke has gone out hunting. Why will they not bring me my baby? Nurse, where is my boy, my bonnie laughing boy?' And then she sat up in bed and stretched out her arms; and the palms of her hands quivered, and the fingers were all wide and outspread with eagerness. But Mary caught her in her arms and laid her down.

'Oh, hush, my poor dear,' she said half sobbing.

'Hush, yes hush! my baby is asleep,' went on the desolate creature, sinking among the pillows again with a contented sigh. 'All night long I have him here; I can feel his little cheek against mine. I hold his warm rosy feet in my hand. My baby, my baby, my only one !'

Her voice became low and indistinct, and the women began to give each other frightened looks. Dr. Arnaud had warned them of this. 'She will rouse but not to reason,' he had said. 'When that comes all will be over with her. You know what I told you,' he had continued, turning to Charlotte, who had wept and wrung her hands. 'Another blow—another shock—and she will not recover from it. Perfect quiet, absolute stillness—perhaps that may be her only chance ; but—but—— ' the little doctor dare not trust himself to say more.

'Dear auntie ! ma pauvre Tante ! try to go to sleep,' exclaimed Charlotte, leaning over her and patting her shoulder ; but the vague wanderings were not to be checked.

They could hear the household moving now. Presently there were faint taps at the dressing-room door, and little whispered talks with Charlotte. Mary heard Dollie's and Grey's and lastly Bertie's voice, and then Charlotte disappeared to change her dress, and have breakfast, and give her orders, leaving poor Mary to drink her solitary cup of coffee in haste, while she looked out drearily on the leafless avenue, and listened to the faint broken mutterings of the invalid. It was a relief when Dr. Arnaud entered, and shared her watch for a time.

He was a small brown-faced man, with smooth shaven gray hair and a dark moustache, and his figure had a neat martial build about it ; his eyes were shrewd and keen, and as he stood by his patient's bedside he cast sundry inquisitive glances at the pale-faced girl who stood dangling her eyeglasses beside him. Evidently he found her reliable, and suitable to his purpose, for, after some minutes of reflection, he beckoned her to the window, and began to talk in the short abrupt sentences that Dr. Arnaud generally used.

'Mademoiselle is not the nurse ? ' interrogatively.

'No, monsieur, I am only a friend ; perhaps I should say a connection of Mrs. Reid.'

'So—an inhabitant of the chateau, n'est ce pas ? '

'Only temporarily, monsieur. I am staying here with another English girl.'

'But mademoiselle has nursed before ; she is not un-used to sickrooms ; one sees that at a glance ; ' and the little doctor bowed and shrugged his shoulders, as much as to say, 'I read you thoroughly ; who is there that could deceive Pierre Arnaud ? ' ' Mademoiselle has served her no-vitiate—is it not so ? ' fixing her with his small sharp eyes.

'Alas ! yes, monsieur. I once nursed an aunt who was a great sufferer for many months.'

'And alone ? '

'Nearly so, except for the help of an old servant.'

'And you were with her when she died ? '

'I have seen many people die,' returned Mary simply. 'I have no horror of death, Dr. Arnaud. I have laid old people and little children in their coffins, and have felt as though I were only composing them for a long sleep.'

'Bon ! ' ejaculated the little man ; 'I knew I could trust that face ; it is reliable ; one can confide in it. Mademoiselle. Morell is nervous and excitable,' he con-tinued ; 'she has the good heart, the sensibilities, but one must not lean on her too hard. A pressure—an emergency—a complication—and pouf—her wits will be flying here and there ; ' and he threw his hands out with a significant gesture.

'What would you have me do ? ' asked Mary, feeling that a crisis was impending that would need all her energies.

'Everything—all that is to be done ; take the command ; this is your territory,' sweeping his arm round as though to embrace the four walls.

'I ! ' returned Mary shrinkingly. 'Miss Morell is twenty years older ; she has the right, monsieur. I must not take so much upon myself.'

'Bon ! Je vous entends bien. We will make all that right. I have my reasons. I nominate you as nurse ; this is your patient, and on no account must you leave these two rooms—on no account,' speaking more decidedly, as Mary looked at him and still hesitated.

'And Miss Morell?'

'Mademoiselle will, of course, help you. Justine also, if you need her, for we must not wear you out. It will not be for long, poor soul! the end may come at any time; le bon Dieu alone knows when. But quiet, perfect tranquillity, soothing when her wanderings become excited,—cela va sans dire,—you understand me, mademoiselle?'

'Perfectly, monsieur. But is there no hope?'

'While there is the life,—you know the rest. Poor madame! she has long been afflicted with an incurable disease, and when you add to this a shock, a broken heart, one dare not hope too much!' and then with a few more shrugs, and adding some straightforward directions, with a promise of returning before evening, Dr. Arnaud took up his curly-brimmed hat, and with another glance at his patient left the room.

Poor Mary! she gave one little sigh as she thought of Bertie downstairs, of the walks and the pleasant fireside talks she would miss, and then she put self and the other dearer self resolutely aside, and girded herself up for the present duty.

For Mary was religious—she was not simply acquainted with religion, neither did she keep it for Sundays, and leave the week-days to take care of themselves; as far as she understood it—and being only a woman, she was liable to make mistakes—she tried honestly and conscientiously to do her duty.

Perhaps she was a little too apt to think that duty must necessarily lie on the path of self-sacrifice; not that she was morbid and thought pleasant things were wrong, but noble acts were magnified in her mind and assumed a largeness and purity of motive that did not always belong to them. Humble-minded herself, she thought the best of everybody—but Maurice was exalted as her hero par excellence—a sort of halo of incipient saintliness surrounded him. In spite of Janet's foreboding, she gloried in his work, his enthusiasm, his forgetfulness of all but his vocation. Strange that a woman of Mary's strong character, who could be a helpmeet to a man like Maurice, should centre all her future hopes, her girlish budding affections, on such an one as Bertie !

What was there in Bertie's character to inspire such steadfast faith in him ? such implicitness of belief in the underlying goodness of his nature, which in spite of his faults and vacillation, his inertness and lymphatic purposes, made her cleave to him with such tender fidelity ? Could mere beauty have won a woman like Mary ?

Dollie might be touched and attracted by his Adonis-like attributes, but hardly Mary; but yet there she was—a woman weak in nothing else but this—but glorying nevertheless in her weakness, and ready with all her strength and all her courage to fight for him, and with him, if it should be against the whole world.

So she prayed her little prayer against selfishness, and tried to be glad that work had come to her in this foreign land, and that others had recognised her usefulness ; and then, leaving thought alone, she took refuge in action, and, summoning Justine to her aid, she soon had the sickroom arranged with exquisite neatness, Charlotte's essences removed, and a few autumn flowers placed in the purple vases.

When Charlotte returned, looking rather crestfallen and subdued after her interview with the doctor, Mary went up to her at once, and spoke to her most affectionately but firmly.

'It was not her fault,' she said ; 'that Dr. Arnaud had given such arbitrary orders ; and she thought it rather hard upon Charlotte. You see Maurice and I are so used to nursing,' she continued apologetically ; 'there is such terrible sickness in the parish sometimes, and one gets hardened and used to scenes of sufferings. Not really hardened, perhaps,' finished Mary, correcting herself in her conscientious manner—for she always took care to avoid anything like exaggeration in speech ; and had she not often come home and cried bitterly over ills that she had no power to remedy ?

'Oh, it is all right,' returned Charlotte, whose ready tears were already flowing. 'Of course you will do better than I. Dr. Arnaud knows that. I do not mind your

taking the lead in nursing ma pauvre Tante. How could
I be such a monster of selfishness? it is only '—and here
the poor little creature buried her face in her handkerchief
—' it is only—only that he should have such an opinion of
me, after all he has said !'

Charlotte cried so, and her eyes were so sad, that Mary
got quite mystified. It was not until afterwards—when
Charlotte got composed enough to indulge in one of her
favourite whispered confidences—that she got a glimpse of
the truth.

For she found out then that Dr. Pierre Arnaud was a
widower, with two little brown-faced boys in frilled trousers
and smart plaid tunics, who went by the names of Gaston
and Jean Jacques ; and that he lived in the great house
with the green jalousies in the Rue d'Equerre ; and that la
chère Hortense was his sister.

'He is a very intelligent physician, and has a large
practice among the best people of Lesponts,' whispered
Charlotte. 'Poor Madame Arnaud was a charming person.
I knew her well, but she was older than he—she must have
been quite middle-aged before he married her ; but she
had distinguished manners and a good dot—so perhaps
it did not matter. Frenchmen have such different ideas—
they are all for les convenances, and for matrimony by
arrangement.'

'Poor Dr. Arnaud! it must be very bad for him and
his poor little boys,' observed Mary sympathetically, who
had taken rather a liking to the brown-faced military-
looking little doctor.

'Oh yes, it is so triste,' replied Charlotte eagerly. She
was looking at all Mary's arrangements in the dressing-
room, and fingering the pillows of the little temporary
couch that had been fitted up for their comfort. 'That
great house, and those empty rooms, and no one but old
Jeannette to look after the dear boys ; and Jean Jacques,
such a delicate child ! He talks to me about them
sometimes, and about himself too. He says we English-
women have such sensibility, and are so full of sympathy,'
continued Charlotte with one of her old dimples.

Mary began to comprehend now. She wondered if Dr. Arnaud thought Charlotte had a dot, or could he really be taken by her youthful airs and fussy good-nature? She was not bad-looking; she was quite young and nice-looking sometimes. Mary understood now why Charlotte always slipped away to make her toilette before he arrived. The braided dresses, the scented handkerchief, the neat little brodequins were all for him. 'She has forgotten her old lover,' thought Mary, as she composed herself on the dressing-room couch for an hour or two's rest, while Charlotte and Justine kept watch. Could she really have loved him? and with the onesidedness of youth Mary blamed poor Charlotte in her heart for thinking of a living Frenchman, while her dead lover lay under the green turf of his foreign grave, not making allowance for the limp clinging sensibilities that made loneliness and a single life repugnant to Charlotte's nature.

'If Bertie were never to tell me that he loved me, if there were no hope for us, and we were never to be married, never to come together in this life, I should care for him all the same, and never want any one else,' thought Mary, as she rested her weary head on the pillow; and, to do her and Bertie justice, they were equally sure of each other, and yet no plighted troth had been demanded or given.

CHAPTER XIII

WHILE Mary slept the sleep of the just, poor Dollie was having a miserable time of it.

Being an honest-hearted little thing, her conscience was still sore with the memory of her past unkindness to her friend; in the spirit of true repentance, she wanted to make it up to Mary, and to atone for her fault by a great deal of extra petting, but no opportunity was vouchsafed to her.

The doctor's orders were stringent; Mary was invisible; when Dollie ventured to turn the handle of the dressing-room door, she was met by a loud 'hush' from Charlotte, or 'ne faites point tant de, bruit, s'il vous plaît, mademoiselle,' from Justine; while through the closed curtains that hung over the doorway between the two rooms, she could see Mary's blue serge dress, as she moved quietly about fulfilling her little duties.

She gave Dollie a cheerful nod when she saw her, but took no further notice; and Dollie went downstairs feeling as though matters were very bad indeed. She had no idea before how much she would miss Mary; the spirit of harmony seemed wanting; everything out of gear in the house; and even the morning-room, their usual resort, looked forlorn and less comfortable¯ than usual. Perhaps Bertie's unaccountable behaviour added to the general dulness; he came down to breakfast looking tired and listless, and his morning greeting was far less cordial than usual; he seemed to have forgotten all about the little Hebe of the previous night. 'How do you do, Miss Maynard?' he said absently. 'What a damp chilly morning!' and then he read his letters and said very little more until the end of the meal.

When Charlotte came in to take her late breakfast, and to retail the doctor's orders, Bertie got up and began striding about the room, rumpling his hair and pulling his moustache, or looking out of the window in a restless, perturbed fashion; then he abruptly left the room, and they saw him no more until the middle of luncheon, when he walked in with a muttered apology for being late, and took his place. Grey's morning had been fully occupied; he had had business letters to write for Charlotte, and some commissions in the town, which he good-naturedly undertook for her, though he would rather have stayed at home and tried to cheer up Dollie.

That little person spent her solitary forenoon in writing to her mother, and playing with Mark Antony; but during luncheon the rain ceased, and a pale watery brightness, as of coming sunshine, began to permeate the room, and Dollie began to feel chirpy again.

'It is quite fine now; it will be a lovely afternoon,' she said, looking across at Bertie; but though he assented he did not take the hint. It was Grey who was watching the girl, and who noticed the wistfulness of her look. Of course he understood her—had he not begun already to read her like a book? 'Do you want a walk?' he said eagerly. 'Of course Mary and Cousin Charlotte are out of the question, but here we are at your service.' Grey did not offer to escort her alone, he was far too keenly alive to the proprieties which hedge in young girls like Dollie, but with both of them it did not matter; and if this illness went on, she could not remain shut up in the chateau without air or exercise. 'Why don't you speak up, old fellow?' he continued, addressing his brother rather impatiently; and Bertie had no option but to declare that he would be delighted to accompany them, though a closer observer than Dollie might have noticed that he looked decidedly bored.

'Two is company and three is none,' says the old
adage; and it was certainly true in this case.   Neither
Grey nor Dollie seemed to enjoy their walk; Bertie hung
heavy on their hands; he would not join in the conversation; he said, 'I beg your pardon?' or, 'What did
you say, Miss Maynard?' every time Dollie addressed
him; as Grey remarked, 'his wits were wool-gathering.'

At last, when they got to the bridge at Laeken-water,
he suddenly remembered that he had a letter from Sir
Charles Howard lying in his pocket that ought to be
answered by the evening post.

'I forgot all about it!   What a bore!' observed Bertie
irritably, with rather a stronger expletive against his stu-
pidity, under his breath.

'Let us go back; it does not matter about going on
farther,' returned Dollie good-naturedly, for she saw he was
really put out by his own carelessness.

'No, no, I will go alone; I shall do it in half the time;
why, your little feet could not keep up with my stride!
Grey will bring you back all right by and by.   I am
awfully sorry, you know, but it can't be helped—good-bye;'
and Bertie hurried off without looking once behind him.

They both stood and watched him, as the tall gray-
coated figure went down the walk with swinging even
strides, until the trees hid him, then Dollie suddenly turned
and looked over the bridge.

It was the same still piece of landscape that she had
once sketched; there were the red roofs and quaint gables,
the bridge with the swans sailing under the arches, the
trees coming down to the shore, the wide sweep of water
with a sunset glow on it.

Down below on the sandy margin Bertie and Mary had
stood for ever so long, talking earnestly together.   What
had they been talking about, she wondered; and then they
had come back to them, laughing and walking hand in
hand, and there had been a happy look in Mary's eyes.

Could it really be that Bertie was in love with Mary?
She had hardly thought so; his manners had been too
brotherly—too openly affectionate, for that construction to

be put on them; and yet, what could his behaviour to-day
signify? was he not absent and disagreeable enough even
for a lover?

'If I had been a wooden Dollie, he could not have
noticed me less,' she thought, with aggrieved jealousy.
'Well, let him be in love with Mary! who cares?—not I,—
only it is a little hard when Mary is not here that he should
treat me in this fashion—and after my kindness to him last
night!' and a pang crossed Dollie as she remembered the
pleasant hour in the old kitchen, and Bertie looking up at
her with kind eyes, and with soft words on his lips, as she
ministered to him in the firelight.

Poor little Dollie! her fancy was touched, though her
heart was as blank as a sheet of white paper—no single
name inscribed on it; she was just in that transition state
when the surface of her mind might be touched by the
physical beauty and winning ways of an Adonis, if not by
this Bertie, by some other Bertie—for at eighteen, an
aquiline nose, and a pair of expressive gray eyes, and even a
stalwart pair of shoulders, will often weigh as heavy in the
scale of feminine favour as more moral qualities, kindness
and courage and such like.   It is later in life when one
understands that beauty and worth do not always go together.   Dollie's mind was vexed, but she could not quite
comprehend the cause of her vexation, and then by some
odd transition her thoughts went travelling homewards—
back to the little green parlour in Abercrombie Road; and
all at once her cheeks were wet, and a little sob rose in her
throat, and before she knew what she was about, the poor
child was crying heartily for her mother.

It was very absurd and babyish, and most unexpected
on the part of a young lady, who is bound to make herself
agreeable to her walking companion.   What would Mr.
Lyndhurst think of her?   And yet, and yet, if Dollie could
be only on her old footstool at her mother's feet with her
mother's arms round her, and the sad gentle face bent over
her, and talk it all out—all the girlish feelings and fancies
—for elder wisdom to disentangle and set right; for the
grace of confession in such cases is that there should be

implicit faith and confidence—why, she could tell her
thoughts, her most foolish thoughts, to her mother, and
never feel ashamed of herself!　So here was Dollie crying,
—absolutely crying, with real tears on her cheeks, and a
real choke in her voice; and what would Mr. Lyndhurst
think?

Mr. Lyndhurst did not know what to think!

He was utterly baffled and discomfited.

Another time Dollie would have burst out laughing over
their ridiculous situation, but she was much too heartily
ashamed of herself for that.

Poor Grey!　He said, 'My dear Miss Maynard!' in a
horrified voice; and then he turned his back on her, and
looked down at the water, and wondered what on earth he
was to say, and what he was to do; and whether she
meant to leave off soon, and what could be the reason
for this sudden agitation?　And then he remembered
Bertie's abrupt departure, and how Dollie's face fell; and
his brow grew very black, and he pulled his moustache
irritably, and walked back to her, looking very stiff and
quite two inches taller.　Dollie saw him coming, and dried
her eyes in a frightened way, and tried to speak, and began
to laugh, and did both together after a fashion that horrified Grey still more.　Was she going to be hysterical?
Here was a pretty position for a young man endowed with
more than a usual amount of good sense and propriety—
left alone on the bridge of Laeken-water, miles away from
the chateau, with a girl who seemed on the brink of
hysterics; and if there was one thing Grey dreaded more
than another, it was anything bordering on a scene; he was
actually getting angry with her.

'Oh, do forgive me, Mr. Lyndhurst,' cried Dollie, becoming all at once aware of the blackness, while a little
round tear, like a shining globule, fell on her glove.　'It is
too silly of me; it is absolutely absurd, but it has been so
horrid all day, and I do so want my mother.'

'Your mother!'　Grey's brow cleared like magic; he
came a few steps nearer, and looked in her face; perhaps
the survey softened him.　'Your mother?' he repeated, as

though doubtful whether he had heard aright, but his voice took its gentlest tones.

'Oh yes,' replied Dollie with a heavy sigh, 'I always want her when things are horrid or go wrong. I would give half I possess, not that that is much,' she said, laughing rather faintly at the remembrance of her scanty store of treasures, 'just to find her sitting in the chateau when we go back,—my dear darling little mother.'

Grey was silent, but his eyes looked kind; he was evidently mollified. 'Poor little thing! poor innocent child!' he said to himself; 'the tragedy of yesterday has upset her and made her nervous; she was looking pale all luncheon-time; we must take care of her. I forgot how sensitive girls are over these sort of things;' and he began to blame himself very unnecessarily.

Dollie heaved another great sigh, and then she looked down on the water and shivered; his want of response was a little depressing.

'Shall we walk on?' he said, misconstruing the shiver, and like a man finding relief in action. Dollie agreed a little sulkily; she thought him cold and unsympathetic; she had no idea what a sudden storm of feeling was roused in Grey's quiet frame by the sight of the little tear resting on her glove; he had never seen her cry before, and had no idea any one could do it so prettily.

Grey had seen children cry, and the remembrance of their contortions and puckered faces and swollen eyelids was very displeasing to him. Charlotte, too, had looked old and plain when she came in that morning with red patches under her eyes, and making up her face into an odd twist as though to force the tears out; but this girl cried so prettily—there were no twists, no contortion of features in her case; her tears brimmed over her cheeks and came rolling down where they would, and the redness of eyes only made her look more pathetic.

Grey meditated on this for a long time; then he revolved the whole thing in his mind, and cudgelled his brains to find something soft and pleasant to say; while Dollie walked rather proudly by his side, thinking him the coldest and stiffest young man that she had ever known.

'I think nothing can replace a mother—her love is so perfectly unique,' he said at last, breaking the silence somewhat awkwardly. He rather derided himself for this bald piece of sentiment afterwards, but Dollie was struck by it, and thought the truism perfectly original.

'Oh!' she said, brightening up, 'I am sure there is no one in the world like my mother; no one half so nice, or so pretty, or so good.'

'Well, I don't know,' returned Grey slowly, for he did not quite agree to this. 'I suppose mothers are pretty much alike, that is, every one thinks their own the best;' and he gave a short sigh,—only Dollie did not hear it,— for he still had a vivid remembrance of the sweet-faced woman who used to kiss him and Bertie in their little cots, and who faded away so slowly and sadly from life while they were still boys. 'Anyhow,' he continued, rather dryly, 'they are never to be replaced.'

'Why, that is true!' replied the girl eagerly; 'any one can have two wives, but there can only be one mother.'

'Two wives!' exclaimed Grey in a tone of perplexity; for a moment flitting ideas of Mormonism and polygamy among the ancients crossed his vision; 'I beg your pardon,' he said, stopping and staring at Dollie.

'Of course I don't mean two at once,' she returned impatiently; another time she would have given a little stamp with her foot, but she was walking decorously beside him, and dare not indulge in any more eccentricity; but how stupid, how very stupid he was! 'When one dies, you know, a man can always comfort himself by getting another. Most of them do it, you know,' continued Dollie, with a swift, bird-like nod, and looking very bright and knowing.

Now what business had that stupid little Dollie to drag in wives with the mothers, when no one was thinking of such a thing? Of course if one applies a match to an inflammable substance there will be an explosion, and latent volcanoes will occasionally break forth.   For Grey got suddenly very red.

'I suppose some men do console themselves in the way you say,' he returned.   'I daresay I am different; but it seems to me as though one could only love once in one's life.' 'He spoke in the driest possible voice; no one hearing him would have believed that his feelings were getting too much for him.

But that silly Dollie would not let well alone ; she had no idea that she was playing with edge-tools.   She only wanted to make him talk a little—to draw him out, in fact— and one subject was as good as another.   So she went on— 'Yes, but she might die early, you know, when you were quite young.'

'Then I would have all the longer to mourn for her,' blurted out Grey, feeling that his time was come, and that there was no help for it—that invisible hands were pushing him over the brink without any will or volition of his own ; and that, come what might, he would speak there and then. Then he stopped, and they both stopped.

They had reached the little bridge leading to the Béguinage ; it was a favourite spot with them, and they had often lingered there to admire the scene.   This evening it looked more peaceful than ever, with its ivied gateway and the broad sweep of water, with the low shrubs and pollards fringing it.   Dollie, as was her wont, leaned over the bridge, and looked down on the silvery water.   Grey cleared his throat, took a comprehensive glance all round at the water, the sky, and the long winding path, and then foolishly enough, as it must be owned, he began.

'Look here, Miss Maynard ; I want to say something ; we have got on this subject oddly enough, and now there is no dropping.   When a man's time is come he must speak, you know.'   It must be acknowledged that Grey was not talking with much eloquence, but on this subject it is not always possible for a man to be fluent.

'Well?' returned Dollie, with her eye still fixed on the water ; her 'well' was not discouraging ; it was purely indifferent.

'It is only three weeks since I first met you,' went on
Grey, with an odd break in his voice, 'three weeks to-day;
and yet it has come to this, that I know that you are the
one woman in the world to me; and so when a man feels
that, he ought to speak, you know.'

'What do you mean?' cried Dollie, facing round upon
him suddenly—she could not believe her ears.   There he
was, leaning against the bridge with folded arms, speaking
in a suppressed, dry sort of voice, but his eyes—at least
they were intelligible enough—their vivid brightness drove
Dollie to the water, this time with angry blushes on her
cheek.   'I don't know what you mean,' she said, feeling
terribly confused, and ready to cry again.

'I thought I was speaking very plainly,' replied Grey.
'You are the woman I love, Dollie—Miss Maynard, I
mean—and for whose loss I should mourn all my life.   I
am not like other men, I fancy; I could not love twice, or
change the object of my attachment.   When I mean a thing
once, I mean it for ever,' finished Grey, with a sigh that was
sufficiently eloquent.

Dollie began to get frightened; she was sure now that
he was in earnest.

'But it could not be like that between us, you know,'
she returned hastily.   'Please don't say any more, Mr.
Lyndhurst; it frightens me somehow.   I am very much
obliged to you, but it could never, never be like that.'

'Why not, Miss Maynard,' he persisted gently, 'when
I love you so much?'

'But you must not love me; you must not go on doing
it when I tell you not,' she returned angrily, for his
persistence terrified her.   'Oh, what would my mother say?
and when I have not known you three weeks;' and Dollie
looked utterly shocked.

'Have I been too sudden?   Shall I give you time—
will you go home and talk to your mother about this?
Please do not shake your head so decidedly; remember this
is life and death to me.'

'But I cannot help that,' she returned, half crying.   'I
never tried to make you like me,—I never thought of

such a thing. It is not my fault if you will go on doing it.'

Her childishness made Grey smile in spite of his pain. Why would she not turn and look at him, and see how thoroughly, how entirely he was in earnest? But Dollie did not dare meet those honest eyes again.

'How can I help loving you when I must go on doing it all my life?' he said rather reproachfully. 'Have I not told you that once means for ever with me; no, it is not your fault; you have never tried to fascinate me, but from that first evening that I met you on the staircase—do you remember it?—I have felt you were different from other women.'

'Oh dear! oh dear!' cried poor Dollie, so dreadfully sorry for him and for herself that she did not know what to say.

'Of course you have made me very unhappy,' continued Grey; but he did not feel quite so unhappy as he ought to have felt. On the contrary, he was conscious of an astonishing amount of obstinacy and strength. If he had been in love with her at the beginning, he was ten times more so now; if he could have spoken out all the thoughts of his heart, he would have said as follows :—

'It is no good your trying to escape me, my darling, for there is no escape possible for you. I am a tenacious fellow; what I will I do, and I have willed this with my whole heart and soul. You may not love me now, but some day I shall make you; for if prayers are heard in heaven and answered on earth, I shall win you for my wife yet.'

But being a slow-tongued man, and shy and embarrassed when his feelings were concerned, he could not say the half of this, but he gave her a shrewd hint of his intention.

'You have made me very unhappy,' he said to her; 'but as for giving up this, you might as well ask me not to go on living. Of course I will never give it up—or you,' he finished under his breath; then aloud, 'I suppose there is no one else,' with a slight hesitation. Dollie shook her head vehemently, but how she blushed at the very idea !

'And I may hope that you do not actually dislike me?'

'Oh, dear no!' returned Dollie, pleased to be able to
say something comforting at last. 'I like you very much,
and I should wish always to be friends.' Why do girls
always say that, always try to retain the rejected lover as a
friend?

Grey's brow cleared a little at this. He began to see
his way.

'Then I may hope to see you sometimes?'

'Oh, of course. I mean, if you like,' turning shy
again.

'I should like it very much, from time to time,' he
replied seriously. 'I do not want to lose sight of you,
or to let you forget me, in spite of—of—my repulse just
now. Now you must be tired; shall we go home? It is
getting quite dark.' And Dollie, who was dying to get rid
of him, eagerly assented.

Grey was acting very magnanimously. Instead of sulking over his defeat, he was marching off, if not with the
honours of war, yet with a good amount of pluck and
assurance.

Of course he had been a fool for his pains; of course
he had been absurd and hasty. Dollie had never shown
him the faintest shade of preference; on the contrary, she
had seemed rather to favour Bertie. What business had
he to take advantage of her girlish nonsense and turn it
into reality after this fashion, and frighten her to death with
his clumsy love-making?

And yet he could not be sorry for what he had done;
out of the fulness of his heart his mouth had spoken.
'When a man feels like this to a girl she has a right to
expect him to say it,' he said to himself; but the mistake
was that Dollie did not expect it, and was utterly and
entirely taken aback by it.

But this only fanned the flame.

No, he could not be sorry about it; he was a little
downcast and anxious, but not more than was good for
him. The thin end of the wedge was inserted; she had
taken it for granted that she would see him sometimes.
He must get his footing in Trevilian Terrace; he must go

to work in the good old-fashioned way, and woo Dollie
through her mother.   It was something to have a purpose
in life, something definite for which to work.   And so it
came about that Grey was not so very unhappy after all,
as he walked home by Dollie's side, hardly trying to talk
to her, but planning ways and means to secure his cherished
plan in the future.

CHAPTER XIV

FEEDING ON HUSKS

NEVER was there a more silent walk.

Grey had said his say, and now his lips seemed re-solutely compressed into silence; while Dollie walked by his side in the gloaming crying softly to herself, and wishing with all her heart that she had never come to Lesponts.

It was a relief to both when the peaked roof and turrets of the chateau came into sight. As they parted in the hall, Dollie flashed one look at him as she ran upstairs. The look mystified Grey, and he pondered over it for many a day. It was proud and yet humble; it seemed to ask forgiveness and to repel sympathy; it seemed to say, ' I like you, but I don't mean to have anything more to say to you.' At least so Grey construed its meaning.

As Dollie fled to the refuge of her own room she men-tally vowed that nothing should induce her to see Mr. Lyndhurst's face again that night. She could not and she would not sit down at the same table with him.

There was nothing for it but to assume an indisposition that she did not feel. True, her head throbbed, but the throbbing hardly amounted to a headache. When she looked in the glass her cheeks were flushed and her eyes were bright in spite of her tears. Dollie stamped her foot and shook her head impatiently over the reflected image.

'You tiresome creature!' she muttered, apostrophising herself. 'Your looks don't pity you at all; you are not a bit interesting or woe-begone.' And then she made her little preparations; and took off her dress and put on her dressing-gown. It was of the softest and tenderest blue, like Dollie's eyes, and her mother had embroidered it with silken pansies and forget-me-nots, so that it was the daintiest and most bewitching of garments; and she took down her long fair plaits, and her hair lay on her shoulders in shining masses; and then she leaned back languidly in her chair, and summoning Romany, made her pathetic little request.

She was tired and her head ached—she thought by dint of much thinking that it did ache a little—and she did not want her dinner; would the good Romany bring her a cup of English tea?

Grey looked up involuntarily from his plate when the message was brought to Charlotte, and then he bit his lip and looked down again. Of course he understood it all. He had half hoped that she would have come downstairs, and that things might somehow have resumed their old footing; but perhaps it was too much to expect. He must give her a little time to get over it, and to become used to the idea of a lover. And then perhaps she would cease to shun him; but how empty, how dreary, the room looked without her and Mary! It may be doubted whether he or Bertie felt more forlorn as they sat through the long evening, pretending to read, but in reality indulging in their own meditations.

If Dollie had wanted her mother before, she wanted her doubly now. Never was there a more homesick little creature. Write to her? Of course she could not write about such things! Fancy her taking up her pen and actually tracing the words : 'My dear Mother—Mr. Lyndhurst has just made me an offer and I have refused him !' Why, she blushed to the very tips of her little ears at the idea. Such things were to be whispered under one's breath. She could have said it between lights from the footstool at her mother's feet; or if she could have got at Mary she might perhaps have brought herself to say a word or two. Mary's sympathy at the present moment would have been of untold value. She might have hinted her trouble and besought help and guidance; but there was Mary out of all reach, and there was no getting at her.

10

This evening with all its misery was an epoch in Dollie's life; it was the first time she had been wholly left to her own resources; those hours of solitary self-communing were not unfruitful of good. She had been brought suddenly to feel the reality and responsibility of her womanhood, and the better and more serious part of her nature was waking up in response. Grey's offer had at least this good effect—it made a woman of Dollie.

She grew ashamed all at once of her trifling dreams and fancies; she took herself to task severely for the pleasure she felt in Bertie's society. 'What business have you to think of him at all, when he belongs to Mary?' she said to herself, becoming virtuous all of a sudden; and she determined as long as she stayed at Lesponts that she would keep both the brothers at a distance. There must be something in the air of the place, she thought, to make them all so foolish, and she summoned her stout English prejudices to her aid, and all sorts of far-fetched pruderies besides, to arm herself against these designing young Britons.

Mary wondered greatly that Dollie did not come to wish her good-night, and half thought of seeking her in her own room, but Bertie frustrated her intention by waylaying her in the corridor again. When he had gone off with his chamber candlestick, Justine, who had been watching them through a crack of the door, came out and summoned Mary, as madame was growing restless again, and so Dollie was forgotten.

Dr. Arnaud had warned them that they must expect a greater increase of fever and restlessness towards night; the day had passed tolerably quietly, but now there were symptoms of excitement, snatches of frenzied talk, of incoherent wandering, which became louder and more intelligible.

The poor mother had ceased to babble of the baby; it was the boy—the youth Walter—who seemed to haunt her brain. Mary shuddered more than once at the dark revelations hinted in her words. There were agonised prayers to his father to do this or that. 'You must not call him that, Marmaduke,' she almost screamed once, seizing Mary by the wrist, as she bent over her, 'our own boy—our only son, Marmaduke.'

'Do you hear me?' she continued in a hoarse whisper; 'what is it you answer?—cruel, cruel. What if he were to sink to the lowest depths of shame?—is he not our son? You are ruining him—you are destroying all his chances. Husband! Do you hear me?—you shall hear me.'

Then again, in still more terrible voice: 'I have lost him—I have lost them both—where in heaven or earth shall I find them? My husband! my son!' Then again—

'Hush! I am not your mother—you are not Walter—Walter died when he was a baby. Who are you—you standing there? That my son? oh, merciful Heaven, never, never!' and a sudden trembling and horror convulsed her frame.

'Oh, hush, my poor dear, hush!' Mary would say to her, soothing her like a child in her arms until the paroxysms had passed away; but again and again it came. There were wild prayers to Walter to spare her—to have pity on her gray hairs and broken heart; commands that he should go away and seek her no more. 'Hide me—hide me from my son; cover me over with earth, and lay me in my grave; only there I shall be safe—only there he will not be able to find me. Call me Marah,' she muttered, 'for the Almighty has dealt very bitterly with me;' and so on.

It was a terrible strain on Mary's endurance; Justine and Charlotte were sleeping in an inner room, but the brave girl would not wake them. 'It is better for me only to hear all this,' she thought; 'she is telling all her troubles, poor soul! by and by she will be easier;' and she thought of Maurice, and how they had once watched together beside a poor man in brain fever, when his wife had broken down, and how Maurice had commended her for her courage, and told her tenderly that she was a ministering woman—'Martha-like as well as Mary-like,' he had said with a smile, 'as all true women should be;'

and then he had broken off and sighed, and she knew
that he was thinking of Janet.

She remembered this; and a vision of the wretched
garret, and the sleeping wife, and the poor sufferer tossing
on his hard pallet rose before her; and then she wondered
what Bertie would have done in such a case, and whether
she should ever watch with him beside sick-beds in squalid
rooms; and then pinched herself, with a little smile—for
she knew she was getting drowsy, and that the mutterings
were growing fainter—and prayed that she might keep
awake until morning, and then drew aside the muslin blind
and looked out on the dark avenue; and all at once the
memory of sleeping disciples in a moonlit garden came
across her. 'The flesh is weak; ah, yes! weak enough,'
she murmured, as she once more seated herself by the
bedside.

When Dr. Arnaud came next morning he stepped up
to his patient, and examined her long and carefully. Mary
answered all his inquiries in a brief business-like way;
she was a little faint and giddy, but she hoped that he
would not notice it; but he had already drawn his own
conclusions from her pale cheeks and heavy eyes.

'Ma foi! but we must not work our best nurse too
hard,' cried the little doctor. 'Come, Mademoiselle St.
John, madame is tranquil. Justine and ma bonne amie
Meess Morell will keep watch. See, I will banish you for
some hours' sleep, and you will be like the giant refreshed,'
And Mary thankfully let Charlotte cover her up on the
chintz couch, where she soon fell into a dreamless sleep.

Dollie meanwhile was facing her ordeal. She could
not have headaches for ever; she could not live up in her
room, or have Romany bringing up her meals; breakfast
was on the table, and she must go downstairs.

She made her entrance into the room rather after the
fashion of a naughty schoolgirl, keeping her head down
when she shook hands with Mr. Lyndhurst; but as Grey
was equally red and shamefaced, it did not matter. They
were evidently afraid of each other. Grey did not once
address her, he left his brother to wait on her and attend

to all her little wants; but his ears were keenly alive to the few shy sentences that dropped from Dollie's lips.

Charlotte did not notice anything amiss—her penetration was never very striking; she kept up a running commentary on things in general that served for conversation. Bertie was much more shrewd in his observation, he looked from Dollie to Grey, and then secretly smiled to himself; there was something in the wind—perhaps he had done them a good turn leaving them yesterday. What a deep fellow Grey was!—but there, it was no business of his; he had enough to do with his own affairs; and with this reflection he took himself off to find employment for his morning.

Grey looked a little perplexed when his brother left the room; he did not see his way clear; he must speak to her; he must try and find out how she intended to spend her day,—she could not be left wholly to her own resources. But while he was hesitating, Dollie solved the difficulty by marching very stiffly to the door, and then, when she was outside it, by running as fast as she could to her own room, where she bolted herself in for the morning, working a little, and reading a little, and yawning a good deal.

At luncheon things were no better. Bertie made himself as pleasant as he could under the circumstances, but this time there was no hint from Dollie about the propitiousness of the weather. She sat up looking very straight and prim, and talked to Charlotte in little cut-and-dried sentences, that might have been taken at random out of a phrase book. Grey lifted his eyebrows more than once in secret consternation; never was there such a demure, withering Dollie !

Charlotte's density and fussiness were rather helpful than otherwise. She took no notice of the uncomfortable state of things, and trotted away after luncheon to wake Mary, and take her own afternoon nap, without questioning Dollie as to what she meant to do with herself.

It was a lovely afternoon, the sun shone out of a cloudless blue sky; a fresh wind, breathing rather of September than November, blew the dry leaves into little eddies and

heaps.   Dollie looked out of her window and longed for a
walk; then she remembered the bridge by the Béguinage
and blushed; finally she put on her hat, and slipped along
the corridor and down the stairs like a little mouse, and
closed the door so softly behind her that Grey, who was
putting on his gloves in the morning-room, never heard her,
and thought she was still a captive in her own apartment.

And so it came to pass that, strolling up the avenue
in the direction of the cemetery, he discovered with a
little shock of pleasure and surprise that the gray dress
before him belonged to Dollie, and that he was quietly
following in her footsteps like a guardian angel—invisible
and watchful.

The fancy pleased him, and he resolved to hold on his
way; but what if she were to turn and discover that he
was following her? that idea was alarming.   He thought,
after all, that he would go back.

But lo and behold, as he hesitated, and as he watched
with far-off admiration the graceful swaying lines of her
figure as it moved between tree-boles and slanting sunbeams,
the gray gown suddenly stopped, and all at once Dollie
faced about, and then began running—yes, actually running
towards him.

She did not seem at all surprised at seeing him, but
all her newly assumed primness fell off her like a cloak;
it was the old Dollie, self-forgetful and impulsive, who ran
up to him, with her little gloved hands outstretched, and
a startled look in her blue eyes.

'Oh, Mr. Lyndhurst, I am so glad you followed me!'
—(who told her he was following her?)—'there is that
man—poor Mrs. Reid's son, you know—sitting on the
bench, and he seems so dreadfully ill;' and Dollie looked
up in Grey's face as though all Solomon's wisdom was
there.

'Never mind him, we will walk the other way,' replied
Grey soothingly; a feeling of rapture came over him that
this dear little creature should be appealing to him again
for protection; but, to his intense surprise, Dollie still stood
hesitating.

'That wouldn't be right, would it?' she said seriously. 'It would be too much like the Levite, you know, passing by on the other side ; one must help even an enemy if he be in distress.'

'Well, you do not want me to go and look at him, I suppose?' asked Grey, very much puzzled by this view of the case.

'I think it would be better; it would be more Christian,' returned Dollie, looking excessively good. 'He is wiping his face, and he seems in such pain, and I thought I heard him groan. I suppose one ought to be kind even to sinners,' she finished, with a pleading glance, that was not without its effect; for Grey said very briefly—

'Very well, let us go and look at him ;' as he would have done if Dollie had pressed him to go and visit all the condemned felons at Newgate.

But when he got to the bench he owned that her charity was right ; the miserable man before them was evidently in severe bodily distress ; one of his paroxysms of coughing had come over him, and he was now stooping over his stick with laboured breath and bloodless lips.

He looked up at them for a few moments without speaking and without surprise; and then again he wiped the clammy drops from his forehead.

Grey eyed him long and attentively ; it was by no special wish of his own that he was acting the Good Samaritan to this man ; but, if Dollie would have it so,— and he shrugged his shoulders mentally.

'You seem very ill,' he said at last in the dry stiff voice with which Grey generally veiled his kindest purposes ; 'do you not think it extremely foolish to be sitting so long in the cold air?'

'Perhaps so,' he replied indifferently; 'not that it matters much in the long run. I have pretty nearly come to the end of everything, so they tell me ;' and his defiant look returned.

'Whom do you mean by they?'

'Why, the doctors, of course ; and a precious lot of fools they are, not to be able to cure a fellow—they say both lungs are gone—as though they expect me to believe them!'

'Well, anyhow, you had better take my advice and go home.'

'All. in good time, sir,' was the cool answer. He seemed reviving a little. 'I just crept up here to see if I could catch sight of one of you. Well, now you are here, you can tell me; how is she?' nodding his head in the direction of the chateau.

Then Grey's sternness returned.

'How dare you ask when you know what mischief you have done?'

'Do you mean that I—pooh, why do you try and frighten me?' but a ghastly look of fear crossed his face.

Grey hardly knew what he should answer; but Dollie, woman-like in her mercy, interposed. Her tender little heart had begun to yearn over this sinner; hardened, cruel, murderous, as he was, he was Mrs. Reid's son, and her own cousin; and then he was dying. Yes, Dollie was sure he was dying!

'You were very wicked!' she said; and her fresh young voice made them both start. 'You almost killed her, but she is not yet dead. She lies there and knows no one, and talks of nothing but the past; you are always in her thoughts; it is Walter! Walter! Walter! from morning to night.'

'She talks of me!' and then to their intense surprise —and because the man's heart was not quite dead within him, and because he was wasted with fear and weakness—the poor wretch before them suddenly burst into tears.

He was ashamed of it after a moment, and wiped his eyes with a ragged handkerchief, and swore at himself under his breath for being such a soft fool; and all the while the Divine spark of grace lay under the miserable wreck and ruin of the man, faintly and dimly burning within him, roused by the sight of the gray head that had lain so near his feet—love and sorrow lying at the feet of the sinner!

Grey held his peace, with a sort of disgust and terror of hypocrisy; but all the woman woke in Dollie, and she laid her hand on Walter's shoulder—noting as she did so the shabby, threadbare aspect of the man—and called him softly by his name, for was he not her cousin?

'I am glad you can cry, Walter; it shows you are not all bad—that you are sorry, I mean.' Henceforth Walter's memory lost much of its blackness in Dollie's eyes; had he not shed tears in her presence? was he not ashamed and sorry? then she said, 'You ought to be very thankful that your mother is still alive.'

He shook his head sullenly; but she had called him Walter, and touched him; and the sign and link of fellowship was not wholly lost on the poor outcast, though he answered her gruffly enough.

'You seem bent, the whole lot of you, on treating me like a murderer,' he muttered. 'What have I done? I wanted to see my mother; I wanted to make her change her mind, and see if things could not be more comfortable. It was Mally's fault; Mally put me on the scent, and forced me to do the whole business; if she dies, it was Mally who killed her, not I. I will not have that on my conscience,' speaking with such loudness and violence that Dollie shrank from him again and crept closer to Grey.

'Who is Mally?' she whispered.

'I suppose he means his wife; he has a wife, I believe.' Then, as though questioning her sweet face, and reading it truly, he continued in a more cordial tone.

'Come, Reid, this will never do; I cannot leave you sitting any longer on that damp bench; why, it is perfect madness! Show me where you are living, and I will help you to get there; come now, do not keep me waiting;' and then Grey nodded to Dollie, as much as to say, 'All right, I will not lose sight of him,' and then she looked gratefully at him and slowly retraced her steps.

It was a tough piece of business for Grey, but he got through it manfully. Walter walked slowly and with difficulty; every now and then there was a halt, and a fit of

coughing. ' I took fresh cold that night,' he gasped.   ' I
was better—I was laughing in my sleeve at all the doctors
before that,—but Mally drove me out that evening; she
said I was a molly-coddle, and that my cough was nothing;
she will be the death of us both, that woman.'

'Good heavens, Reid, are you speaking of your wife?'

' A nice wife !' he growled; 'the curse and torment of
my life.   I slipped the noose round my neck when I was a
mere lad, and she has been helping me down hill ever
since.   Why am I without a cêntime?' and he shook his
empty pocket. ' She has spent the allowance, every farthing
of it.   Last night she pawned one of the blankets off the
bed ; but there was no coffee for breakfast—no soup for
dinner.   When a man is half starved as I am, there is not
much chance for him.'

Grey's hand was in his pocket, fingering a napoleon, but
on second thoughts he withdrew it.   ' How do I know if he
be speaking the truth?' he said to himself.   I know poor
Mrs. Reid has always allowed him a good income—at least
a sufficient income.   I will go with him all the way, and
see how matters really stand with him.'

They were threading the long dull street in the centre
of which is the church of the Redemptorist, and after a few
moments they had turned into a narrower one.   Walter
stopped before a high shabby-looking house, with some
children playing noisily in the small back court ; the entry
was close and dark, the stairs steep and with awkward
twists and turnings.   Grey followed his heavy climbing
footsteps with some difficulty ; they seemed ascending to
the very top of the house.

'This is my suite of apartments,' said Walter with a
covert sneer in his voice, as he threw open a door.   ' We
had better ones in Paris, furnished with crimson and gold,
but they were not to Mally's taste.   Mally, I have brought
a gentleman to see you ; put on your company manners
and bid him welcome.'

The tone of his voice was indescribable ; there was a
mixture of defiance and despair in it; it seemed to say,
' Look at her, Mr. Lyndhurst—look at the couple of us ;

there is a wife for a man.' Grey followed him in and stood
hat in hand. The woman dozing by the stove—a fireless
stove—roused up stupidly and looked at them ; she was a
gaunt, almost an aged woman, and as she pushed back the
black handkerchief that covered her gray hair, Grey looked
at the harsh outlines of the face, the dull crafty black eyes,
and the coarse cruel nature of the woman was plainly
visible to him.

Poor miserable Walter ! Heaven help him indeed !
He had married as a boy a woman old enough to be his
mother ; and he was still young, and, but for his degrada-
tion, a fine handsome-looking man, and she was an old
woman, only with the womanhood, the softness and sweetness and the goodness of it, gone out of her.

Grey looked at her, and then round at the comfortless
bare room ; there was an inner chamber with a bed, on
which some rumpled bedclothes were lying, and by it an
empty packing case, and an old greatcoat flung on it ; the
window was dirty and high up in the roof ; there was a
round table with a bottle and some glasses, and a pack of
soiled cards ; two of the chairs were broken—such were the
squalid quarters where Mrs. Reid's only son was lodged.

'Come, rouse up and speak to him, Mally,' continued
Walter recklessly ; and then he rubbed his hands and looked
at the cold black stove and the empty bottle, and chuckled
and shivered, and coughed his dry hard cough ; and the
evil spirit that Dollie had partly exorcised came into him
again.

'What do you mean by your havers, waking me out of
the blessed sleep, which is all I've had for the two past
nights ? ' returned Mally viciously ; and then, as her dim,
stupid eyes took in Grey standing trim and resolute by the
door, her tone became cringing : 'And is it the gentleman
you are leaving out in the cold, Walter ? ' she exclaimed,
for Mally was an Irishwoman, and though she had married
a gentleman, or thought she had married one, the old
brogue still came up sometimes. 'Put a chair for the
gentleman, Walter. Is it one of your grand relatives ? '
peering at him with her greedy black eyes.

'A very distant connection,' returned Grey with much decision. 'Look here, Mrs. Reid—I am speaking for your good—if you have any influence with your husband, keep him away from the Chateau de St. Aubert.'

'Ay, ay, he is right there, Mally; if she die—if my mother die,' hissing out the words with a concentrated tone of hatred and bitterness, 'her death will lie at your door.'

Mally shot a vindictive look at him ; possibly a torrent of Irish abuse would have been launched at him but for Mr. Lyndhurst's presence ; as it was, she returned sulkily to her seat, cowed by Grey's tone and manner. He saw his advantage, and followed it up without hesitation.

'You will gain nothing by attempting an entrance to the house. Your unfortunate mother lies between life and death,' he went on, turning to Walter ; 'a few weeks, a few days, may see the end of all ; will you give me your word that you will do nothing to disturb her peace—at least not peace—you have robbed her of that for evermore—but the quiet which is all the dying ask ? '

There was an irresistible shudder, but no answer ; only Mally said in a shrill whisper, ' Don't let them make you promise anything, Walter ; they want to get the money for themselves ; ' but Mr. Lyndhurst took no notice of her.

' Promise me that,' he continued. ' Give me your word of honour to be guided by me in this, and I will guarantee that you shall be no loser ; none of us can tell what arrangements your mother may have made concerning her property. You are the best judge how little claim you can have on that, but as long as she lies in this state, unable to decide for herself, I will take care that a proper weekly sum, sufficient for your comfortable maintenance, shall be allowed you. I have influence enough with Miss Morell to pledge my word for that.'

Mally's eyes grew greedy. ' Ask him how much, Walter,' she said under her breath ; but Grey heard her and turned sternly upon her.

' Why do you interfere ? this is none of your business,' he said harshly ; ' it lies between your husband and me. I will not trust you with his money. Do you think that I cannot see how you and your shiftless ways have helped to drag him down?' He was surprised at himself for daring to provoke the termagant in her, but his anger against her was great.

'Look at this room,' he continued; 'is this the place for a man by birth a gentleman? why is not your husband on a sickbed? Why are you not nursing him instead of driving him out to meet his death on this chill November evening?' And Grey having worked himself up to this pitch of indignation took up his hat, despite Mally's whining protestations, and began climbing down the stairs again.

Walter followed him. 'I promise,' he said in a sullen tone, when they had reached the lower passage.

'You are wise,' returned Grey briefly, and then again he fingered the napoleon, but a glance at the drawn and wasted face before him, so terribly altered in the last two days, seemed to change his purpose.

'No, I will not give you money to-night; I dare not, with that woman upstairs. I will do better; I will send you in some nicely-dressed food from a restaurant, and some fuel, and to-morrow I will speak to Dr. Arnaud about you; you shall have medical aid at once.'

'It is no use,' replied Walter despairingly, 'but thank you, thank you kindly, all the same. Perhaps you are right about the money; she would drink it all; she has been at her old tricks again to-night. Would you believe it, Mr. Lyndhurst,' he went on with a loud laugh, 'that Mally was a handsome, buxom-looking creature when I saw her first—a little too old perhaps for a lad like me, but as fine a woman as a man need see.' He paused a moment and went on: 'I saw her first in Dublin acting "Mrs. Halley" in the "Stranger"—was it Mrs. Halley? I forget names so—but I know I lost my heart to her. Till the child died, she was not a bad sort of wife to me; but then she took to drinking—she says I taught her—and then it was all up with us.'

'I never knew you had a child,' observed Grey in surprise.

'Yes, a little girl; we called her Isabel, after my mother,' with a sudden quiver in his voice; 'such a pretty little creature! just the image of Mally, black-eyed and roguish.   Oh, but that was a bad business!' breaking off with an oath.

'Tell me about it,' said Grey kindly—he wondered if Mrs. Reid had ever heard that there was a child—and Walter complied, though with some reluctance.

'Well, Mally would go on acting—though she promised me to give up all that sort of thing at our marriage.   We were well off, and I was a soft young fool, desperately in love, and confoundedly jealous.   But no, she had the stage fever, and act she would.

'She used to go out night after night, and leave little Belle—we called her Belle—in the care of a mere girl.   I was out too, for the gambling mania was strong on me; but I always went up and kissed little Belle in her crib, and had a game with her, and I used to bring her home toys and sweets, for which she paid me in kisses—for she was a happy little creature.'

He stopped and leant against the banisters.   'No, I can't go on; it is too horrible.   Mally was prancing on the stage one night, and I was losing my money over the cards —curse them—and the girl was gallivanting with her lover, and the crib-curtain caught fire; that wretch of a servant-girl' (here Walter had added a stronger word) 'had left the candle too near, and the door was open, and somehow the window too, and—and Belle was too badly burnt to recover— she was quite dead, the darling, when I came home in the gray morning.'

He stopped again, and Grey thought he heard him sob in the darkness.

'That's all I can tell you.   Then Mally took to drinking because she said the child's screams were always in her ears, and she grew into what you see her; and as for me——'   Walter struck himself heavily on the chest, and gave a bitter little laugh, but Grey grasped his hand.

'I will come and see you again; we will have some more talk together,' he said; and his voice trembled with feeling.

'And you will tell me about her?'

'Yes, I will bring you news of her; go back and be patient with that poor creature. Good-bye, I will come again to-morrow;' and then as he strode from the door and hurried down the street, he blessed Dollie in his heart for first holding out the olive branch of peace to the poor wanderer.

CHAPTER XV

MALLY

As Grey walked back in the twilight, he told himself that he had done a right thing in holding out a helping hand to that poor sinner. The picture of the miserable man sitting on the bench in the sunset with Dollie's bright face beside him; the remembrance of the poor wretch in his dreary garret, with the shrewish face of Mally peering out from the black handkerchief, rose before him, and the disgust he had first felt at the encounter, faded into a mixed feeling of horror and pity.

Good heavens! that such lives should be lived out! such pitiful parts played in the broad light of day! and then Grey softly whispered to himself the old pathetic words, 'The only son of his mother, and she was a widow.' Ah, how terrible it all was! and the young man walked on in a softened and subdued frame of mind.

He had never come across misery like this, and it affected him strangely. In his quiet way he had made himself useful in his generation; he had taken great interest in a working man's club, that his vicar had lately formed; and during the previous winter he had devoted two of his evenings to teaching algebra and the rudiments of Latin to an advanced class. In this way he had secured an entrance into half a dozen homes belonging to the more respectable artisans; and it had latterly grown a pleasure to him to seek out these humble friends, and by intelligent conversation and the loan of his scanty library, to cement a good understanding and sympathy that should be of mutual benefit.

Many of Grey's friends called him visionary, or an enthusiast, for leaving the beaten tracks of a so-called young man's life; but he had small respect for these busy mockers. 'Some fellows pass their lives in laughing at everything,' he said once to Dollie, to whom he had shyly spoken of his work; 'they are always thinking of what will please number one; they make a sort of fetish of it, and everything that comes under the head of duty is offered up to it. The selfishness of some fellows is amazing.'

'I think it is very good of you to give up so much time to your poorer neighbours,' replied Dollie gravely, feeling that some word of commendation was necessary. What a good young man he was, to be sure! Dollie was not quite certain if she liked good young men.

But to her surprise Mr. Lyndhurst grew suddenly very red.

'There is no goodness in it,' he said rather abruptly. 'I am fond of work; I like teaching almost as much as Bertie abhors it; and then these fellows are so intelligent, and so much in earnest!

'Why,' continued Grey, warming up into enthusiasm in spite of himself, as he touched upon his favourite hobby; 'it is quite a pleasure to me to go and see some of these men in their homes. There is Joe Puckell, for example, the head of my class, and a first-rate mathematician; when I sit there talking politics to Joe, with his pretty little wife sewing beside us—she is a dressmaker I believe—I find it as hard to get away as many fellows do to leave a ball. I never knew a more interesting talker in any sphere of life than Joe Puckell. And then there is Sam Green;' but here Grey pulled himself up adroitly, for Dollie was politely stifling a yawn. She did not at all want to hear about Sam Green; she was rather ashamed of her want of interest afterwards, when, on that very evening, she heard Mary questioning Grey quite eagerly about this same Joe Puckell; she thought he looked rather reproachfully across the room at her as he answered.

Grey quickened his footsteps as much as possible; it was growing late, and he wanted to see Charlotte before dinner. What was his surprise, then, as he walked up the courtyard, to find the door of the chateau open, and Dollie standing on the threshold in her white dress, looking out anxiously into the moonlight.

'Oh, there you are!' she said in a tone of relief, as he hurried up to her, scarcely daring to believe his eyes. 'What a dreadful time you have been; I was getting quite frightened, thinking something must have happened to poor Walter. Now you must tell me all about it, everything from beginning to end,' commanded Dollie with sweet peremptoriness.

'Not now; there is no time for so long a story. Come to the morning-room after dinner, and I will tell you and Charlotte together; there is so much to arrange; we three will talk it over together.' But Dollie persisted; she had been waiting ever so long; she did not want her dinner— dinners were such slow stupid things. She wanted to hear about Walter; he must tell her at once. But she might as well have spoken to the wind — Grey was simply inflexible.

'Not now, by and by,' he said laughingly. He felt as gay and light-hearted as a boy as he ran upstairs. The barrier was broken down between them; that she should be waiting for him, and she should be speaking to him with her old animation and eagerness—surely poor Walter had done him good service; and he whistled softly to himself as he hurried dressing, that he might be the sooner in her presence again.

But Grey's triumph was brief; his inflexibility had affronted Dollie, and she had resolved to punish him. She had waited for him all this time, had been anxious on his behalf, and he had refused to gratify her. 'He may be good, but I cannot bear stiff proper young men,' thought Dollie, marching in her stateliest manner to the dining-room. Grey found her there alone when he hurried down; she was waltzing in the firelight with Mark Antony. He had a fleeting view of the dog's stiff reluctant movements, and a white dress floating softly towards him; and then Mark Antony's four paws were on the carpet again; and

Dollie was standing motionless looking into the fire, a little
flushed and panting, but with the corners of her mouth
drawn downwards.

'Where is Charlotte?' asked Grey, looking round, and
then drawing near the fire; but Dollie immediately withdrew.

'I do not know.'

'And Bertie?'

Dollie gave a little shrug in imitation of Charlotte, and
stooped down to pat Mark Antony; but the waltz had
ruffled his feelings, and he took refuge behind Grey.

'Is Mary still invisible?'

'I believe so.'

'What is the last report from the sickroom?'

'I do not know; shall I ring for Justine and ask?'
This was not promising, and Grey was silent; but after a
few moments he began again, but this time not in the
form of interrogation; he quite understood he was being
punished, and a little latent fun appeared in his eyes.

'It is such a lovely night,' with emphasis.

'So I see,' with marked indifference.

'I quite enjoyed my walk home. I did it in twenty
minutes, I am sure. Let me see—it was five minutes to
six when I passed the church of the Redemptorist, just
after I parted with poor Reid.'

'Please do not fatigue yourself,' interrupted Dollie,
looking very severe and uncommonly pretty. 'Charlotte
is not here, and it would be a pity to repeat yourself. Ah,
here comes your brother;' and naughty Dollie woke up
from her languor and nonchalance, and began to rouse
herself. She had so much to say to him that she could
not see Grey offering his arm to take her into dinner, and
he was obliged to content himself with Charlotte. During
the whole of that meal she bore herself in an unusually
flighty manner, eating little, and talking only to Bertie.
When Grey spoke to her, she answered in monosyllables,
and with an air of being interrupted; but Grey took his
punishment very cheerfully, and after a time confined his
conversation to Charlotte.

He had no idea that the girl was actually annoyed; the fact was, Dollie was disturbed in her mind. In her anxiety about Walter she had forgotten all about that unfortunate talk on the bridge by the Béguinage; for the moment it had escaped her memory. She had been pleased with Grey—grateful to him for obeying her wishes; and she had waited for his return with real impatience and longing.

His laughing repulse had angered her; she had been forward—she ought not to have been there waiting for him in the hall. No wonder he treated her like a child when she acted like one. She remembered that she had pressed close up to him in her eagerness, looking up in his face, and a peculiar expression had come into his—a certain look that always made her feel hot and shy. Perhaps he misconstrued her motives and thought; but here Dollie frowned angrily, and shook herself free of such dreadful ideas. One thing was certain—if she were dying of curiosity she would not go into the morning-room after dinner. She would hear it all from Charlotte afterwards. But she little knew Grey's pertinacity; as she went into the drawing-room he suddenly started up, and followed her.

'We are waiting for you, Miss Maynard, please; Charlotte is free for the next half hour.'

'I am not coming,' returned Dollie, quietly taking up her book. She spoke quite gently and primly, for she was half afraid of him by this time. 'I want to finish this volume; I shall hear it all from Charlotte to-morrow.'

She opened her book as she spoke, and seemed intent on finding her place; but looking up after a moment, she found that Grey, instead of taking his dismissal, was standing looking at her with kindly amused eyes.

'Now, Miss Maynard, I call this too bad.'

'So do I, to keep poor Charlotte waiting.'

'Charlotte will have to wait a little longer if you are going to give me trouble. No, I do not intend to go unless you come with me. Aren't you a little hard on me after walking all those miles to do you a service? You asked me to go and I went,' finished Grey very solemnly.

'Thank you; you were very good, but I am sure Charlotte will not like waiting.'

'Neither do I like it,' returned Grey in a quiet, good-
humoured voice. 'Come, Miss Maynard, you are a little
vexed with me, I see, because I did not answer your
questions; but you will forgive me, I know, and not refuse
to help me in this very real work, when souls and bodies
too are at stake. Come.' And his voice was so patient
and pleading, and his eyes were so kind, that Dollie suddenly felt ashamed of her ill-humour and suspicion, and
gave him her hand, and let him lead her unresistingly to
Charlotte.

It was well that she did not see his smile and the
brightness of his face as they crossed the dark passage, for
she would certainly have made some excuse and gone back.
His look was demure enough when he began his story, to
which Dollie—now quite oblivious of her book—listened
with breathless attention, while Charlotte was scarcely less
interested.

What was to be done? He must be rescued and comforted—that was the conclusion to which the two women
came at once. Grey must go again to-morrow; he must
find decent lodgings, and some one who could cook and
attend to his comforts. If he were dying—did Mr. Lyndhurst really think he was dying?—his last days must be
made as comfortable as possible.

'Take care of his poor body, and perhaps he will have
time and opportunity to repent,' said Dollie with great
solemnity, and Charlotte dried her eyes, and added—

'Yes, dear Grey; and you must talk to him, and tell
him how very wicked he has been, and how he has broken
ma pauvre Tante's heart, and what a wretched, unhappy
life he has caused her to lead. But there, Mary is waiting
for me, and I must go. Good-night, ma chère,' to Dollie,
and waving her hand to both, Charlotte bustled away.

When they were left alone, Grey moved a little nearer
to Dollie, as though he would bid her good-night too.

'Are you going?' she asked rather hurriedly.

'Well, yes; I must shut myself up for the rest of the

evening, as I have half a dozen letters to write—one for
the next Indian mail,' and then he hesitated, and his tone
became almost humble. 'I wish you would promise me
one thing before I go.'

'What is that?' but Dollie's eyes sank, and her colour
rose under his fixed look.

'Promise me never to be offended again about such a
little thing; it was such a little thing, you know.'

She coloured still more at that, but answered 'Yes'
readily enough. She would have liked to have told him
that she was angered more at herself than him; that she
had been forward, thoughtless, altogether childish,—but
there was no telling him that. His manner—gentle as it
was—recalled too forcibly that evening by the Béguinage,
and she began to feel in real earnest that the man before
her was not one with whom she could trifle.

'Now you know your power over me, I am sure you
will be merciful,' he went on; 'even a trifling word can
hurt when one feels as I do. Be natural—be your own
self with me; we are to be good friends, you know;' and
then he smiled at her and went away.

Dollie never knew why the tears rushed to her eyes
when she was left alone, but somehow the simple dignity
of the young man—his gentleness and unselfishness—
touched and subdued her. How good he was! how altogether friendly and pleasant except for that one terrible
mistake! Oh, if he were only as nice and good-looking as
Mr. Bertie! but how could such darkness and angularity
find favour in any girl's eyes?

'It is just like a story-book—the wrong one always
comes in novels,' thought Dollie to herself in a vexed way.
'There are mistakes, complications, all sorts of worries;
but how unpleasant it is in real life. I never knew it
could be so horrid to have a lover,—at least a lover who
was not wanted. If it had been,' but there she sighed, and
the current of her thought changed. She began to think
more kindly of Grey; he had asked her to be natural,—to
be her own self with him,—not to tease him with childish
humours. Well, it was a little thing to ask after what had

passed between them. She had been obliged to hurt him terribly in one thing, but at least she could be good friends with him; she would be natural, as he said, and do kind little things for him. He could not misunderstand her,— he was too wise and keen-eyed for that; but at least she must make herself agreeable to all her aunt's guests as long as she remained at the chateau. But oh! if she could only go home to her mother!—and at this point of her meditation Dollie again indulged in a hearty fit of crying.

Never had an offer caused more floods of tears.

She woke the next morning in a calmer frame of mind, but on going downstairs she found Mr. Lyndhurst alone in the salle-à-manger, reading by the window. To her surprise he beckoned to her somewhat mysteriously.

'I have something to show you,' he said. 'Read that;' and he put a crumpled piece of paper into her hands. 'It was brought to me just now;' and Dollie, with some difficulty, managed to decipher the scrawl.

'Come to me at once,' it said. 'I have had a terrible night. Mally is dead!'

'Dead! and you saw her yesterday! How very dreadful! What does it all mean? Shall you go?' asked Dollie, looking rather pale.

'Yes; I will just have my breakfast first. Will you pour me out my coffee?' And as she hastily obeyed, 'Now I want you to do one thing more for me. Will you go up to Charlotte and ask her for the address of that woman who lives in the Rue de St. Jean?—I forget the number—the one who has two rooms to let. Charlotte thought her a likely person to take care of poor Reid.'

Dollie left the room at once. 'I saw Charlotte and Mary too,' she observed on her return. 'Mrs. Reid seems worse this morning; they had a dreadful night with her; they were both up; Charlotte is such a piteous object, with black rings round her eyes; and poor Mary looks sadly tired.'

'It is too much for Mary. I must speak to Dr. Arnaud if this goes on much longer,' he said, pushing away his plate and rising hastily. 'What a sad state of things it is! I shall find you here, I suppose, if I want any advice or help about things ?'

'Oh yes, I shall be here,' returned Dollie very demurely; but in her heart she was pleased. It was nice of him to treat her in this friendly way, and make use of her; evidently he had a good opinion of her sense and capability, and then Dollie settled down as comfortably as she could to her solitary morning; for Bertie, as usual, was working off his restlessness by an interminable walk.

Meanwhile Grey was not long in finding his way to the tall narrow house in the Rue de St. Antoine. The door was open, and he climbed up the steep stairs without pausing to ask questions.

A muffled 'Come in' answered his knock. Grey thought the room looked a little less deplorable than it had done yesterday. A small fire burned in the stove. The bottle and glasses had been cleared away, and a coffee-pot replaced them; but in the seat that Mally occupied yesterday Walter was sitting, or rather crouching, with his face hidden in his hands. When he looked up to greet his visitor, Grey almost recoiled, his countenance was so altered and ghastly; evidently the man had had an awful shock.

'Well,' said Grey kindly, taking the cold, shaking hand, 'I did not expect to receive such news this morning. How did it happen?'

Walter stared at him stupidly. 'I don't know.'

'You don't know!'

He shook his head.

'Come, this will not do, Reid. I do not think you understand my question; you have been having some wrong sort of comfort this morning; is it not true that your wife is dead?'

'Yes, she is in there,' pointing with his trembling hand to the door of the inner room. 'Yes, it is true; you shall see her presently. Poor Mally! she was the curse of my life; but I never thought she would end like this.'

'But how did it happen?' demanded Grey again rather sternly, for he saw clearly that the man's faculties were clouded; evidently he had had recourse to stimulants to deaden thought.

'That is just what I cannot tell you,' he persisted. ' I had gone in there to lie down; my cough was terrible, and I thought it no use trying to sleep. But about one or two o'clock I must have fallen into a doze——'

'Well?'

'I had left her in here,' dropping his voice almost to a whisper; 'she was pleased with the fire you ordered for us, and she would not leave it. I think she must have had some money by her, for I know she got some spirits some-how.'

'I feared that,' was Grey's sole rejoinder.

'I must have been asleep, for I woke up with her calling me, "Walter, Walter." It was her way; I do not know that she wanted anything; most likely the fire had gone out and she found herself in darkness; but I did not answer, and pretended to be asleep. I have often done it before to keep her tongue quiet. I thought she would be coming in presently in search of me; but she only called once, "Walter, Walter;" I can hear it now.'

'And what then?' asked Grey, for he seemed to pause in uncontrollable horror.

'And then I heard her move, but not towards this door. She had missed her way,' whispered Walter, in a voice that made his listener's blood curdle. 'You know how close the stairs are to our room, and how steep they are. I could hear her strike them again and again—such heavy thuds! I knew what had happened, but I lay and could not move. When they brought her up they thought I was asleep, but I think I must have fainted.'

'Did they understand—the people of the house, I mean?' asked Grey, feeling a grave question might be involved.

'Yes,' he groaned; 'they knew her ways. No one thought of blaming me. Do you think I was to blame,' he asked piteously, 'because I did not answer? She was always calling me out of my sleep for nothing, but to make me swear at her; she loved to provoke a scene.'

'I think you ought to have watched her more closely;
you should have taken the poison from her.'

'Impossible,' was the answer; 'you do not know Mally.
Why, she was as strong as any man; and look at me, a
poor broken-down creature. Come and look at her,' he
continued, rising feebly from his chair.   'She did not
suffer much, they say; she was quite dead when they lifted
her up;' and Grey reluctantly followed him into the other
room.

Poor misguided Mally!   There she lay with the black
handkerchief still binding her gray hair. After the first
moment of repulsion, Grey was surprised to find how
youthful and handsome the features looked, the wrinkles
were quite smoothed out; in her prime she must have been
a fine-looking creature. Walter spoke out his thought.
'Ay, she was a bonnie creature once, when I first knew
her.   Poor Mally! but it was the terrible death of little
Belle that led her first wrong.   She was a bad wife to me,
a blight over my whole life; but I never wished her such
an end as this;' and he spoke with real feeling.

'Now, I have told you all, and you will not go away,'
he continued, when they were back in the other room.
'I cannot be left alone with that,' he continued imploringly.

'I cannot leave you here to-night, certainly,' replied
Grey.   'I am going now to try and find you some clean
respectable lodgings.   I have a great deal to do.   I must
see the people of the house, and the doctor; and there is
plenty to settle.'

'I wish I could come with you,' said Walter wistfully;
'but I am so weak, I can hardly cross the room.   Do not
be longer than you can help; come back before it grows
dark.   I am no coward; but a man needs to be strong
indeed before he is left alone with that!'

'I will come back before dark if you promise me one
thing.   Take nothing but what I send you—a little soup
and some coffee.   Take plenty of that, but nothing else,
mind.'

'I promise,' returned Walter, with abject submission.
'I only took some brandy, because of the faintness and

terror. Ah! I see you do not trust me, but I will keep
my word for all that. I am not such a fool as to offend a
good fellow like you ;' and he gave a miserable laugh as he
went back to his chair ; but before he left Grey saw that
he had relapsed into his old crouching attitude, and was
hiding his face in his hands.

What was to be done? Grey was at his wits' end ; he
must be away the greater part of the day, for lodgings
might be hard to find, and there was much to settle ; he
must get money, too, from Charlotte.

If only Bertie had not started off for that insane twenty
miles' walk ! and then there was Mary shut up in the sickroom, and utterly exhausted—Charlotte too ; but Charlotte
would be no manner of use. Dollie—would he ask
Dollie? would it be fit for her, a mere child, to remain
hours alone with a corpse, and a miserable object like
Walter? There were people in the house, he remembered
—women and children—whom she could summon to her
aid ; and he would look in on her whenever he could. If
she were frightened, she could easily refuse ; but he was in
a sore strait, and he thought he must ask her. One thing
was certain, he dare not leave Walter alone ; he might go
out of his mind with terror ; he might destroy himself ; he
—well, it was no use conjuring up horrors—Dollie was a
woman after all, and a very courageous one ; he must go
home first and talk to her.

CHAPTER XVI

WHEN Grey opened the door of the morning-room, he found it empty,—the bird had flown; the salon and salle-à-manger were both deserted; but as he paused in the hall in some perplexity, he thought he heard the sound of Dollie's voice behind the red baize door that shut in the kitchen and storerooms.

As he pushed it open, he could hear her plainly; she was scolding some one volubly.

'Are you not ashamed of yourself, Kâtchen?' exclaimed the shrill young voice; 'you are in a horribly stingy humour. I must have some more grain for these poor things—they are absolutely starving.'

'Hein!' mumbled Kâtchen; 'not one grain more, I protest. Is it Kâtchen who will rob the mistress on her dying bed? No, not for all the meess Anglaises that ever were born. Chut! are not their crops full already? What you dare, meess—out of my very hand! Where is mademoiselle? will she see her old Kâtchen insulted in her own cuisine? I will resign; I will have justice. I will it say; never more shall that jeune meess enter here to break my heart.'

A burst of girlish laughter interrupted Kâtchen. 'Have you a heart, my little old Kâtchen? It must be the size of a pin if you could see all these beautiful pets starving, and not allow me a grain. Another handful; yes, I will have it. There, miser, avaricious wretch that you are!'

'Meess!' screamed Kâtchen; but here Grey in much

amusement put an end to the duet. As he opened the door a great ray of sunlight met him; the red-brick floor, the gleaming brasses, the bright tins, were all touched by it. Kâtchen's withered old cheeks were flaming, as she hobbled across the kitchen with a long iron spoon in her hand. She looked to him, with her knotted gray hair and small angry blue eyes, like some malevolent fairy—so wrathful and so diminutive. She shot angry gleams at him as she retreated to stir her pot-au-feu. 'These barbarous insulaires!' he heard her mutter between her closed teeth. Evidently Kâtchen was in one of her worst humours; woe betide Charlotte if she crossed her path now!

Grey smiled to himself as he stepped up to the low window, and then he was silent. He was not prepared for the pretty picture before him.

The window looked out on a sunny courtyard, with some stone steps bordered with yellow lichen. There was the red-peaked roof of the stable, and a gilt vane over it; a well with a covered top stood in the centre; and the air was full of the fanning of wings, and the sound of soft gobblings, and peckings, and swellings of inflated throats; for there, surrounded by a hundred pigeons—at her feet, on her arms, her shoulders, even her head—stood Dollie, bareheaded, in her little blue gown, and with her fair hair shining like gold in the sunshine, laughing for very glee out of mischief and the fulness of life.

The stones were strewn with Indian corn and great yellow peas; and amongst them strutted pigeons with brown ruffs, white fantails; and carriers with green and purple necks, black and gray pigeons; and others in various-coloured plumage, with little feet and small sleek heads—now with contented coos and now with vixenish pecks, like fine ladies at a feast. Dollie laughed and watched them, amused at their greediness, and threw up her strong young arms, tossing a trumpeter into the air— where he turned a somersault, and then betook himself to the stable roof, and sat in a row with a pouter and two brown ruffs, looking down on the others like wallflowers or chaperones at a ball, swelling with discontent and ruffling themselves.

And then she caught up a small carrier, and kissed and cuddled it, and held it between her warm hands, caring nothing for its frightened pecks; and then there was a footstep and a sudden whir of a hundred wings, and looking up at the sound, she saw Mr. Lyndhurst standing on the horse-block, watching her. Her first thought was vexation at being discovered in such a childish amusement, but the momentary cloud dissolved before the gravity of his look.

'I wanted to speak to you; I was obliged to follow you here,' he said apologetically. 'If you will come in, I will explain my errand.' And Dollie actually obeyed him without a word; she only laughed once as Kâtchen shook her fist at them as they passed.

'Never mind, my good Kâtchen, you will be in a better humour to-morrow,' she said amiably; and then she smoothed down her dress and composed her face to listen.

No, he had not done wrong to seek her, he felt, when he had told his sad tale. How she flushed over it with sudden sympathy and interest! 'Wait for me; I will not be an instant,' was all she said; and almost before he had finished listening to her retreating footsteps she was beside him again, panting a little, and fastening her long gloves with fingers that trembled with eagerness, but otherwise quite ready and composed.

'You will not be afraid if I were to remain away for some time?' he said rather anxiously, as they walked rapidly down the avenue; 'and you will promise me one thing—not to go into the inner room,—indeed you must promise me that;' and his voice took the slight touch of peremptoriness that Dollie had unconsciously begun to obey.

'I think I can promise you that,' she replied very gently; 'I have never seen any one dead, and I do not think that I should dare cross the threshold. Mary is different—she is older and more experienced; she has attended a great many death-beds already—old men and

women and little children; is it not strange? And she
is only a girl!'

'Ah! Mary is an exception; I have never met any one
like her. She has been helpful and self-reliant from a
child; and then her training has been in a severe school—
she is a deaconess in all but the name.'

'Yes, she is very good,' responded Dollie, with a sigh;
and then they were both silent until they reached their
destination.

If Grey had doubted the wisdom of his plan, in a few
minutes he doubted it no longer. That day Dollie was to
appear in a new character.

Directly she caught sight of the miserable garret with
its skylight, and the bowed crouching figure near the stove,
a change seemed to pass over her, and womanly brightness
and pity began to shine in her eyes.

'I am come to sit with you, Walter,' she said quite
pleasantly and indifferently, as though the poor broken-
down wretch before her had been a well-known and favourite
cousin; she took no notice of the somewhat vacant and
stupid stare with which he received her. Uninvited, she
laid aside her jacket and hat, and then, to Grey's surprise,
she took out a baby's sock from a fairy reticule, and commenced knitting.

'Do not let us keep you; you have to be busy, you
know,' she said, dismissing Mr. Lyndhurst with a brisk
business-like nod. 'I shall talk to Walter and amuse him
until you come back.' And Grey had no excuse to linger;
but if Dollie could have heard that muttered blessing that
swelled her lover's heart as he left the room! And once
more the vow was registered that he would win her yet for
his wife.

It was a strange experience for Dollie, but she bore her
part bravely; her presence seemed to soothe the wretched
man, and after a little while he dropped asleep. He dozed
fitfully, and always woke in terror; then she would speak
to him brightly, and mend the fire, or even hum a light
air, though perhaps her voice was not as clear as usual.

At noon a tempting little meal from a neighbouring

restaurant made its appearance, for Grey had not forgotten
Dollie's young and healthy appetite; but she had much
trouble in inducing Walter to take even a few mouthfuls
of food. A sick horror seemed to be upon him; his
hands shook so that she had to lift the soup to his lips.
As she put it down he looked up at her with almost a
senile expression of imbecility.

'Did you hear? There it is again, "Walter, Walter."
She is wanting me in there;' and he actually tried to
stagger to his feet, and then failed for weakness, and
clutched her arm as she stood by him.

Dollie's lips turned a little white, but she determined
not to be silly.

'Hush! you have been asleep and dreaming, Walter;
no one is calling. Shall I sing to you a little?' and she
broke into a simple childish hymn, and then stopped, half
terrified, as the sound of a hoarse sob broke on her ear.

'What is the matter?' she asked in a voice of the
sweetest pity, for the shaking hands were covering the
man's face again.

It was long before she drew it from him. Those words,
that air,—he had heard them last at his mother's knee;
through the guilty past there had come back to him the
memory of an innocent childhood.

'I was a little fellow,—just Belle's age,—and she used
to sing it to me on Sunday evenings,' he groaned. 'I
remember her velvet dress, and the diamonds on her fingers,
and how she used to stroke and kiss my curls. I had
curls, I remember; ah! and so had Belle—poor Mally
used to be so proud of them,—but Belle is dead, and
Mally lies yonder, and she—' (for the divine word mother
would not form itself on his lips)—'and she is dying, while
I——' but the rest of his speech may not be repeated; it
fell on Dollie's shrinking ear like the cry of a lost soul in
torment; now indeed the twin scorpions of remorse and
anguish were preying upon their victim. Would Dollie
quail and leave him at those fearful words? Would she,
his earthly good angel, desert him in his hour of retribution
and woe? No! for as he groaned and hid his face, the

small white fingers rested on his shabby coat-sleeve, a sweet girlish voice repeated, trembling, those words so applicable to all sinners : 'I will arise and go to my Father.'

What was she telling him in a voice so broken with tears? what old-world story of a lost son in a far-off country—of a miserable hireling feeding on husks—of a starved and stricken wretch returning to the home he had left?

A long way off, yet met, discerned, and welcomed! Ah! yes, he had heard it before—the robe, the shoes, and the ring,—he knew it now; they called it the story of the Prodigal Son. Ay, but not such a prodigal as he. But what was she telling him—'This story is for you, Walter; you must go to your Father too. But there is your mother first; you must ask her forgiveness; she will not refuse it; are you not her son?'

More and much more did she tell him, in stammering, broken sentences, some half intelligible—for she wept so —some penetrating like keen iron into the bruised and guilty heart. 'Too late, too late!' that was all the answer he gave.

'Too late! Hush! in all God's world—His living world—there is no such word. Do you hear me, Walter? —no such word. Do you know what I mean to do?' and as he looked up at her, stirred by a certain fervour in her voice, she went on still more eagerly—'I mean to watch my opportunity; I shall tell no one, not even Mary; but when I see that she can understand me, I shall tell her—you know whom I mean—that you are sorry, and she shall send you a message of forgiveness before she dies.'

He shook his head.

'She will never do that. I have sinned too deeply.'

'Yes, too deeply for any but God's and a mother's forgiveness. Now I will sing you that hymn again, and then we will talk no more about this.'

And so it was that Grey, returning heated and weary in the dusk, heard the sweet sounds floating down the staircase, and found Dollie singing with the tears still wet on her cheek, and Walter listening with averted face.

12

They both started at his entrance, and Grey felt rather than heard the sigh of relief with which the poor little watcher greeted him.

'Have I been too long?' he said, looking at her keenly; 'but there was so much to do. Now I have a fiacre at the door, and everything is ready. Come, Reid, we are going to leave this dismal hole. I have found you more comfortable lodgings.'

'Must I go in there first?' the bewildered look returning.

'No, certainly not; you must get to bed; and I have sent for Dr. Arnaud. Come, rouse yourself and make the effort;' but though Grey spoke sharply, he was secretly dismayed at the ravages the last few hours had made in his appearance—it was a dying man he was supporting; he knew that now.

What a relief it was to Dollie to be leaving that gloomy street behind! she had done her part bravely, but the strain had been terrible. She leant back looking almost as exhausted as Walter, as they drove on slowly. By and by they stopped before a neat-looking house with green jalousies looking out on the canal.

A brisk-looking woman in widow's dress received them, and ushered them into a small comfortable apartment. A pleasant warmth was diffused from the closed stove; a coffee-service stood on the little round table; through the open door Dollie caught sight of a trim little bedroom, with a brass bedstead with snowy quilt, and a black polished armoire, and a strip of gay-coloured carpet. Poor Walter! no wonder he looked round him as though he were in the vestibule of paradise.

'Do you mind waiting here a little?' asked Grey. 'Dr. Arnaud will be here directly, and after that I shall be able to leave him in Madame Probin's charge; and we can go home together;' and Dollie nodded assent.

The little doctor eyed her rather shrewdly as he entered. 'These English demoiselles, what will they not do? They care for good deeds more than for les convenances,' he said to himself, with an expressive shrug, half of admiration and half of dismay, as he went in to his patient.

'He thinks that he cannot last more than a week or two. That last chill has done for him,' said Grey, as he and Dollie returned to the chateau in the starlight. 'Madame Probin is an excellent nurse, and her son Pierre is a stout strong fellow, and can help in lifting him when he gets worse; and to-morrow I must call on the English chaplain, and interest him in his story, poor fellow. I do not see we can do any more for him. Oh, by the bye, he asked if you would go and see him again to-morrow?'

'Yes, certainly.'

'Then I will take you; but I fear your day has been too much for you.'

'Do not let us talk of it,' she returned with a shudder; and Grey thought she came closer to him. 'Such days age one; but I think they teach one something too. Poor Walter! I am sure he is penitent;' but neither to him nor to any one but her mother did she ever speak of what had passed between her and the poor sinner.

CHAPTER XVII

THE next day Dollie paid her promised visit; but Walter seemed in a feverish stupor, and scarcely recognised her, and she returned home sadly disappointed and downcast. Mr. Mayne, the English chaplain at Lesponts, had also called, but his ministrations had hardly elicited any response.

Moved by a sense of helplessness and depression at the misery by which she found herself surrounded, and fettered by a promise she hardly knew how to perform, Dollie became grave and absent. Mr. Lyndhurst was necessarily much engaged, and Bertie had become a wanderer on the face of the earth, and brought back every day Belgian sand and dust on the soles of his feet, and hung about the rooms day after day looking moody and tired and far from companionable, until Dollie grew sick of solitude and her own thoughts.

So one day she crept up into the dressing-room where Mary lay sleeping, braving Justine and Charlotte; and when Mary woke she found her beside her, looking very meek and tired.

'Dear Dollie, you ought not to be here; Dr. Arnaud has forbidden any one but the nurses to enter this room,' remonstrated her friend.

'Then I will be one of the nurses too,' returned Dollie decidedly. 'I shall tell Dr. Arnaud so when he comes. Why, look at Charlotte; her eyes are quite red and swollen from fatigue, and you are looking so grave and pale that I scarcely recognise our bright-faced Aunt Mary; but I will not be treated any longer like a child, and ordered to be quiet, and to keep out of the way;' and Dollie's tones waxed ominously vehement, despite their lowness. 'She is my mother's aunt, and I insist on being with her sometimes.'

'You are very wrong and very childish, Dollie,' replied Mary with a flush on her pale face, for the girl's pertinacity troubled her. 'Well, I have no right to forbid you; but you must speak to Dr. Arnaud;' and then she turned away wearily. Was it the strain of these painful watchings, or some secret presentiment of coming trouble, that was beginning to oppress her spirits so heavily?

Dr. Arnaud began to suspect the former reason. He therefore yielded a suave consent when Dollie made her modest little petition in the prettiest French she could muster. Charlotte and Mary were so tired, might she not help them a little by keeping watch sometimes?

'Mais oui, certainement,' replied the little doctor. 'If mademoiselle will be reasonable and tranquil and tread softly and not raise her voice above the ghost of a whisper; silence, repose—that is all that can be done for madame.'

'Yes, yes, I understand all that,' replied Dollie hastily; and she stole away to carry the good news to Mary, while Dr. Arnaud muttered, under his trim moustache, sundry exclamations of astonishment concerning 'ces demoiselles Anglaises. C'est inconcevable, c'est incroyable,' Justine heard him murmur, 'thou art behind the times, Pierre Gaston Arnaud.' And ever after he spoke of 'cette blonde demoiselle avec les cheveux magnifiques' with a certain respect in his tone.

Poor little Dollie! she nearly repented of her self-will when she found herself on the other side of the heavy curtains. The gray-haired recumbent figure, lying so prostrate among the down pillows, the unconscious muttering, the sudden starts and tremors of delirium, the room orderly and darkened, Justine with severe disapproving face, going to and fro with list slippers, filled her with secret dismay. If it were so terrible by day, what must

the nights be? No wonder Charlotte shrank back from
such vigils and left them to Mary! It was Mary on whom
the night watch now devolved, while Charlotte or Justine
slept soundly in the adjoining room.

'Dear Mary, you have such nerve, such courage, and I
am such a coward,' Charlotte would say; 'I cannot remain
with ma pauvre Tante alone at night; I should be terrified
out of my senses; and Justine says the same. By day
it seems less terrible;' and Charlotte's blue eyes grew
frightened and pathetic as a child's.

'It does not alarm me,' returned Mary quietly; and she
spoke the truth; but none the less did she dread the
weariness and monotony of those endless nights. Her
strength was great, her constitution good; but six days
and nights, with only broken snatches of sleep, were enough
to try the most practised nurse. It was with a sense of
relief, therefore, that she learned that on the evening in
question Dollie insisted on taking the earlier part of the
watch.

'Charlotte and Justine must go to bed, and you must
have a good long nap on the dressing-room couch,' pleaded
Dollie. 'If we loop back the curtains I shall feel as though
you are in the same room with me. If I take that armchair against the wall I can see you plainly, and then if I
feel uneasy I can just say, "Mary! Mary!" and you will
come.'

'But you do not know how lonely it is: all in the chateau
sleeping, and no one but yourself to listen to that sad talk.
You are not used to it; your mother would not like it,
Dollie.'

'My mother would like me to do my duty,' returned
Dollie stoutly, and speaking all the more firmly because of
secret qualms within. What if she were frightened? Was
she going to own her cowardice to Mary? She must share
the watching, and wait her opportunity for Walter's sake.
She had promised, and no terror, no amount of fatigue or
difficulty, should turn her from her purpose; for Dollie had
a touch of Puritan blood in her, and could degenerate into
sheer obstinacy on occasions.

It so happened that it had been a quiet day with the invalid. Dr. Arnaud had paid his evening visit, and had expressed himself more contented with the condition of his patient. 'I trust you will have a fair night,' he had said; but neither to Mary nor Charlotte did he hint his conjecture of an approaching crisis. 'It may be reason and death within the next twenty-four hours, or there may be no lucid interval at all,' he said to himself. Dollie was not in the room when he added a final charge or two; neither did he suspect for a moment that there would be any change of nurse for the night. Some one was always sleeping within call, he knew that; and nothing more could be done than had been tried already.

'I have prepared her. When the end comes she will be ready for any emergency,' he thought, with a half-compassionate, half-admiring glance at Mary's composed face. 'My best nurse is tired, but to-morrow, unless a change comes, she will rest, and la blonde demoiselle will take her place; and then he went off and had a long whispered talk with Charlotte in the dim hall underneath the swinging hall lamp.

Bertie strolled out of the morning-room, and heard the final words—

'Good-night, ma chère amie. I may tell Hortense, then?'

'Yes, if you think it right, Dr. Arnaud.'

'Très bien! To-morrow or the next day; what does it matter? I have thy promise. Gaston and Jean Jacques will not long want a mother. Hortense is excellent, but she is a disciplinarian—a little hard—dur—what do you call it? She has prejudices; Madame Arnaud had none.'

'And you are quite sure, Dr. Arnaud?' whispered a bashful voice.

'Quoi—am I sure of what? Of your goodness, mon ange?'

'Confound it all!' said Bertie, waking up to a sense of eavesdropping, and very nearly laughing outright. The sound of his retreating footsteps startled Charlotte, and she scudded away like a frightened hare, while Dr. Arnaud drew on his thread gloves complacently.

'Va, for les convenances, this English courting is not unpleasant,' he said to himself as he lighted his cigar and stepped out into the courtyard.

'Madame Arnaud had a fine figure and a large dot; but one remembered sometimes that her parents were plebeian. But Mademoiselle Charlotte has charming manners—such sensibility, such softness, such confiding ways. My little Jean Jacques, thy father has done well for thee and thy brother. Hortense may grumble, but one can but be firm. Thou knowest how to manage women, and thy own ménage, Pierre Arnaud,' he finished, quite oblivious of the fact that he had been notoriously henpecked by his former wife, and had been sister-ridden ever since.

Meanwhile Charlotte had betaken herself, all smiles and blushes, to Dollie's room. Dollie, who was robing herself in her blue dressing-gown, listened to her confused recital with an averted disdainful face.

'Do you mean to tell me, Charlotte, that you are seriously contemplating marriage with Dr. Arnaud?'

'My dear Dollie, I have just told you all about .it. "Will you be ma bonne amie, and the mother of my poor little Gaston and Jean Jacques?" that is what he said. "You are Protestant, I am Catholic; but that need be no hindrance. The priests are no friends of mine; thou shalt have religion for both, thou shalt teach me. I shall be an apt scholar. I shall have the grande passion like an Englishman. Thou shalt avow a tendresse for me." He said all that, Dollie.'

'And you have forgotten *him*—Captain Hervey?' and, as Charlotte commenced weeping and said, 'Never, never, dear Dollie!' she went on severely—

'How can you be so weak, so fickle, Charlotte? What is a little French doctor to compare with an English officer, a hero like Captain Hervey? If such an one had loved me, had chosen me out of the whole world, had given me his faithful heart, I would have kept true to him living or dead all my life. I would have mourned for him like a widow all the rest of my days,' cried Dollie, with her blue eyes kindling. Charlotte was absolutely cowed by her vehemence.

'So I did, dear Dollie. I wore mourning; the best crape at eleven and ninepence—yards and yards of it for ever so long. People said it suited my complexion; as though I cared for that! I cried my eyes out,' continued the little woman; 'but nothing would bring Percival back to life; there he is, my hero in his grave on Cathcart Hill; and here I am, a foolish little creature, but so lonely, Dollie;' and here Charlotte's voice became almost too pathetic. Dollie's heart began to soften in spite of herself.

'When one is lonely, one seeks distraction; a friend appears a good thing. I have no one in the wide world but la pauvre Tante, and she will not be long here. Dr. Arnaud has been my good friend; he has shown affection and respect. My heart warms to his motherless children.'

'And you love him?'

Charlotte shrugged her shoulders. 'My dear, you must not be so romantic. I have been young once, and loved; but I think I have buried sentiment in Percival's grave. 1 like Dr. Arnaud. I have a respect for him. He pays me charming compliments. He is a good man. He is well off. I have a moderate dot. Well, then, where is the objection?'

'I make you my curtsey, Madame Arnaud the Second!' returned Dollie mockingly, with her blue robe floating into all manner of graceful folds. 'Dry your eyes, Charlotte; you must keep them bright for your French lover. When Dr. Arnaud comes, I shall curtsey to him also. I shall say: "I congratulate you, Monsieur; you will have a charming wife. Jean Jacques will have an affectionate mother." Two halves make one whole; you can muster a heart between you! good, excellent, my dear Charlotte! He pays you plenty of compliments; what can you desire more? Adieu, bonne nuit! and plenty of sugared dreams to you!' and wicked Dollie ran off, leaving poor Charlotte open-eyed with astonishment.

This little passage of arms refreshed Dollie. She looked so bright-eyed and determined when she made her appearance in the dressing-room, that Mary grew quite subdued. She watched her, growing more drowsy every minute, while

Dollie's needles flashed through the silken sock. 'Knit one, purl one,' she said sleepily, before she fell into a sound slumber.

So Mary slept, and Dollie sat erect in the great arm-chair against the wall, dividing her attention between her knitting, the fire, and the great carved bedstead. Now and then a movement made her heart beat faster; and she would steal on tiptoe and stand for a moment looking down on her helpless charge, longing and yet dreading to hear some sound break the stillness.

She grew more used to it presently, and began to knit up all sorts of vague thoughts with her silk. Pleasant dreams began to flit before her imagination; scenes of reconciliation, peaceful endings to a life so fitful and so full of woe, forgiveness sought and obtained, through her influence as peacemaker.

Now, to the end of her life Dollie steadily maintained that she never closed her eyes or slept a single moment that night; but, whatever might be her convictions on the subject, one thing was certain—that before very long a fair head was nodding against the velvet cushions, and that the knitting needles had somehow found their way to the floor.

For Dollie was young, and had a healthy appetite for sleep; and had never known the drowsy stillness of a sick-room, and the pine knots were diffusing a spicy odour, and spluttering pleasantly every now and then; and Mary was breathing as softly and evenly as a child. And so—and so the silk unravelled itself, and Dollie's golden head nid-nodded like a buttercup in a breeze, and all her wits went wool-gathering like young lambs at grass.

And how it came to pass she did not know, but all at once she thought she was in the green parlour in Abercrombie Road, and that her mother was call-ing to her, 'Dollie, Dollie;' and starting up in a fright, with her eyes wide open, she heard it again, only in weaker tones, 'Dollie, Dollie,' and found it proceeded from the bed.

Poor little Dollie! how her heart went pit-a-pat

as she crossed the room! for there was Mrs. Reid leaning on her elbow and regarding her with a strange fixed
look, and yet with something of her old kindness in her
eyes.

'Dollie, is that you, my dear?' The tones were very
feeble and low. Dollie's heart gave a great leap of joy.
She knew her, then; she spoke in her old voice; was the
opportunity come so soon? Oh! if Mary would only go
on sleeping—if she could have her to herself a little
while.

'Yes, dear Aunt Reid, it is I,' she said; but her voice
trembled so, she could hardly speak. 'Are you better?
Will you let me give you this?' handing her the composing
draught that was put in readiness beside her; but Mrs.
Reid waved it away with a movement of impatience, and
sank back wearily on her pillows.

'Not yet,' she said feebly; 'that is what they give to
make me sleep, and I have something I want to say first.
How long have you been here, Dollie? I have been
watching you for some time, poor little one; how tired you
were! Why have they let you do this?'

'I wanted to be with you, dear aunt.' She had never
called her by that name before, but now it seemed to come
naturally.

'It is not you who have been nursing me? I thought—
I thought, but I am not sure, that it was Mary who was
always beside me.'

'She never left you, except for a little rest,' returned
Dollie earnestly; 'she has been with you night and day.'

'So I thought. Was there no one else—no one,
Dollie?'

'No one but Charlotte and Justine, and sometimes Dr.
Arnaud.'

'And no one else?' persisted the sick woman; and now
a bewildered look came into her eyes. 'When I am very
ill I get confused; but surely—oh yes, I know he was here
too.'

'Do you mean Walter?' she whispered; and as Mrs.
Reid closed her eyes, and her lips seemed to form 'Yes,'

something seemed to rise to Dollie's throat and almost
choke her. Must she speak—should she dare? Was not
the opportunity too good to be lost? And yet, if she
should kill her! 'O God! give me wisdom,' faltered the
poor child; and then, before she knew, the words came
rolling out.

'Walter! Oh no! He is ill too; he will not live long;
Dr. Arnaud told us so.'

'Walter ill!' Were the words groaned, or simply
breathed? How could Dollie through her blinding tears
see the spasm that passed over the livid face?

'Yes, and Mally is dead, and his little child too. They
called her Belle, after you. He told me all about it—what
a dear little creature she was, and how she had your eyes.
He said it was a punishment because of his wicked life,
and then he cried so, and seemed so sorry; he said there
was no hope, that it was too late to ask your forgiveness,
that he had broken your heart and killed you, that his
mother and his God had cast him off, and that there was
nothing for him in this world and the next.

'Hush! you shall not speak—not yet,' went on Dollie,
with a sob. 'Do you know what I told him? "Do not
cry, Walter"—that is what I said. "Do you say it is too
late? There is no such word in all God's world—mothers
are not like that. I will go to her; I will watch till her
poor brain wakes up and she understands and can hear me,
and I will tell her you are sorry; and she shall send you
her love and forgiveness to cheer you on your dying
bed——"'

'Dollie, how dare you? Oh, Dollie, and I trusted you
so!' And there was poor Mary standing by the bed, with
her face pale with fright and her limbs shaking. 'How
could you—how could you——' But Mrs. Reid's voice
stopped her.

'Mary! come here, Mary. In all the world I have no
one to depend upon but you; I know I can trust you,—is
this true, all—all that this girl has said?'

'Yes, yes, my poor dear; it must be true;' and Mary
knelt on the bed, and stretched out her strong protect-

ing arms over the agonised creature, as though she would shield her.

'Then bring my son home to die under his mother's roof;' and as she said this the strength of her voice relaxed, and as she fell back upon the pillow, her face was as the face of the dead.

CHAPTER XVIII

AT LAST

HER face was as the face of the dead, but not yet was the broken heart at rest. They must needs call her back to life and her sorrow again—not until the appointed time comes can the weary ones of earth lay down their cross and take their long sleep. The time had not yet come for Isabel Reid—a few more hours, a few more days—that was what they gave her.

There was wild confusion that night in the chateau. Grey, waking from sleep, heard hurrying footsteps along the corridor, and dressing hastily, found Dollie crouching outside the door of the sickroom crying as if her heart would break.

'She is dead, and I have killed her,' she said, looking up in his face with such woe-begone eyes that Grey felt quite frightened for her. 'Mary and Charlotte and Justine are all in there, but they can do nothing—nothing. I have told her about Walter, and killed her.'

'Nonsense,' he returned vigorously—for though things were serious he would not have her talking like that. 'Have they sent for Dr. Arnaud? It may be a fainting fit, you know;' and then he pushed past her and made his way unceremoniously into the room, putting the frightened women aside.

A moment's observation confirmed him in his surmise. 'All right—go on with your remedies while I fetch Dr. Arnaud,' he said to Mary, who, even at this moment, looked alert and composed. He took no more notice of the poor little penitent in the blue gown—time was too precious for that. Dollie could hear him unbolting the great oak door, and striding out into the darkness; and the promptitude of the action gave her a certain sense of comfort—perhaps, after all, she was not dead!

The poor child was still on guard when he returned with Dr. Arnaud; she looked after them piteously when they entered, leaving her still outside. But she was not to be left long without comfort; not many minutes passed before she felt a light touch on her arm, and there was Grey looking at her with a world of pity in his eyes.

Poor Dollie! She tried to gasp out, 'How is she?' but her tongue refused to articulate; she could only clasp her hands in an agony of suspense and doubt; but he understood the unuttered question.

'Do not look like that,' he said kindly; 'things are not so bad after all. Consciousness is returning.' And as Dollie covered her face with an exclamation of thankfulness, he continued briskly, 'Now I cannot leave you here in the cold any longer; there is a fire in the dressing-room; you must come there, and Romany shall make you some coffee—come;' and before Dollie could answer, he had gently lifted her from her low position, and in another moment she found herself in the armchair, stretching out her numb hands over the welcome blaze, already half comforted by the warmth and brightness.

The heavy curtains were closed; through the thick folds they could faintly distinguish the low tones and movements in the adjoining room; there was the couch from which poor Mary had risen to a new shock and terror. Grey quietly moved away, and after a short interval returned with the cup of steaming coffee. How grateful it was to Dollie—shivering in the early dawn of a wintry morning. 'Now, tell me all about it,' he said quietly, as he took the empty cup and replenished the blaze, and Dollie obeyed as readily as a child.

'Do you think it was very wrong?' she asked meekly when she had finished.

Grey hesitated a moment; if he had spoken out his thoughts he would have said—

'What childishness—what folly—what inconceivable imprudence—to talk in that way to a woman just recovering from brain-fever! Could any one in their senses be so utterly ignorant? You are an honest-hearted and well-meaning little blunderer; that is what you are, you foolish child!' But what he really did say was this—

'It was a risk—but you meant it for the best. I think Providence sometimes takes our mistakes and turns them to account; good may come out of all this.'

- 'Do you really think so?' she asked breathlessly.

'I am sure of it. Now promise me not to fret any more; you were frightened, you see; and that made you feel so uncomfortable. Dr. Arnaud will not leave the house for some hours. Now you must go to your own room and try and sleep a little, and by and by we will talk again about this;' and after a little more persuasion Dollie yielded.

The day wore on—it was an anxious one to all in the chateau. There were long consultations in the dressing-room between Dr. Arnaud, Mary, and Grey. Mrs. Reid had recovered, but not to speech; life seemed slowly ebbing; but as she lay her eyes followed Mary wistfully—weary sunken eyes, yet with a gleam of entreaty in them. Towards evening Mary could bear it no longer, and she followed Dr. Arnaud into the next room.

Grey was there; he had promised Mary to linger within reach.

'I can endure it no longer,' she said; and her voice was very moved. 'You fear, you hesitate, Dr. Arnaud; you say it will be bad for both of them. But I tell you my honour is at stake—a dying command is imperative; you must go for Walter, both of you, and bring him home.'

'Mademoiselle, je vous donne ma parole, que——'

'Stay, Monsieur, you must hear me. I have thought—I have thought until my head seems bursting;' and she put her hand up to her forehead. 'Listen to me, both of you. "Mary, there is no one in the world that I can depend on but you." Alas! that was what she said; was it not pitiful? "Bring my son home, that he may die under his mother's roof." What could be plainer?'

'I tell you it will kill them both,' returned the little doctor angrily.

'Monsieur, she is dying now; one can see it in her face. What will a few days or hours matter in comparison with peace and rest of mind? All day long her eyes have called to me; they say, Remember I have trusted you; where is my son? There is the night coming, and how am I to bear their pleading? Kill her indeed! Why, I tell you,' continued Mary, with a sort of passion in her voice, 'that she cannot die. Until he comes you will keep her in torture, hovering on the borders of life and death. Now I shall go back to her and say to-morrow he will come, and she will believe me, and her poor eyes will close. On your peril, then, if you fail to bring him;' and then she turned herself quietly round and left them.

Dr. Arnaud shrugged his shoulders. 'Est il possible? Mademoiselle makes one's hair to stand on end; one has to obey her and commit murder; it will be a case for the guillotine to bring him out of his bed, to introduce him into that room,' with a wave of his hand and another shrug. 'Madame, I have brought Monsieur your son, behold him. He has been a goat, a scapegrace—bon ciel! the prodigal himself; embrace him. Make the scene—what can follow but the deluge? He bien! I wash my hands; I make them clean; I protest; and I obey.'

'It is an unlucky business; but I suppose she is right,' returned Grey, who found himself somewhat moved by Mary's eloquence. If it had been Dollie—well, perhaps he might hesitate; but Mary, so calm and quiet and reasonable! he had a sort of conviction that she must be right after all.

And that night the poor staring eyes closed, and Mary laid her weary head on the same pillow as she sat beside the bed, and slept too; and for once there was peace and rest in the sickroom.

But with morning came revived consciousness and restlessness; bodily weakness was great, but the dormant

13

faculties of the brain roused up and asserted themselves. Again the wistful glance followed Mary; the ears seemed strained to listen; at every footstep, at every sound Mary noticed the nervous twitch or convulsive start; the hands seemed groping for something on the quilt.

'No, he has not come yet,' Mary would say, softly hushing her like a child; 'you must be good and patient; you know you can trust us,' and then the head would turn on the pillow again with a weary sigh.

It was late in the afternoon when Mary heard the wheels of a fiacre in the courtyard, and then a slight commotion in the entry, and knew they had brought him. Mrs. Reid had heard it too; her eyes beckoned Mary at once.

'Fetch him!' that was all she said; but how the poor face quivered with expectation! how the hands groped and worked on the coverlet!

Mary hesitated a moment, and then she looked at Justine meaningly, and left the room.

How long it seemed—minutes, hours—before he reached that door! Mary watched him anxiously as he commenced his toilsome ascent leaning on Grey's arm, and followed by the little doctor grumbling at every step.

'Ciel!' they heard him mutter; 'Quelle bêtise!—thou art a disgrace to thy profession, Pierre Arnaud, to permit such doings;' and there was a fresh groan and shrug at every pause.

He stood at last on the threshold of his mother's room —a worn shabby figure, panting and breathless, with the great drops of perspiration standing on his forehead. 'Mother, I have come home to die!' that was what he said; and at the word 'mother,' a great light came into her eyes, and all her features quivered with ecstasy.

'Walter!' she cried feebly, and tried to raise herself and could not; and stretched out her trembling arms. 'Walter, my son, my son; come back to God and me!'

And as he sank, half in repentance and half in feebleness beside the bed, the weak hand touched his hair and lingered there. What was this they heard her whisper?—

'For this my son was dead, and is alive again ; he was lost, and is found.'

For a little while they left them undisturbed ; they had nothing to dread now. It was the last flicker of life—they knew that ; but how peaceful were those closing hours !

They had placed him where her dying eyes might rest upon his face ; now and then he stroked her hand, or called her mother ; and then that strange sweet smile came to her lips, but she seldom spoke. Once they heard her murmur, 'My baby, our baby, Marmaduke !' Was she tracing in that worn, bowed figure and sunken face the bold beauty of her long-lost boy Walter ?

'Mother, tell me once again that you forgive me before you die,' he cried ; and then again she smiled. And now there was a change upon her face.

Forgiven ! oh yes ; what need to tell him that, when she had cradled his head upon her dying breast, and laid her thin cheek to his ? Forgiven ! when such a smile as that greeted him ? Even now, when speech was past, she signed to him to kiss her ; but, as his lips touched hers, there was a sigh, a slight quiver of the face—the soul of Isabel Reid was at rest.

CHAPTER XIX

NEARLY a fortnight had elapsed since the Chateau de St. Aubert had lost its mistress; and since then another sad catastrophe had happened. Poor Walter had only survived his mother five days; what Dr. Arnaud had secretly feared had come to pass—he had broken a blood-vessel during one of his paroxysms of coughing; and in his enfeebled condition there had been no rally, and the end had been very sudden.

Grey and Mary had nursed him; and during the last few hours Dollie had crept in to bid her ill-fated cousin good-bye. There had been no smile or sign of recognition; but Grey, who was bending over him, was sure that the white lips had formed themselves into the words ' God bless her!' and he cheered her greatly by assuring her of this.

' You see good has come out of evil after all,' Grey said in his quiet way, as he and Dollie stood together over the morning-room fire. The next day he and Charlotte were to start for England, to convey the mother and son to their resting-place in Crome churchyard; for such were Mrs. Reid's instructions for herself. It was doubtful whether Grey would return to the chateau; but Bertie was to remain to watch over the two girls, and, if necessary, to escort them to London. Dollie had written to her mother, begging to be recalled at once; but Mary was too utterly spent to do anything but lie on the sofa and sleep. The shock of Walter's sudden death had utterly broken her down after her anxious watch and nursing. 'Sleep, chère made-moiselle; nature must have its way. You have spent your substance for the present; the vital energies are exhausted. In a few days you will be refreshed, revived, re-born like the phœnix. Now you must be like a little child, an infant, and sleep and eat, and do nothing at all.' And Dr. Arnaud was right; for a few days Mary did literally nothing but sleep.

This was Grey's last night in the chateau, and he knew it. Charlotte was upstairs making her sad preparations, and Mary was in her own room. Bertie was strolling up and down the avenue in the moonlight in company with his cigar; and Dollie, in her black dress, was hanging over the morning-room fire, looking very dull and subdued, when Grey came in and found her.

There had been a little desultory talk between them, and then Grey had launched off into graver subjects.

'After all, good has come out of evil,' he said; 'uncertain as it was, it has not turned out such a mistake; she might have died any moment, and so might he. One cannot judge of results in such a case.'

'I am glad you think so,' returned Dollie earnestly. 'Do you know what I tell myself? Now they will meet in heaven reconciled; there will be nothing to make right, to explain—first the mother's forgiveness, then God's. Some-how they seem to go together.'

'I think that we may hope so.'

'Yes, of course; there is no forgiveness without repent-ance; to repent means to get up and do something; not only to be sorry, but to make the step forward. I explain it badly, but this is what I mean—when Walter came to his mother, he found his Father too.'

Grey bowed his head; somehow he had no answer ready. A young man's reticence approaches these subjects reluctantly.

'He did the right thing,' went on Dollie dreamily; she was talking to herself more than him. 'God would not be hard on him, because he was too ill to pray; we think too much of forms, of mere words. He was sorry, and came home; and then he lay and suffered. Ah, poor Walter! how he suffered! now it is all right, and they have met; and he is showing her little Belle—and, oh dear! one must not think too much,' as a recollection of Mally and her wretched end recurred to her mind.

Grey thought it better to turn her thoughts.

'We must not judge. Do you know what I heard a clergyman say once?—that if we were ever fortunate enough to reach heaven, we shall encounter three surprises.'

'Well?' interrogated Dollie, and her eyes grew bright with feeling.

'Our first surprise will be,' returned Grey very slowly, 'to miss many whom we fully expected to see there; our second surprise, to find many whom we never thought to meet there; and the third will be to find ourselves there;' and as Dollie hung her head, he quickly changed the subject.

'I wonder when we shall meet again;' that was what he said after a few minutes' silence.

Dollie, who was thinking deeply, looked up a little startled.

'You will not be long gone; Charlotte says four or five days, not longer.'

'I am not thinking of returning here,' was the unexpected rejoinder, 'unless circumstances are very different from what I imagine them to be. I must get back to my chambers and work.'

'But Charlotte——' stammered Dollie. Somehow this view of the case had never occurred to her; it was odd, and not quite pleasant, to think of bidding Mr. Lyndhurst goodbye. After all, he had been very kind—kinder than she liked to remember—especially during the last few days; what would she and Mary have done without him—he had been so quiet, so helpful, yet so unobtrusive?

'Charlotte cannot travel alone,' she said the next instant.

'Then Dr. Arnaud must fetch her,' replied Grey, with a quizzical smile; for both he and Bertie were immensely amused at this Anglo-Belgique alliance. 'What is the good of a fiancé If he is not at the disposal of his fair lady. Poor Charlotte! the "funeral baked meats do coldly furnish forth the marriage tables." Poor little soul, she is a perfect Niobe!'

'You see she has lived here so long, and was really attached to Mrs. Reid. In spite of her affectations, Charlotte has plenty of heart.'

'Yes, and by and by it will be given to Dr. Arnaud and those droll brown-faced little boys of his. Did you ever behold such a scene?' continued Grey, with a smile at the remembrance—'"My sons, embrace this lady who has promised to be your mother; salute her, Jean Jacques, and thou, Ton-ton chéri." I think Ton-ton chéri hung back and put his thumb in his mouth.'

'It was droll, but I thought it rather touching at the same time,' returned Dollie. 'Charlotte looked very pretty and motherly, and her red eyes did not matter. Dr. Arnaud is not so bad, after all.'

'No; he is clever and fair-dealing. And after all, there is no accounting for tastes. So you see England will be our next meeting-place,' continued Grey with pardonable egotism. 'I wonder how soon I may venture to call at Trevilian Terrace, Abercrombie Road.'

Dollie changed colour a little at that. 'My mother will be very pleased to see you, and Mr. Bertie too,' she returned very primly, and pursing up her lips. Her manner was not quite encouraging; but then she knew her mother's horror of young men. 'What will she say? Oh, how I wish he would keep away, at least for a month or two,' she thought, and then blushed at her own ingratitude.

But Mr. Lyndhurst, like a wise man, took no notice of her obvious confusion.

'I shall come very soon,' he announced decidedly. 'I am longing to make your mother's acquaintance. I have few friends, and not many houses are open to me. Now I must wish you good-bye,' he went on, and Dollie thought she heard a sigh. 'This has been a sad ending to a pleasant visit, but I think it has made us all know each other better; it is worth a whole season of ballroom

intimacy,' continued Grey, with a forced smile, for he
hated to part with the girl. 'Ah well! good-bye; I shall
not see you to-morrow;' and then he hesitated and said,
'God bless you!' but in such a low tone that she hardly
caught it, and looked at her a little strangely, she thought,
as he left the room.

This conversation had taken place five days ago, and
since then she and Mary and Bertie had been alone.

What quiet days they had seemed! how silent and
deserted the old chateau with its closed rooms! Justine
had joined the other servants; the great red-baized door
shut in Kâtchen's scolding voice and the voluble Flemish
talk of the others. Now and then Dollie would glide through
them to feed and pet her favourite pigeons, but generally
the three sat quietly together in the morning-room, working
or reading or talking low in the twilight. At night the
girls would go up together hand in hand, their black dresses
flowing behind them; Bertie would watch them from the
hall; at the top of the staircase they would turn round and
wish him a subdued good-night, as he stood there under
the swinging oil-lamp.

Dollie used to feel dull and *de trop* at times. Somehow
Mary and Bertie always had so much to say to each other;
now and then she fell out of the conversation, and could
not regain her place; the others did not seem to notice
her silence much. Mary would certainly appeal to her at
times, but Bertie would go on eagerly with his subject. It
was all right of course, but it made Dollie a trifle sad; she
began, unconsciously to herself, to miss a certain kind
face; if somebody were there, she thought, she would
never sit silent and neglected. Little attentions that she
had hardly noticed were recalled now to mind. 'A friend
was a nice thing, after all,' she said to herself, with a spice
of discontent in her thoughts.

But if Dollie found it dull, they were halcyon days to
Mary and Bertie. Never before had they been so
much together, or had enjoyed such unrestrained intercourse.

To Mary it was simply delicious—a new experience in

her life—to lean back in her easy-chair, and do nothing
but rest and be waited on by Dollie and Bertie. As Dr.
Arnaud prophesied, nature effected its own cure. Mary
slept as placidly as a new-born baby the first two or three
days, and then her tired eyes grew bright again, and her
languid frame vigorous and alert. 'Now we have our
chère Mademoiselle Marie back again,' exclaimed the little
doctor, rubbing his hands with satisfaction; and to Bertie
he expressed afterwards his surprise and admiration at
'this physique superbe, this constitution so robust, this
mind so admirably balanced and self-composed — this
specimen, in short, of a perfect Englishwoman.'

One evening they were sitting together as usual; the
girls in their low chairs with their feet on the rug; Bertie
opposite, with the book from which he had been reading aloud lying open on his knee; the story was an
interesting one, but, much to Dollie's regret, they had
strayed off into talk as usual. Bertie had been volunteering
some information about his life at Stoneyhurst, about
which he expressed himself in a somewhat lugubrious
fashion, which Mary was striving hard to combat.

'The one fault seems to me,' she said decidedly, 'that
it is too comfortable and luxurious a life; you do as you
like from morning to night; as far as work goes, you are
as fine a gentleman as Sir Charles himself.'

'Ralph and I work three hours every day—from breakfast to luncheon,' replied Bertie half sulkily. 'I do not call
a tutor's life particularly easy; it is grind, grind, with no
special results. It is not that Ralph is without brains, but
he is indolent and desultory.'

'But when the morning work is over, you are free for
the rest of the day,' persisted Mary; 'you and Ralph seem
to have a fine time of it—you fish and shoot and ride,
and in the evening enjoy the best society; while poor
Grey is shut up in his den with only law books for
companions.'

'I do not call that a fair comparison,' argued Bertie; 'I
only wish Grey and I could change places; his work is
harder, of course, but then there is some chance of getting

on. Here I am, very comfortable, I grant you, but after all I am only a tutor with eighty pounds a year.'

'Yes, but you will not always be a tutor,' returned Mary hastily, for there was a meaning inflection in Bertie's voice. 'Sir Charles is rich, and has great influence, and Ralph is his only child. Do you recollect how grateful he was when Ralph had scarlet fever and you helped to nurse him? Many tutors would have been afraid of infection and have only thought of themselves.'

'Oh, nonsense!' was the answer, for Bertie hated to be reminded of his good deeds. He had been very much commended and patted on the back for his behaviour at the time, and had won both Sir Charles's and his wife's hearts by his devotion to the invalid. 'What is the good of bringing that up again and making such a fuss over it? It was all in the day's work; one need not make a merit of doing one's duty.'

But though Bertie spoke crossly enough, he was secretly pleased that Mary should recall it. He remembered how anxious she and Maurice had been, and how even Mrs. St. John had written to him and enclosed a list of directions for disinfectants.

'Is Stoneyhurst a pretty place?' interrupted Dollie, who was tired of keeping silence. How she wished they would go on with the book! But no; Bertie liked better to watch Mary. In his eyes she had never looked nicer than she did this evening. Her new black dress suited her; her slight paleness only made her look interesting; and the softness of her gray eyes was very winning. What was there about her face that he loved so? She had not half Dollie's attractions, and yet in his mind there was no comparison.

He roused himself rather reluctantly to answer Dollie's question.

'Is it a pretty place? Well, I suppose so. There are plenty of fir-woods, and the walks are nice. The Hall is not a bad sort of place: there is a big park, and the garden is all laid out in terraces. Lady Emily is as proud as a peacock about her garden! I wonder what Charlotte would say to see her in her old hat and shawl pottering among her roses. Charlotte would not think much of her toilette.'

It must be confessed that Bertie was not a good hand at description. Dollie tried in vain to get some idea of Stoneyhurst. 'The big park and the terraces and the fir-woods'—she could not frame it somehow in her own mind.

'But the house itself?' she persisted. 'You are so tiresome, Mr. Bertie; you never will give one a proper notion of a place.'

'Oh! the house is like most other houses,' he returned indifferently; 'a great red-brick place, with queer windows, and a lodge, and a rhododendron shrubbery. Why do you want to know?' he went on provokingly; 'the drawing-room is as big as a barrack, and has three fireplaces, and the chairs are good for a nap.'

'We will not ask him any more questions, Dollie,' returned Mary, laughing; 'he is in one of his bad moods, when there is no getting anything out of him. I will tell you all about it. There is a picture-gallery upstairs, and a certain Lady Cecilia Howard in a yellow satin and a pearl neck-lace, who walks about, in red-heeled shoes, when all good people are asleep; and an old gentleman in a periwig and plum-coloured velvet coat, who is said to carry his head under his arm on Hallowe'en; and all sorts of interesting curiosities: and there is the blue room, where Sir Charles sits; and the yellow drawing-room; and the damask room, which is Lady Emily's; and the octagon room, where a certain sulky young gentleman, who shall be nameless, spends his hard-working life; and—and——'

'Why, you seem to know it all as though you lived there!' exclaimed Dollie, opening her eyes, at which Mary blushed; but Bertie broke in, in a little whirl of affected anger—

'Oh yes, you describe it very well, and you are right to laugh at me; but I should like to know who would work harder than I if I could only get a chance? I cannot go on teaching Ralph for ever; and yet what is a fellow to do? A navvy can turn his thews and sinews to account;

but just look at me. I am stronger than most fellows; I can ride, shoot, and pull an oar with any man, and yet because I've crammed a little Greek and Latin, I must grind at teaching or starve. Take orders, as Grey says. No, thank you; no curate's pittance for me. A man must have a vocation for that sort of thing, you know.'

'Yes, indeed,' returned Mary earnestly; 'I am glad you think in that way, Bertie. I could not imagine you a clergyman.'

'I am not good enough, am I?' he returned, with a sort of laugh; 'rather a poor sort compared with Maurice. Why, he is the grandest fellow I have ever known,' he continued, with a burst of enthusiasm that brought the tears to Mary's eyes; but she answered him rather sadly—

'I sometimes think that he is too good to live. No, not that exactly, for of course there are other men as good as he; but I fear sometimes that he will wear himself out. Do you know, Janet writes such poor accounts of him. If I were not going home I should be anxious. By the bye, I wonder we have not heard from Charlotte. She will surely return to-morrow.'

'Justine had a letter, I believe,' put in Dollie; 'she was very mysterious over it this morning; she and Romany have been busy upstairs all day; but I cannot get anything out of them.'

'Ah well, I daresay we shall hear to-morrow,' returned Mary complacently. She was in no hurry for Charlotte's return.

With Charlotte would come bustle, movement, the break-up of all this pleasant time; then would be the return, the parting with Bertie, the long blank of months during which she would not see him or hear from him. If they could only write to each other sometimes; but what would Janet say if he were to propose such a thing? And Mary sighed as she thought of the home criticism that would attack such an unconventional proceeding on her or Bertie's part. That was the worst of these sort of understandings; they had no rights or privileges to counterbalance their drawbacks.

Mary sighed, and Bertie echoed the sigh. Too well he understood it. He could read her heart as clearly as his own. He knew they must part soon; that in all honour he must leave her without one word or pledge of affection.

What would Maurice say if he were to induce her to engage herself to him, when the engagement might extend over an indefinite number of years? And yet he thought that he could answer for her as well as himself that they would be far happier if they could only pledge their love to each other.

What if, after all, he were to speak to her and ask her to decide for them both? He knew already what she would say. She would bind herself to him, and take up her life and her work cheerfully, and put faith in herself and him. She would not be impatient or fret, as other women would. She would wait for him until her brown hair got gray streaks in it, and the freshness of her youth would be gone, and he would never hear a word of complaint or regret. If he dare only venture! if Maurice were not to look sternly at him and call him dishonourable!

'I think I must do it, that I must say one word to her. It will half break my heart to leave her this time,' thought poor Bertie, growing suddenly weak at the sound of Mary's sigh. After all, the matter was for them to decide; no brother, not even Maurice, had a right to stand between them if they loved each other!

'I will get her alone to-morrow, and have it all out with her before Charlotte comes,' he decided, not knowing, poor fellow! that the golden opportunity had already gone. Had he spoken, who knows, things might have been different between him and Mary.

But even as the gleam of the sudden resolution flashed into his eyes, Dollie sat erect in her chair and put herself in a listening attitude.

'There, did you hear it? I was sure there were wheels in the courtyard. Listen—ah, that is Charlotte's knock,' as there was a thundering peal at the hall door. 'That accounts for Justine's mystery; she knew all about it this

morning.   It is one of Charlotte's surprises, bless her fussy
little heart!'

Was it Charlotte?   Mary and Bertie exchanged glances,
and as though by a sudden impulse moved closer together.

'Oh, Mary, is our pleasant time all over?' cried Bertie,
in a tone of regret, and he took her hand ; somehow the
action seemed natural.   Mary did not draw hers away.
There they stood together, poor young creatures! hand in
hand, with their Nemesis waiting for them outside, like the
avenging angel, to drive them out of paradise.

Dollie did not notice them ; she was putting back the
thick tapestry curtain that hung before the door.   Any
change was welcome to her, even Charlotte's arrival.   She
opened the door and went out into the dark entry, and
ran—dear little soul—straight into her mother's arms!

CHAPTER XX

'BUT where is Aunt Mary? why does she not come out to welcome us?' exclaimed a brisk, decided voice, breaking somewhere out of the darkness. Mary gave a great start, and loosened Bertie's hold of her hand as though she had been stung. Again they exchanged glances — this time almost of dismay. The voice was Janet's.

'What is in the wind now? Why has she come to spoil everything?' groaned Bertie. Poor fellow! this sudden arrival of his enemy filled him with all manner of dire forebodings. Were the Fates against him? 'Mary, what does it mean?' he cried, trying to detain her.

'Hush, how can we know?' but Mary had turned a little pale too. 'Here I am, Janet,' she said, striving to speak naturally, and advancing to the tall cloaked figure that stood peering impatiently into the dim corners.

Bertie followed her sulkily enough. What a scene the hall presented at that moment! There was Charlotte chattering volubly to Romany and the driver of the fiacre; Justine and Ursula were bringing in wraps and packages; on the oak bench in the farthest corner were Dollie and her mother, closely locked in each other's arms; and there was Mary taking off Janet's cloak, and trying to look pleased at this sudden invasion.

Janet laid aside her wrappings willingly enough. What a handsome creature she looked, as she stood smoothing her glossy hair with both hands under the dim light!

'Now, I am ready,' she said, taking Mary's arm, but

scarcely noticing Bertie. She swept past him on her way to the morning-room, with her head erect, and a strange sort of eagerness on her pale face; the folds of her long dress quite enveloped and extinguished Mary.

'Dear Janet, this is such a surprise,' said Mary mildly, as her sister-in-law again stooped over her and kissed her cheek. Such demonstration was rare with Janet, save with her husband. She was seldom prodigal of caresses; now her fingers stroked her face in quite a motherly fashion.

'Poor Aunt Mary! how pale and thin you look! what would Maurice say if he saw you now? We must take care of you, and give you plenty of attention and petting to make you forget all this dreadful time.'

'Thank you, Janet,' returned Mary gratefully, 'but I have had a nice time to rest, and am feeling myself again —ready for any amount of work you or Maurice like to give me. Now you must tell me what has brought you all this distance, and what could have induced you to leave Maurice and the children?'

'We wanted to talk to you, Mary, and Maurice was not well enough to come;' and now a very perceptible shade of embarrassment crossed her face. Mary noticed it.

'Is not Maurice well?' she asked anxiously; and again the cloud rested on Janet's brow.

'Is he ever well?' she demanded in the low, vehement tone that Mary had somehow learned to dread; for it always betokened a stormy argument or mood of discontent. 'He is worse than usual; his cough will not let him rest at night, and yet he will not consent to see a doctor. I got frightened last week—he looked so ill and exhausted —and spoke privately to Dr. Raven. I felt I could not any longer bear the anxiety.'

'Well?' interrogated Mary, as Janet paused and turned her dark eyes moodily to the fire, 'you were perfectly right; and what did Dr. Raven say?'

'Oh, it was the same old story,' and her bosom heaved with repressed feeling; 'he is killing himself, that is all. He will leave me a widow, and his five children fatherless.'

'Now, Janet, you know this is not right,' returned Mary, taking her hand, for she knew how much to allow for exaggeration. 'I am sure Dr. Raven never said that.'

'No, of course not, he only left me to infer it. He said Maurice was killing himself by inches—he used that very expression, Mary; he said there was no cause for present anxiety, as far as he could judge, for he had not examined him; but he had seen a great deal of him lately, and had made up his mind that he was the wrong man in the wrong place.'

'You mean that the air does not suit him?'

'The want of air I mean, and the work. There has been a terrible amount of sickness lately—low fevers, and two or three very serious cases. Maurice has hardly given himself time to take his meals, and when he comes home at night he is too exhausted to sleep; and then there is his cough.'

'Oh dear!' sighed Mary; 'how badly you have wanted me. If I had been there Maurice need not have worked so hard.'

'You would have done your best, I know that; but you could not have lightened his burden much; in such a parish as ours, so much responsibility rests on the curate. And that is not all—both Lettice and Rosie have been ill.'

'Ill! you told me in your last letter that they were poorly—but ill?' Poor Aunt Mary! were anxieties never to cease? Lettice too, who was Aunt Mary's darling!

'Yes, it was the same sort of low fever that was going about—a feverish cold, Dr. Raven called it—but I know it was more than that. Lettice kept her bed five days, and she looks very poorly still. Of course, as Dr. Raven says, Lime Street is not exactly the place for delicate children.'

'But how could you think of leaving them if Lettice be not quite strong?' asked Mary in some astonishment. Janet was too devoted a wife and mother to lightly desert her post.

'Ah! thereby hangs a tale,' returned Mrs. St. John with

14

a little forced laugh. 'I have a long story to tell, and I must make sure that we shall not be interrupted. Where is my room? we might go 'there.'

'But you are in need of some refreshment. Where are the others? I have hardly spoken to Mrs. Maynard; and what has become of Charlotte?'

'Of course they are all in their own rooms,' returned Janet decidedly. 'Mrs. Maynard will have no eyes for any one but her daughter for the next hour; we were just in time for table d'hôte at Ligne, and that is only an hour and a half ago. I want nothing but you, Aunt Mary,' again linking her arm in Mary's.

'Then we will ring for Justine and find out which room has been prepared for you,' was the cheerful rejoinder. Mary was making the best of it, but what had become of Bertie? She found Janet tolerably correct in her surmise. Charlotte was bustling about in the upper regions, with two maids to wait on her; and Dollie was closely shut up with her mother.

'Madame has had tea served for her; would madame require the same?' asked Justine, looking with awe and admiration at madame's regal beauty. No, Janet did not desire tea; she moved forward eagerly, still holding Mary affectionately by the arm. Once Mary looked back; yes, surely out of that dim corner some figure was slowly moving; yes, there he was rumpling his hair and looking after them wistfully, as they moved away from him farther and farther, until he could see them no more. A gleam of firelight, a closing door, and he was left out in the darkness.

Meanwhile in a quaint little octagon room at the end of the corridor called la chambre verte Dollie was making tea for her mother.

Mrs. Maynard sat in the great armchair drawn up close to the fire; her bonnet was laid aside; the firelight gleamed on her reddish-brown hair and worn delicate features; her eyes brightened, and then grew dim with feeling, as they rested on Dollie's happy face.

'My darling, how thankful I am to see you again!' she exclaimed.

'Not more than I am to see you, my dear little mother,' returned Dollie, flying to her for the sixth time, and covering her with kisses. 'Where is your cap, motherling? You don't look yourself without it. Your hair is prettier than mine, but you look too young—oh, far too young to be my mother. I shall get it out, if it be at the very bottom of that great yellow portmanteau; you must look just as you do at home; and then I will sit at your feet and admire you;' and Dollie acted up to her words.

'My darling, it is for me to admire you;' and indeed the widow could hardly take her eyes off her treasure; would not any mother be proud of such a daughter, she thought, as she watched her girl's graceful movements about the room. Dollie's figure was very pretty, and the little head was so heavily weighted with its fair plaits, and her face was so bright and animated, that one forgot the high cheek bones. 'But my Dollie looks different somehow,' she continued; 'a little older and more womanly.'

'Nonsense, mother,' and then Dollie blushed suddenly under that affectionate scrutiny, for was there not a secret, a tiresome little secret, to be told some time? Mrs. Maynard saw the blush, and a pang crossed her; what new experience had befallen her girl in these five long weeks of absence? and then she put the thought away from her in true coward fashion, and made believe it was her fancy, and that the fire had suddenly scorched Dollie's fair cheek, and turned her attention resolutely to another subject that she had at heart, and about which she must talk to her girl.

'Well, Dollie, you never told me that you were surprised to see me here; I have travelled all these miles, just to see my little daughter and fetch her home.'

'Mother, how good of you! but I should have come home safely all the same if you had sent for me; you got my letter, I suppose.'

'Yes, they forwarded it to Crome. Were you not astonished that I summoned up courage to go to the funeral? Mr. and Mrs. St. John persuaded me to go. Do you know, I was grieved to see how ill Mr. St. John is looking.'

'He works too hard, I suppose,' returned Dollie, and then she continued eagerly : 'I am glad you went, mother ; it would have pleased poor Mrs. Reid if she could have known it. Were you not sorry when you heard what had happened—that you had not accepted her invitation, I mean?'

'Yes, Dollie, it will be a matter of lasting regret to me,' replied her mother gravely. 'Poor Aunt Isabel ! how little I knew her and her sorrows ! Mr. Lyndhurst and Charlotte told me all about her illness, and poor Walter's—my Dollie did a piece of angel's work there.'

'Mr. Lyndhurst ! ' exclaimed the girl involuntarily, but this time her head was bent down, and her mother did not see the blush.

'Yes, he was kind enough to give me a good many particulars ; he seems a nice young man,' continued Mrs. Maynard innocently, 'pleasant and gentlemanly, somewhat above the average of young men. I took rather a fancy to him.'

'I am glad of that,' returned Dollie rather incoherently ; 'at least, I mean he is all that ; but Crome Park—how did you like that, mother ? '

'Oh, it is a fine old place, Dollie, a grand old house. Mary is a fortunate girl.'

'What do you mean ? ' exclaimed Dollie, almost starting to her feet ; for the moment she had forgotten all about Mrs. Reid's property.

'I mean,' returned Mrs. Maynard, smiling, 'that your friend will be no mean heiress. Mrs. Reid has left her Crome Park, and the greater portion of her money.'

'Crome Park to Mary ! ' in spite of Charlotte's hints she could scarcely believe her ears.

'Yes, the will was a very strange one ; hardly a satisfactory one. Evidently my poor aunt was a woman of strong prejudices ; she had likes and dislikes. There is a handsome allowance for Charlotte, the same she had promised her during her lifetime ; and another large allowance to be paid monthly to her poor son, but this will revert to Mary.

'To Mr. St. John she has only left one hundred a year, and the same to her husband's connections, Grey and Cuthbert Lyndhurst, and also to you; to myself she has been more generous, for there is an annuity of three hundred a year settled on me for my life; you see I was her own niece, Dollie.'

'Yes, mother; but how kind, how thoughtful! she knew you were poor, and had to do without comforts to which you had been accustomed. Why, mother, four hundred a year between us, and the pension besides! why, we shall be quite rich! We can leave that horrid Abercrombie Road; we can travel, and do all manner of nice things;' and Dollie clapped her hands as though all the riches of Crœsus had come to her; it never occurred to her for a moment to envy Mary.

'It has relieved me from a great anxiety; but, Dollie, if I die, you will be poor again; the pension and annuity will end too.'

'As though I cared what would happen to me then!' returned Dollie scornfully, as she threw her arms round her mother's fragile figure. 'If I were poor I could work, but I suppose a person could live on a hundred a year.'

'Yes, yes, and of course a hundred things may happen before that,' observed Mrs. Maynard, feeling that the time would soon come when she must part with her child. 'But, Dollie, my dear, there is one part of the will I do not understand, and which made Mr. Lyndhurst look grave—Crome Park is left to Miss St. John, but only on one queer condition, that she does not marry Cuthbert Lyndhurst.'

'Mother!' burst from Dollie's indignant lips; and then a frightened look came over her face.

'Can you explain it, my dear? is there anything between her and this young man? What can my aunt mean? She evidently dislikes him, and yet she has left him an equal portion with his brother; what can be her motive in acting so strangely?'

'Oh, I do not know; she has always been hard upon him, always. I think Mrs. St. John talked to her when she was staying here last year; you know how severe she can be,

mother; they say that he is indolent, desultory, irresponsible, and all that sort of thing.　Mrs. St. John has always
been terribly afraid of some entanglement between him and
Mary.'

'But, my dear, if this were true—you are so young to
judge in such cases.　Miss St. John seems a very superior
person; they may be right in saying that he is not good
enough for her.'

'But who would be good enough for her?' returned
Dollie with a burst of feeling.　'Mother, you do not know
how I have grown to love her; she is so different from other
people! she is so thoughtful, so unselfish, so truly humble-
minded!'

'Just so, and her sister may therefore be correct in
thinking that Mr. Cuthbert Lyndhurst is far from being her
equal.'

'Has she been talking to you too?' cried Dollie in despair.　'She is so clever, she can twist a thing round and
make you see it from her point of view; she is not fair to
him; and poor Mrs. Reid was hard upon him too.　He is
very nice; why,' continued Dollie, taking up the cudgels
most warmly for her poor Adonis, 'he is one of the nicest
young men I know' (she had never seen above three in her
life); 'he has so much in him when you come to know
him, and he is so kind and bright and pleasant, and so full
of fun!'

Mrs. Maynard regarded her daughter with a careful
brow.

'This is not a very long list of moral qualities, Dollie;
if it were his brother now—no one could object to him.
And you really think Miss St. John cares for the poor
fellow?'

'I am sure they care very much for each other; when
Mary is in the room Mr. Bertie seems to have eyes for no
other person.　Oh, mother, I am certain that they want to
be engaged, only he is so poor.　How cruel, how desperately cruel Mrs. Reid has been!'

'Nay, my dear, you must not be so hard on my poor
aunt.　Consider the circumstances—she was a conscientious,

almost a morbidly conscientious woman; the property is large; as she says in her will, she was anxious to find an heir who would be a faithful steward of her bounty, one who would carry out her wishes and care for good works; if Miss St. John married, she would be in subjection to her husband; Mrs. Reid was therefore only acting up to her sense of duty in stipulating that this husband was not to be Cuthbert Lyndhurst.'

'But why should she not have made Mr. St. John her heir?'

'Their church views differed. I do not think she cared for him much, and she had taken such a dislike to his wife. Charlotte tells me Mary won her heart from the first—" I have never known a sounder, sweeter nature," she said to her before the first week was over.'

Dollie leant her cheek on her hand and sighed. Here was a complication; presently she looked up and said with a little spirit—

'It is all no use; she will not take the money; she will never give him up.'

'But, my dear!'

'It will just bring things to a crisis, that is all. They are not so poor now; at least Mr. Bertie has a hundred a year left to him; they will be engaged and wait for him to get on a little better; and Crome Park will have no mistress. By the bye, mother,' continued Dollie, opening her eyes very wide, 'you have not told me what the will says in case Mary declines the property.'

Mrs. Maynard shook her head. 'No one knows about that; there is a sealed codicil that is not to be touched; no one but the lawyer knows what provision she has made for such an emergency, and his lips are silenced; if we could only peep into that codicil, Dollie! Mrs. St. John is certain that, in the event of Mary's refusal to inherit, the property would be left to the many charitable institutions in which Mrs. Reid was interested. Mr. St. John thinks the same; but no one can be sure.' And again Dollie bent her head upon her hands to think.

By and by her mother touched her softly.

' Well, little one, what now ? ' for the girl was in a brown
study, and her eyes had a fixed far-off look ; she woke up
slowly at the sound of her mother's voice.

' I am trying to think it all out,' she said at last very
slowly; ' I am trying to put myself in Mary's place, and to
feel how she feels.   I know what Mrs. St. John will say to
her ; she will persuade her into things ; she will put the
matter so cleverly that she will drive her into a corner ;
she will appeal to her feeling, to her unselfishness ; she will
ask her to sacrifice herself for the sake of her brother and
his children ; and she will say it over and over, and there
will be no silencing her ; this is why she has come, that
she may have her to herself ; ' and when she had said this
she rose very stiffly and slowly to her feet.

' Where are you going, my dear ? ' for there was a sudden
look of determination on her face.

' I am going to Mary, mother,' was Dollie's prompt rejoinder ; ' and I shall tell her that all the sisters or brothers
in the world must not make her give up Mr. Bertie.'

CHAPTER XXI

'BUT, Mary——'

'Janet, will you be merciful and leave me? No one shall influence me in this. Do I not tell you that this is a matter of life and death to me? why will you not believe me?' and in Mary's eyes there was a sad, almost a hunted look, and her lips were tightly pressed together as though she were in severe bodily suffering.

'Yes, I will go directly, but you must hear me first. What is there in this young man that you must sacrifice us all to him?'

'I love him,' was the answer.

'For shame, Mary! you make me blush for you. Is this our sister Mary who is so lost to all feelings of propriety? How can you be so unfeminine as to avow partiality for a young man who, by your own account, has never said one word to you?' and Janet's face was dark with passion, and her eyes flashed angrily. For a whole hour had she been arguing—pleading even with tears—and yet there was no result. 'Mary, you are beside yourself; you know this is wrong.'

'I love him and he loves me,' returned Mary in the same calm, inflexible tones. 'Words! oh yes, one would have them too, but when heart speaks to heart—when one knows and understands — you cannot put things wrong between us, Janet. I tell you we understand each other.'

'But there is no engagement, no pledge, no promise—not one word to bind you to him,' persisted Janet; she felt that she must abandon her ground and take up another point in her argument. 'Even if you love him, there is nothing to prevent your changing your mind.'

'Nothing on earth can change it.'

'He cannot reproach you,' went on Mrs. St. John, affecting not to hear her; 'it will not be jilting or casting him off; if you were engaged to him, could I ask you to do anything so dishonourable? I am a wife myself—I gave up everything I valued in life to marry Maurice.'

'And why may I not do the same, Janet? why should you try to interfere with my life? You have had yours; is there a love on earth like Maurice's? Why are you not satisfied with him and your own happiness, and leave me and Bertie alone?'

'Because I cannot see you committing suicide, and not try to save you. He is not worthy of you; he is——'

'Oh, for Heaven's sake spare me all that again!' returned Mary almost with a gesture of despair. 'How can I help your opinion of him? You are prejudiced, and have set Mrs. Reid against him; cruel, cruel—ah, you did me an evil turn there, Janet.'

'I meant it for the best,' returned Mrs. St. John, with an angry flush, for the words stung her. Had she been cruel to Mary? nay, she had not intended that. 'How could I know what would happen? how could I foresee such things?'

'Still you were unjust,' was Mary's answer; 'you have always been harsh in your estimate of him, and yet he has never done you harm. Janet, when you talk against him —when you speak in the way you are doing now—you anger me so that I am ready to vow to you what I have already vowed to myself, that I will never marry any one but Bertie.'

There was an instant's silence, and then Mary repeated her words, this time more firmly—'No, I will never marry any one but him.'

'Well, and what then?' and Janet threw up her head, and a quick gleam passed over her face.

'I do not understand you,' replied Mary, looking at her.

'What if you do not marry any other man? am I forcing you to take a husband? Good heavens, Mary, that you should think such things of me! I, who am Maurice's wife! Should I be so false—so utterly false to my creed—as to tell you to marry any one whom you did not love? No, no, better live single all your life—better a thousand times live and die an old maid than that.'

'Then for once we agree, Janet.'

'Oh, Mary, do not look at me like that; do not be cold, so unlike yourself. I will not talk any more against Bertie; you shall think of him as you will, and I will not contradict you; but why need you marry him? why need you marry any one? can you not make yourself happy with us?'

An inexplicable look passed over Mary's sad face, but she did not answer; only in the depths of her heart she cried, 'Oh, my darling! my darling! happy without you? —never, never.'

'How often women make up their minds to live single!' continued Janet; 'sometimes they become sisters of mercy; they devote themselves to their work; they are not unhappy. Why do I demand such a sacrifice you ask me?—it is because I cannot stand by and see you throwing yourself away.'

'Again!' exclaimed Mary wearily.

'Yes, again and again, until I can make you see with my eyes. Am I thinking of myself? Do I covet these riches for my own sake? You know I am not so base; I would starve rather than interfere with your happiness; but, Mary, when I think of Maurice, I could find it in my heart to kneel to you.'

'Janet, Janet!' and Mary covered her face with her hands; she wanted to shut out that beautiful pleading face from her view, but the eloquent voice was not to be silenced.

'What! you turn away—you will not hear me!' exclaimed Janet in such a tone of agony that Mary could hardly bear it. 'You will refuse Crome, and throw yourself away upon this worthless lad! Mary, how can you be so

selfish, so hard-hearted?   Do you know what will happen?
Maurice will stay where he is; he will be too poor to move.
What is a hundred a year more when there are five mouths
to feed, and all our little capital is eaten up?   This year we
are in debt—ah! you did not know that.   Never mind,
we shall pinch and set ourselves straight; we shall have
enough; there will be no fear of starving.   But he will
not move; every month he will grow weaker—more unfit
for his work; then will come decline; by and by they will
give us no hope—it will be too late for change, for rest,
then—Oh, Mary, Mary!' and Janet suddenly threw herself
upon the ground and caught hold of her dress, 'for my
husband's, for Maurice's sake, do not refuse Crome.'

'Janet, you are breaking my heart.'

'No, no, it is mine that is to be broken—mine and my
children's.   What will Lettice do without her father?   How
am I to live when the treasure of my heart is taken from
me?   What is your love compared with mine, Mary, who
have known his every thought for fourteen years — my
sainted, noble husband!'

'Janet, will you rise?   I cannot speak to you like this.
Hush! there is some one at the door; no one must see
you in this state;' and as Dollie's tap was impatiently
repeated, she half raised half pushed her to her feet.   'Go
into that room,' pointing to the inner door that connected
hers and Dollie's,—for Janet had insisted on accompanying
Mary to her own room,—and Janet, exhausted with her
own passion, and sobbing hysterically, made haste to hide
herself.

When Dollie advanced into the room, she looked round
her suspiciously; she was not in time to catch sight of the
retreating skirts of her enemy, but her quick instinct detected a sort of disturbance in the atmosphere.

'Where is she?' she asked in a quick eager whisper, and
would have peeped through the curtained archway that
divided the rooms, but Mary stopped her.

'Come here, dear, I want to speak to you,' she said;
and as Dollie reluctantly obeyed her she put her two hands
upon her shoulders, and looked at her for a moment with-

out speaking, as though she were trying to read her thoughts.

She was somewhat the taller of the two; and as she stood thus, the younger girl looking up into her face, saw that there was a drawn, pallid look about her mouth, and that her eyes were full of a great sadness; but her voice was quite calm.

'Dear Dollie, you have heard it all, and you are come to talk to me; is it not so?' and as Dollie nodded vehemently she went on in the same passive tones.

'You want to tell me not to give him up—to be true to my own heart and to him. Ah, yes! I can read your thoughts. Now, Dollie, listen to me a moment. I am sure you love me a little?'

'I love you dearly, Aunt Mary;' and Dollie looked ready to cry.

'Then do not speak to me to-night—no—not one word —I could not bear it,' as Dollie seemed inclined to interrupt her.

'Indeed, you do not know all that I have been through. I have had a great shock; and then Janet would talk. I asked her to go away again and again, but there was no stopping her. It is quiet I want, Dollie—quiet for this one night.'

'And you shall have it, my darling!' cried the warm-hearted girl, suddenly putting her arms round' Mary's neck, and stroking her face like a child's. 'Don't fret about it, Mary; they shall not make you unhappy; no one shall make you give him up for all the stupid parks in existence. There, there! I won't say another word; you shall not be teased by me;' and Dollie clapped her hands over her own ears and ran out of the room, that Mary might not be troubled to answer.

In another moment she would have been flying down the corridor, but some one who was lurking outside the door caught her in boyish fashion by the sleeve, and stopped her.

'Oh, do wait a moment,' implored Bertie's voice. 'I have been waiting here ever so long; I saw you go in just

now, and a moment ago Mrs. St. John brushed quite close
to me.'

'Mrs. St. John!'

'Yes; she did not see me; she was crying, I think; and
she went in there,' pointing to a door nearly opposite them.
'There is something in the wind; I said so to Mary.
Dear Miss Maynard, will you do me a favour? will you
take a message to Mary? ask her to come out and speak to
me a moment.'

'I dare not, Mr. Bertie; please do not ask me.'

'But why not? it is not so very late,' he pleaded; 'only
just ten.   They have locked up the morning-room, but
there is still a fire in the hall; the lamp is out, but there
will be light enough to see each other's faces.   Tell her to
come to me a moment, for I will not sleep until I have
found out what all this means.'

'I dare not,' persisted Dollie, shrinking from him.
'She looks so ill, and I am sure her head aches badly;
and she has begged me to leave her in quiet.'

'Then I will knock at the door myself,' returned Bertie
recklessly; and he would certainly have acted on his words,
but it opened suddenly, and Mary's pale face appeared.

'Good-night, Bertie,' she said.

'Will you come, Mary?' he asked eagerly.

'No, I heard what you said to Dollie; I am sorry, but
I cannot come.   Will you not say good-night to me?' and
she held out to him a cold hand, and looked quietly and
sadly in his face.

'What does she mean? why does she look so unlike
herself?' exclaimed the poor fellow, when the door was
again shut, and they heard the key turning in the lock.
'She has never refused to speak to me before.   You are
not going to leave me too, Miss Maynard?' he continued
reproachfully, as Dollie faltered out 'Good-night.'

'No, you shall not go; I will not be treated in this
fashion!' and before Dollie could quite comprehend what
he was about, he had tucked her arm unceremoniously
under his and was leading her down the staircase.

'Mr. Bertie, I must go back to my mother,' cried Dollie,

really frightened at this persistence; but she was no match for his determined will.

'You shall go back to her in five minutes,' he returned, taking up the poker and making the pine knots blaze till every corner of the great hall was brilliant with firelight.

'Why are you afraid of me to-night? you were kinder to me that evening when you were Hebe, and brought me all manner of good things;' and Bertie's eyes looked persuasive and affectionate. Dollie glanced up the dark staircase, and then she hesitated; perhaps, after all, she could keep her mother waiting for five minutes.

'Do not speak so loudly; you do not know that she may not be listening.'

'Who? Mrs. St. John?'

Dollie nodded.

'Why has she come?' he asked eagerly. 'Directly I heard her voice I knew something was wrong; she has not travelled all these miles for nothing. I have never heard of her leaving her husband and children before.'

'Mr. St. John is not well.'

'That is all the more reason for her to stay with him.'

'Yes! but she wanted to talk to Mary, and to bring her the news. What! have they not told you, Mr. Bertie?' and Dollie looked at him half frightened, half puzzled. How was she to avoid answering his questions?

'You forget that every one has been avoiding me all the evening,' he returned angrily. 'Look here, Miss Maynard, you need not be afraid to tell me; of course I know that something has happened—something about the money and Mary.' He pronounced the last word hesitatingly, and with a peculiar softness of intonation; and then a thought struck him, and he said very quickly, 'I see it all—she is Mrs. Reid's heir!' and again Dollie nodded. How cleverly he had guessed it! oh, if she could only slip away now!

'I am not surprised,' he continued after a moment; but Dollie thought he looked rather pale, as though the news was unwelcome. 'One could see what a fancy she had taken to her, and how she trusted her. Well, she might have told me herself, and allowed me to congratulate her.'

'Perhaps she has no wish to be congratulated,' returned Dollie.

'Why not?' he asked, turning sharply round on her. 'Is it not a matter of congratulation for a girl so poor as Mary to be made mistress of a grand place like Crome? Yes, she ought to have told me,' he continued, leaning his head on his hand, and looking rather sadly at the fire. 'She need not have thought that I was such a selfish beggar that I should not have been glad of it for her sake;' and then he sighed, and looked anything but glad.

'You have something too,' went on Dollie, hardly knowing what to say; and she quickly repeated the list of bequests and legacies that her mother had given her. Bertie brightened up a little as he heard of the moderate sum that was his share.

'Between three or four thousand to each; that will bring us in a hundred a year,' he said with some animation; and then he thought again and shook his head and sighed; why, he would not have two hundred a year, and she would be mistress of Crome!

'What are you two doing there?' said a voice, speaking softly to them from the top of the dark staircase. 'Miss Maynard, your mother is looking for you; she has just been to my room. I told her I knew where to find you. Is that Bertie? what a glorious fire! may I warm my hands at it a moment?' and Mrs. St. John advanced to them, looking dignified and graceful, and with no traces of her late emotion perceptible on her face.

Dollie looked at Bertie and fled; it was cowardly, but how was she to help him? and there was her mother waiting—her poor tired little mother!

Bertie made no sort of effort to detain her. He gave an inward groan as Mrs. St. John placed herself tranquilly on the oaken settle, and spread out her white hands to the flame. She took no notice of the young man's discomposure, as he sat rumpling his hair and eyeing her with keen wrathful looks. What did she want with him? What mischief was she going to brew at this hour of the night? For Bertie had an instinctive feeling that this tall graceful woman, with the beautiful face and the deep voice, was the evil genius of his life.

Presently Mrs. St. John turned to him, and there was a smile upon her face.

'So little Miss Maynard has been telling you the news!'

'What news?' demanded Bertie curtly, for he would have scorned to understand her.

'About Mary's good fortune,' she returned cheerfully. 'I wonder why Mrs. Reid attached such a condition to her will. What have you done, Bertie, to make that poor woman think so badly of you.'

'What condition? I do not understand you,' he inquired; but a faint thumping at his heart made him feel queer for a moment. What did she mean? How he hated her smile!

'I thought you said Miss Maynard had been telling you the news,' returned Mrs. St. John in real or affected astonishment. 'Dear me, how very awkward! I am hardly the right person to tell you. Old people get strange fancies in their heads sometimes; but that she should have thought such nonsense as that! Well, if you will have it'—for Bertie's gray eyes were literally flashing their question at her—'there is a condition—a very absurd and unnecessary one, as you will allow, and very distressing to poor Mary's sense of modesty—that she cannot inherit Crome without promising first that she will never marry a certain Mr. Cuthbert Lyndhurst.'

'Good heavens, you lie, woman!' had almost risen to Bertie's lips as he sprang to his feet, and then he checked himself; and something cold seemed to creep over him—a conviction that she was speaking the truth.

Was that what Mary's manner meant? Was that why she had avoided him? He remembered the coldness of her hand, and the sadness of the look with which she had regarded him. Would Mary, his own true-hearted Mary, give him up for this? No, he knew her too well for that. And the flash died out of his eyes, and a great softness came into them,

Janet saw it, and she leaned forward and touched him eagerly.

'Bertie, may I ask you a question? Is there anything, anything' (with a slight emphasis) 'between you and Mary?'

'Why do you ask me that? No, you have no right to ask,' he returned almost rudely; but she angered him so.

'Ah! but I have a right,' she returned, speaking very gently. 'She is our sister; we love her better than any one in the world; how can we help desiring her good? When I heard the contents of that will,' she went on slowly, evidently choosing her words with difficulty, 'and knew of the rich gift that had come to her, I said to my husband: "Mrs. Reid has done right; she could not have chosen more wisely. Mary will be the Lady Bountiful of the place; she will be the benefactor of old and young, the friend of rich and poor; she will reign like a queen, for she has a royal nature;" this is what I said to him.'

Bertie was silent. How was he to answer her? was it not true? But yet his Mary!

'Heaven has been very good to us,' went on Janet in the same equable tone. 'As my husband says, it is often darkest before dawn. The last few years have been very anxious. I daresay Mary has told you we have been getting poorer and poorer; our little capital has dwindled sadly; and Mr. St. John is such a bad man of business—they say the clergy are, as a rule—and so we have sunk rather heavily into debt. And that is not all'—her voice breaking a little in spite of her resolution—'his health is failing; unless he has rest and change, a country cure, and easier work, the doctor fears there will be danger of decline. Think if he were to go into a consumption! what would become of our children? and now,' clasping her hands, 'Mary will save us. She is rich—rich; she will come to our aid; she will save Maurice; she will be good to me and the children; she will be our best blessing, our generous, true-hearted sister.' Her manner changed and she stretched out her hands, and as he looked at her in his wrath and pain, her magnificent eyes were full of tears, which slowly brimmed over on her cheeks. 'Bertie, you have a good heart; you are a gentleman; do not ruin me and my children; do not come between us and Mary. In robbing her of her fortune you are robbing us all; you are making me a widow and my children fatherless, when a little—a very little—might save his precious life. If you have a heart, and it is not hard as iron, you will go away and leave her to us;' and when she had said this she slowly turned herself from him and went up into the darkness again, leaving him to sit beside the dying logs until far into the night, until his heart grew cold within him, and all the dreams of his life blackened slowly into ashes before his eyes.

CHAPTER XXII

MAURICE'S LETTER

WHEN Mary had heard Bertie's voice she had gone to him and had bidden him good-night, and had sent him resolutely away from her, and then she had turned the key in her door, and sat down to think.

But first she took Maurice's letter from her pocket and read it.

The envelope was still unopen, as when Janet had handed it to her two hours ago. Since then she had pressed her more than once to read it, but Mary had refused. Her brother's words should be sacred to her; she would keep them until she was alone.

Maurice, her own dear brother, could he help her? could any one help her in this awful strait? What had he said to her? and then she smiled in sad fashion and shook her head at the playful commencement. But before she had finished, the tears were raining down on the paper.

MY DEAREST MARY (it began), my bonnie Mary, and so you are to be mistress of Crome ! I have had all the children down and have told them. Lettice said nothing, but she turned very pale ; evidently the dear child fears to lose you. But Hatty and Rosie and May were more outspoken. 'Will she be as rich as the Shunamite, father?' asked May. We had read the story that evening. I am afraid I was wicked enough to answer her in the same fashion, and to assure her that you would have vineyards and olive presses, and men-servants and maid-servants, and oxen and she-asses in abundance ; bless their dear little hearts ! children are so literal. May actually mistook my fun and believed me. 'What will she do with such a lot of donkeys, father?' she asked ; and then Lettice struck in in sober and rather sad earnest : 'Father is only joking, May ; he wants us to understand that Aunt Mary is very rich, and will have all she wants, and a grand place to live in, and she will go away, and oh, father——' and here the darling actually trembled like a leaf, and laid her head on my shoulder, for she is weak still and poorly, and I felt she was crying. I tell you this that you may know how Lettice loves you, as indeed they all do.

Well, we made it all plain presently, and Lettice cheered up, and we had a long, long talk. Bee interrupted it now and then by calling out in her shrill little voice : ' Mammy, does oo' know auntie is a rich 'oomans—a werry, werry rich 'oomans?' with inimitable waggings of her little head ; and in her prayers that evening she said of her own accord, ' Thank God for making auntie rich 'oomans, for ever and for ever, Amen.' Poor babe ! as though our riches were to follow us !

But the rest of us had a grand talk. I wish you could have heard it, Mary. Lettice thought you would build a church ; Hatty a hospital for incurable children, because you were so sorry for little lame Jemmie; Rosie's opinion pointed to alm-houses. May was dubious, only they were all to live with you, and drink new milk every day, and have little gardens of their own, and donkey rides, for the child's head still ran on the she-asses ; and then I stopped them, and I told them that whether Aunt Mary built churches or founded hospitals, or endowed alm-houses, one thing was certain, that whatever she did she would regard herself as her Master's steward, and all these rich gifts would be as a loan to her, to be laid out in His service. For I know your heart, my darling sister, as I know my own, and while others are congratulating you—poor Janet, for example, but you must bear with her, she is so happy about this— you will be shrinking as though from a burden, with a full understanding of added work and responsibilities. ' What ! all this for me ! and souls and bodies perishing round me for lack of a little ; ' this is what you will say to yourself, and your eyes will grow dim, and your heart heavy as though a weight were on it.

But courage, my beloved ! open your arms wide to receive the Divine bounty ; gold is not dross to those who know how to spend it. Do you remember the parable of the talents ?—all for His use, who called the poor His brethren. Mary, you will not fear, not very much now, will you?

One word more, my dear, for I am writing a sadly disconnected letter, I fear—a sudden thought has struck me—that condition. What could Mrs. Reid mean? Can there be any ground for such suspicion?

Men, even brothers, are slow in such matters, and somehow I have always believed our Aunt Mary's heart to be free ; but if I be wrong, if there be any inward disquiet—anything to cause you regret in after life, put away this gift from you ; better a peaceful heart than a royal kingdom. I think you will understand me, dear.

Now I am weary, and Janet looks at me reproachfully. ' What ! not finished yet !' her eyes seem to say. No ! not till I have blessed

you, my own dear sister; there, may God bless you and help you
to a right decision! if there be need for decision.—Your loving
brother,   MAURICE.

The tears were raining down on the paper now—those
last few sentences, how almost illegible they were! Evidently
his hand had trembled, shaking either with fatigue or
emotion; perhaps his cough had troubled him; there was
a blot, and the last few words looked like an old man's
writing.

What if Janet were right, and Maurice should die?

'If there be any inward disquiet—anything to cause you
regret in after life—put away this gift from you.' What!
he could tell her to do that, when all his grand heart was
sunning itself in the prospect of this new gladness, when
he was rejoicing from his inmost soul that she was to be
the dispenser of such royal gifts. 'Open your arms wide
to receive the Divine bounty,' and then as though by
an afterthought and in a sad minor key, 'but not at all
costs—better a peaceful heart than a kingdom;' it was
as though he would say, 'Be true first—be generous
afterwards.'

'Oh, Maurice, Maurice! tell me what I ought to do,'
cried the poor girl, hiding her face in her hands; and then
in thought she was by his side in the old shabby study.
Janet and the children were upstairs; he had sent them
away; they were alone.

Now she was speaking; now she was telling him all her
heart; clear as crystal her thoughts came leaping out under
the kindness of his eyes; he was holding her hands in his;
he was encouraging, aiding her to speak. 'No secrets
between us; am I not the priest as well as the brother,
Mary?'

There, it was all spoken. Now, what would be his
answer? would it be, 'Cast this temptation from you;
overcome your own heart; crucify its best affection; take
up your appointed cross of loneliness and heart desolation,
and walk in the path that Providence has ordained for your
feet'? or would it be, 'Be true to yourself, Mary; do not
be blinded by a specious sense of duty; self-sacrifice that

involves misery to another is not always accepted ; do not betray your love for the sake of these riches ; live your own sweet life, my sister ; God will give us strength to bear our own burdens'? Oh, would he not say all this? Yes! and more than this.

· He would send her away from him healed and comforted, not counting the cost, but seeing things as they were with a far-sighted large simplicity, a child-like abiding in a present duty ; leaving the vast margins of the future to widen as they would out of the mists. 'To-day do rightly, to-morrow also, but leave results with God ;' that is what he always taught.

And she and Bertie would be comforted. Stop! let her follow out this thought slowly, carefully. What if the chateau clock were striking midnight? would there not be nights many and long enough in which to rest or grieve? The fire was dying slowly down, but her hands were over her eyes and she did not see it. Darkness—and yet all sorts of images flashed and wavered before her ; silence— and yet she could almost hear the throbbing of her own temples, the heavy beatings of her heart. But what of that, when she must think it all out?

She was his wife now : this was the next thought. Their slender incomes united would make such things possible ; they would not have to wait long, perhaps not more than a year or two ; they would be poor, but neither would mind that much ; they were together, and the outer world with its criticism and fashion and cut-and-dried philosophy would be as nothing to them.

How bright would be that hearth-fire! She would have little to give to others, but out of the fulness of her happy life she would reach out ministering hands to all that needed her. She would go to her daily labour among the sick and suffering and the ignorant ; and when her work was over, there would be the evening rest, and the face of her dearest friend to greet her. Hush! let her pass over that quickly.

Peace in their home!—and in the household in Lime Street a growing sense of trouble and despondency, deeper lines on Maurice's face, and the pinching hand of care planting heavier furrows in Janet's white forehead, an added gloom in the dark eyes, a sharper key in the fretful tone.

Maurice would go among his people, and the voice that grew daily weaker would speak the same brave words as of old. There would be no faltering of courage, no change in the sudden sweet smile that always greeted his wife. But Janet, oppressed with the day's struggles, with small sordid cares, and miserly hoardings for some dearly-coveted delicacy for his sickly appetite, would have no answering smile for him. 'Careful and troubled about many things' —alas, poor Janet!—about her husband's failing health, about her children's growing sickliness, about the load of daily-increasing debt that was dragging them down!

No possibility of change now, no relief from the squalid courts and alleys, the smoky atmosphere; no green lanes, no fragrant hedgerows, no morning song of larks for them! Who would hire that worn-out servant, faint with ministering to his Master's brethren? Who, looking on that tall stooping figure and hectic flush, would bid him come and rest and refresh himself?

Ah! the shadows were growing deeper; he cannot work now—he is dying, nothing can save him; too late—too late now! Whose is this passionate voice breaking out of the darkness, as St. Sauveur's clock chimes one? this groping hand clutching her dress? 'What is your love compared with mine, it says, who have known his every thought these fourteen years? Mary, for Maurice's sake! What will Lettice do without her father? How can I live when the desire of my eyes is taken from me?' The fire is out now; but in the darkness there is a figure kneeling with outstretched arms, as though in mortal agony.

'Anything but this—all that I have, but not Maurice's life, not my only brother! It cannot, it must not be! Bertie, you cannot ask it. I dare not—I dare not!'

The next morning Mary's place was vacant at the breakfast-table; but an hour or two afterwards Dollie encountered Bertie walking disconsolately up and down the passages.

'Mary wants you,' she said with a little tremor in her voice, and not daring to look at him lest he should see she had been crying; 'she is up there,' pointing to the door of the room that had been Mrs. Reid's private sitting-room.

'Mary wants me!' repeated the young man, and there was a blankness and perplexity in his face; and then he looked at her again as though he scarcely understood the message. But as Dollie nodded without speaking—for she dared not betray herself—he darted up the stair, and scarcely waiting for permission to enter, turned the handle and went in.

Mary walked across the room and gave him her hand, but without speaking; and then he saw that she was not alone. Mrs. St. John was sewing by the window.

'You sent for me, Mary?' he said eagerly; but Janet, looking up from her work, saw that his face was almost as pale as Mary's, and that there were dark circles round his eyes.

'Yes,' she answered, casting down her eyes, 'there was something I ought to have told you last night, only— only——' Her voice shook a little, and she tried to recover it, but he interrupted her.

'But if I know it, Mary?' and as she gave a little start indicative of surprise, he went on, 'Mrs. St. John was good enough to enlighten me last night.'

'Oh, Janet! and you never told me!' and Mary's tone was a little reproachful. Janet's colour heightened, but she had too much tact to show resentment at this moment.

'If Bertie recollects,' she said quietly, 'it was Miss Maynard who first informed him of the news. I interrupted their talk last night, and then found he knew all but the one clause. It was better I should tell him, was it not?' and Mary winced at the meaning tone; but again Bertie struck in—

'Look here, Mary; never mind who told me. I had to know, you see. What does all that matter to us? Of course you meant to tell me, and of course I know why

you have sent for me; but all the same I will not have
you speak.'

'But, Bertie——'

'Now, Mary, I will not have it. You shall not distress
yourself on my account. What is the use of being a man
if one cannot help the girl one loves? You have sent for
me to say that everything must be over between us, that
you are going to give me up; but, Mary, you shall not say
that to make yourself miserable. I mean to speak first, for
nothing on earth would induce me to stand between you
and Crome. Do you understand me?'

'Oh, Bertie!' and now Mary's eyes were full of tears,
and she could not answer him.

'It is I who am giving you up,' went on the poor fellow,
speaking in a half-choked voice; 'I have been thinking of
it all night, and I knew this morning you would send for
me. You have your brother and the children, and—and
it would not be right for you to do otherwise. So, though
I love you, and shall love you all my life, I would not
marry you even if you would have me,' breaking off with a
lame attempt at a smile. 'So you see it is not you, it is I
who have done it and given you up.'

'Oh, Bertie! How good, how generous you are!' said
poor Mary; while Janet, in spite of her antagonism, felt a
growing respect for this young man, who was at once so
gentle and so manly, and who was trying in his boyish
awkward fashion to shield the woman he loved.

'Now, there is nothing more to say; and you must not
fret about it, because you have always done what is right
and kind, and I shall understand, you know.' And as
she stretched out her hand silently to him, the gratitude
and the wistfulness of her eyes moved him to a recklessness
of courage, and he forgot they were not alone.

'Mary, you will let me kiss you once before—before we
wish each other good-bye,' he said, and there was almost a
sob in his voice.

Her only answer was to turn her face to him and let
him kiss her on the lips. 'God bless you, Mary!' he
said; and as she looked up at him trying to frame the

word 'Good-bye' with her lips, he suddenly threw her hands from him and went hurriedly away.

Mary remained standing for a few minutes where he had left her, and then Janet came up to her and touched her gently.

'Dear Mary, he is gone; he will not come back.'

'Gone! and I never said good-bye; I scarcely spoke to him. Are you sure?' and her look was so piteous that Janet's heart was touched, and she put her arms round the girl.

'Dear, he has acted nobly; he has spared you everything—he has made it so much easier for all of us; you and he will both feel better about it by and by; and oh, Mary, you have saved us all!'

'Yes; and Bertie, my Bertie, has gone,' returned Mary; and then she turned from her sister-in-law and walked feebly to the couch; it was not that she was faint, but that all her strength had suddenly gone from her, and that she could only lie there, spent and utterly exhausted.

Janet did the best she could for her by leaving her alone. Now and then some one came to the door, but she sent them away with a whispered word—'Mary was too tired to talk.' Now it was Charlotte with her fussy inquiries, now Dollie with a sorrowful pleading face, and once it was Mrs. Maynard; but Janet was resolute, and refused to open the door.

It was a long weary day for both the women. Janet tried to write to her husband, but the task was too difficult for her; Mary's pale face and closed eyes damped all the triumph of her joy. Maurice must wait; she could find no words for him.

Towards afternoon there were unwonted sounds in the chateau—footsteps passing up and down. Mary raised her head languidly, and looked at Janet.

'Yes, dear,' she said, answering that look; 'they are bringing down his portmanteau; he is going now. Indeed, Mary,' touched by that uncomplaining sadness, 'it is better, far better so.'

'Yes, yes,' she answered; and then rose slowly to her

feet and walked to the window. There he was in the courtyard bidding good-bye to Charlotte. Would he look up? He was standing bareheaded, and the sharp east wind was rumpling his fair hair. Yes, he was looking up now; their eyes met; and Mary waved her hand to him. 'Good-bye, Bertie, my Bertie,' Janet heard her say; and then she went back to her couch, and turned her face to the wall.

CHAPTER XXIII

A FEW days after Bertie's abrupt departure from the Chateau de St. Aubert, Mrs. St. John and Mary returned to England.

· Dollie and her mother remained behind, very reluctantly on Dollie's part, but Charlotte had appealed to them with many protestations and tears. In six weeks she was to become the wife of Dr. Pierre Arnaud, and the mistress of the large corner house in the Rue d'Equerre. Would they leave her alone in the great desolate chateau to weep over the memory of ma pauvre Tante? Would they abandon her to Justine's tender mercies at this critical, this most interesting period of her life? When would she require more the good offices, the sympathy, the support of her female friends? This, and much more, did Charlotte sob forth, to Dollie's secret chagrin and scorn, and to Mrs. Maynard's infinite perplexity, until Mary stepped in with a word or two that weighed down the balance.

'I do think you ought to stay, Dollie,' she said one evening when they were alone together. It was two days after she had bidden good-bye to her lover; the first day her strength had been utterly spent, and there had been no effort possible to her; then she had turned her face to the wall and wept, and it had seemed to her as though she had tasted of the bitterness of death.

But the next day she had come among them again, and had sat there very grave and silent, but conveying by her manner that she wished for no expression of sympathy; she looked so ill that Dollie and her mother exchanged

glances of dismay and sympathy; Dollie could have fallen
on her neck for very love and pity, but a certain passive
resistance and constraint in Mary's manner forbade her.
Once Janet spoke over-tenderly to her, and she had flushed
up with sudden irritation.

'What do you mean, Janet?' she had said; 'I am
well, quite well;' and soon after that she had asked Dollie
to walk out with her. Janet looked after them wistfully,
but they did not invite her to join them. When they had
gone a little distance, Mary took Dollie's arm and leaned
on it rather heavily, but she was very silent.

They had gone in the direction of their first walk towards the cemetery; Dollie, who was in no mood for
churchyard musings, would have passed on, but Mary
pressed her arm, and gently guided her towards the entrance.

'It is so cold and damp,' shivered Dollie, looking up at
the gray skies and bare tree-tops; but Mary took no notice.

By and by they were sitting on the little bench over-
looking the convent graves.

'Sister Veronica, aged twenty—do you remember?'
Mary had said very softly, as though some thought struck
her, and then she had made that remark, 'I do think you
ought to stay, Dollie.'

'But it will be so horrid remaining behind after all that
has happened,' returned Dollie, fidgeting as she spoke.
'Do you know, I quite hate the chateau—I feel as though
it were haunted; we have been so happy and have had
such lovely times, and now everything has ended so
miserably;' and Dollie crunched the pebbles impatiently
with her feet.

'Yes, it will be very dull,' replied Mary, with a sigh,
'but all the same I think for poor Charlotte's sake that you
ought to do it; it will be so lonely for her, and she has been
very kind to us, poor little woman! and the change will do
your mother good.'

Dollie made a wry face—she was only half convinced.

'But I shall want you every hour of the day, Mary,' she
said in a coaxing voice. 'I never had a sister, and somehow we seem like sisters. I shall be thinking of you, and

fretting about you, and—oh dear—I don't think Sister Veronica aged twenty was so much to be pitied, after all; she got over all the horrid part of life so quickly.'

Mary smiled—a wan pitiful little smile it was.

'I am not so sure of that, Dollie; perhaps it is not intended for us to get over the horrid part so quickly; we ought not to "take ourselves down from the cross"; it is better——' her lip quivered, but she went on quietly, 'it is better to live the life intended for us as bravely and as patiently as we can. By and by there will be no more pain;' and then her manner changed, and she started up from the bench and walked hurriedly down the narrow path.

'Yes, it is cold, and the air feels as though it were going to snow. Janet was right, and we had better not defer our return after to-morrow. Will you promise me to stay, dear Dollie? It would hurt me for you not to do right; one cannot always please oneself.'

'Oh, Mary, what a rebuke you are to me!' returned the younger girl with tears in her eyes. 'Stay! I will stay six months if you wish it.'

'No, only six weeks—until our poor little Charlotte becomes Madame Arnaud. You must write and tell me about it; everything you do; and how your mother likes Lesponts. You must take her to the Béguinage and Laeken-water; and—and—oh, how cold it is, Dollie!' and now Mary began to shiver, and wrap herself closer in her mantle.

'And you will write to me, Mary?'

'Yes, yes, of course I shall write. I must tell you about the children and Maurice, and my plans; and when you come back, you and your mother must come to me at Crome, and—and—we shall be so comfortable,' but at this point Mary's voice became husky, and she walked on faster. Before they reached the chateau they were overtaken by a sharp hailstorm, and arrived wet and weary, to find Janet waiting for them anxiously in the porch.

'Oh dear! what a dreadful storm! you must be thoroughly drenched,' she exclaimed, laying a detaining hand on Mary's wet cloak; but she eluded her grasp.

'Yes, we are very wet, and I think I will go to my room and rest, Janet,' and Mrs. St. John let her pass with a sigh.

Dollie had promised to stay, and so she tried to make the best of it. It was very dull seeing Mary off at the station, and walking back alone across the Grande Place; the very carillon vibrated sadly to her ear. How empty the chateau felt that evening! how trite and meaningless Charlotte's incessant chatter; for once her mother's presence hardly seemed sufficient. The rooms were haunted, but not in ghostly fashion; Grey's dark face lurked in corners; his kind eyes and smile seemed to follow her; the firelight shone on Bertie's fair hair, rumpled into a halo; she could hear his voice—his very words—and Mary answering him.

'Would you like to go to bed, Dollie, my dear?' asked her mother, noting the girl's restlessness. It was better when they got upstairs, and she could put her head on her mother's lap and let her pet and talk to her. What wonder if she were weary and unstrung after all that had happened, thought the widow, and she was very tender and solicitous over her child.

But after a few days it was better; Dollie ceased to miss her friends quite so keenly, and her natural buoyancy asserted itself. She had to do the honours of the chateau to her mother; Charlotte was far, far too busy. She had to act as cicerone, and show her the beauties of the dear old city. She must see all Dollie's favourite haunts—St. Sauveur's, St. Jacques, Notre Dame, and the Hotel·de Ville; and then, but only when all the other sights were exhausted, she took her to Laeken-water and the Béguinage.

How very quiet Dollie was all the walk! She made no answer to her mother's exclamations and little ejaculations of surprise and pleasure. 'This is the prettiest walk we have had yet, Dollie,' she said quite innocently; 'why have you left it to the last?' and Dollie flushed up and looked foolish.

But that night she took heart of grace, and told her little story.

'I thought I ought to have no secrets from you, mother,'

she said, looking very good and demure: how the widow
thrilled and trembled over her girl's recital. The next day
she went out alone, and took that walk again. She stood
for a long time on the bridge that led to the ivied archway
of the Béguinage. 'It was here that he told my Dollie that
he loved her,' she said to herself, and again that thrill had
passed over her. Was the danger averted? or should she
have to fear for the future?

'And you refused him! you actually said no!' she
exclaimed. Now, indeed, her girl was a woman.

'What could I do? One is, not obliged to accept
people because they ask one,' returned Dollie a little loftily.
The narrative had excited her; it sounded better in the
retrospect. 'Of course I was sorry, and I told him so,' she
went on, feeling all at once as though she had acted very
creditably—after all she had not done so badly.

Then suddenly Mrs. Maynard changed colour, and her
manner grew very nervous.

'Oh, Dollie, my dear, if you had only written to me!
and I have asked him to call—actually to call.'

'How could I write about such things?' returned Dollie
in a shrill little voice. 'Mother, how you do talk! And
what does it matter if you have asked him to call? We
are very good friends; he has been kind to me, and has
done so much for Mary and for us all; we settled all that
—that he was to call, I mean—and that I was to be glad
to see him. I daresay he will come, and be dreadfully
disappointed to find the house empty,' continued Dollie in
the most matter-of-fact way, as though she had refused half
a dozen offers, and had settled the same number of disconsolate lovers. And it was after this that Mrs. Maynard had
taken her second walk to the Béguinage.

Dollie and her mother found plenty to do all day, and
in the evening Dr. Arnaud always came and stopped a
couple of hours. He was a brisk wooer, and carried on
what he called his 'English courtship' with a mixture of
bonhommie and gallantry that amused Dollie.

'Oh, Charlotte, how I do wish I could have a lover like
Dr. Arnaud!' she exclaimed once, to his fiancée's delight.

16

'Mother, would it not be nice? Dr. Arnaud comes in like this,' planting her little feet in the first position; 'he carries his curly-brimmed hat under his arm, he bows, he flourishes his hand. "Mon amie! I trust I find thee well this evening? Jean Jacques and Ton-ton chéri send thee their felicitations, their love.' How hast thou passed the day, my Charlotte? how have thy energies diffused themselves?" Is it not so?' and naughty Dollie twirled an imaginary moustache, and assumed a sprightly sentimentality.

'Dear Dollie, you are so droll!' laughed Charlotte, while Mrs. Maynard held up a warning hand.

'Droll! how can you be so hard-hearted, so unsympathetic, mon ange?' mimicked Dollie. 'What do you call him when you are alone? Pierre?—Pierre, mon bien-aimé!' and then she leant her dimpled chin on her hand and sighed plaintively. 'Mother, it is hard—there is an inequality in fate after all. Why are these blessings denied to me, Dorothy Maynard? Why may I not have a lover as erect as a little tin soldier, with a well-waxed moustache and a head like a highly-finished scrubbing-brush? Can you conceive anything more adorable?'

Once when Charlotte was arraying herself for one of these evening visits, Dollie ran up to her with a coaxing face: 'Do let me dress you to-night, Charlotte. I will promise you that Dr. Pierre Arnaud shall go home more in love than ever.'

Dr. Arnaud hardly knew his fiancée that evening, the little witch had so metamorphosed her. Charlotte wore her mourning dress with a muslin kerchief crossed over her bosom; the thin golden hair was tucked up under a little cap; a single white flower nestled at her throat; her blue eyes looked as round and innocent as a child's; a little pink flush tinted her worn cheek.

'Mon ange, thou art charmante, adorable to-night!' Dollie heard him whisper; and even Mrs. Maynard owned that Charlotte had never looked better.

It was soon after this that the three went for a week to the gay city of Brussels. Charlotte had bridal purchases to make, and the trip would be a treat to Dollie.

They took lodgings in the Rue de Trône, behind the king's palace, where Dollie had a sunshiny little bedroom with a painted ceiling, and a pink-and-white bed in an alcove.

What descriptions Dollie wrote of that visit—of the park, the cathedral, the picture-galleries! What hours she spent, gazing into those wonderful shops, with their blaze of colour—of jewels, their fairy-like fabrics and lace!

There is a street here full of the most gorgeous shops (wrote Dollie); we are for ever climbing up and down it, Charlotte and I, and we cannot tear ourselves away.

Aladdin's lamp must have conjured up those marvellous things; everything is a mass of colour; even the confectionery and the flowers are beyond everything! how I wish I could have Fortunatus's purse! There is an emerald tiara that is ravishing, and a dress of cobweb lace that Titania might wear, and a wreath of forget-me-nots in China that take all the colour out of Charlotte's eyes. Oh dear! I never dreamt or imagined that things could be half so beautiful.

And then she went off on another description.

We have had such a horrid day (she wrote next)! I am afraid it will haunt me all my life long, but it was all that stupid Charlotte's fault, and she said we ought to go. It was horribly wet, and we went splashing through great pools; there were no shops—nothing but dull-looking streets, and a few people clattering along under their umbrellas.

Mother wanted to go back; but no—Charlotte said we must not leave Brussels without seeing the W—— Gallery, and actually she compelled us to undergo all the horrors.

Oh, Mary, such pictures! the work of a madman!—at least his work must have driven him mad. The poor little mother looked quite scared. 'A diseased imagination, Dollie, my dear,' she whispered; 'please come away; these pictures will get into our brain and haunt us!' and she actually put down her veil and walked into the next room. But I was obliged to stay; and now the whole thing seems to me like a nightmare. They were such terrible pictures, Mary! such awful subjects! My head got confused over them; the whole room seemed full of grotesque figures, writhing limbs, bloodshed, and madness. The very titles were appalling—'Hunger and Madness and Crime,' 'The Resuscitation of a Person Buried Alive,' 'The Suicide,' 'The Vision of a Beheaded Man!' Can you conceive such subjects? There was the face of Lucifer hurled from heaven, so diabolically beautiful that it riveted one's attention; and a Napoleon in the infernal regions—the most perfect impersonation of unyielding pride—it reminded one of a description in Dante.

I took refuge with mother at last; for the moral, or rather the immoral, atmosphere seemed to choke me. What right have they to torture healthy minds with the diseased imaginations of a crazy painter? genius that borders on frenzy ought to be deprived of his palette. I perfectly raved as we splashed through the pools again. That night all my dreams were horrid; I found myself wondering what you would say to it all, Mary.

Dollie's letters were very clever and amusing; she wrote all the thoughts that came into her busy little head. By and by her topics changed; they were back again at the chateau. There were quiet days—plenty of work, Dr. Arnaud's visits in the evening. Then came the wedding. Dollie wrote that Charlotte had behaved fairly well, and had looked very nice. The great event sobered her; her little affectations had dropped off her—she was quiet, simple, and subdued.

After that they had seen her in her own home, the evening before they left Lesponts. She came running down the staircase to meet them, followed by her youngest stepson. She wore her little cap, and looked flushed and happy.

'Pierre likes me in it,' she said simply; and then she patted Gaston on the shoulder. 'Is he not a great fellow?' she said, in quite a motherly fashion, looking down affectionately into the queer little brown face. 'Make thy bow, Ton-ton chéri;' and Ton-ton chéri made an odd little grimace, and stuck out his brown paw. 'They are good boys; they are dear boys, and I love them and their father dearly,' cried the little woman, with sparkling eyes.

'Whom hast thou there, Madame Arnaud?' interposed a brisk voice. 'Hé bien! our good friends! my Charlotte, make them welcome. Let us offer them the best hospitality that the house contains. You behold us, madame, mademoiselle, the happiest family in Lesponts. My wife there is our good angel, our beneficent genius. Jean Jacques and Ton-ton chéri cease to weep for a lost mother. Le roi est mort, vive le roi—n'est ce pas? Can we not transpose the sentiment? the mother is dead, yet the mother lives. Bon ciel! how is a man with any degree of heart to inter-pret such fidelity, such nobleness?'

'Mon ami, coffee is served in the salon, and Hortense waits there,' interrupted Charlotte, with a blush and dimple; and her blue eyes rested tenderly on her husband.

'Poor little woman, she is very happy!' observed Mrs. Maynard, as she walked through the silent streets that evening. 'Her husband and those boys adore her. Well, she is not wise, but she has plenty of heart; and men like Dr. Arnaud can put up with a fair amount of coquetry. Perhaps, after all, she will be happier with him than with Captain Hervey.'

'Perhaps so,' returned Dollie absently; she hardly heard her mother's observation. This was their last evening in Lesponts. Christmas was over and the New Year; they were crossing the Grande Place for the last time; the crescent moon was rising behind the Tourdes Halles; there were bright facets of stars set in the dark wintry sky; a strong wind blew keenly across the market-place. Dollie stood still a moment, and looked round her—at the dark peaked roofs, at the closed shops and cafés, the old mediæval houses. Just then the carillon rang out. 'Good-bye,' it seemed to say to Dollie; 'good-bye, golden days; good-bye, happy dreams; will they come again? will they ever come again?'

'Dollie, my dear, it is too cold to stand,' remonstrated the mother gently; and the girl roused herself obediently, and hurried on. 'Good-bye, golden days and happy dreams. Ah, poor Mary!' she sighed; 'will they come again? will they ever come again to her?'

CHAPTER XXIV

IT was late on Saturday evening when Mrs. St. John and Mary drove through the crowded streets of the East end of London.

Saturday night in Whitechapel! Mrs. St. John leant back and closed her eyes as though she would shut out the sight, but Mary sat erect and watchful. This was Maurice's battle-field—the scene of his labours.

How well she remembered it! and yet how strange it looked after those long weeks of absence! There were the flaring gaslights; the butchers' shops; the 'buy-buy' of the impatient salesmen; the open stalls; the rough, pushing crowds; the pinched faces of anxious men and women; rags and tatters—there they were—tawdry finery; plenty of white-faced babies trying to find refuge from the bitter wind under the thin shawls—Whitechapel on its gala night —lit up with its diadem of gas—and behind her an old mediæval city, grass-grown and buried in sleep, and a chateau haunted by dismal memories.

'Oh, Mary, why does it look so much worse to-night?' groaned Janet; but the girl did not answer. She sat with her hands folded in her lap, and a wide, far-away look in her brown eyes. 'Good-bye, golden dreams!' what if the carillon had said that to her too ; this was the life that was waiting for her !

By and by they were standing on the pavement at Lime Street; Mary hung back, and let Janet precede her into the house. The entry was very dark, but she could hear

Maurice's fondly - uttered 'Welcome home, my darling,' before his outstretched arms received her. 'Thank God, I have you both again,' he said, as he extended a hand to each, and drew them gently in. What a greeting for Aunt Mary then; they were all there—Lettice and Hatty, Rosie and May, down to little Bee. Janet caught up her darling in a moment, and nearly smothered her with kisses. What a beautiful creature she looked, standing. there with her child in her arms, and a sweet smile playing round her lips! Lettice had timidly removed her wraps. The tall figure showed to advantage in the straight, black draperies; some of her dark hair had escaped from its coil; her face looked animated and eager. How it changed and softened as she looked up and caught her husband's eyes! her colour deepened like a girl's; it was just so she looked when he saw her first, and all his honest heart had gone out to her.

'Janet, how well you look! I have never seen you look better,' he said; but his voice spoke volumes, and Janet blushed again.

'I am so glad to see you and the children,' she said simply, as she moved closer to him; 'but you are looking thin, Maurice—no better than when I left you,' and the light suddenly died out of her face.

'Why, of course not,' he returned lightly; 'I wanted my wife. Children, tell your mother how much we missed her, and how we longed for her and Aunt Mary. Well, Mary'—and here he held out his hand to her, and looked at her with a kind smile—'so Bee's rich 'oomans has come back!'

'Yes, Maurice, I have come back;' and she lifted her quiet eyes to his; and then she drew May towards her, and beckoned the others who were standing aloof shyly, and said a pleasant word to each.

'Lettice, light the candle for Aunt Mary, and take her up to her room,' interrupted her mother, who was watching them. Perhaps she wanted to be alone with her husband—perhaps she noticed that Mary's face was pale, and that there was a tired look in her eyes, and feared that

Maurice would notice it. As she spoke, Mary rose rather quickly and followed the child.

A large front room at the top of the house had been allotted to her; it was rather a bare-looking apartment, with three high, narrow windows, and a small iron bedstead. It had brown wainscoted walls and roomy cupboards; the cupboards were full of heterogeneous articles belonging to Mary's parochial labours—piles of books in neatly-stitched blue calico covers, layers of old threadbare garments patched and repaired for gifts, balls of lists, ragbags, newspaper cuttings, a formidable medicine-chest, mended toys, and half-finished illuminations. The great round table was full too—a heap of tracts to be covered for distribution lay beside the well-worn copy of Thomas à Kempis, a work-basket, an inkstand, a shabby old desk, and a rag scrap-book, on which some gaudy pictures were pasted—for this room Mary had loved to call her workshop or her hospital, for here the children and she had often effected marvellous cures.

How many toys had they not neatly repaired?—dolls with broken arms and legs, with dejected sawdust bodies, had been here refitted with new limbs, and their emaciated frames renovated; waxen heads, devoid of hair, smirked blandly under new flaxen wigs; decapitated trunks were united to wonderful rag heads, with painted eyebrows; and an agreeable caricature of the lost visage, while faded blooms were revived with the skill of a Madame Rachel. At the bottom of the largest cupboard there was still an army of sick or wounded dolls waiting for Aunt Mary's skilful surgery.

If Mary's ministrations had not been valued among her adult patients, she would still have been hailed by every little curly-haired Arab 'as their favourite friend and toy-mender.' Mary's heart had often been touched by the dreary, neglected state of the children. Some had literally nothing to amuse them; one baby had the sole of an old boot which it was making believe to cuddle; another had picked up a broken flowerpot, and was gloating over the fragments with a 'Pretty, pretty.' Could nothing be done for these poor innocents ? Toys were not to be bought where bread was often wanting; but Mary thought of another plan—she organised a raid on the nurseries of her friends ; she bore down upon the more respectable inhabitants, and carried off armfuls of broken or disused toys. Then began those wonderful afternoons, which were called the 'Hospital Saturdays.' Then was the round table cleared, and the head surgeon and her dressers brought out their limp patients, and operated on them to their hearts' content. What beautiful cases of compound fracture ! the painted rag heads were rocked tenderly by and by against the grimy little bosoms. Jemmy Stokes was made happy by a cart that actually moved on wheels ; wonderful Noah's arks, with animals such as never had appeared, and never would appear on this earth, tumbled out of that memorable refuge.

'Let me paint the zebra, Aunt Mary,' May would plead.

'Zebra, my dear !' Aunt Mary answered, putting up her eyeglasses, and regarding the blue and scarlet stripes critically ; 'that must be some extinct species belonging to the antediluvian period, before zebras wore tails, and had only three legs.'

'Oh, I forgot its tail,' returned May, in a conscience-stricken voice. How the children revelled in these Hospital Saturdays. Aunt Mary always told them some story as they worked; sometimes she sang to them ; now and then the door would open stealthily, and a man's face would look down on the four flaxen heads.

'I wonder if there were any toys in the cottage at Bethlehem,' he heard Hatty say once ; but before Mary could answer, Lettice had responded in her dreamy way—

'Not bits of painted wood like this ; but of course He used to play with the birds and flowers. Don't you remember that picture, Hatty, with the doves ? He is stroking their wings and cuddling them ; and they look as contented as though they were in their nests, the pretty white things ! and there is the mother and the young St. John looking at Him.'

'How sorry He must be for all the dirty little babies in Sloane Court!' struck in Rosie.

'Ah, but He is pleased that we are mending toys for them,' put in May. The children always spoke of such things in simple, literal fashion; to them the Holy Child was no abstract idea, no vague impersonality; they lived with Him; they thought out their childish thoughts in His presence. To them this toy-mending was one of the corporal works of mercy; it was as holy in their eyes as the incense and gold of the Magi. He had been a child Himself, and so He understood and loved children, and in this way their childish hands grasped the very skirt of His mantle of mercy.

'Hospital Saturday!' and there was Bee's 'rich 'oomans' looking round the room with sad, wistful glances. How bare it looked to-night! and yet a bright fire blazed in the grate, and two candles—unheard-of luxury—burned in the china candlestick; the old easy-chair, with its worn cretonne covering, looked inviting and restful. Mary sank into it with a sigh, and Lettice knelt down on the rug.

'Would you like to be alone, Aunt Mary? Shall I go down and leave you?' asked the child timidly; she had never seen her aunt look so tired and grave before.

That roused her. 'No, dear, no; am I very stupid, Lettie? We will go down together by and by, when father and mother have had their talk. Come closer to me, my pet; have I grown strange to you all at once? Why, what a thin little hand! You have been ill, my darling, and there was no Aunt Mary to nurse you.'

Lettice shook her head.

'I wanted you so badly,' she whispered, laying her head against her arm. 'You seemed so far away, one could not see you, somehow. I could not bear being such a trouble to poor mamma, she always looked so tired.'

'You foolish Lettie! Mothers do not think it a trouble to wait on their children when they are ill,' replied Mary, pinching her cheek. How thin and white it was! and she was beginning to stoop, too, like her father.

'Ah, but Rosie was ill too; and then there was father

not well, coughing dreadfully, and not able to sleep properly. Mamma used to look so worried when she brought me my food or medicine; she never had time to sit down and talk as you do, and she never smiled or said things that made one feel happy. She was always telling me Rosie was cross, and that father was so bad, and that I must make haste and get well and help her. Once she came back and found me crying, but I was not well enough to stop when she told me, and then she was vexed with me, and said I was selfish and fretful, and that I added to her burdens; but I could not help it, indeed I could not, Aunt Mary.'

'My poor little girl, of course not;' and she sighed as she thought of Janet's sharp tones admonishing the sensitive child. Fretful and selfish! Lettice never had been that in her life. When would Janet understand that beautiful nature?

'If mamma had only kissed me I should have felt better, but she went away without bidding me good-night, just as she does when she is displeased with us. I don't know what I should have done. I was so miserable, and feeling so hot and sick too, only father came up to me.'

Mary looked relieved. 'Go on, dear,' she said encouragingly. 'Of course father put everything right?'

'Yes, he was so kind; he seemed to understand, and never scolded me at all; he turned my hot pillow, and moved the light where the shadow should not dance before my eyes; and he bathed my face, and told me to lie as quiet as I could, and I should soon feel better; and he called me his dear patient little daughter, and said I was a good child, and how much he loved us all; and I don't remember any more. I think I must have fallen asleep, for when I woke, there he was still watching me. I know mamma was very kind to me the next day.'

Mary was silent; she knew Janet always repented of these irritable moods, but all the same the words haunted her—'What would Lettice do without her father?' Heaven help those poor children if they were ever to be left solely to the care of a mother so exacting and so peremptory!

Already Lettice's sweet obedience and simple faith had
been sorely tried.

'What now, my dearest?' for the child's forehead was
wrinkled with some perplexity and care.

'Oh, I don't know,' throwing her arm affectionately
over her aunt's lap; 'it is so nice to talk to you again
that all sorts of queer thoughts seem to tumble out of one's
head, like the animals in May's Noah's Ark. I think I
must have been naughty and foolish to think such things.'

'What things, pet?'

'Oh, that mamma did not love me as well as the others;
she so often says I tire her when I talk, or that I am
awkward and silly. Hatty gets on better than I do, though
she is often scolded. Oh, if I were only as pretty as Bee!'
and the look of unhappiness deepened on Lettice's face.
This would not do at all. Mary sat upright, and her tone
became bracing; these morbid fancies must not be encouraged, and she turned away resolutely from the underlying truth.

'Lettice, I am surprised at you—you disappoint me.
What was it you promised me?'

'Yes, I know, Aunt Mary, but——'

'Hush! no buts. Is not this being selfish, Lettice?
is not this selfishness in its most subtle form, cherishing,
watching, dwelling in self? Do you think love measures
and deals with quantities? so much to you—so much to
Bee—to Hatty. Can you question love, to whom you
owe existence? Oh, Lettice, this is wrong—wrong.'

Lettice hung her head, and a tear stole down her thin
cheek. 'Pet, am I hard on you? Who loves you better
than Aunt Mary, even when she scolds you.

'Listen to me, my dear one; this is your fault; you
are over-sensitive; you think too much of yourself; an
unkind word crushes you; a look chills you. Be more
generous; the sun is behind the clouds. If your mother
reproves you, it is not that she does not love you. Poor
mother!'—she went on pleading for Janet, even against
her own conviction—'think how harassed she is! how
full of troubles! You are a child, Lettice; you cannot

understand the burdens that lie upon her shoulders. If she could smile and look happy, she would; when you were a baby, she used to play with you as she does with Bee.'

A strange startled look came into Lettice's eyes.

'Aunt Mary, are you sure? did—did,' her voice trembling with eagerness, 'did she ever smile and look at me like that?'

'Yes, of course, Lettice, my child. What have you got in your head against your mother? I was very young then, not much older than you, but I well remember her going to the little cot that stood near her bed, and stand looking down on it with such a smile; and once when I was very impatient, she said, 'Hush, Mary, I must have a good look at my baby.'

'Mamma looked at me like that!' she said no more, but such a radiance lit up her face. Janet would hardly have known her child at that moment, the plain irregular features were so transformed with that inward light; those few words had put to rest something that had threatened to destroy the girl's peace. Now she could be patient, she could endure, since her mother loved her, and had looked at her like that.

Nothing further was said on the subject; for a little while they sat in silence. Lettice's thoughts were happy ones; Mary's had strayed back to her own troubles, to that dim borderland where they were henceforth to abide —a region of infinite possibilities but of little hope. By and by she roused herself, but with difficulty, and they went down together hand-in-hand.

Meanwhile Maurice had said a word to his wife that caused her a little solicitude—'He thought Mary did not seem quite like herself.'

'You must not judge of her to-night,' responded Janet hastily; 'she is tired from her journey.'

'Yes, but you are looking so fresh yourself,' he returned. 'It is not fatigue I mean; she has a worn anxious look, and she is so very, very grave; I am afraid this money is a source of trouble to her.'

'Consider what she has been through,' replied Janet

evasively, but her heart beat a little faster from nervousness. How she dreaded the keenness of Maurice's eyes! What if he should question her more closely about this money? She knew her husband, his high-souled sense of honour, his hatred of intrigue and double-dealing; with all her faults, her ambition, and worldliness, she had never lied to him or deceived him—she had been as absolutely true as he.

This was the first time she had ever acted without his guidance; what if he were to discover that she had so intrigued for his sake, that by subtle arguments and tears she had induced Mary to give up all her prospects of happiness for the sake of himself and his children?

What if he had seen her abased in the dust for his sake! Would he not have spurned her from him with something like scorn? Would not his anger be bitter against her that she had so humbled herself and him? Ah, he must never know what crooked paths she had trodden on his behalf; Mary would not betray her, and she must answer him by evasion, as she was doing now.

'Consider all she has been through,' she had said to him. 'Maurice, you do not know, but Charlotte has told me, the whole history of those terrible days. Mary behaved like a heroine; she thought of every one but herself; she spared herself neither day nor night—is it a wonder if her nerves be worn? Some day I will tell you about it all, but do not speak to her to-night.' But Maurice would give no promise; he thought that it might be as well for him to say one word to his sister.

Janet had sufficient tact not to press the point; she was quite aware that with all her husband's softness of heart he had a tenacity of will that nothing could move; with all his love for her, she had never succeeded in influencing him against his judgment.

Janet's only chance was not to leave them together, but here the Fates were against her. Bee, who was excited by her mother's return, woke crying, and refused to be comforted by Biddy's blandishment. 'Tell mammie I want 'omes and 'eavens; go away, you stupid old Biddy; Bee doesn't love you; Bee will have 'eavens and 'omes.'

'Oh, my naughty Bee,' sighed her mother sorrowfully. But there was no help for it; she must sit down in the rocking-chair, and let Bee put her fat arms about her neck. Lettice, in her little bed in the other room, heard her low-voiced singing, 'There's a home for little children,' and turned on her pillow with a smile—she was looking at Bee just as she used to look at her.

And in the room downstairs Maurice was talking to his sister.

'Well, Mary,' he said, as the door closed upon his wife, 'you and I must have a word together. Tell me, my dear, did you get my letter?'

She looked at him in surprise. 'Yes, Maurice, of course I did.'

'And was it not a kind letter?'

'Very, very kind.'

'I never had an answer to it,' he returned quietly; and Mary changed colour and looked down.

'I sent you a message through Janet,' she returned in a very low voice; 'I tried to write—indeed I did; but somehow the words would not get themselves written; I was too tired, I suppose, and everything was so confusing.'

'Poor Aunt Mary!' he answered tenderly. 'You have had a terrible time, I hear; you must tell me all about it sometime, when you are rested, and we have leisure for a good long talk. How I have thought of you through it all! how I have gloried in your means of usefulness! You have behaved like a heroine, Janet tells me; but, Mary, you and I never thought for a moment of the reward.'

'No, indeed,' very faintly.

'Look at me, dear, a moment. There is something in your face that perplexes me—are you sure that this money is not a source of trouble to you?'

The hands that he was holding turned very cold, and for an instant the sudden revulsion of feeling was almost too much for her, and she feared that she would burst into tears, but the next moment she had rallied.

'I think it is a trouble to me,' she answered so truth-
fully that she deceived even him ; 'I have never cared for
riches, I never wanted them ; and at present I feel rather
burdened by a sense of responsibility. Oh, Maurice, help
me ; what am I to do with it ? '

'Is that all your trouble, Mary ? ' looking at her rather
anxiously.

'What do you mean ? ' she faltered, 'are you afraid that
I am not sufficiently grateful for the fortune that has come
to me ? Indeed, I am thankful for it, more thankful than
ever to-night ! ' but how her lip quivered as she said it !
'It was given to me, and of course it was the right thing to
keep it—how could I doubt it ? Now you will teach me
how to spend it, you and the children ; ' and a feeling of
gratitude swelled up in her heart as she looked at his worn
face—thank God she had had strength to do the right thing !

Maurice had no idea that his next words were robbing
her of her best comfort—'What have we to do with it ? it
is your own money,' he said a little stiffly, for pride was
Maurice's chief fault.

Then she looked at him pitifully.

'Oh, do not say that ! do not make me sorry that I
have grown rich,' she said in a loving voice. 'Think of
all the years I have lived here, and how I have been a
daughter as well as a sister to you. Have I ever refused
to be beholden to you and Janet ? then why should you be
too proud to accept anything from me now ? '

That appealed to his generosity and touched him.

'Mary, my dear sister ! '

'No, I am not your dear sister if you could say such
things to me. Why should you deprive me of my greatest
pleasure ? are not your children mine ? do I not belong to
you as much as they ? Maurice, I did not think you could
be so hard.'

'No, no ! ' he said soothingly. 'I am not hard.'

'Then take that speech back again. It is not my own
money—it is yours, it is Janet's, it is the children's. You
shall not separate yourselves from me, and leave me out in
the cold alone.'

'My dear,' he returned, quite conquered by her earnestness, 'how you talk! Do you think anything can separate us? you shall not look so unhappy over it. What is it you want me to do?'

'Oh, I will tell you that by and by,' she said more lightly; and rising from her seat, she threw her arms round his neck and kissed him gratefully. She had conquered— oh yes, she knew that—conquered by the very force of her goodness and earnestness and truth; by and by she would tell him what to do and he would do it. Maurice loved the right and he would never be proud with her again—no, her brother, for whom she had given up all, would never be proud with her again.

CHAPTER XXV

AT this moment Mrs. St. John re-entered the room, and the conversation became more general; both brother and sister were content to let the matter rest for the present; neither did the one absorbing topic of interest revive until the following evening.

Janet, who had been living in a sort of dreamland for the last few days, found it strangely difficult to take up the thread of her home life; she woke the next morning with the old weary feeling that it was Sunday, Maurice's hardest-working day in the seven—when he neither spared himself nor allowed others to spare him; when he gave himself body, soul, and spirit to his people; when the claims of wife and children were as nought compared with them—a day when a sense of separation and divided sympathy seemed to creep over the wife's oppressed sensibility, as she sat in the great square pew in the old city church, with her children beside her, trying to drag her weary thoughts to the level of a meagre devotion.

'Be ye not unequally yoked together.' Why did those words of the apostolic injunction haunt her at times, as her eye wandered over the monumental tablets on the opposite wall? Was it her fault that she could not raise herself to her husband's standard? was it not rather her misfortune that he had hung the millstone of her frailty about his neck? He had married her knowing of these difficulties in her nature, but hoping that mere contact with his earnestness would ennoble her. Could she love him, and yet not tread in his footsteps? How could he know that she would grow to regard his work as her rival—that she was hardening her heart and becoming stiff-necked in her secret opposition? Alas! poor Janet—so loving yet so rebellious,—she was no Santa Maura to bid her husband preach from the cross!

And yet Janet thought herself a religious woman; she was strict in her observances; she could talk fluently on doctrinal points, and had a strong but sad leaning towards Calvinism.

Her religion was cold and severe. Maurice once told her half jestingly 'that she would have made an excellent Pharisee.' She was punctilious in her attendance at the week-day services; she ruled her household rigidly in the matter of Sunday observance—even Bee had her Sunday books and sacred puzzles. Her husband would protest at times against such Puritanical usages, but in such matters Janet would have her way, and he would shake his head at her and yield the point. 'Do not be too hard on them,' he would say sometimes; 'above all, let the children love Sunday;' and in his leisure moments he would gather them round him, and tell them some enchanting story or allegory—stories in which some hidden truth would be so cunningly wrapped and disguised that they digested it unconsciously.

Janet often wondered why her children were so listless and tiresome over their Sunday lessons; they would stumble over their Catechism and sacred history in a heavy uninterested fashion. 'I wish all the kings of Israel had been killed by Herod,' Rosie once said in an aggravated whisper to Hatty. 'I tie knots in my handkerchief—one for Joash and one for Jehoiakim, but I never can remember who comes first; you might as well remember the animals in the ark.'

'I cannot think what I have done that I should be punished with such stupid children,' Janet said once in an aggrieved voice to Mary.

'Hush! they are not stupid; look at them now,' Mary answered, pointing to the group before them—five fair

heads all mixed up together; five pairs of blue eyes wide
open and intelligent; five earnest, happy faces. 'Oh,
father, how lovely! but how are we to cast our shadows?'
asked Hatty—for he had been repeating to them Adams's
beautiful allegory of *The Shadow of the Cross.*

'Stupid Hatty!' cried Bee, cuddling her father's boot;
'you shan't have no shadows; 'Oosie and me shall have
them all, and live in the great big garden.'

'Maurice, it is time for the children to go to bed,'
broke in the mother somewhat impatiently. Perhaps she
felt a little lonely and out in the cold—all those faces
turned from her to their father, all those twining arms
about and round him. Maurice looked up quickly, and
caught the shade on his wife's face.

'There now, run away, my darlings, and kiss your
mother!' he said. 'It is a long story, and we will finish
it next Sunday; and God bless my little Bee!' lifting up
the laughing child, and kissing the dimpled arms and
neck; and Janet smiled as he put her in her arms.

When Janet came down to breakfast that morning with
her grave Sunday face she found Mary in her old place, as
usual, cutting thick bread and butter for the children, and
pouring out coffee for Maurice.

'I am late; I must have over-slept myself,' she said in
a dissatisfied voice, as Mary looked up and wished her a
bright 'good-morning.' 'Good-morning! when it is
drizzling and wet,' looking out at the courtyard and blank
wall with a shiver. 'I suppose you will go to church
with us, Aunt Mary, and miss the Sunday school this
morning?'

'Miss the Sunday school?' returned Mary in a tone of
surprise; could Janet really think she would shirk her
duties in that fashion? Janet looked still more dissatisfied
as Mary turned from the table and tied on her bonnet.

'You have made a miserable breakfast, and have eaten
nothing,' she went on complainingly.

'Never mind, I will make up for it at dinner-time,'
returned her sister cheerfully. 'Now, Maurice, if you are
ready we will go.'

Mary taught her class, and then sat among her children in the gallery; her prayers were said to an accompaniment of hobnailed boots kicking against the floor; ducking heads and whispered messages interrupted the flow of her devotion; sometimes a marble or an apple would be produced during the first lesson, and Mary and the young pale-faced teacher would have a hard time of it. The hymns, too, were occasionally marred by a dissentient voice chiming in a different key or tune. Mary once detected a popular street melody that was being whistled by a rosy-cheeked urchin.

'That is not the tune, Tommy,' remonstrated Mary in a whisper.

'Laws, teacher, ain't it now? and sich a bootiful tune — quite 'eavenly - like — downright stunnin',' returned Tommy in an unabashed voice. It was Tommy who was the Mohawk of the class, and whose marble once rolled over the gallery right on the verger's bald head.

'I 'it 'im! wasn't that a queer start? Didn't I do it furst-rate, and no mistake?' cried Tommy, as he was led in awful custody down the gallery stairs. 'My, supposin' I had made an 'ole in his 'ead.'

'You will live to be hanged, Master Tommy,' returned the pale-faced young teacher, who was slightly irascible— he was an excellent young man, but a little narrow and dogmatic in his views. Tommy thought nothing of the sound cuffs administered outside the hallowed precincts; he had much harder blows than that every day of his life, when his mother failed to sell her watercresses.

'He can't 'it a cove, not him!' Tommy observed contemptuously to a shoeblack who was watching the proceeding; 'butter fingers, and no mistake! Why, you should just see the old 'ooman lay to; she stings rather— oh laws!' and Tommy stuck his hands in his ragged pockets, and marched off whistling to enjoy a free fight between a tipsy sailor and his mate.

Poor Mary! she was not allowed much peace that morning. During the sermon most of the younger children fell asleep and dropped off their forms; some were picked up and shaken by the pale-faced teacher; others were propping their heavy heads against Mary. The vicar went droning on, excellent man, with his secondly and thirdly, and his slow summing-up of practical points. Janet sat erect, with her little girls in a row beside her; when the service ended, it may be doubted whether she or Mary were the more tired.

But there was no rest for either of them yet. While Janet and her children plodded through the kings of Israel, and turned the sweet Sunday hours into a long weariness, Mary and her brother went out again through the wet drizzling streets. Maurice had his baptisms and his catechising and his children's service, and Mary spent her afternoon in a great underground room, in a building that was used for all sorts of miscellaneous purposes. Mr. Denoon and Maurice had organised a workman's club and a young man's institute; there was a lending library and a course of evening lectures; and in the basement story Janet spent purgatorial hours over her mothers' meetings.

On Sunday afternoons about twenty or thirty boys and youths belonging to the night-school were wont to congregate. This was Mary's special work, and one that yielded her entire satisfaction; it was singular to see the influence she possessed over these raw lads; there was not one of 'our boys,' as she called them, who would not have pulled off his old coat and fought a dozen rounds in defence of 'teacher.' One new recruit had already been soundly thrashed because he was caught mimicking Mary's way of putting up her eyeglasses. 'A low cadgerin' cove, to take off teacher's specs,' was the remark, as Mary's champion dealt the last facer that brought his antagonist to the ground.

They were a rough ragged crew, these lads who gathered Sunday after Sunday in the great underground room with its brick floor and wide cheerful fireplace. When the class was over a plain plentiful meal was set out on the long tables; the pale-faced young teacher, who was a tailor by trade, and a Timothy in name and heart, dropped in to help Mary in her arduous task of cutting

great hunches of bread and butter.   An old widow who
turned a mangle in the next court boiled the water for
their tea.   At the last moment Maurice would look in to
say grace and give a few cheery words to the lads.

Poor fellows! this weekly meal was a new experience
in their hard poverty-stricken lives.   Some of them were
costermongers; two or three had no settled home, and
were mere waifs and strays picking up a livelihood down
by the river-side; the others lived in the foul reeking
courts and alleys with which the place abounded.   The
space, the warmth, the good plentiful food, and the
beaming face of their teacher gave to these poor fellows
their first idea of a home.   An eccentric old sugar-baker
was the benevolent provider of the weekly feast.   ' Laws,
we do have our tea sweet and 'ot, and no mistake; and as
much bread and butter as we can stow away,' cried one
poor lad, whose usual lodging was an archway in the
neighbourhood of Farringdon Market.   ' When' one is
warm and comfortable the hymns don't matter so much;
one can holler them pretty freely.'

To Mary this was a sacrament of love; no hour in the
seven days was so sweet to her as when she stood among
her 'boys,' dealing out the food to them with her own
hands.   As the clock struck six her labours were ended.
Sometimes, but not always, she would go to evening
service to hear Maurice preach; at other times, when she
was tired, or when Janet wanted to be set free, she would
go quietly home and spend the evening with the children.

How they loved these evenings with Aunt Mary.   The
'Sunday populars,' as Maurice once called them, were
valued almost as highly as the 'Hospital Saturdays'; then
it was that they sat round the fire in the winter, or at the
open window in the summer, and sang their favourite hymns
one after another.

Bee would lie with her head on Mary's shoulder, crooning an accompaniment in her baby fashion.   When they
had finished she would imperiously demand her favourite
'mammie's 'omes,' as she called it; nothing else satisfied
her; it was Bee's lullaby, but she liked it best when her

mother sang it. 'Mammie, 'oo has a lovely voice,' she would say, when Janet had sung through the oft-repeated melody in her low vibrating tones; ''oo shall be a dead angel too one day, and have a great big harp all to yourself.'

But to-night Mary was tired, so she went down to the church and sat alone in the great square pew; and the quiet service refreshed and strengthened her, and then she and Maurice walked home silently together.

Janet received them with rather a cloudy aspect; the day had been a trying one to her, and she felt jarred and out of tune, and there was Maurice coming in with his tired face, and the exhausted, spent look his wife knew so well.

He threw himself down on his easy-chair and put his arms behind his head, a favourite position of his. Janet brought him some wine without speaking, and put back the damp hair from his forehead; she knew nothing soothed him so much. She never found fault with him, however much he tried her; but to Mary she was somewhat given to speak sharply; her first words were in the old dissatisfied tone.

'The children were so disappointed that you went to church, Mary; poor things, they had counted on your spending your first evening at home.'

'I am very sorry,' replied Mary in her gentle way; but she said no more, she could not well tell Janet that she was in too sore a mood to enjoy the children's innocent voices. The day had been a weary one to her, and she felt tired and overstrained; how could Janet or any one know of the dull pain that was now her companion night and day?

Maurice raised himself lazily to look at her; a half-amused, half-proud look twinkled in his eyes.

'Think of our heiress sitting in the gallery amongst all the dirty boys and girls of Whitechapel,—a disguised princess among shoeblacks! Did you feel very odd, Aunt Mary?'

'I felt much as usual,' she returned calmly. 'Oh, by the bye, Maurice, since you have begun on this subject, I will tell you what has come into my head. Wednesday is your leisure day; so Janet and you and I must go down to Crome.'

'Oh, indeed!' observed her brother, closing his eyes in a provoking fashion.

'When a thing has to be done it is no use putting it off,' she went on in the same matter-of-fact tone, as though she were repeating a lesson she had learned by heart. 'I must see the house and speak to Mrs. Pratt. I suppose you could leave the children for one night, Janet. Lettice and Biddy would look after them. That would give us time to look all over the place, and we could go down to the Rectory and speak to Mr. Champneys.'

That made Maurice open his eyes.

'Why, what do you know about Mr. Champneys?' he asked in unfeigned surprise. Mary and Janet exchanged looks; they had been over this ground before. Janet left off manipulating her husband's hair; her fingers were not quite steady. But nothing could be more unconcerned than Mary's manner.

'Oh, Mr. Champneys is the old rector of Crome, whose wife is in such bad health that they will be obliged to go to the south for a year or two. Mrs. Reid told me all about them. He wants a curate in charge, Maurice—a hardworking conscientious man—and I think you will just suit him.'

Mary was looking into the fire, so she missed the flash of Maurice's eyes that answered her; but Janet saw it, and trembled.

'And who told you that I should be willing to resign my work here?' he said in a voice that to his wife was almost awful in its strong indignation. For once she forgot her usual tact and threw herself foolishly into the breach.

'Oh, do not speak to her in that way, Maurice,' she said, taking Mary's defence upon herself; 'you do not know how good she is, and how she is thinking of us all. If you will not spare yourself, if you will go on killing yourself by living in this horrible place, at least be persuaded to leave it for the sake of your children.'

Maurice was tired and irritated, and the appeal angered

him. 'Always the same old story!' and he spoke with a
sort of passion in his voice. 'Why do you always tempt
me, Janet, just when I am weakest? The children—always
the children!'

'But are they not your first duty?' she replied, almost
weeping, but still holding to her point. Why was Mary so
silent? Had she nothing to say?

'No; they are not my first duty!' he almost shouted
at her; for he was a man of strong passions, though he
generally kept them in check. 'Should I have married if
I had thought that? if I had believed that my wife and
children were to be stumbling-blocks and hindrances in my
way?'

'Listen to him, Mary!' exclaimed his wife bitterly.
'He repudiates us; he tells me that I, his wife, and his
innocent children are as nothing to him.'

But he interrupted her reproaches and silenced her by a
look. 'No, I did not tell you that, Janet. Why do you
say such things and grieve me to the heart? You are
wrong—all wrong. My children's welfare is the dearest
thing to me on earth. But have I not other children? am
I not bound to my people by a tie as holy and as binding
as my marriage vows? Why should I divorce myself from
them though the one woman whom I love bids me do it?
Must we do evil that good may come, Janet?'

A storm of conflicting feelings passed over Janet's face;
anger at this opposition to her will, despair at his blindness,
passionate love for the man whose will overpowered and
bore down hers, veneration for the moral strength that
remained unshaken by her arguments.

'Mary, speak to him!' she implored. 'I can say no
more. You hear how he turns upon me,—how he treats
my anxiety for him and the children as an unholy thing
that must be trodden under foot. Maurice, you shall not
tell me that again, that I tempt you; I will never open my
lips if the children be dying one by one round us.'

'Janet, my darling——' But she turned away from
his offered hand for the first time since their marriage, and
left the room.

Maurice looked at his sister with a face of dismay.   She had never acted like this before—never.   Had he gone too far ?   Had his sternness broken her heart ?   Was she not, with all her faults, the truest, the tenderest of wives ?

'Go to her,' whispered Mary; 'no one but you can comfort her.   To-morrow, when we are quiet, we will speak of this again.'

CHAPTER XXVI

'So, Mary, this is what you and Janet have been plotting against my peace?'

The quiet time when they should be alone together had come the very next day. The brother and sister had set out together on one of their interminable rounds, and their business had brought them beyond the confines of the parish.

Now in the heart of the city—that great palpitating busy heart—there lies a certain quiet nook, gray with age, and silent with repose.

One turns into it suddenly, from the roar and the pressure of the great moving crowd of men and vehicles. The surging mass of human faces ceases. Here there is silence, a perpetual hush, a stillness, where one can speak and be heard, where the eye can rest on a narrow strip of sky, on gray old buildings, on the flagged pathway. And here Maurice and his sister had paced up and down for the last half hour. The few passers-by took scanty note of them; perhaps from their bent heads and earnest faces they may have judged them to be lovers. Lovers! what an incongruous idea to a business man in the full light of the day!

Mary had been talking and Maurice had listened. He had said nothing to her of the terrible night he had passed, of Janet's wild weeping when he had gone up on his ministry of comfort, of the long sorrowful talk they had had together—all this had been sacred to Janet's husband.

'Tell me all that oppresses your poor heart,' he had said to her; but even as he spoke the current of her words seemed to suddenly freeze up within her. The time had gone by when she could tell him all. Henceforth there must be one subject untouched between them—a secret gnawing of remorse for a woman's pain that was beginning already to make itself felt.

Ere long there was silence between them; but while Janet slept Maurice lay open-eyed in the darkness thinking over her words. Was he wrong after all? self-willed? stubborn in his notions of what was his duty? Could it be that these two women were right? Was the time come when his Master should call him to work in a less crowded corner of the vineyard? Had he been unfaithful to his charge that he should be banished to feed 'those few sheep in the wilderness'?

What if they were right and his strength was failing, absolutely failing? and then, for he was singularly self-forgetful and careless in such things, he took himself in hand, and questioned himself, as though he were his own patient.

His voice had been weaker lately; more than once Mr. Denoon had spoken to him and urged him to spare himself and rest a little; and the churchwarden, who sat in a pew at the back of the church, had remarked that 'he thought he was getting hard of hearing, as he had not heard half of Mr. St. John's sermon!' If he were to lose his voice, would not all his hopes of usefulness be marred?

Then there was his cough; he had not shaken it off as he had last winter; it clung to him, and seemed to undermine his strength. He was aware too, now he came to think of it, that he had hours of lassitude that were very hard to bear; certain feelings of exhaustion and faintness of which he had not spoken to Janet; a sense of weariness in his devotions that were new to him; a growing irritability that not all his efforts could control. And then with a sort of shock he remembered that their mother had died in decline, not exactly consumption, but a slow kind of wasting that had carried her off in the prime of her young womanhood. Did Janet know that? he wondered; was it this that kept her so fretful and anxious? did she fear to lose him?

He would like to live a little longer, he thought, for her and the children's sake. In spite of his hard work, life was very sweet to him, and he had enjoyed it with a fulness of content which only such a nature as his could know. Like Mary, he had created his own heart sunshine; his own happiness had radiated round him until it had drawn others into its magic circle. No, he did not want to die yet, not unless his Master should call him; he had not worked sufficiently, he had not bound enough sheaves together, he had not gained souls enough; he had done nothing, nothing to earn his rest.

He was in the heat of the battle now—fighting a hand-to-hand conflict against sin and disease and death. He had snatched victims from the grisly enemy; now and then he had rescued some weary soul from being trodden under foot. What if he were to go apart for a little and watch beside the standards. Would such watching be inglorious? And then he almost made up his mind that he would rest a little.

And so while Mary talked in her sensible way, he had listened in silence. ' So this is what you and Janet have been plotting against my peace,' he said at last, and there was still a trace of bitterness in his voice.

She turned and looked at him with her quiet smile. With all his passionate love for his wife, his sister's influence was the greater. On most points they thought alike; they had the same interests, the same single-minded aim— to do good, to live for others, to merge all selfishness and self-seeking in their work. This was their notion of life. Maurice's motto was ' Love to God and my neighbour.' Janet said, ' My neighbour means my husband and children; beyond them there is a great world outside of which we need know nothing.'

' Well, Mary, and what does that smile mean?'

' We are not plotting against you, Maurice,' she answered

simply. 'We are thinking with you; putting ourselves in your place; trying to feel as a clergyman's wife and sister ought to feel.'

'And what is the result of your thoughts?'

'It is contained in two well-known proverbs, "Prevention is better than cure," and "Half a loaf is better than no bread."'

'Which means, I suppose, that if I do not leave my work, my work will leave me?'

'Exactly so; we must not over-drive the willing horse. Maurice, you have no idea of the pace you have been going lately. It is my belief that you are so worn out that if we took you out of the traces too suddenly, you would collapse utterly. Seriously, you have been working too much; the oil is spent in your lamp; you are drawing on your strength too heavily.'

'And you think my next bill of health will be dishonoured?' in a half-joking voice.

'We seem talking in metaphors, but what I mean and what Janet means is this: you have overtaxed your strength; if you do not believe us now, you will soon be convinced by your own feelings. You are no longer fit for this large parish; you want less work, less responsibility.'

'I am to fill a sinecure's place in my prime; I am to go and rust in a country village, and preach to a few clodhoppers!'

'Maurice, Maurice!' for his tone was very bitter. 'It is not like you to say such things. Are there no souls in the country? Will you measure your work by quantity? Are you sure—do not be angry with me for suggesting such a thought to one so good and wise, so immeasurably my superior—are you sure that there is no self-pleasing, no love of excitement in this?'

He stopped in the middle of his walk, and looked her full in the face. 'You have me there, Mary; that is what my conscience told me all last night. Who taught you these things? what gave you so deep an insight into human nature?

'We are all miserable sinners,' he went on, 'the very best of us. Here I am priding myself on my purity of aim—quite sure of the integrity of my motive—and all at once there is an arrow launched between the joints of the armour—"a certain man at a venture;" eh, Mary? and there I am wounded, stricken in conscience, knowing that I love my work and my own will above everything; and humiliated by the very notion of physical weakness.'

'It is very hard,' she assented, hardly knowing how to answer this outburst.

'Yes, it is hard,' he repeated, mistaking her meaning; 'but it is right. I see it now; it shall be done. Mary, shall you mind going home alone? I want to go into the church for a little;' and she understood, and left him.

He came in by and by, and went straight into his study. His wife took him some tea, and he thanked her, but did not invite her to linger. Now and then he had these moods, when some care was heavy on him; he would sit with his hand pressed on his forehead, and would neither speak nor hear what was said round him. At such times Janet would move about with a certain awe, watching him with tender, reverential eyes from a distance, but not daring to approach him. 'What is it, Mary?' she whispered, as she carried away his empty teacup.

Mary shook her head. 'You had better wait until he tells you himself; he is thinking over what I said last night, and it all troubles him;' and Janet restrained her curiosity, and took up her work in silence.

It was a dull evening. The children had gone to bed, and the two women sat alone together. Janet had her mending basket beside her, but Mary made no pretence of working. She sat in a low chair, with Dollie's letter in her lap, and her eyes fixed on the fire. The past and the future seemed mixed up together in the glowing coal pictures, beyond all efforts to disentangle them.

When the door opened, they both started. Maurice came in shading his eyes from the light; then he stood behind his wife's chair, and took up an unfinished garment.

'You are always at work, Martha,' he said; for in his playful moods he would tease her by calling her Martha. His tone made his wife's heart beat.

'You would not like me to be idle?' she responded cheerfully. 'I am clever at making old clothes look like new. Look at this frock of May's; it was torn almost to shreds, and see how neatly I have mended it.'

'Yes, I see,' he answered absently. 'Do you not wish you had been a mother in Israel, Janet, during the forty years' wandering, when there was nothing old or worn out? Well, wife, put by those things for a moment and listen to me. I have spoken to Mr. Denoon.'

'Maurice!'

'Do not interrupt me just for a moment. I met him after you left me, Mary, and he walked with me a little. I told him that I was afraid that two very wise women belonging to me were right, and that I was not as strong as I ought to be; and then I asked his opinion.'

'Well?'

'I was surprised to find that it coincided with yours. It seems that he has been uneasy for a long time,—he feared that I was doing too much, and losing my voice. "Though it will break my heart to lose you, St. John," he said very kindly, "and I never expect to replace you, I must own I think your wife is right. Go into the country and vegetate a little; in a few months you will be twice the man you are now." Those were his very words.'

'And you will go to Crome?' asked Janet breathlessly.

'Yes, if Mr. Champneys will have me; it is not such a bad place for a country cure of souls. I shall not be quite buried alive, shall I?—why, my darling, what does this mean?' as Janet leaned against him, and covered her face with her hands to hide the starting tears.

'Only that I am so glad—so thankful,' she whispered. 'Mary, thank him for both of us; tell him what a burden —an almost unendurable burden—he has lifted off me. Oh, Maurice, how can I ever tell you how grateful I am to you for this?'

'Nonsense!' he said, bending down to kiss her; but

18

his eyes glistened in sympathy; 'what a fuss over a worn-out curate! Take your triumph mildly, Janet, for I am beaten and humiliated enough;' and then he took the seat beside her, and laid his hand on hers. Never had he so much needed the comfort of her presence as he did now that his heart was so sore and downcast within him. 'Now you will be happier and more satisfied, will you not, my dear?' he said after a pause; 'and you, Mary?'

'Oh, I am so glad,' she answered quickly. 'Think how lonely I should have been—you and Janet and the children here, and I in that great house miles away.'

'And now we shall be all together,' observed her sister-in-law joyfully.

'Yes; the Park and the Rectory are not a quarter of a mile apart—at least so Mrs. Reid told me. You see, Maurice, the will enjoins nine months' residence in the year, so we should have been utterly separated.'

'And now we shall be near enough to quarrel every day,' he returned, trying to joke. 'We shall have to be very careful not to offend the lady up at the great house, Janet. Do you mean to find fault with my sermons, and patronise the poor curate-in-charge by asking him to dinner on high days and holidays?'

She passed that over with a smile.

'We shall be together just as we are here,' she replied simply. 'I shall come down to the schools, and Janet will have her mothers' meeting and blanket and coal club; and we will set on foot a lending library, and winter evening lectures—all the things you have started here; and it shall not be our fault if Crome be not a model village.'

Maurice gave her an approving glance, though he sighed furtively; but Janet interposed with a touch of reproof in her voice.

'But, Mary, you must not spend all your time as you do here. The circumstances will be very different; society will have its claims on you; you will have to take up your position in the county.'

'I am afraid society will have to do without me, then,' she returned quietly; but there was a certain inflection in her tone that warned Janet that she was touching on dangerous ground. Mary, with all her softness, shared her brother's inflexibility of purpose.

'And when do you intend to go into residence, my Lady Bountiful?' asked her brother playfully.

'Not for three weeks or a month;' she answered him quite calmly, as though she had long ago made up her mind. She had thought it all out during those quiet days at the chateau, when she had sat amongst them—not speaking, but weighing all her future life and its responsibilities. 'I have so much to do here,' she went on, 'and you must help me, Maurice. I want my boys to have a treat; we must take them to the Crystal Palace, you and I, and show them a glimpse of fairy-land. Then the ragged schools and the night schools must have a tea and supper; and Janet's mothers too, and every child must be made happy. And there must be gifts of clothes and toys——'

'And a general jubilee and rejoicing in Whitechapel,' added Maurice; but how proudly and tenderly his eyes rested on Mary! Was not this a sister for whom to thank God? Could any man wish for a dearer and better? Janet caught the look, and a vague discomfort and uneasiness stole over her. It was not that she was jealous of Mary,—strange to say, she never had been jealous of her; but a sense of her own inferiority jarred on her. They seemed to breathe habitually a purer atmosphere than hers —to move in a region where she could not follow them.

She was again behind—left out in the cold; and yet the pressure of her husband's hand lay warm within hers.

'And in a month we are to lose our sister from under our roof,' observed Maurice regretfully.

'Yes, and she will be so lonely without us,' added his wife.

'That cannot be helped,' returned Mary cheerfully; 'busy people are never long dull, and I daresay you will spare Lettice to me. One of the other children might come to me by turns; the country air will do them good, and you will have less to look after, Janet;' and Janet assented gratefully.

'You think of everything and everybody, Aunt Mary,' she said; for she was touched by Mary's love for her children; and then a little remorse seized her,—she had robbed Mary of her happiness, and yet she was already heaping coals of fire on her head.

The next day Mary had an unexpected trial to encounter: Grey Lyndhurst called.

He had hesitated for a day or two—not knowing how far his visit would be welcome to Mr. St. John and his wife. But they were old friends, and he had received many kindnesses at their hand, and he was unwilling to give them up. The meeting between himself and Mary would be full of awkwardness,—all the more that there was a strong bond of friendship between them; they had a mutual respect and admiration for each other. Latterly, her feeling of kindness for him had increased, and she had grown to regard him in a sisterly fashion.

Mary was alone when he called, for Janet was at her mothers' meeting. She was sitting by the fire trying to fix her attention on a book when Grey was announced.

He did not look at her as they shook hands, but he noticed that a moment afterwards she had drawn her chair back into the shadow, so that he could not see her face; and when the fire leapt into a blaze, she took up a little screen and held it up between her and the flame.

It could not be denied that both were very nervous. Grey talked about their journey; asked after Mrs. St. John, and expressed regret at her absence; made a few commonplace remarks on the weather, the state of the roads; and then took up the book Mary was reading. Mary answered him quietly, but her voice was not as clear as usual; a certain mannerism, a turn of the head—something inexplicable and undefinable reminded her of Bertie. She had never before noticed a likeness between the two; a great yearning to ask after him, to hear only his name mentioned, came over her. Would it be wrong? would not the omission of any such inquiry be strange?

Mary was wonderfully simple and child-like in her nature. She had so little self-consciousness that she seldom paused

to ask herself how things would look to others. Janet
might be shocked perhaps; but then her sense of propriety
was always taking alarm.

And so her next words startled Grey, making him drop
the book he held in sudden confusion.

'How is your brother?' she asked very quietly; 'how
is Bertie?' And there was absolutely no faltering in her
tone; it was Grey who got red and hot all over.

'Bertie!' he stammered; for he quite lost his presence
of mind. 'Oh, he is not very well.'

'Not well!' and now the hand that held the screen
shook a little. Bertie the strong, the vigorous, not well?

'Oh, it is nothing particular,' returned Grey hastily, feeling he had made a slip. 'He was out of sorts, slept badly
when he was with me, and seemed a little down about
things in general. One could not expect otherwise. You
must give him time, you know, to get over things a little,'
went on Grey incoherently, utterly out of his depth and
floundering in deeper water still.

Mary ignored the latter part of his speech as though
she had not heard it; and yet every word Grey spoke
seemed burned into her brain. 'Out of sorts, sleeping
badly, down about things in general. Oh, Bertie, Bertie!'
But she did not show her pain.

'Is he with you still?' she asked quite calmly.

'Oh no,' Grey answered; 'he left yesterday for Stoneyhurst. Sir Charles telegraphed for him. Ralph is ill
again; there is some talk of their going abroad in the
summer—to Davos or the Engadine.'

'Oh, that will do him good; it will do Ralph all the
good in the world.' But Grey was quite aware that she
had not meant Ralph.

Then she changed the subject, but not too abruptly, and
began speaking of Dollie and her mother, and how she
hoped that they would come to her at Crome when the
days got longer and the spring flowers were out. And how
it happened Grey never knew, but as they talked and the
twilight deepened he found himself telling Mary all about
it—how he had grown to love her friend, and how inexor-

able Dollie had been ; and a great deal that he had never
thought to tell man or woman, but which seemed drawn
from him by the sympathetic chord in Mary's voice.

Mary did not hide from him how moved and interested
she was by his confidence.   She put down her screen and
let him see her face now : her eyes were sad, but full of
kindness.

'Thank you for telling me this,' she said, when he had
finished.   'Dear Dollie ! how could you help loving her
when she is so sweet and innocent?   Now you must go on
telling me about things, Grey, just as though I were your
very own sister.'   And then her poor lips trembled a
moment, for had she not hoped to be his sister?   'And
when they come to Crome you must come too and do it
all over again, and I will help you, and we will all help
you.   Hush ! there is Janet, and we cannot talk any more.'
And as the young man looked gratefully at her, she held
out her kind hand to him in silence, and then moved to
welcome her sister-in-law.

CHAPTER XXVII

CROME PARK

It was in the glimmering dusk of a wintry afternoon in December that Mary first saw her new home.

After a slight hesitation Mr. St. John had acceded to her plan. The children were left with many injunctions under Biddy's charge. Both he and his wife looked round many times to catch the last glimpse of the five heads clustered at the window of 'father's study.' Lettice had been made happy by an extra kiss and a few parting words from her mother. 'Remember, I trust you, Lettice; be a good child and take care of your sisters for me.'

It was still early when they alighted at the little country station. An old-fashioned barouche with a pair of fine bay horses was waiting for them. As Janet threw herself back on the cushions she looked somewhat disparagingly at the somewhat faded linings.

'You will find things rather out of repair,' she said, addressing Mary. 'I noticed when I was here before that the carriages wanted doing up. You see it is so long since Mrs. Reid lived at Crome. Some of the furniture is shabby too. You will have plenty of work cut out for you during the first few months.'

'I daresay,' returned the young heiress listlessly. Janet's remarks were a little trying. What did she care just now if the cushions were faded? She was looking out at the long country road, at the fields and hedges. The hedgerows were black and bare; a keen wind blew in at the open window, making Maurice shiver. His sister did not notice

it ; her eyes were fixed on the somewhat cloudy sky. A
faint mist rose from the fields ; the whole landscape looked
chill and inhospitable.

'It is very pretty here in summer,' observed Maurice,
replying to her unspoken thought ; but she did not answer
him or turn her head. Just then they had come to a little
white lodge, very unpretentious-looking, and not at all
ornamental. The gate was opened by a very old woman
in a poke bonnet. A broad winding carriage-road led
through the Park, which was not large or particularly well-
wooded, and where a few sheep were feeding ; and then,
almost suddenly, as it seemed to Mary, there seemed to
rise out of the ground a long and somewhat low red-brick
Elizabethan house, with the firelight playing on the antique
windows, and through the open door a vista of a large hall
with heavy marble columns, which brought back to her
mind a vivid remembrance of Mrs. Reid's dream.

That confused her, and for a moment she forgot her
rôle; but as with her wonted humility she drew back to let
Janet precede her, Maurice quietly put his wife aside and
held out his hand to Mary.

'Welcome to your new home, my dear,' he said, in a
voice loud enough for the servants to hear. 'Mrs. Pratt,
this is your mistress, Miss St. John. My wife, I think, you
know already.'

Mrs. Pratt curtsied, and then looked a little critically at
the young lady who shook hands with her so pleasantly.
But there was something in Mary's face that, despite its
want of beauty, always prepossessed strangers in her favour
—a frankness of look and smile that won them at once.

'Oh, she is not to be compared to Mrs. St. John for
handsomeness ; she is a real beauty and no mistake, and
carries herself like a duchess,' observed Mrs. Pratt afterwards
to her husband, who had performed the function of butler
in the old time, and who, with her niece Rhoda, made up
the present establishment. 'But I tell you what, Pratt,
our young lady is good if she is not bonnie.'

'Oh, aunt,' interrupted Rhoda, 'I think she is good
and bonnie too ; she has such a sweet smile when she

speaks. The other one is handsome, but she is terribly
sharp, and looks all round her at once, as though she were
given to pick things to pieces before putting them straight'
—which speech showed that Mistress Rhoda was tolerably
shrewd in her observation.

When Maurice had made his little speech, Mary had
shaken hands with the old servants, and had said a few
appropriate words; but though she smiled and looked
pleasant, the dream-like feeling was heavy on her. She
almost thought she must pinch herself to be sure she was
awake.

'It will soon be dark; let Mrs. Pratt show you the
principal rooms,' observed Janet, thrusting herself forward,
for she never liked to linger long in the background. She
thought Mary was a little too familiar with the Pratts, and
was not carrying herself with sufficient dignity—why, she
had actually shaken hands with Rhoda, the rosy-cheeked
niece! They formed into a little cavalcade after that, Mrs.
Pratt leading, Maurice and his sister following, and Janet
and the others bringing up the rear.

Mrs. Pratt made a few concise observations on everything. 'The largest room in the county, used as a sort of
picture gallery of the Talbot family,' she said, as she threw
open the door of the great drawing-room hung round with
portraits of dead and gone Talbots, from whom Crome had
been purchased. The firelight played on the soft blue
damask couches, and on the dark oil paintings. After a
cursory glance at its splendour they went through the
dining-room with its large anteroom, and the billiard-room,
and the gun-room, and a large bay-windowed apartment
that was fitted up like a library, and lastly into the morning-
room, the pleasantest apartment in the house, with its
two windows looking out on different views of the park,
with easy-chairs and couches covered with old-fashioned
chintz, sprawling carnations, and vivid green leaves, a
terrible eyesore to Janet, whose taste in such matters was
perfect, but to Mary there was something warm and rich in
tone, that harmonised with the quaint windows and old tiled
fireplace.

But what impressed her most was the strange perspective seen from the house. The windows—some of them mullioned or with small lozenge panes, while others were more modern—reached nearly to the ground, with low broad window-sills ; the park stretched to the back of the house—nothing from this side broke the greenness. As one walked up the hall and through the anteroom, one was conscious of a curious effect and trick of perspective. A hillside seemed to lie outside the windows ; the green wave seemed to spread upward ; one's feet would climb it presently ; but as the window was approached the fancy vanished. There was a pleasant clipped lawn, with pheasants on it ; a few palisades divided it from the park proper ; there were trees planted well away from the house, hiding the stable and farm building ; through a little gate there was a small sunny flower-garden, with an arbour and a long walk and a sun-dial ; a peacock and his mate usually strutted along the path, which was known as the 'peacock's promenade.'

The sun-dial was green and mossy with age, and on it was faintly and almost illegibly traced, ' I watch the hand of Time.' When Mary paid her first visit the next morning, she found the peacock perched on it, spreading the glories of his tail in the wintry sunshine. The quaintness of the place, its quietness, and the warm tone of the high red-brick wall, with its southern aspect, where peaches ripened, and underneath which blossomed hundreds of roses in summer time—all delighted her.

Later on it became her favourite resort. Here, on summer evenings, she would pace, book in hand, with Topaz and Sapphire strutting behind her ; on wet days she would betake herself to the arbour, with her faithful attendants still beside her, and her great black collie at her feet, listening to the patter and trickle of leaves, and watching the thirsty vegetation drinking up and bathing in the warm summer shower, and then hanging out myriads of green fingers to dry in the sunshine.

' We have got ready the mistress's old room for Miss St. John,' observed Mrs. Pratt, as they hastily concluded their survey of the lower rooms. Mary felt as though she were to be shut out of the outer world as she entered the apartment allotted to her. A little side staircase led to it; there was a narrow passage, with a small room where all the alarm bells hung; then a large anteroom, bare-looking and almost devoid of furniture, but with a grand view of the park and the lodge; this led to a still larger one, where the great crimson canopied bed seemed almost lost, where the big wardrobe, large enough to conceal a dozen people, seemed a mere speck against the wall—a vast room so dimly lighted by the blazing fire and half a dozen candles that shadows seemed to lurk everywhere.

Janet lingered behind the others with a trace of anxiety in her face.

'You need not keep this room, Mary; not beyond this one night, I mean. There are others smaller and far pleasanter, though I must own,' with a laugh, 'they are most of them as big as barracks. This is so lonely, with the great anteroom and belfry,—unless, indeed, you fit up the outer room for your maid.'

'I do not mean to have a maid,' returned Mary, with an amused twitch of her mouth at the idea, as she took off her hat and warm jacket, and thoughtfully contemplated herself in the long pier glass.

'I do not think Mrs. Pratt was much impressed with her new mistress. I do not look much like an heiress, do I, Janet? You would suit the character far better. Why, what a plump homely sort of body I look beside you!' linking her arm in Mrs. St. John's, and drawing her in front of the glass. But Janet had no personal vanity, and she scarcely deigned a glance at herself; she only cared for her beauty because Maurice admired it.

'You always look very nice, Mary,' she returned in a perfectly matter-of-fact way; 'heiresses need not be handsome. If you would only be a little more dignified, dear, and hold your own ground with these people. Mrs. Pratt is inclined to be familiar—most old servants are; and you need not have shaken hands with that girl. But by and by you will know these things better,' checking herself as she remembered Mary must not be snubbed now. 'And about this room, there is not the slightest occasion for you to sleep here after this one night, if you take a fancy to one of the others.'

'Thank you, but I think it will suit me on the whole,' returned Mary a little gravely, for this lecture was not particularly palatable. 'It wants a little more furniture, which I daresay we shall find in some of the other rooms. A round table to remind me of my old room in Lime Street —dear old room!'—and she sighed—'and an easy-chair instead of that stiff-looking one, and a couch for lazy times; and I must do away with that tremendous erection,' pointing to the tent-like canopy. 'I rather like the size and vast emptiness; it gives one room to breathe; and the anteroom will make a splendid hospital,' she continued, quite ignoring her sister-in-law's horrified face.

'Hospital, Mary!'

'Well, workshop, then; the rubbish corner where Jack-of-all-trades and his satellites may be busy to their hearts' content. Now I think of it,' went on Mary, rubbing her plump white hands with a mischievous enjoyment, for she dearly loved to plague Janet, and throw word pellets at her as she stood on her moral pedestal environed by proprieties, 'now I think of it, we will have our "Hospital Saturdays" here. Dr. Mary and her dressers will still volunteer surgical aid to the sick and wounded dolls of the East End of London;' and then Mary laughed, but her eyes were a little wet, for what had become of the light heart that accompanied the busy fingers? But Janet merely stared at her, too aghast for words. Was it thus that the young mistress of Crome would take her place in the county?

'I think we had better go down to Maurice,' she said a little stiffly, feeling that Mary was becoming too much for her; and yet not daring to lecture her too freely in her own house.

The morning-room looked the picture of comfort as they entered it. Preparations for 'meat tea,' a favourite meal in Lime Street, were being duly set forth. Maurice lay back in the depths of an easy-chair, gazing at the spluttering pine logs that were diffusing a shower of mimic stars. Pratt, who was placing a dish of cold game on the table, was haranguing him.

'Ay, ay, he was contrairy-like from a boy,' he was saying; 'a fine lad, a noble lad, but with a spice of devilry in him even then; and the old master was no better,' and then Mary knew they were talking of poor Walter.

'Now, Mary, we are all pretty well famished, and I am longing to try that game pie,' exclaimed her brother; and then he took her playfully by the shoulders, and inducted her into the seat behind the great silver urn, though Mary hesitated and looked dubiously at Janet.

'No, Mary, it is your home, not mine,' returned Janet, answering the look; but her voice was a little constrained; perhaps for the first time the thought crossed her mind that an injustice had been done to Maurice—he had been set aside in favour of his younger sister. If things had been rightly ordered, it would have been she, not Mary, who had been mistress of Crome.

The reflection was tormenting, and kept her silent for a while; but there was Mary, pretending to eat, but leaving her food almost untouched, and talking to Maurice as fast as her tongue would go. And she would talk of nothing else but 'Hospital Saturdays,' and what she and the children would do; and what games of Badminton they could have in the long gallery at the top of the house; and how she would have a little pony for them, that they might ride alone in the park, and a donkey for Bee—a white donkey, with long ears, and a pannier. And would Maurice speak to Jem Anderson, the dog-fancier, for she wanted a collie—a real Scotch collie—to go with her and the children in their walks?

And then, just as Janet was getting interested, she strayed off to the old subject, and began plying her brother with questions. Did Maurice think it was too far from London to have her boys down for one day?—a long summer day—just to show them what was meant by the country.

'Some of them have never seen a green field or a hedgerow in their lives, poor fellows! and they don't know

what cricket is; and their only game is chuck farthing, or
playing with an old set of greasy cards.   Think of Tommy
or Miles Stokes or Bob Scratcher let loose on the grass,
and scampering about like shaggy ponies.   And then
there are the mothers, Maurice—oh, I am always so sorry
for the mothers.   It is washing and sewing and scolding
from morning to night—work doing, and never done—
tired, ill-fed bodies and cross tongues, poor souls!   Could
not something be done for them, Maurice?   Could I not
have them down, two or three at a time, and fit up one of
the attics for them, and let them have two or three days of
quiet and good feeding, with lovely sights of green fields
and growing flowers to refresh their poor dim eyes?'   And
Mary's voice grew tremulous with inward excitement.

'Softly, softly, my Lady Bountiful,' returned her brother,
smiling, and evidently well pleased; but his wife interrupted him with a few stinging words.

'Now, Maurice, how can you listen to such nonsense?
Mary, I am surprised at you; would you bring down
disease and vice and dirt into this lovely place, to infect
your house and Maurice's new parishioners?   Do you
suppose respectable servants would put up with such specimens as Polly Tyler or Mrs. Watkins?   It would breed a
moral pestilence in the house, even if you escape actual
contagion;' and Janet tossed her head in her wrath—
never had her prejudices, her sense of what was right and
fitting, been so utterly outraged.   Mary looked a little
crestfallen; both of them turned to Maurice.

'Think of our children—of Mary and her position,'
exclaimed Janet.

'Think of our poor people, and all our means of doing
good,' put in Mary sorrowfully.

Maurice looked benevolently at his women-kind, and
then he patted his wife's hand as though she were one of
his youngest children.   'Do not fret and worry, Janet,'
was all he said to her; 'you may trust me,' and then he
turned to his sister, and a sort of luminous softness came
into his eyes.

'It was a kind thought, my dear, and spoken just like

Aunt Mary; but you remember the words of our favourite old saint, St. Francis de Sales, "make haste slowly"; think as much as you like, but let your thoughts ripen slowly, like the peaches on the south wall; unripe fruit is apt to disagree with one, unripe thoughts lead to incomplete actions.'

'Oh, Maurice!' and then she added in a forlorn voice, '"Et tu, Brute!" are you also going to damp me?'

'No, no,' he returned earnestly, 'I am going to help you by every means in my power; we will work together, Mary, if I ever come here; we will link this parish to my old one, and work for both.

'But Janet is right,' he continued, after a pause; 'you must not fill your house with all the ragged mothers in Whitechapel; we cannot interpret things literally, or "go out now in the highways and hedges, and compel them to come in"; we must spread our feast another way. I have a better idea, if your funds allow, and you are still in the same mind. Would you not like to take a little cottage somewhere, furnish it simply, and leave some trusty woman in charge—some "widow indeed," like old Mrs. Hales— and then invite your mothers, two or three at a time, and let them enjoy a week of country air; would not that plan suit?' as the disappointed look vanished from Mary's face.

'I think it a beautiful plan,' she replied gratefully. 'Maurice, you are so clever and wise, and can grasp an idea at once. I see I was wrong about bringing them here; of course Mrs. Pratt would not like it.'

'I am glad you have come to your right mind,' observed Janet curtly. If you do not mind, Maurice, I think I will go to bed, as I am rather tired from the journey.'

Janet might have said more truly that she was tired of all this talk; her mind was full of plans and ambitious projects; she wanted to talk to Mary about the house and the furniture, and her future establishment; and there was the plate chest and the jewellery to inspect the next day, and she thought they might have gone over the list together; but no, there they were, having one of the old Lime Street discussions, bringing back all the horrid

associations that she longed so vainly to shut out of her
life—Mary's boys, and the mothers, and old Mrs. Hales,
and Maurice gravely promising to unite the two parishes in
his thoughts and work.

It would be far better to retire to her luxurious room,
and sit by the fire and read or think. Maurice was quite
aware of the reasons that induced his wife to retire. He
lighted her candles, and wished her good-night a little
gravely.

'I am afraid we have tired her,' he said, with a slight
compunction, as he sat down opposite to Mary. 'Poor
dear Janet, how she loathes Whitechapel! I verily believe
the feeling is constitutional with her, and that she cannot
help it;' for his tenderness caused him to make large
allowance for her.

They sat for an hour or two discussing their plans, and
riding their mutual hobbies. As he told his wife afterwards, 'It was one of Mary's times of refreshment when
she could have her brother to herself, and talk out all her
thoughts;' but even Maurice did not know how Mary's
sympathy and reciprocity of ideas went far to reconcile
him with his wife's deficiencies. Mary could always enter
into his plans; he could never weary her. Never were
two women so unlike, and yet how dearly he loved them
both! He went up presently, and found his wife contentedly reading a novel by the fire.

'How late you are, Maurice!' she said; 'but I was too
comfortable and tired to stir.'

'Poor Janet! how we must have bored you downstairs!' he said remorsefully, as he stroked her glossy
black hair, as it swept over the back of her chair. 'What
are you reading, love? *Lorna Doone?* ah, a capital book!
I must have another peep into it some day. Now, we will
read the Psalms together, and then you must go to bed;'
and, as usual, Maurice's will was law. Janet would not
have read another page, however much she might have
longed for it.

Meanwhile the young mistress of Crome had stolen up
the little staircase and past the belfry-room, as it was called,

and the empty anteroom, and was standing before the fire, looking down into the flame.

It was the first night in her own house !

'My house, my servants, never ours—how lonely it makes one feel, just the use of that one little word,' she thought. 'If it were not for the children I should be far more desolate than I am—bless their dear little hearts! how they will rejoice in this place! I am glad I thought of the pony—that will be beyond their wildest imaginations. And how well Maurice looked this evening! he seemed in such excellent spirits, and hardly coughed at all. Thank God I have had strength given me for the sacrifice. I think I have acted rightly, and if I were only sure that he did not suffer'—but here she broke off, and then knelt down and said her prayers. She did not trust herself to think; the pain was far too fresh and vivid for that; such thoughts would only unfit her for her daily life; but it always did her good to pray for him. She would plead for her dearest friend, as she called him, with an earnestness she could not use for herself; and when she had finished, she put up her humble thanksgiving that she had been enabled to overcome her own selfishness and to live for others. And then as she thought of her beloved ones who so needed her, and of the great army of Christ's sick and poor who were outside her own life, holding out feeble hands for succour, a great wave of love and pity swept over the girl's heart. 'Inasmuch as ye did it unto them ye did it unto Me,' she repeated softly; and this was Mary St. John's last waking thought that night.

CHAPTER XXVIII

DOWN AT THE RECTORY

WHEN Maurice came downstairs the next morning Pratt informed him, with a trace of wonder in his voice, that the young mistress was out on the 'peacocks' promenade'; 'has been out ever so long, all over the place before it was light!' finished the honest butler, secretly marvelling at this strange proceeding on the part of his young lady.

'Why, it is nine now; we early folks think this quite late,' returned Mr. St. John; looking admiringly at the green perspective from the dining-room window. 'Is breakfast ready, Pratt? I will go and look for her;' and he started off briskly in direction of the garden.

He found Mary standing by the sun-dial, reading the defaced inscription. The whole scene lingered as a sort of lovely sketch in Maurice's mind ever afterwards—the long walk bathed in crisp wintry sunshine, the red southern wall, Topaz spreading his shining tail to the admiration of his humbler mate Sapphire, Mary looking quaint and homely with her red woollen shawl pinned over her head and arms, the old sun-dial with its mossy lichen-covered stones. '"I watch the hand of Time!" what a strange inscription, Maurice,' observed Mary thoughtfully, as he stood by her. 'Poor old sun-dial, I wonder how long it has been here? how many years of patient still waiting, wetted by rain, frowned on by clouds, blown upon by all the adverse winds of heaven, and only sometimes cheered by a tardy sun!'

'A true picture of a faithful life, little moralist!' returned her brother; 'an old veteran decayed and worn out, but watching still. If this sun-dial could speak, what strange stories it would tell us of some of those old Talbots! Perhaps some cavalier in Charles's time may have wooed his lady-love just here; or in that arbour yonder some fair creature in hoop and brocade and powdered hair may have listened condescendingly to her beau in plum-coloured velvet and ruffles, with a Topaz and Sapphire of an earlier generation strutting and flaunting beside them!'

'Yes, one could make up all sorts of romances,' observed Mary gravely, for she was not thinking of love stories; other thoughts had come into her head. Would she pace up and down here on summer evenings when she was an old woman, she wondered, a contented tranquil old woman, counting her peaches and gathering rose leaves for her pot-pourri? Perhaps Lettice and Hatty and their lovers would come and whisper by the sun-dial, and she would look at them smilingly; or rather Lettice's and Hatty's children, for she would not be so very old then; and when they had gone, she and the old sun-dial would be alone together! ' "I watch the hand of Time;" I could say that too,' she thought.

'Janet will be wondering what has become of us,' observed Maurice, surprised at her unusual gravity; and Mary drew her little shawl closer round her face, and accompanied him to the house.

They found Janet standing at the open window, looking as fresh and bright as the morning itself. She had some white asters pinned in her dress; she held out some to Mary.

'Think of waking up every morning in this sweet place!' she said, drawing a deep breath of intense pleasure. 'It does not feel like December at all; there is only just wind enough to ripple the grass. Does it not look like a green sea, Maurice, flowing round the house? I have been into every room, Mary, and some of the furniture is lovely; such carved oak, and some Indian cabinets! very little will be needed to make it perfect.'

'You must give me the benefit of your taste by and by,' returned Mary gently; for she loved to see Janet happy, and would not have damped her for anything. As for Maurice, he looked at his wife with delight—her eyes were as clear and limpid as a child's, the fretful chord had gone from her voice; if she were happy, it would be well for all of them, he thought; and he began to contemplate the change with a less degree of pain.

After breakfast they walked down to the Rectory. It was about a quarter of a mile from the lodge gates; the churchyard and the garden were separated only by a privet hedge; the church was built of gray stone, and had the venerable appearance of extreme age; a mantle of ivy clothed it picturesquely. Maurice was delighted with its outward aspect, but he warned Mary that the inside was less satisfactory.

'It is sadly out of repair,' he said; 'some of the wood-work is decaying, and the seats in the south aisle are worm-eaten.' And when Mary inspected it afterwards under the Rector's supervision, she owned that he was right.

There was a forlorn, neglected air about the whole building. There was some fine oak carving in the choir stalls, and one or two beautiful painted windows; but the font was broken, the high pews looked dilapidated, and the rusty velvet cushions on the altar made Maurice and his sister exchange horrified looks.

The churchyard was pretty, but choked with weeds; in the sunniest corner was the great red granite monument under which lay Isabel, the relict of Marmaduke Reid, with her husband, and their son, Walter Henderson. It was a large unornamented slab, but a beautiful Spanish chestnut stood near it, and the turf was smooth and cleanly trimmed. Mary thought it a charming nook; she planned with Maurice how they would have a border of flower-beds, with rhododendrons and flowering shrubs, and a seat under the chestnut tree, where they could come and sit some-times, and where Maurice could compose his sermons in summer time.

'They will be veritably "meditations among the tombs,"' he said playfully.

They had been received very kindly by Mr. Champneys

and his wife. Maurice and he had met before, and letters had already passed between them. While the two clergymen were closeted in the Rector's study, Mrs. Champneys took the ladies over the house, or sat chatting with them in her pleasant bow-windowed drawing-room.

The Rectory was a picturesque gabled house; the red-brick walls were almost hidden in ivy that climbed to the very chimneys; a wisteria hung over the porch; there was a slightly-sloping lawn, with a mulberry tree in the centre, and a few flower-beds. An extensive kitchen-garden, planted with a row of apple and plum trees, was shut off from the flower-garden by another privet hedge.

The Rectory was large, but in a sad state of dilapidation; the upper floor was unfurnished, and in many of the rooms the paper was hanging from the bare walls, revealing the lath and plaster. Janet shook her head over it, but Mary gave her a reassuring glance and whispered, 'You can all come to me while this is being made fit for the children,' she said; and her sister-in-law felt consoled.

'We have no children with us now, and the house is far too large for us,' observed Mrs. Champneys, wrapping her shawl more closely round her, and coughing somewhat feebly as they descended the broad old staircase. She was a thin, dark-eyed woman, with a very soft voice and manner. Life had passed somewhat sadly and monotonously with her; for years her world had been bounded to her husband's study, and to the quaint bow-windowed drawing-room, with its old-fashioned furniture and Indian screens, and great blue jars of faintly-smelling pot-pourri. The upstairs room was full of appliances for an invalid's comfort, and there was a side window in it with a view of the church and the Spanish chestnut, and just a pinky gleam between the leaves in summer time of the granite monument.

At present the trees were bare, and the slab was conspicuous enough. Janet started when she saw it. 'I am sorry this window looks out upon the churchyard,' she said, 'as otherwise it would be my favourite window.'

'It has always been mine,' returned Mrs. Champneys

mildly. 'Ah, you are young, my dear, and like a bright prospect!' looking at Janet's beautiful face with visible interest. 'In spring when the leaves are out you will see nothing but the church and the trees. I have often sat at that window on Sunday morning listening to the singing—I used to tell my husband I had been to church too.'

Both Janet and Mary took a fancy to Mrs. Champneys; but they were less favourably impressed with the Rector. He was a grave old man, with a dry, abrupt manner; very scholarly and precise, but terribly unpractical when they came to deal with him.

He had spent his life in a hermit bookworm sort of fashion, not going much among his people, but poring chiefly over old folios in his study. With a sufficient income he had yet contrived to involve his money accounts; from sheer shortsightedness and want of interest he had suffered the Rectory to fall into a state of shameful dilapidation—dangerous in so old a house: with the exception of the rooms he and his wife occupied, there was hardly a sound floor or roof in the place. Maurice whistled in a low voice to himself as he contemplated the rooms in which his little girls were to sleep.

'Mr. Champneys wants me to take the curacy at the beginning of February, and he and his wife will not move out until the very last moment; even if Mr. Denoon consent to part with me then, how are we to make that floor habitable for the children?'

But Mary only laughed at his dismayed face. 'You must all come to me,' she said; 'Janet and I have already settled that. There is so much to be done that you may be thankful if you get in by June;' and after that they all went down to look at the church.

Mr. Champneys and his future curate in charge found so much to discuss that the two women grew weary of pacing up and down the aisles; and Mary at last proposed that they should walk slowly down the road, and that Maurice should follow them.

'Do you think you will like your future home, Janet?' she asked, as they stood for a moment looking at the ivy-covered gables of the Rectory. To her surprise, Janet's eyes filled with tears.

'Oh, Mary,' she said, 'it seems almost too good to be true. Think of waking up morning after morning in that dear old room, with the sun shining on the ivy; and to open one's window and feel the sweet country air blowing over one's face; and to see the children wetting their feet in the dews; and Maurice——' but here Janet stopped as though her feelings were too much for her; but she said presently in a low voice, 'and we shall owe it all to you.'

Mary looked at her with one of her old sunny smiles—they had become rare now.

'You and I will have plenty of work putting the old place in order,' she said. 'I want you to sell your shabby old furniture, except a few things that we all value, and we will fit up the children's rooms with new iron bedsteads, and little toilet tables draped with white and pink, and some prints on the wall, and a little cabinet for their treasures; and there must be new carpets in the drawing-room and dining-room; and the curtains in the study were faded. I mean to make it the beau ideal of a country rectory,' finished Mary with an enthusiasm that contrasted strangely with her indifference about Crome Park.

'But, Mary, this will cost you too much,' returned Janet doubtfully.

'What does it matter what it costs?' retorted Mary with sublime generosity. She would not have moved a finger to purchase a new cretonne for her morning-room, or to replace the faded lining of her carriage, but Maurice's and Janet's home should be as perfect as she knew how to make it. True, the furniture would be the Champneys', not theirs, but the rooms should be brightened by new carpets and hangings, and the upper floor should be converted into a sort of child's paradise; she and the mother would have their own way there.

'Oh, but, Mary, think when they come back, and we have grown to love it, and to look upon it as our home; will it not be too hard to turn out?' For it was part of Janet's unhappy nature that she could not abide

in present happiness, but must be ever straining her
mental vision after possible shadows.

'Nonsense!' returned Mary stoutly, for she had scant
sympathy with the want of faith which, as she always truly
observed, lay at the bottom of such doubts. 'Perhaps
they will never come back. Mr. Champneys is not so very
old; but he seems to me inclined to shirk his work. If
Maurice suit him he may keep away for years; and what
is the use of looking forward? and who can tell what may
happen?' Mary spoke thus hastily, but she little knew
the changes that the years would bring.

Perhaps Janet felt her words deserved rebuke, for she
took the lecture very quietly, and Mary went on with their
previous discussion.

'As to expense, you need not trouble your head about
that,' she said; 'for since I have talked to Mr. Senhurst,
I have been quite bewildered with the amount of money
I have to spend. I had no idea Mrs. Reid was so rich.
I must talk to him again, and get him to give me a little
advice, for Maurice seems so helpless about money matters;
you and I must arrange things by ourselves, Janet.
Maurice evidently thinks that the Rectory being rent free
he will be able to live comfortably on his curacy; and,'
with a little amused laugh at her own duplicity, 'I do not
see that we need undeceive him.'

'How do you mean?' asked Janet, rather bewildered
by Mary's manner.

'Well, I will have another business talk with Mr.
Senhurst, and get the reins more firmly in my hands, and
then I will inform you more decidedly of my plans. I
want to put aside a certain sum for Maurice's benefit,
that could be paid to you in monthly instalments for the
use of the house. You have always managed all the
accounts, Janet; and I do not see that we need trouble
him.'

'Oh, Mary!' but Janet could not utter another word,
but in her secret heart she thought 'She is heaping on me
coals of fire.'

Mary misunderstood her emotion.

'Oh, you poor thing!' she exclaimed, 'how you must have suffered from the strain of all these years. You took all this burden on yourself to spare Maurice; no wonder you so often looked fagged and tired out.

'You shall not have another day of anxiety if I can help it,' she went on in a pitying voice. 'You shall bring me all your bills, and we will pay them together; and I will be your banker, and you shall draw on me. Seriously, Janet, what a pity it seems that the will has hampered me with the care of this great house!' for they were now crossing the park; 'it seems to me such a waste of money keeping it up just for one stupid young woman; and all the time I would rather live in a little cottage about the size of the lodge, and keep chickens and bees, and plant my own cabbages.'

'Oh, Mary!' sighed Janet, 'you do not seem to me to care for one of the good things that have come to you;' and a cloud came over her face.

'Oh yes, I do care,' she returned very quickly. 'I care very much to see you happy, and to hear Maurice laugh as he has done this morning. Ah, there he is!' as they heard the long strides behind them; and Janet stood still and waited for him with such a smile on her face.

The remainder of the day passed less pleasantly to Mary. After luncheon Janet had her way, and they inspected the storeroom and the plate-chest; and sundry cases of jewels were brought out of the strong box and displayed to Mary's wondering eyes.

'Are these all mine? Can I not give them away?' she asked; and as Janet replied, 'Certainly not,' in her old dictatorial tones, she persisted. 'But I can lend them to you; you can wear them, you know.'

'My dear Mary, a clergyman's wife!' for Janet was very orthodox in her views, and would not have done anything unbecoming her station for the world. She had given all these things up when she had married the poor curate.

'And you used to be so fond of diamonds. I remember you told me so once,' observed her husband regretfully, as he laid a sparkling aigrette against her dark hair; but Janet put up her hand gently and removed it.

'I do not want ornaments for myself,' she said; 'I shall enjoy seeing them on Mary.'

Mary held her peace like a wise woman, and did not tell her that she never meant to wear such things. What would be the use? It would only provoke an argument. She put away the glittering gems in their cases; probably she would take them out again to show Dollie, who loved such things. When Maurice, in almost boyish fashion, wanted to fasten a ruby serpent round her wrist, she drew back almost impatiently. 'Don't, Maurice, we have no time for such nonsense,' she said quite sharply. When Mrs. Pratt came in to carry away the cases she left the room, and stole softly down the darkening hall. Maurice found her a long time afterwards standing beside the open door, looking out on the gray dusk.

'Mary, it is so chilly, you will catch cold,' he said. 'The carriage is coming round directly, and Janet has gone upstairs to get ready;' but Mary hardly answered, and for some minutes she did not move.

'Yes, the sacrifice was made willingly—willingly; but they should not deck the victim;' those were her thoughts. When Bertie should hear of her, no one should tell him that the young mistress of Crome wore grand attire and adorned herself with jewels. She would be as simple and unobtrusive in her personal dress and habits as though she were still living in Lime Street. If Janet found fault with her plainness, she would turn off the subject with a laugh. No one should influence her in this matter, not even Dollie. For his sake she might have learned to care for dress; but now the opinion of the outer world was as nothing to her.

'They want to bribe and coax me into forgetting you, Bertie,' she said to herself, and she laid her head against the cold marble pillar and cried a little; and then she dried her eyes and made her resolve, and that comforted her.

'What does it matter if Janet does tease me a little?' she thought. 'I can have my own way in spite of her;

and one day, perhaps, she will understand;' and then she went upstairs.

'Good-bye, you dear beautiful place, until I see you again,' cried Janet enthusiastically, as they drove rapidly away from the hall-door. The park looked barren and chill; but through the open door there was a vista of brightness. But Mary leant back in her place and did not answer; only one month of freedom, she thought, and then the red walls of Crome would close round her—like a prison—for evermore.

CHAPTER XXIX

THE next month passed over only too quickly. Mary, on looking back to it, secretly marvelled at the rapidity with which it passed, and at the daily strength given to her.

'My meal wastes not, and my cruse of oil does not fail,' she wrote once to Dollie, in answer to some words of sympathy expressed by her; but this quaintly-phrased assertion was all she ever said on the subject. And yet whole pages of self-pity would not have been more eloquent, for it spoke of a daily want and a daily famine replenished from a supernatural fount, of a strength not her own, in which she lived and worked.

It is a true saying that busy people are seldom long unhappy people; that nothing so exorcises the demon of inward disquiet as work rightly undertaken, and carried on without flagging. There would have been no room for the seven other spirits in the swept and garnished apartment of the parable if it had not been empty. And Satan's work is done by desolated hearts as well as by idle hands.

In speaking of this time in her life afterwards, and always frankly acknowledging it as a time of trial, Mary once said : 'I was always so busy that I had never time to think, until I was alone in my own room at night, and then I was often so tired that I could do nothing but sleep; now and then I had hard times, but I was helped through them;' and ever afterwards her favourite 'sermon,' as she called it, to people in trouble used to be—'Never mind what you

feel or how you feel; leave all that alone; only do something—never be idle a moment.' So, during these last days
that she spent under her brother's roof, Maurice's keen eyes
discovered nothing amiss, and even Janet, who watched her
narrowly, wondered and rejoiced as she heard Aunt Mary
laughing in her old fashion with the children, or listened to
her light footstep running up and down the stairs. True,
the laugh soon ceased, and there was often a sigh after the
smile, and sometimes a tired wistful look came into the
brown eyes. But if responsibility were making Mary graver,
who could blame her?

Mary was having her own way, and Whitechapel was
holding high day and holiday that Christmas. The ex-
pedition to the Crystal Palace had been organised and
triumphantly carried out, at the cost of ten hours of intense
fatigue to her and Maurice. Janet's mothers had been
bidden to a feast, such as their imagination had never
conjured up, and gifts of clothes and money had been
transferred to the toil-worn hands, as Mary and Janet
wished them good-night; on Twelfth-night a gigantic
Christmas tree and cake, with a magic lantern, and refresh-
ments of buns and oranges to follow, had allured all the
children of the ragged school and Sunday school, to the
great delight of Lettice and Hatty and Rosie, who were
allowed to help in the distribution.

'Oh, mammy, look at the dolls burning,' whined one
little white-faced mite, clinging to her mother's ragged gown.
Poor little gutter child! she evidently believed that she was
invited to be present at a mighty auto-da-fé; and another
little fellow of tender years called it a great burning bush,
with a lively remembrance of teacher's lesson last Sunday.

'Ain't it 'eavenly?' observed Mary's favourite plague,
Tommy Stokes, in an aside to another curly-haired Arab.
'Wot lots of candles and goodies! I call that stunnin' of
teacher, that's wot I call it.'

Tommy's opinion proved general, and during the last
week of her stay in Lime Street, Mary tasted the mixed
delight of excessive popularity. When she moved abroad
a password seemed to spread through the courts, and a

ragged train, grinning from ear to ear, escorted her to her destination. This was embarrassing. On one occasion an impromptu serenade was got up by her boys, 'her special and particulars,' as Maurice styled them.

The intention was good, but the performance was sadly marred by a deficiency of suitable and sound instruments. The band on inspection was found to consist of a banjo, very much the worse for wear; a wandering hurdy-gurdy that had been pressed into the service; a broken-winded accordion; and two or three Jews' harps. In consequence of these defective arrangements the concert had been chiefly vocal, and had been restricted to two of the best-known melodies, 'Rule Britannia' and 'God save the Queen.'

'Teacher won't know we means it for her,' objected one lad, Phil Harmon, who was a 'coster' by trade and tolerably acute for his years. This was a general poser, and felt to be such even by the hurdy-gurdy, who was of foreign extraction, and carried white mice in his waistcoat pocket.

'I say, you chaps, I've got an idea,' announced Phil, after a long silence, during which there had been much pulling of grimy locks and dejected whistling; only it must be added that Phil prefixed his observation with a strong expletive or two, language not being particularly choice in Whitechapel. 'Couldn't we alter a word just here and there, that might tell her wot we are up to?'

'In course; you're a sharp 'un, Phil. What a soft lot we are not to think of that!' returned his chum, Dick Sawers. 'Go it, old chap; tune up,' to the hurdy-gurdy, who showed his white teeth as he ground at his melancholy instrument.

So Mary, wondering at this unusual burst of loyalty from her boys, was much amused and edified by Phil's transposition—

> Send her victorious,
> 'Appy and glorious,
> Long to reign over us,
> Teacher, we mean.

'Pitch it high, sing it loud, you fellars, and keep it up,'

shouted Phil; 'laws, isn't it fust-rate? there's no mistaking that—"teacher, we mean."'

'Thank you, Phil, thank you all, boys,' said Mary, trying to stifle her amusement with becoming gravity. The drollery was too much for Maurice, and he was obliged to retire hastily. It was Janet who seemed most touched by the proceedings, and who cut the home-made cake with lavish hand, and distributed the slices with mugs of hot elder wine; but Janet could afford to be hospitable now. The boys looked askance, and held back like sheep in a pen as that graceful vision appeared on the threshold; it was teacher they wanted. When Mary came out a few minutes afterwards, their faces cleared, and they ceased elbowing each other in their shyness; it was only the hurdy-gurdy who held out his white mice to Janet with an engaging smile, and 'Grazia Signorina bella'; the rest of the lads had clustered round Mary with eager looks.

'Wasn't it fine and clever of Phil, teacher? Now you knows wot we means—'appy and glorious, and all that sort of thing.'

'Yes, yes,' interposed Mary hastily, for the corners of her mouth would unbend; 'it is very kind of you, boys; now eat your cake and drink the wine, for it is beginning to snow.'

Besides this mutual interchange of civilities, Mary was busy in other ways. There were long business consultations with the lawyer, Mr. Senhurst, and not a few purely domestic in character, with Janet; sometimes these talks lengthened into arguments, in which Mary, though tired, always came off victor. Janet was beginning to see that Mary would set about things in her own way.

But on the whole, Janet was tolerably contented, and unusually affectionate; during the last few days she seemed hardly to like Mary being out of her sight. Sometimes when Mary was engrossed with her work and writing, she would sit looking at her until her eyes filled with tears. Mary did not notice it, but Maurice did, and he was not a little touched by this new gentleness and solicitude on his wife's part. 'If Mary were her own sister she could not be

fonder of her,' he thought; but it was not only affection on
Janet's part.

'Dear Mary, I cannot bear to think that you are leaving
us to-morrow,' she said the night before her departure.
She was standing by the fire in Mary's room; Lettice and
her aunt were packing some old books away in the cupboard; Mary was on her knees working busily. 'The
only comforting thought is that you will soon have finished
all this drudgery, and will have time to rest.'

'Time to rest!' ejaculated Mary with a horrified face.
'Oh, Janet! wish me anything but that; we mean to be
busy—Lettice, do we not?' for Lettice was to accompany
her to Crome—a clear month of heart contentment and
satisfaction to the careworn but childish Lettice.

She smiled a silent assent to Mary's question, and then
went on piling up the books. To work with Aunt Mary
was better than to play with other people; to spend a whole
month alone with her in her beautiful new home was almost
too much happiness. Was she not to sleep in the room
next her aunt? and Boy, the new black collie that Maurice
had procured for his sister, was to sleep in the little bell-
room outside. What long walks they were to take together!
what quiet cosy evenings they were to spend alone, with
only Boy to keep them company! Lettice's nights had
been almost sleepless with the anticipation of this wonderful
visit.

'I wish you would leave all that for me to finish,' continued Janet, watching them with discontented looks; for
she wanted Mary to come and sit by the fire and talk comfortably. But she might as well have spoken to the wind.
Mary only looked up at her with a good-natured laugh, and
went on packing her books.

'Do not wait, Janet, if you are tired,' she said; 'I am
as fresh as possible, and could go on working until midnight. Lettie, darling, it is time for all good little girls to
be in their beds; run away, dearie, I can do the rest by myself.'

'Oh no! let me help you,' returned her sister-in-law with
alacrity. This was what she wanted, to get rid of Lettice

and have Mary to herself. And yet there was nothing for her to say that the whole household might not hear. Lettice rose reluctantly, but she was far too obedient and well-trained to hesitate. Janet kissed her affectionately.

'What am I to do without you for a whole month, Lettice?' she said, putting her hands on the child's shoulders, and looking at her with a sort of proud tenderness; for Janet was secretly proud of Lettice's cleverness. 'What a cruel Aunt Mary to rob me of my eldest daughter!'

'Hatty has promised to be very good and help you, mamma,' returned Lettice with her usual shy diffidence. She was always a little shy and awkward with her mother; but how her heart beat with joy and excitement at the thought that her mother would really miss her!

'Oh yes, Hatty will do very well, but all the same I never want to get rid of any of my children,' replied Janet, patting her gently, and then motioning her to the door. 'Do not talk to the others, Lettice; go to sleep as fast as you can.' And Lettice said, 'Yes, mamma, I will try,' and went off and lay contentedly awake through the next two or three hours, wondering when the night would pass, and the wonderful day begin.

'Do you know, I think Lettice is certainly improved,' was Janet's next observation. 'I am not sure after all that she will be so very plain when she grows up; she has nice eyes, and when her face lights .up and looks intelligent, there is something quite attractive about her.'

'I always thought so,' was Mary's quick reply, for this qualified praise did not suit her. 'She is far above the average of girls in my opinion; of all the children, Lettice takes most after her father.'

'Well, yes, perhaps so,' in a softened tone, for Janet did not like parting with her child.

'She is a darling, and will make the dearest little companion,' continued Mary enthusiastically. 'It is so good of you and Maurice to spare her to me for so long!'

'Good, Mary?'

'Yes, indeed; and I am very grateful to you both.'

'Please, do not say so,' returned Janet hastily, 'as

20

though we do not owe you all—everything. Oh, Mary,' and then she came behind her and took hold of her, 'do tell me that you are contented about things, and that you are not so very unhappy.'

The books dropped from Mary's hands; then she picked them up again steadily, and put them in their places; but Janet still stood behind her, holding her by the shoulders.

'Oh, Mary, if you could say just a word to ease me!' ·

Then the answer came, but Mary did not turn her face.

'I am quite content about things, and I am not so very unhappy,' she said; and her voice was low, and quite steady. If her lip trembled as she said the words, and if there were sudden tears in her eyes, Janet was no wiser.

'Look, that is all quite tidy,' she said, rising from her knees, and speaking in her usual voice; 'how dusty I have made myself! Now I have only my clothes to pack, and then I shall have finished.'

'Let me help you,' replied Janet, brushing something suspicious from her cheeks, and turning to the window under pretence of looking out on the night. 'Why, it is snowing,' she continued after a pause. 'Oh, Mary, it will be so cold at Crome! and you would not be persuaded into buying a sealskin.'

'Thirty guineas for a winter mantle, and my own is quite good! No, indeed,' was the uncompromising answer; for this had already formed the basis of a stout argument; but as usual, Janet recapitulated the various heads in her next sentence.

'But, Mary, how absurd! how can you be so obstinate when I have already told you over and over again that your jacket is badly cut and quite old-fashioned? You remember you got it a bargain at the summer sale at Vendale and East's. Thirty guineas is not too much for you to give under your present circumstances; besides, it will last eight or nine years as good as new. There is nothing like a sealskin for beauty and comfort and durability.'

'Very well,' replied Mary, who had heard all this before;

'then we will get you one next winter, Janet. Maurice shall help me to choose it.'

'Nothing will induce me to wear it,' returned Janet with spirit. 'Oh, Mary, how can you be so incorrigible?' but she said no more, and the packing proceeded smoothly. It was Maurice who interrupted them at last, and scolded them both for keeping each other up; but as his lecture lasted for half an hour, during which he persisted in sitting on Mary's box, and haranguing the tired women on all sorts of foreign subjects, it may be doubted whether his interference was quite beneficial. Mary got rid of both of them at last, and sat down on the rug for a good hour staring into the fire, while Lettice lay in the adjoining room gazing open-eyed into the darkness, and thinking it a dozen nights rolled in one, and longing for sleep to come and bridge over the weary hours of waiting.

Mary had made up her mind that she would not arrive at Crome before dark; there had been a battle royal on the subject with Janet, but she had adhered to her resolution.

'Fancy flitting into your new home like a bat,' observed Mrs. St. John rather irritably, 'instead of driving up in state!'

'I should like to walk in, only Lettice and I would lose ourselves and wet our feet,' returned Mary quietly.

Mary had worked so hard the previous night that there was nothing for her to do, and only a prospect of a long morning with Janet and the children. Plenty of snow had fallen, and the gray cloudy sky contained promise of more. It was raw, chill, and uninviting; nevertheless, Mary put on her thick boots and her waterproof and went out with Maurice. Neither of them appeared until dinner time, when they came in powdered with snow and looking cold and tired.

'What a bad day for Mary's journey,' observed Maurice, warming his numb hands at the fire; 'nothing will induce her to put it off, I suppose?'

'It is not a long journey, and she has already been out needlessly,' returned his wife dryly; and Mary understood at once that she was considered to have sinned in so absent-

ing herself; but she only laughed and observed cheerily,
'That's right, Janet; what a sensible woman you are !' and
shook out her wet jacket.

At last the hour for their departure came. Maurice
went with them to the station. Mary was very silent at the
last, and let Janet and the children cling about her as they
would; even to Maurice she said but little.

'I hope you will not be dull, Mary, alone in that big
house,' he said rather anxiously, as he stood leaning against
the window of the train.

'Oh no, I shall not be dull with Lettice and Boy,' she
returned, stooping down to caress the dog; and then as he
bade God bless them both, she raised her head and smiled
at him; and Maurice wondered afterwards why her smile
had seemed so sad !

During the journey she did not speak much to the child,
but sat looking at the falling snow. Just before they got
out of the train it ceased, however, and the drive down the
smooth white roads was delightful to Lettice; but the intense whiteness of the surrounding country and the light,
neither clear nor dark, produced the same dream-like feeling in Mary that she had experienced on her first visit—
a sensation that she was somebody else, and that she was
not living out her own life, that presently she would wake
up and be her old happy self again.

But to-night the feeling of unreality was stronger and
still more curious. In vain she reasoned with herself as
they drove through the park; in vain she told herself that
this was her home, where she and she alone was to live out
her life, for others not for herself; that she would only
leave it to be buried under the Spanish chestnuts in Crome
churchyard. The idea all at once became incongruous and
impossible. She gave it up at last, and listened to Lettice's
awestruck raptures. Then came the welcoming lights and
the open doors of Crome, and the Pratts' kindly attentions.

'Dear Aunt Mary, are you not glad to be in your new
beautiful home ?' exclaimed Lettice, when at last they were
left alone. Rhoda, the rosy-cheeked housemaid, had
escorted them to their rooms, and had assisted at Lettice's

modest toilet; and the snug meal in the morning-room had
been somewhat marred by Pratt's officiousness, as he disregarded his young mistress's hints, and persisted in handing round the dishes; but at last they were alone, and
Lettice was in her favourite seat at her aunt's feet.

'Do you like my house?' returned Aunt Mary with a
smile. 'Are you sure it does not disappoint you? that it
is big enough and grand enough even for Hatty?'

'I think it is fit for the Queen,' was the earnest answer;
'but nothing is too good for you, Aunt Mary. Oh,
how lovely to think we shall be alone together in this
beautiful place for a whole month! and that to-morrow I
shall see the peacocks and the pheasants and the park!'
and again Mary smiled. The childish talk pleased and
soothed her; she even felt some regret when Rhoda came
with the silver candlestick to escort Lettice to her room.
For a moment she felt as though she must keep her with
her this first night, as though she could not be left alone.
But Lettice's eyes were bright and feverish with excitement,
and her cheeks were so pale, that her aunt's unselfishness
prevailed. What did it matter if she were lonely this first
night? would she not often have to spend solitary evenings
with nothing but her own thoughts to keep her company?
And yet when the door closed upon Lettice and her
attendant, and she could hear their retreating footsteps
across the hall, she could have called them back; but she
refrained, though tears of unutterable loneliness and longing rushed to her eyes. Such loneliness, such longing, such
an indescribable craving for the touch of a hand and the
sight of a face that was dearer to her than all the world
beside!

But now a strange thing happened to her, and one that
would seem incredible to most good folk, who deem
women but fools sometimes with their absurd fancies, not
dreaming that their philosophy may be at fault sometimes,
and that there may be marginal possibilities beyond even
their conjectures.

For as Mary sat alone that night in her beautiful new
home, sick at heart and trying vainly to keep back the

unbidden tears, thinking of Bertie, and wondering where
he was and when she should hear of him again, a
sudden feeling of nearness and warmth and comfort came
over her.

And how it came she knew not, and what it meant she
hardly cared to ask—women are such strange credulous
creatures, and so given to all manner of fond superstitions.
But all at once her eyes got bright and a sort of glow of
inward satisfaction pervaded her, and she said to herself—
but not aloud, for the whole thing was inward and inexplicable—'Bertie is near me, or else he is thinking of me
as I am of him;' and this communion of sympathy seemed
to destroy the feeling of loneliness and steep her in sudden
happiness. When Mrs. Pratt came in an hour later she
found her sitting looking into the fire as placidly and contentedly as a child. She was even surprised to find how
late it was, and took her candlestick with a half-laughing
apology.

But the next morning, as Lettice and she were crossing
the hard crisp snow in the wintry sunshine, on their way to
the peacocks' promenade, Pratt met them and pointed out
to Mary the clear unmistakable marks of countless footsteps
right round the house.

'The gardener and me have been tracing them ever so
far,' he said solemnly, pointing to the mysterious footprints.
'They are right across the park as far as the lodge gates,
and not a creature has been up to the house since last
afternoon! Some of them followed the carriage tracks,
and they are right round the house. Should I speak to the
police? I could easily take one of the horses and ride over
to Canterton; it is not many miles, and the horses are
roughed.'

'Look here! Aunt Mary,' interposed Lettice eagerly;
'what a lot of footmarks in one corner!' and Mary followed
her. The window belonged to the morning-room, where
they had sat last night; and the track of footsteps had
turned and doubled and retraced themselves. Pratt shook
his head and pondered heavily.

'I am thinking it looks suspicious, ma'am, and I had

better be riding over to Canterton ; that is what Atkinson and Mrs. Pratt and me think.'

'Oh no, Pratt, thank you, leave it alone; it was only some poor wanderer; I am not at all afraid,' returned his mistress decidedly; and she took Lettice's hand and went off to the peacocks' promenade, leaving Pratt still shaking his head very dubiously.

'Are you quite sure it is all right?' asked Lettice rather doubtfully.

'Yes, dear, quite sure!' returned Mary; and her step was firm, and there was a glow on her cheek as she answered. Later on she left Lettice feeding the tame pheasants, and came back alone and stood by the morning-room window, looking long at the footprints.

'I knew it!' she murmured to herself; 'somehow I felt it. Oh, Bertie! it is so like you!' And from that moment she believed with a faith that needed no convincing that her lover had actually kept watch and ward like a faithful sentinel outside the walls of Crome that night.

CHAPTER XXX

If Mary had been like other girls she would certainly have commenced her new life with vague expectations that would have been doomed to disappointment. A presentiment that something out of the common must happen each day would have kept her restless, turned sweetness to acerbity, and moved her to brief passing moods of discontent. But Mary was wiser in her generation. Her first evening in her new home had been blessed indeed; but she was reasonable, and knew such comforts must be rare. Human nature cannot go now as heretofore among the tents and fill their own little measures with such heaven-sent manna; such consolations are sparingly scattered through a lifetime; even if it be given to one to entertain angels unawares, one is not conscious of such visitants until they have left.

So she neither expected nor questioned, but simply rested in the possession of her sweet secret, not breaking the sacred seal of silence, but folding up her treasure, and laying it apart in her heart, as careful and thrifty souls fold up some precious fabric too good for daily use.

She had so much to do too, those first few days; she had to gather up the reins of office, and literally, as well as metaphorically, to set her house in order.

So while Lettice, for the first time in her life, enjoyed the sweets of liberty and wandered at her will about the place, feeding and coaxing the live pets, from the peacocks and tame pheasants down to the horses, and the black cat

and kittens that lived in the stable loft, Mary looked over
her hoards of plate and linen, altered rooms, readjusted
furniture, brought curious old things to light, and inspected
and hired servants to complete her modest establishment.

Mary had determined from the first that there should
be no extravagance or useless show; the house should be
properly kept up, and with a due regard to hospitality;
Pratt should have a boy under him, and there must be a
good kitchen-maid to assist his wife; two housemaids
would keep the place in good order, and Rhoda should be
reserved for Janet and the children. Bee would require
constant supervision, and there would be ample scope for
needlework; but she laughingly declined Mrs. Pratt's
suggestion that Rhoda should be considered as her own
maid.

'My good woman,' she said in an amused voice, ' you
do not know me, or you would not propose such a thing.
I am a most independent person, and not at all a fine
lady. What should I do with a maid? I think, with the
gardeners and coachman and odd man, as you call him,
we shall muster a very respectable household for a single
woman with no encumbrances. I do not want to work any
of you too hard, but at the same time I do not wish to
burden myself with a number of useless dependants.'

'Our young lady has a head on her shoulders!' was
Mrs. Pratt's verdict as she went downstairs after this consultation. 'For all her softness and mild speaking and
her pleasant way of smiling at one, she is as firm as firm
can be. It is my opinion, Pratt, that if she had once
made up her mind about a thing, nothing would move her.'

'What's the odds as long as she keeps things straight
and comfortable?' returned Pratt, who had already conceived a great respect and liking for his young mistress.
'Ah! the old missis knew what she was about. It wasn't
likely she would take such a powerful fancy to a high-
flying, touch-me-not sort of person as Mrs. St. John!' for
Janet was no favourite in the servants' hall at Crome.

'I am not denying you're right, Pratt,' replied his wife,
'but I am thinking she is a bit soberer and more staid

than her age warrants. What is the use of your putting
all that polish on that plate? I'll be bound there is not a
dance or a dinner-party to be given either this or that side
of Christmas. She is all for good works, and feeding the
poor, and such like things.'

'And what's the odds?' observed Pratt again; 'I hope
I know my duty and can live up to it, if I don't wait at
another dinner-party as long as I am here,' and his leather
worked still more vigorously at the silver branches of the
great epergne. 'If good works is her hobby, I suppose we
must put up with the faults of our betters. Some folks of
her age—for she is only a slip of a girl, after all—might
have turned the old place out of doors, and made us that
miserable we should be fit to hang ourselves. Supposing
it had been Mr. Walter, now,'—and as Mrs. Pratt put her
handkerchief to her eyes and said, 'And right you are,
Pratt,' the brief argument ceased.

Mary's first occupation was to alter her own room, and
the changes she introduced were so judicious that even
that critical personage Janet pronounced it a model of
comfort.

The huge canopied bedstead had been removed, and a
small brass one of old and very exquisite workmanship
had been transferred from one of the other rooms. The
vast empty space was partially occupied by a round table,
an old-fashioned lounge, and some cosy-looking easy-chairs.
A carved cabinet to match the wardrobe had been filled
with Mary's favourite books, and a fine old print of the
San Sisto Madonna hung over the mantelpiece. In one
corner there was a hanging cupboard of china, which gave
a pleasing tone of colour to the room. The anteroom
was at present fitted up for Lettice's use; but Mary
eventually intended to turn it into a sort of nondescript
workroom, where she and the children might busy themselves on wet days.

But her greatest pleasure was in fitting up and arranging
the rooms that were to be allotted to Janet and her
children during the months that the Rectory would be
uninhabitable. A suite of pleasant rooms, some of them

opening into each other, was being already prepared for them.

The disused billiard-room would make an excellent playroom or schoolroom for the little girls, while the room adjoining, which was already fitted up as a study or library, should be set apart for Maurice's use. Janet could occupy the morning-room, and Mary planned how she would surprise her, by choosing a more tasteful cretonne.

'Poor Janet!' she said to herself, 'I do believe that ugly or ill-chosen colours make her positively uncomfortable. Those sprawling green leaves and carnations, which are so quaint and old-fashioned to me, would make her eyes ache with a sense of glare and incongruity. She will not know the room when she comes; it shall be the perfection of a country morning-room;' and though Mary loved that room best in the house, because of those remembered footprints underneath the windows, she heroically resolved that Janet should call it hers during her stay, and that she would pitch her tent elsewhere—a piece of self-sacrifice that Janet nipped in the bud by vowing that it was Mary's room, and that she meant to sit principally in Maurice's study, where she could superintend the children's lessons and be at hand if he wanted her.

All these plans for her brother's and sister-in-law's comfort kept Mary busy and her heart warm. The mornings used to fly, while she and Rhoda worked first in one room and then in another. It was often a surprise when the gong sounded, and Lettice came running up three steps at a time with Boy behind her, to tell her luncheon was ready.

The afternoons were devoted to long rambles. The snow had soon melted, and as neither Lettice nor her aunt minded wet boots or miry lanes, they and Boy had soon made acquaintance with the surrounding country, often losing themselves and coming home tired and famished to the meat tea, that for Lettice's sake had taken the place of the more formal dinner. In the evenings they read aloud and worked; and when her little companion went to bed, Mary wrote long letters to Janet and Dollie.

Sometimes, but not often, they would drive. Randall

the coachman was compelled to exercise his horses by himself; Mary found these drives so tedious, but for Lettice's sake she would sacrifice herself sometimes. Once they had a delightful day : they drove into Canterton and had dinner at the quaint old inn, and then wandered about the town and attended service in the cathedral.

To Mary this was such a treat that she promised herself to repeat it with Maurice and Janet. How Maurice would enjoy it, she thought. To her the stupendous cathedral was a perfect vision of beauty and rest, and the sweetly-intoned service seemed to lull her into unutterable repose.

Another day Randall drove them to Featherston. That was a marvellous day to Lettice. That gray wintry afternoon was set apart as a sort of epoch in her life, when she and Mary crossed the little high windy churchyard, and below them lay the sea, and the slow, booming rush of the waves breaking on the shore. This was Lettice's first view of the sea.

Lettice would have stayed for hours, but Mary felt a sort of oppression, looking over the long gray waste of waters and listening to the dismal wash of the waves ; a heavy gray sky brooded over them, a mingled sense of monotony and restlessness seemed to invest her outward and inward world. It was a relief when Randall turned his horses' heads homeward, and they went back through the long dark roads among the glimmering hedgerows. Lettice nestled up to her aunt cosily in the darkness. Mary felt warm childish hands stealing to her neck.

'Oh, dear Aunt Mary, what a lovely afternoon ! and oh, I am so tired and happy !' And this was what Lettice said nearly every day; she was always 'so tired and so happy'; and the pale thin cheeks were filling out and rounding into oval curves, and the blue eyes seemed to get colour and light. 'Janet would hardly know her child,' she wrote. She was almost sorry that she made this remark, innocent as it was; it drew forth such a response from Janet.

Can you wonder at it (replied the anxious mother)? Lettice looks well because she is breathing sweet country air ; for the first time she is leading a child's natural life. Before this she was merely pining through a sort of sickly existence.

With all your love for Lettice, you hardly know her as well as I do [a private query from Mary at this point]. She is so terribly sensitive. I believe she takes after me in that; and all these wretched sights and sounds by which we are surrounded, these rags and tatters that you and Maurice find so alluring, oppressed and weighed on her spirits. Why are there so many unhappy people in the world? that is what she was always asking; and even the sufferings of the dumb creatures, the over-driven cattle and jaded horses, seemed to fret her tender spirit.

But all my darlings will owe their deliverance to Aunt Mary's brave act of self-sacrifice. Oh, Mary, Mary! what do we not owe to you, my dear?

Mary put down the letter with a rising flush and sigh.

'Poor Janet! If it be a sacrifice, why will you keep piling up the faggots in this manner?' she thought in her vexation, and then was angry with herself for her irritability; but she said as little as possible of Lettice in her next letter. Somehow she found Janet's gratitude very hard to bear sometimes. But one thing rejoiced her; she found a grand opening for work for Maurice and herself, and on the afternoon she discovered that, a dull weight seemed lifted off her, and she felt as though she could breathe more freely.

For a painful conviction had been stealing over her that Maurice's energies would rust in this small out-of-the-way parish. The village was straggling, and, with the exception of a few cottages near the church, the inhabitants were fairly well-to-do. Some of the parishioners were wealthy people, and lived in the great houses enclosed in grounds, towards which the young mistress of Crome cast looks of disfavour, for she would willingly have eschewed her richer neighbours and confined herself to intercourse with her poorer ones. As for taking her place in the county, as Janet wished, Mary registered a 'never' in her downright fashion.

There were schools, and they were tolerably well attended, but the mistress was a flighty-looking inefficient sort of person. Mary thought the children looked dull and listless, staring at strangers in stupid rustic fashion, and evidently somewhat in awe of their teacher.

I think Miss Leigh singularly ill adapted for her post (wrote Mary). If I am not mistaken, the children suffer under a system of petty tyranny, and yet there seems no method, and hardly a form of discipline. The school needs reorganising, and I shall be greatly surprised if you do not change your teacher within the next six months.

Mary with her young companion roamed up and down the village, paying visits here and there, and every day she grew more puzzled and discouraged. For what would Maurice find to do?

All the people went to church, and nodded and slept through the sermon. The women carried their prayer-books wrapped up in blue spotted handkerchiefs, and often had a nosegay beside; there were one or two picturesque smock frocks, and one old woman in a scarlet cloak and drawn black bonnet who was the very picture of a country dame. Mary found she was stone deaf, and could not read. Yet there she was always in her place, with her great book in its blue wrapper, dropping her old-fashioned curtseys in the churchyard when any of the gentry passed. It was all very rural and quaint, and the peaceful atmosphere was not without its charms. But how could Maurice's vast energies concentrate themselves on this group of gaping rustics and those pews full of feathers and finery where the so-called county people worshipped after their own fashion? Mary's knowledge of her brother's character was almost unerring, and she was not a little troubled in her mind. But one afternoon Lettice and she had discovered about a mile and a half from Crome a little village called Brotherton.

It was one of those out-of-the-way places that seem to have dropped down accidentally, and without any special purpose. The whole village consisted of a winding street, to which a miry lane gave egress, with a dismal winter setting of ploughed fields and bare hedgerows.

The lane was unpromising—a mere succession of ruts filled up with black oozing mud; so Mary left Lettice sitting on a fallen log, with Boy to guard her, and continued her researches alone.

She was glad afterwards that she had not suffered the

child to accompany her.   The cottages at first sight looked
comfortable and picturesque; they had thatched roofs, and
small enclosures for gardens and piggeries, but a nearer
inspection was less favourable.

Some of the windows were broken, and the damp was
exuding from the walls; palings were broken down; the
gardens were mere rubbish heaps; untidy-looking women
and ragged children came to the doors as Mary passed.
There was no church, for Brotherton was an offshoot of
Crome parish; but neither was there a mission-room—not
even a cottage service.   The only attempt at saving the
Brotherton souls was made in the small Dissenting chapel,
where sundry itinerant preachers were wont to dispense
doctrine hot and strong, and with a pungent odour of
brimstone and fire to those who would listen to them,
thereby insuring nightmares to the many and conviction to
the few.   But even the hireling Josiah Culpepper was
more faithful to his self-imposed trust than Mr. Champneys
—writing gentlemanly sermons in his study and preaching
them to his slumbrous congregation — wholly forgetting
'those few sheep in the wilderness' at Brotherton.   Mary
gave a shake of her head at the Dissenting chapel, and
another at the small beer shop adjoining; and then she
went into an all-sorts shop, where cheese and tallow candles
and marbles and string and such like small gear were dispensed by a little old woman in horn spectacles and a
mob cap.   Mary bought some stale biscuits for Boy, not
without a doubt of their wholesomeness, for they were so
aged and soft of their kind; and she asked Mrs. Weevil
a few questions—Anne Weevil being the name put over
the door.

'And you have no school for the children?   I suppose
some of them come over to Crome?'

'Ay, a few; not above two or three.   The little 'uns
fright the birds, and the big 'uns work with their fathers
and mothers in the field.   It is a longish bit to Crome'—
Croome, as she pronounced it.

'And you have no cottage service? no clergyman comes
near to visit you?'

''Deed, that we have,' returned Mrs. Weevil indignantly. 'Haven't we got Josiah Culpepper, who comes and preaches in the chapel yonder most Sunday evenings? Eh, he is a rare one is Josiah; he is such a powerful screamer that he makes folks jump off their seats with the starts he gives them. There's Sally Mokes at the alehouse —she nearly went into a fit with his pointing at her, and his saying such horful things; not but what Sal takes her drop too freely like the rest of them!'

'And does Mr. Culpepper never tell the people about heaven?' questioned Mary, horrified at this account of Mr. Culpepper's eloquence.

'I don't mind—maybe—I do not remember,' returned Anne Weevil, weighing the biscuits and wrapping them in the corner of a newspaper. Boy merely snuffed at the biscuits disdainfully when they were presented to him afterwards, the tallowy flavour not recommending itself to his olfactory nerves. 'But I think he is fondest of talking about the other place; he has a powerful sort of mind that deals most freely in the 'orribles. But you see, ma'am,' and here Anne leaned her skinny arms on the counter, and looked at Mary severely through her spectacles, 'you gentle-folks are all for Canaan, and milk and honey, and we poor critters don't have much of that sort of thing to bless ourselves with. There's Josiah now—he is only a tailor, but his wife took and drank herself to death, and his eldest girl has gone to the bad; and they say his boy is the idlest, most aggravatin' young varmint that ever was, and always being taken up for poaching; and so Josiah takes a sort of delight of painting things up black. Why, take it all in all, he is the dismallest preacher I have ever heard since I came to live at Brotherton, five-and-twenty years ago. Shall I be putting you up some sweets along with the biscuits?' but this Mary declined; and as one or two slipshod women were now approaching the door, she hastily broke off her discourse; and with another long look at the place, she picked her way along the miry lane, and rejoined Lettice and her four-footed companion.

CHAPTER XXXI

MARY paid Brotherton another visit, but this time she left Lettice at home. A leisurely house-to-house visitation and an inspection of the comfortless interiors under the picturesque thatched roofs, where stonecrop and lichens flourished, soon satisfied her that here Maurice and she would have full scope for their energies; and that evening she sat down and wrote off pages of description.

Maurice kept the contents of her letter to himself; 'it was only business, and treated of parochial matters,' he told his wife; and Janet, who had taken up the first sheet somewhat eagerly, dropped it at once as though it burned her fingers; but she could not fail to notice that Maurice's eyes brightened, and his whole frame expanded, as though he beheld the battle from afar.

A neglected village wholly given to idolatry, men and women alike worshipping the foul fetish Drink, bound hand and foot by ignorance, and delivered over to the tender mercies of Josiah Culpepper! here was work enough!

Brotherton with its miry lanes and dilapidated dwellings, its pigsties and dust-heaps, and rankly-growing gardens, began to haunt his waking and sleeping dreams; the draggled, dim-eyed women and sunburnt ragged children met his thoughts at every turn; already in imagination he had ridden lance in hand against his brimstone-breathing adversary, and lo! Josiah Culpepper lay in the dust. Once, when Janet thought he was sleeping, he suddenly electrified her by saying out loud, 'Confusion to that fellow Cul-

21

pepper! he is like a nightmare to me; I must have a talk to that woman about him.'

'Who do you mean?' asked Janet, who was rather bewildered.

'Why, Anne Weevil, to be sure; oh, I forgot you did not know who I mean—the old woman who keeps the all-sorts shop at Brotherton.'

Janet had never heard of Brotherton either, but she guessed rightly when she said to herself with a sigh that Mary must have fallen into the hands of Philistines.

Mary would have agreed with Janet on this point, but the Philistines she meant were of a different order, and gave her far more trouble.

About a fortnight after their arrival at Crome, several people called up at the Park, as it was called in the place; on their return from their walk or drive, they would find cards lying on the great silver salver in the hall.

Mary took them up and inspected them so gloomily that Lettice felt puzzled.

'Aunt Mary, you are staring at those cards as though you were looking right through them and into the people,' she said at last; and Mary smiled grimly, and dropped them almost as Janet had dropped her letter; but Lettice read the names aloud.

'Colonel and Mrs. Fullerton, Combe Lea. What a pretty name! oh, I remember now; it is that old ivy-covered house by the church. Mrs. and the Misses Ducie, The Glade. Where was that I wonder? And Mrs. Woodyard of Crome Cottage. Oh, that's down by the church too!'

Then another day. 'Oh, Aunt Mary, the Rolf Egertons have called! Don't you remember that dear old place Randall pointed out? He called it the Priory, and he told us particularly that the Rolf Egertons lived there, and that the old gentleman was as rich as Crœsus.'

'I should say they are richer, Miss Lettice,' struck in Pratt, who stood by, and who often put in his word with the privilege of an old servant; 'but they are nobodies for all that. Why, Miss Brettingham of St. Norbert's, though she is as poor as poor can be, won't even call on them, because she says they are not the real quality, but just Brummagen-like, all tinsel and show.'

'Now, Pratt, you know I dislike gossip,' observed his mistress mildly, for she was loath to hurt the old man's feelings.

'Gossip! I am only telling you the truth, ma'am,' responded Pratt, somewhat injured; 'what I was waiting to observe, ma'am, was that Sir George and Lady Vendale have called this afternoon, and Miss Vendale was with them.'

'Indeed!' returned Mary, taking up the card listlessly; but Pratt still waited, and his manner became pompous.

'They asked most particularly after you, ma'am, and if you were not lonely being here with only Miss Lettice; and Lady Vendale said she was one of the old mistress's greatest friends, and you must look upon her as your nearest neighbour. I am bound to say she spoke up as kind and free as any lady need, and so did Sir George.'

'Where do they live, Pratt?' asked Mary with a sudden sinking of heart; this was not what she was prepared to meet, an invasion of wealthy Philistines. How galling must be her servitude if she must be dragged at the chariot wheels of her richer neighbours! And yet was not even this a part of her discipline?

Pratt's countenance smoothed, and he answered with alacrity, 'Well, they live at the Hall, a little higher up, just as you turn to the right from the lodge gates; it is the Hall proper just as this is the Park, and of course they are our next neighbours.'

But Lettice again interposed, for she had a childish interest in all her new surroundings, animate and inanimate. 'Oh, Aunt Mary, don't you remember that nice-looking old gentleman with white hair, riding with his daughter?—at least, we guessed it was his daughter—and you said what a fine-looking girl she was. They turned into the gates with the great stone balls on the posts.'

'That's it, that's the Hall, Miss Lettice!' exclaimed Pratt. 'That was Sir George riding with Miss Diana; he

rides out with her every day.   She is an only child, at
least, since poor Captain Manley died in India.   That was
an awful blow to them ; Lady Vendale has been an invalid
ever since.'

'Ah, well, we will call on them, Pratt,' returned his
mistress half interested, and yet desirous to close the
subject, for she preferred to form her own opinions of her
neighbours, and Pratt's gossiping tendencies must be crushed,
she thought.   When the old servant withdrew, satisfied that
he had made an impression, Mary heaved a great sigh and
went up to her room, and then she sat down and had a
battle royal with herself.

'What a sour dismal old misanthrope I am getting !'
she thought; 'I am actually afraid of my kind, unless they
are dressed in rags ; and yet it is not that I am afraid, but
that my spirits are too unequal to cope with light-hearted
people.   I have nothing in common with young ladies now.
They think of tennis and balls and lovers, while I am de-
barred from dwelling on such subjects.   Dollie is different,
dear sweet little Dollie ; ' and then her thoughts travelled
back to the old chateau, till a great stab of pain roused her
from her reverie.

At first she determined to wait for Janet, and pay her
return calls with her.   It was just what Janet would enjoy,
but on second thoughts she remembered that her sister-in-
law never willingly took the second place ; she had a way,
perfectly unconscious to herself, of engrossing the attentions
of strangers and centring them on herself; not that Mary
minded this in itself, but her common sense, which was
seldom in fault, told her that she was more likely to stand
on her own merits and take her own ground if she were to
go alone.   Janet would receive their visits later on her own
account, and could exercise her fascinations *ad libitum*.   Mary
began to think the thing would be done more simply alone.

So, one cold dreary afternoon, when there was a prospect
of snow, she started off on her rounds with Lettice, somewhat scandalising the neighbourhood by not taking her
carriage, thereby bringing down on her devoted head the
longest lecture Janet ever gave her.

'Nonsense,' was Mary's downright answer when Mrs. St. John paused at length from want of breath; 'I did not intend to give my neighbours an impression that I was a fine lady.   Every one knows I have a carriage, and I told them that I liked walking better.   Why, we did not walk a mile; did we, Lettie?'

'It is the look of the thing, not the distance.   Your first calls too, Mary; and of course you went in that old-fashioned jacket.'

'Yes, of course; I had nothing else,' was Mary's blunt rejoinder, but she did not inform Janet that she had wholly forgotten to put on her best bonnet.   She wore her black felt hat that had been a little damaged from being caught in a snowstorm.   No wonder the Egertons pronounced her dowdy, and shook out their satin flounces with a little disdain, when they talked over their visitor at the dinner-table that evening.

'She is a very ordinary person, papa,' observed Caroline, the youngest daughter, a sprightly handsome girl.   'She is rather stout—at least plump—and uses eyeglasses; and was dressed just in an ordinary serge dress, without a bit of crape.   Amelia would not have thanked you for the whole costume.'   Now, Amelia was the Egertons' maid, a very fine lady in her own way.

'Humph! you are a little hard on her, Carrie,' observed Rolf Egerton—most people called him Rolf Egerton without the Mr.   'I met her in the shrubbery, and she struck me as a sensible, pleasant-spoken young woman.'

'Young woman—that is just it; you have hit the nail on the head, papa,' and then Carrie giggled, and the other sister, Sophy, giggled too.

'What are you girls laughing at?' asked Mrs. Egerton, who carried an ear-trumpet, and wore a gorgeous ruby satin, which matched her plump cheeks rather too exactly.   'You are always having jokes with your father that you can't repeat.'

'Bless me, don't be so cross, mamma!' returned Miss Carrie tartly, for there were tempers at the Priory.   'Papa is calling Miss St. John a young woman, that's all; and

somehow the term just suits her.   She looked just like a
Sunday school teacher, who thinks feathers and artificial
flowers delusions of the evil one,' and Carrie giggled again
at her own wit, wholly oblivious of the footman beside her
chair.

'Nonsense, Carrie!' returned her mother sharply, for
she had followed this speech pretty closely; 'it would be
better for your father if you and Sophy thought a little less
of dress.   Young woman, indeed!   I call Miss St. John a
very nice, lady-like person.   When she saw my trumpet
she came and sat quite close to me, and I could hear every
word she said without asking her to repeat it once; that is
more than some of your fine friends would do, Carrie.'

'Mamma has never forgiven Isabella Hawkes for laugh-
ing when she tried to speak through her trumpet,' observed
Carrie in a low voice; and at the recollection both the
sisters indulged in a laugh, in which Rolf Egerton joined.
Mrs. Egerton's fretfully-uttered 'What now, what now,
Rolf?' was suffered to pass unheeded and unanswered.

Miss Brettingham's opinion was hardly more favourable
when she stepped across to Crome Cottage, to indulge in
afternoon tea and scandal with her intimate friend Mrs.
Woodyard.   The two women were strange contrasts.
Mrs. Woodyard was the widow of an Indian officer, and
was a languid, discontented sort of person.   She had been
a great beauty in her youth until the Indian suns had faded
her pretty pink-and-white complexion, and made her old
and sallow before her time.   Since then she had lived on
the prestige of past charms and present ill health; to dress
in perfect taste, and to detail the novel and varied symptoms
of each day's experience were the chief objects of her life.
Most of her friends found her wearisome, and it could not
be denied that there was much sameness in her discourse;
but she was not without her good points.   She was amiable
as far as her ailments permitted her; if her friends would
listen to her list of symptoms patiently, there was nothing
that she would not do for them in return.   Most people
failed in this, and interrupted the first opening sentences;
they thought her gloomy and full of whimsies, and in-

sisted on turning the conversation into a more cheerful channel.

Miss Brettingham had once listened patiently to an account of two long illnesses and one bereavement, as she sat there one hot summer afternoon, with only a patient 'Oh dear !' and 'Indeed !' uttered at proper intervals in the right tone.   Mrs. Woodyard was grateful, and Miss Brettingham became her friend for life. Henceforth she had secured a listener after her own heart.

Miss Brettingham was not what is popularly called an attractive woman ; she was a thin, eccentric sort of person, rather out of date as to costume, and delighting in what Miss Carrie maliciously termed a 'Noah's ark style of fashion.'   For she insisted on wearing thick black curls that nearly obscured her thin high cheek-bones ; and her turned silks and frayed satins were marvellously scanty ; only on rare occasions certain pieces of point lace and a diamond brooch formed part of her dress, but except on these gala-days she was remarkable for her old-fashioned dowdiness.

No one but the Rolf Egertons ventured to laugh at her, however, and they only under their breaths ; for though Miss Brettingham was poor, and St. Norberts was the very smallest of cottages, with tiny rooms and small grates, and a childish handmaiden to open the door, Miss Brettingham had a pedigree that struck terror in the stoutest of her neighbour's hearts, and on which she lived and nourished her somewhat meagre existence.   Never was there such a pedigree ; never did a stiffer carriage or a more Roman nose eke out its ponderous dignity.   What did it matter if Miss Brettingham's gown were shabby, or that her skirts were so ridiculously scanty, when her manners were so superb and her voice so aristocratic?   Was not her accent that of a Brettingham of Brettingham?   Did she not roll her 'r's' just as her great uncle Sir Willoughby Brettingham used to roll his?

And then she was such an admirable listener ; she would sit bolt upright in one of Mrs. Woodyard's deliciously-cosy chairs—for, as she often remarked, 'loung-

ing was not her fault, and she thanked Heaven she had a
straight spine'—with her small, finely-shaped hands, Brettingham hands, lying crossed over each other in her lap.

'Oh, my dear,' she would often say, 'what a mysterious
Providence! Here I am blessed with the regular Brettingham constitution—robust and hardy—with every nerve in
order; and there you are a martyr to an over-sensitive
organisation.'

'And what do you think of our new neighbour at
Crome, Arabella?' asked Mrs. Woodyard languidly. The
little drawing-room at the cottage looked snug and inviting
in the winter twilight; a little shaded lamp diffused a half
light; the tea-table was drawn up to the fire; there was a
fragrance of hot spicy cakes, such as Miss Brettingham,
with all her aristocratic tendencies, loved; the tea was
strong, with a peculiar, scented flavour, and the cream was
of the richest yellowish kind. What could be more comforting to the palate of a maiden lady who had no nerves,
and who could indulge pretty freely in the delicious poison?

'Humph!' observed Miss Brettingham, putting down
her cup and becoming a little more rigid in attitude; 'well,
if you ask me, my dear Adelaide, I may as well express my
opinion candidly; candour is always the best under all
circumstances!' for Miss Brettingham was somewhat
diffusive in talk and slightly addicted to repetition; 'and
I must own I find Miss St. John singularly disappointing.'

Mrs. Woodyard raised her heavy eyelids; she had handsome eyes when she opened them fully.

'Indeed! I thought her rather an amiable sort of person.
She showed a great deal of sympathy for my helpless condition. She made some very sensible and pertinent
remarks; one especially.'

'Yes, yes, I daresay,' interrupted her friend, who was
unwilling to direct the conversation into the old channel;
'she may be very pleasant and kind-hearted, and any one
seeing you for the first time, my dear Adelaide, would feel
their sympathies excited and stimulated. I am not denying
Miss St. John may be a very good sort of person in her
way but she has a lamentable ignorance of the usages of

society. We stumbled somehow on the subject of pedi-
grees,' and here Miss Brettingham coughed slightly; ' I
was pointing out to her the Dean's picture and my uncle
Sir Willoughby, and she put up her eyeglasses and laughed.
" Do you know, Miss Brettingham," she said in the coolest
possible way, "I have no idea what sort of pedigree we
have, or if our family came in with the Conquest; or if
they found us here; perhaps my brother would know !"
and then she went on quite seriously, for she was not
joking a bit, " I am afraid I am rather a heretic in these
matters; I should like my ancestors to have been good
brave men, who did great deeds for their country, and led
pure God-fearing lives ! but it would not make a bit of
difference to me to know one of them was chief baker
or head candlestick-maker to that horrid William the
Conqueror, who had no business to come over here with
that pack of hungry thieves he called his barons !" My
dear Adelaide,' and here the Brettingham hands were
uplifted with ineffable horror, 'after that display of crude
ignorance and rank dissent from all our noblest institutions
and—' here the right word was not forthcoming, and she
substituted ' Charterism '—' how can I regard her but as a
very dangerous and ill-judging young person ? '

There was diversity of opinion too at the Glade, whither
Mary had betaken herself on the following afternoon. The
Glade was a pretty house, and Mrs. Ducie and her daughter
Mabel just matched it ; for the house was many-gabled and
had a verandah running round it, and the rooms were full
of old china and articles of vertu and bric-à-brac ; and Mrs.
Ducie and her daughter were both pretty women, of a rosebud style of beauty—only whereas the daughter was very
fresh and pink, and had all sorts of little dimples in her
cheeks, the mother was rather white and waxen, and the
dimples had worn away into hollows; but they were both
dainty creatures, and matched the old china.

'What a very downright outspoken young lady !'
exclaimed Mrs. Ducie, when the garden gate closed upon
their visitors. Jack Ducie, a cousin, one of the suspicious
order, who was perilously handsome, and was quite aware

that Mabel thought so, had just come striding back through
the window, thereby making his aunt shiver, a fact of which
he took no notice.

'Jack, why will you always come in that way?' remonstrated Emma Ducie, an exceedingly plain young woman,
with prominent teeth and a sensible face. People said it
was a pity that Mrs. Ducie's stepdaughter lived with them,
for she was so ugly that she quite spoiled the harmony of
prettiness that pervaded the house; but as usual people
were at fault. A great deal of the inner comfort of the
Glade was owing to Emma; it was she who bore the
weight of the domestic burdens on her broad shoulders,
whose intelligence and unselfishness moved the secret
springs of the machinery, so that things worked smoothly
and well.

Mrs. Ducie and Mabel might be as ornamental and
useless as they liked; and they both liked to waste a good
deal of time: at the Glade there was plenty of novel
reading got through with feet on the fender in the winter,
and a good deal of ornamental gardening, rose clipping,
and tennis in the summer. Mabel sketched and painted,
and her mother was an adept in crewel work; they both
had pretty voices, and sang in an artless lark-like fashion,
only the elder lark was a little flat sometimes. Emma used
to listen to them as she mended and planned and contrived, for the Glade could not boast much wealth.
'Emma is such a good old thing, she is always busy!'
Mabel would say, patting her cheek affectionately.

'Yes, I am always busy; there must be bees as well as
butterflies, Mab!' Emma would answer good-humouredly.
It was all right, all in the proper order of things; she
neither sketched nor painted nor sung; rose-clipping was
not to her taste, neither was tennis; she would sooner put
in a dozen patches than read the novels Mabel loved; but
though it was all right that she should be the slave of the
lamp, the family drudge, and that she spoiled the rosebud
mother and daughter dreadfully, she could scold Jack upon
occasions like the present.

'You have no business to disregard your aunt's wishes,

and come in that way !' she said in her abrupt fashion ;
but Jack only laughed ; who cared if old Emma scolded or
not ?

'A very downright sort of person !' repeated Mrs.
Ducie, who was engaged in quilling some dainty lace
ruffles for her own pretty hands. Emma never did this
sort of fine work.

'Rather too bracing and matter-of-fact for my taste,
madre !' burst out Mabel. 'She never noticed our china
at all, not even the Louis Quinze teapot. I observed all
the time she talked she looked at you or Emma. Jack and
I were quite beneath her notice.'

'Yes, we were quite beneath her notice !' repeated
Jack, pulling his moustache and sidling up to his cousin.
'Never mind it, Mab ; we shall get over it.'

'Oh, but I made up my mind to like her !' pouted
Mab. 'It sounded so romantic, a young girl living all
alone in that great big house. She is not very pretty,
Jack, but she is not bad-looking. Now I suppose you will
go and make love to her, and perhaps, after all, you will
not have to go to India !' for Jack Ducie was a lieutenant
in the —th.

'Oh yes ! of course I shall make love to her,' replied
Jack calmly, as he looked his cousin in the face ; but the
look made Mabel blush a little and betake herself to her
drawing. Jack was not actually her cousin ; he was more an
offshoot of the Ducie family, and the connection was not
very near ; but it pleased Mabel to treat him on occasions
as though he were her own cousin, a position in which
Jack languidly acquiesced, for it invested him with all sorts
of privileges, and spared him a great deal of trouble in his
wooing.

'Now, Jack, don't be talking nonsense,' interrupted
Emma severely ; she was always ready to repress this
young man on all due occasions. 'Miss St. John is far too
sensible to give you the slightest opening. I am seldom
wrong in my first impressions, and I call her a thoroughly
nice lady-like girl.'

'She is just Emma's sort,' put in Mabel mischievously ;

'they will soon be vowing eternal friendship and all that sort of thing. It was love at first sight, that is what it was. Miss St. John was so struck with Emma that she could not notice the Louis Quinze teapot.'

'She is a worker, and I like workers,' replied Emma, not at all ruffled by this attack or Jack's laugh. 'She was her brother's right hand in his parish. Mrs. Champneys told me so the other day, and now she means to take up Brotherton. She was full of it, though you stopped her by laughing, Jack.'

'And I was very grateful to Jack,' interrupted her stepmother. 'Fancy dragging in Brotherton on a first visit!— a dreadful place like that, and a disgrace to the whole neighbourhood, as I have told Mr. Champneys over and over again. The very name rasps one's nerves like an east wind. Miss St. John is very practical, but she is more to your taste than mine. Mabel and I like a more feminine clinging sort of person; don't we, Mab?'

'So do I; I like clinging sort of people,' put in Jack eagerly; 'I like a girl who can smile and blush and look pleased when a fellow talks to her. Eh, Mab?'

'Oh, go away; you are shaking the table and making me spoil my group of flowers,' returned his cousin with another pout. 'Why don't you go back to your regiment and not waste all your time loitering in our little drawing-room, you idle good-for-nothing Jack?'

'So I will go back, when you have given me—you know what!' he returned in so low a voice that his aunt did not hear him. Probably Mabel heard, for she went on with her work industriously for the remainder of the afternoon.

CHAPTER XXXII

DIANA

THE first decided encomium was pronounced by Colonel Fullerton.

'I do like that girl; she is such a thorough specimen of a frank, open-hearted English girl,' he said, as he re-entered the morning-room, where his wife was occupied with some intricate needlework.

Mrs. Fullerton looked up with a little glimmer of a smile. 'I saw you approved of her, Reginald,' she said quietly; 'I could see that by the way you talked to her.'

'Sensible women are not so plentiful as they used to be,' returned her husband with a twinkle. He was a largely-built, well-preserved man, who carried his stoutness and his gray hairs with soldierly dignity. A certain bonhomie still lingered as a sort of offshoot of youth.

His wife exactly matched him. She too was a large comely woman. Her white curls and fresh girlish complexion blended pleasantly together; and under her comfortable amplitude there beat one of the gentlest of hearts. People called them a striking-looking couple, and all their sons and daughters had been tall handsome men and women. But the daughters were married, and the sons had scattered themselves over the face of the earth, and only the parent birds remained in the snug home-nest at Combe Lea.

'I liked her way of speaking; girls are so frivolous nowadays, they never seem to be serious about anything. Do you know, Margaret, she reminded me a little of Adela.'

Now Adela was the one daughter they had lost. She had died in the bloom of early womanhood of some strange mysterious disease, and it˜was generally understood that she was her father's darling, and for some time the Colonel had not held up his head.

When Colonel Fullerton had pronounced this name with a little effort, his wife looked at him softly and attentively, and then she seemed to ponder. The likeness had not struck her, for Adela had been very beautiful, and Miss St. John had only the brightness and colouring of youth; but now it seemed to her that there was a certain sweetness of manner and pleasantness of tone that recalled their girl, and from that day Mary found warm friends and partisans at Combe Lea.

At the Hall, too, she and Lettice were most kindly welcomed. It was somewhat late in the afternoon when they paid this visit. By some sort of intuition Mary had left it to the làst, fully understanding by Lady Vendale's messages that some kind of friendliness might be expected; and she was not disappointed.

When the outer door was opened they stepped at once over the threshold into the very centre and circle of home. The family had gathered in the hall for tea. It almost dazzled Mary, passing from the dark drive at once into that circle of fireside comfort. She stood still for a moment, almost forgetting to give her name.

Just picture to yourself my surprise (she wrote to Janet afterwards). I thought from the size of the house we should have to cross wide passages and lobbies, but when the door opened there was Lady Vendale in her high-backed chair pouring out tea, and Sir George standing with his back to the fire patting his dogs. The hall is such a beautiful old place; it is wainscoted with oak, with some fine old carved cabinets, and settles and stands of guns and stags' antlers. The staircase is shut off by an immense screen, but an upper gallery runs across one end; and it is so funny seeing figures passing to and fro—Lady Vendale's maid with a lighted candlestick, Sir George's valet with some clothes over his arm—it was rather like a scene in a play. Sir George is a fine-looking man with a florid face and white whiskers; his wife has been very pretty, but she is a sad invalid, and her face has a worn, sickly look, but she seems far younger than her husband. Miss Vendale is very handsome, and has pleasing manners. I think we shall like her; she is their only child now, and they seem to dote on her. They all welcomed me in the kindest manner, and treated me more like an old friend than a stranger.

There could be no doubt that Mary was pleased with her reception; she had found some of her other neighbours damping and a little repressive—Miss Brettingham and the Rolf Egertons, for example; but here she was received with outstretched hands and genial smiles. The warmest and snuggest seat was found for her close to Lady Vendale's chair. Lady Vendale with her own hands removed the obnoxious jacket, and interposed a glass screen between her and the fire. Diana Vendale brought her the little stand for her teacup, and plied the shy Lettice with cake. Sir George's favourite black hound, Wolf, laid his slender nose in her lap, and regarded her movements wistfully. From where Mary sat the glossy eyes from a tiger-skin glimmered and shone in the firelight. It was all so quaint and picturesque and yet so home-like, no wonder Mary was fascinated.

She had seen Diana in her riding-habit, but she admired her far more in her dark closely-fitting serge dress, moving about the dusky hall. She was a tall handsome girl, with the low broad forehead and the classical features that one sees in old Greek statues; only there was nothing cold or statuesque about her; on the contrary, there was brightness and colouring and exuberance of life only to be seen in very young and healthy natures.

One did not perceive at once her extreme youth, she was so Juno-like and commanding, and her reserve with strangers gave a certain gravity to her manners. But Mary, who was quick in her discernment, soon found out that her mind was as fresh and almost as unformed as a child, that she was shy and sweet of nature, and quite unspoilt by the adulation she received. Though she was in reality mistress of the Hall, and ruled parents and domestics alike, her tyranny was a very loving one, and when occasion demanded it she would submit herself as docilely to her father and mother as though she were an infant in their hands.

She had been a very high-spirited creature once, as wild and tricksy as a young unbroken colt; but the death of her only brother, the companion of her young lifetime and only her senior by a few years, had cast a shadow over her brightness and imparted a tinge of seriousness to her nature. Her mother's ill-health had further quieted her. Mary detected the underlying earnestness, and her interest at once deepened.

'I have seen you riding several times,' Mary said to her, trying to draw her into conversation; for hitherto only Sir George had talked, and his wife had thrown in a mild observation now and then.

He answered for her now, for Sir George was one who loved the sound of his own voice.

'Yes, Di was the first to point you out to us. "That's our new neighbour, Miss St. John!" she said at once; and then we wondered who the child could be. So your brother is going to be curate in charge, is he? Well, well! a little change of diet will not hurt us. Mr. Champneys writes good sermons, but somehow they do not check one's napping tendencies. He is always preaching against Socinianism and the Arianism of the nineteenth century. I am a poor theologian, and I often cannot make out what he means; my wife there finds fault enough with him.'

'There is no warmth in his sermons, they are so cold and lifeless! she sighed; 'they always remind me of Ezekiel's dry bones! To what school does your brother belong? is it the High, Low, or Broad Church party? I hope he is not very extreme in his views.'

'Maurice is a very good churchman, but he rather prides himself on belonging to no particular school; he is very hot against all narrowness and intolerance. I heard him once say that these divisions of parties seemed to him like rents in the seamless robe! He has a reverence for all antiquity, and is a great lover of Hooker and George Herbert.'

'That sounds well, that sounds well,' replied Sir George, rubbing his hands. He was not largely acquainted with Hooker, but it was his custom to fall asleep on Sunday afternoons over George Herbert's *Church Porch*; it was as good as a narcotic to him. Diana had once slily substituted Keble's *Christian Year*, and his nap had been spoiled for that afternoon. 'Augusta, I should not be surprised if Mr. St. John turns out a man after your own heart, the very model of a country parson.'

'He is earnest and lives for his work,' returned Mary, who could never say enough in her brother's praise; and then she commenced to talk to these kind people about Brotherton. She soon found that though Sir George fidgeted and called it a pigsty of a place, and a pest and plague to the whole neighbourhood, he was not ill disposed towards its reformation, and even offered a twenty-pound note on the spot towards fitting up a mission-room; though he argued with Mary a long time on the desirability of at once ejecting Josiah Culpepper. Diana meanwhile kept her large eyes fixed on them both and made no comment, but she evidently thought a good deal.

'But, Sir George, you are surely not advocating rank dissent; Josiah Culpepper simply frightens these poor people; temporary excitement produced on overwrought minds seldom results in lasting good.' Mary was quoting largely from Maurice.

'Well put, well put, my dear Miss St. John; but let me remind you of one thing—the lower classes differ from us in these matters; a washerwoman, for example, likes her doctrine to be hot and peppery; the quiet sort that suits my wife would seem tame to her. How do you or I know that Josiah Culpepper may not be doing a great work in Brotherton, though he does spice his discourses a little too strongly?' and Sir George rubbed his hands in a pleased argumentative way, as though he had put the matter very cleverly.

Mary looked at him with a little smile.

'Have you ridden through Brotherton lately, Sir George?'

'Humph! well—no. Di and I generally keep the straight road to Canterton.'

'If you would go there to-morrow, I do not think that

you would be favourably impressed by Josiah Culpepper's
work. "Ye shall know them by their fruits ;" is it not so,
Lady Vendale ?' and when she had said this, she rose still
smiling, and took her leave.

'A very superior girl that; you must cultivate her, Di !'
was Sir George's observation as he closed the hall-door
behind his guests.

Mary's next meeting with Diana was on the evening
before her brother and sister were expected. She had had
a busy day superintending the last finishing touches; and
late in the afternoon she left Lettice coiled up in one of
the morning-room windows, and went out for a solitary
stroll.

As she passed the Hall gates Miss Vendale came out
with her great black hound beside her. She was wrapped
in furs, and looked handsomer than ever; but she stopped
at once on seeing Mary, and held out her hand with a
pleased smile.

'I am so surprised to see you. I thought only Wolf
and I were fond of this gray gloaming. Father always
laughs at me about my partiality for dusky prowls; I shall
tell him you share the same taste.'

'I have always been fond of walking on a winter's
afternoon,' replied Mary in an animated voice, for she was
gratified at Miss Vendale's cordial greeting. 'There is
something in the general grayness that fascinates me ; the
world has lost its matter-of-fact glare and becomes dim and
indistinct. In London I often felt an odd sort of pleasure
in watching the street lamps being lit; the sudden brightness in the long gloomy streets, the soft perspective when
one looked down one of the glimmering roads, the quiet
brooding sky overhead, all had attractions in my eyes.
People would laugh at me ; but even bricks and mortar are
not without certain beauties.'

'I should not laugh at you,' returned Diana seriously.
'Ah, I see you have read Ruskin to some purpose. Which
way are you going, for I should like to talk to you a little ?'

'Let us go back to the Park,' was Mary's reply; 'the
wind blows so that we can hardly hear each other's voices.

The fireside is the'best place for an undisturbed chat ;' and as Miss Vendale made no objection, they were soon seated in the morning-room, with Lettice still coiled up in the window.

'I have been thinking over what you and my father said about Brotherton,' began Diana somewhat abruptly. 'Father is so good, but he thinks a cheque or a twenty-pound note will set everything right ; he is always vexed if any one talks about Brotherton to him, because he says it is such a disgrace to the place ; but when your brother comes, what will he say to us ? '

'I am afraid he will give you very little peace until every abuse is rectified,' answered Mary candidly.

'And he will tell us that he is ashamed of us ; that there is Lazarus at our gate, lying unfed and untended. Poor father ! he will not be able to enjoy his Sunday naps for a long time. Do you know, I am beginning to be afraid of your brother ? '

'Oh no ; you must not look upon Maurice as a sort of clerical Josiah Culpepper,' returned Mary. 'He is very much in earnest, but then he is so gentle. He never frightens people into doing their duty, but when there is something to be done he tries to interest them, and to put things clearly before them. He always finds excuses : people did not know, they did not think, or else they would have done otherwise. "Always impute good motive, unless you are sure of the contrary," is a favourite sentence of his.'

'I like that,' returned Diana thoughtfully ; and then they fell into an eager discussion about Brotherton ; and Mary spoke enthusiastically of her brother's work in London, and of his failing health and impaired energies ; and though she said nothing of her own share in his labours, her hearer quite understood how things had been between the brother and sister, and marvelled not a little at the absence of all mention of Mrs. St. John.

Once she volunteered a question, 'Does not Mrs. St. John work too ? ' but she was sorry that she made the remark when she saw the uneasy colour rise to Mary's face.

'Janet has her children and the house ; she is not as

much at leisure as I am,' was the perfectly truthful answer, and Diana tried not to feel that something lay behind the simple words.

It was late when Miss Vendale took her leave, which was not until she had exacted from Mary a promise to come up to the Hall the following week, and spend a long afternoon with her and her mother.

This budding intimacy soon ripened into warm friendship during the months that ensued. Mary's pleasantest and most congenial hours—apart from her work with Maurice—were spent up at the Hall. Janet's good sense so approved of this new source of interest that she actually forbore to reproach Mary with leaving her sometimes to her children's companionship; and if Mary's unselfishness ever took alarm, and she would offer to give up one of these pleasant invitations, she would say quite kindly and cheerfully, 'Oh no, dear Aunt Mary, you have given up quite enough for us. I like you to be with Diana; she is such a thoroughly nice girl.' Mary's chief trouble was with Dollie, who became furiously jealous, and who always wrote Miss Vendale's name with inverted commas. 'I suppose you never pass a day without seeing your new friend, Miss Vendale,' or, 'I imagine my opinion is not worth much in the matter, but if you ask Miss Vendale,' and so on, until Mary lost patience, and wrote a downright scolding letter to the naughty little thing, asking her if she knew a certain fable in Æsop; and whether she meant to resemble that unamiable and thoroughly despicable quadruped; and if she were never to possess a feminine acquaintance except a certain touchy Miss Dorothy. And then in a postscript, as though her heart melted at the thought of her own severity—

Oh, Dollie, how I do long for June, when you and your mother will come to me. Tell Mrs. Maynard she is very tiresome to put off her visit until then; if the house be full I could easily have found room for you two. But perhaps she will prefer Crome when it is quieter; and seriously, Dollie darling, I shall be so pleased to make you and Diana acquainted with each other, for I am sure you will love her. She is far nicer than Emma or Mable Ducie, though Emma is a very sensible woman.

Dollie felt ashamed of herself when she read this letter.

Oh, Aunt Mary (she wrote, in a sudden burst of penitence), how can you be so good to me after my shabbiness and meanness? You shall have a dozen Dianas, my poor dear ! if they will only make you happier, and help you to forget what had better be forgotten. And though I will not promise to love this one, I will be very well-behaved and nice to her. I was only afraid that as she was so very good, and handsome, and clever (adjectives all underlined), that you might forget your poor little Dollie (and so on, and so on, through a page or two of affectionate protest ; and then rather abruptly, as it seemed to Mary)—We have seen Mr. Grey Lyndhurst two or three times ; he is very polite and attentive, and brings us flowers, and mother seems to enjoy his visits. I have coaxed her into taking lodgings at Brighton for the next two months ; Abercrombie Road is too dreadful after Lesponts. When we have accomplished the flitting I will write to you again. If I can only keep her there until we come to you in June, would not that be delightful ?

And as Mary folded up the letter she wondered whether this plan of Dollie meant anything more than restlessness and a desire for change, or whether she was anxious to avoid Mr. Grey Lyndhurst's visits. But on this subject Dollie was reticence itself.

CHAPTER XXXIII

MAURICE'S NEW WORK

WHEN Mary welcomed her guests the first evening she was surprised and disappointed to find Maurice looking ill and depressed, and Janet anxious and rather tearful. Even the children's joyous exclamations failed to evoke a smile. He was very affectionate to his sister, and said all sorts of loving things to her as she pointed out her plans for their comfort : the luxurious study, the children's playroom, the suite of spacious bedrooms which they were to occupy for so many months, the fires, the flowers, the thousand and one little details over which her affection had busied itself —all attracted his attention, and drew an answering word or smile. 'Oh, Mary, my dear sister,' he said at last, and there was a volume of unspoken eloquence in these few words, and then, as though he could say or look no more, he sank down wearily in his study chair, and Janet made a sign that they should leave him alone.

'Oh, Janet, is he worse?' asked poor Mary; and a great fear woke up in her heart. Janet shook her head, and one or two tears fell.

'Oh no, it is not that,' she said, looking round the beautiful room that had been set apart for her. 'It is the wrench from his old life that he is feeling. He is half breaking his heart over it, and when he frets like that he breaks mine too. Run away, Bee, my darling,' as the child peeped in at them through the half-closed door. 'I want to talk to dear Aunt Mary. Run to Lettice, my pet !' Then speaking in the disconsolate voice that Mary knew so

well, and hoped never to hear again—'Oh, you do not
know how dreadful this last week has been. I could enjoy
nothing; not even the children's anticipation and my own
pleasure at coming here. He used to come in evening
after evening and sit down opposite me, looking so unhappy,
and leaning his head on his hand—you know his way.
And once, when I spoke to him, and tried to cheer him up,
he was almost sharp with me.'

Mary shook her head, incredulous but smiling. 'No,
no, Janet, you do not expect me to believe that, I hope.'

'Well, not sharp exactly; but he was terribly reproachful. "You don't understand, Janet. It is not your fault,
my dear. No, you cannot comprehend how I have carried
these poor creatures in my heart; and now I must forsake
them." That was what he said.'

Mary was silent. She understood now. Alas! how
could a woman like Janet comprehend this grand priestly
soul? This was what ailed him, then. Well, she would
go to him by and by—she who was his humble helper, and
who could sympathise with him so entirely.

'It is so hard!' continued Janet fretfully, for she was
overwrought and excited, and things were strange about
her. 'Just when I was so happy, and one's life was beginning to arrange itself after one's wishes! And now, just at
the moment of realisation, for everything to be spoiled!'

'Nay, my dear Janet.'

'How am I to enjoy things when I see him look like
that?' she protested. 'When you showed us the rooms, I
could hardly say a word; and yet my heart felt bursting.
When the children cried out in their glee, I felt inclined to
hush them.'

'Poor little souls! I am glad you did nothing of the
kind,' returned Mary, who had been much edified by their
raptures. Through the half-closed doors she could hear
them chatting to Rhoda. 'Now, you are to be quiet. I
will not let you talk any more. To-morrow when you wake
up to your new life you will feel quite different about
things, and so will Maurice. Do not force yourself to feel
happy or to enjoy. You are too spent and weary;' and

then she put her gently in an easy-chair, and brought her a
footstool, and kissed her softly between her troubled eyes.

'You are to rest and do nothing for the remainder of
the evening. Rhoda will come to you by and by, when
she has put the children to bed. Now, I must go down to
Maurice;' and then she left her half comforted. Mary
was such a tower of strength to them; she understood
them both so well. She would go and talk to Maurice,
and lift him out of his despondency.

'Oh, Mary, what a blessing you are to us both!' she
murmured, as she leant her tired head against the cushions
that Mary had placed. When Lettice peeped in a few
minutes later she thought mamma was asleep, and gently
withdrew. The firelight, the scent of the flowers, the deep
luxurious stillness and sense of utter rest, had lulled her
into a half-waking dream, and in her sleep Janet smiled
and looked so beautiful that the child lingered for a moment
half fascinated.

Mary was quite prepared for her brother's mood. When
she entered the study he was sitting in the attitude Janet
had described, leaning his head on his hand, his tall figure
bowed partly from weakness and partly from despondency.
He looked up at her and smiled faintly as she quietly drew
the chair beside him, but volunteered no word, and for a
little while they sat silent, both occupied with their own
thoughts—Maurice brooding heavily, and Mary thinking
how she could comfort him.

He roused himself at last with difficulty.

'I am poor company to-night, my dear; where is
Janet?'

'She is tired, and I left her to rest; you will let me
stop with you a little, Maurice?' Then very softly—'I
understand all about it, my dear brother.'

He lifted his eyes at that. 'What do you understand,
Mary?'

'What you are feeling, and how sore and heavy your
heart is. You are telling yourself all manner of hard things
—how you have failed, and how your work is taken from
you. Is it not so, dear?'

'Yes,' he returned with a sigh. 'I am afraid I am only an unprofitable servant. I wanted to work where the harvest was plentiful and the reapers few; and now in the heat of the day my strength has failed.'

'Oh, Maurice, can anything be nobler than such failure?'

'Mary, you must bear with me to-night, for I am sad at heart at leaving my people, and all this luxury seems to oppress and stifle me.'

'Oh!' she said, and then caught her breath and stopped. Had it not stifled her too?

'I feel bewildered and oppressed,' he continued; 'strangely so, for I am not ill, and nothing has occurred to vex me. If I were superstitious, which, thank God, I am not, I should say some presentiment of approaching evil troubled me. Mary, have I been weak to listen to you and Janet? Can I be sure that I have followed a plain leading of Providence and not the mere instincts of affection?'

'My dear Maurice, why do you distress yourself with such doubts? It was an act of self-preservation, taken for the sake of your wife and children.'

'Well, perhaps so; a man's household must be his first duty, be he priest or layman. The life I planned for myself could only be carried out as a celibate. But, Mary, I must own myself disappointed.'

'In what way?' she asked, lifting her quiet eyes to his. Their mute sympathy seemed to draw out the secret sting of his pain.

'With myself—with everything—with the checked purposes and aims of my life. When I married, when my darling gave up her luxurious home and estranged all her belongings to become my wife, I said to myself that not even she should come between me and my work. I was dedicated—wedded to it, and yet it has come to this, that for her and for the children's sake I must renounce it.'

'For your own sake too, dear.'

'For my own sake? I would rather have stayed at my post until I died. What death could be more glorious, Mary? Ah, you do not know—not even you—how I have

loved those poor creatures.   I seemed to carry them in my
heart—their life was my life—I lived among them.   I was
poor, and could understand their poverty; I knew their
thoughts and sins and temptations; fallen as they were,
they were not foul in my sight.   Under the scars I could
see the reflection of a purer humanity.   Why should not
the woman who was a sinner touch me since she touched
my Master?   And now,' he continued in a tone of grief, 'I
have forsaken them; who will love them and understand
them as I have done?'

'Oh, Maurice!' and now there was soft rebuke in her
voice.   'Has the Church only one faithful servant?   Are
they all hirelings and not shepherds?   Do you think the
Master who has stricken you with weakness has no one to
take your place?   My dear brother, what cloud is upon
you?   Where is your faith?'

'I do not know,' he returned humbly; and then almost
in a voice of awe he continued, 'Who taught you such
wisdom, Mary?   Nay, why should I ask that?   God is
surely rebuking my discontent and presumption through
your mouth.   Am I the only faithful servant?   Ah, you
had me there.   Shame on me for giving way to such
despondency!'

'Nay, Maurice, it was your weakness, not you, that
spoke.   We are so dependent on our poor bodies.   Ill
health makes one despondent.   When you were stronger no
one had clearer views, or was less prone to melancholy.
This is pure exhaustion and brain weariness.   The Philistines are upon you to-night.   Had you been less tired I
meant to have talked to you of Brotherton.'

'I had forgotten Brotherton,' he returned, and then he
was silent for a few minutes.   But under his shaded hand
Mary could see his pale lips moving.   By and by, when he
uncovered his face, she almost started at the sudden sweet
brightness of his smile; it was almost heavenly.

'Thank you, Mary; thank you, my own sister, for speaking the truth to me, and bearing with me in my dark mood.
It has passed now; yes, thank God, it has passed.   I see
it all now; how ungenerous, how rebellious I have been.

I would work for Him, but I would not lay aside my work at His bidding. I would not trust those poor creatures to His care who'—his voice breaking—'died for them. I would choose my work, and order my life, and murmur at failure, which was the hardest part of all. Mary, how am I to preach to others when I am so faulty myself? God bless you, dear, for lifting the burthen off my soul! Now I must go to Janet and ask her pardon for making her so unhappy.'

And Janet, waking up from her brief refreshing sleep, found, to her surprise, her husband leaning against the mantelpiece, watching her with tears in his eyes.

'Are you ill, Maurice? Is anything wrong?' she exclaimed, starting up in sudden anxiety at his moved, tender look.

'No, love, nothing is wrong. I have been ill, but am well again—ill in mind, not body. So you need not look so anxious.

'Janet,' he continued, 'I have made you miserable the last week, but you must forgive your husband, darling. Now I mean to be happy with you and the children, and to take what God gives me. You and I must love Him better in this beautiful place.'

'Yes, Maurice,' whispered Janet, leaning her head against him, and her bosom heaved under its sudden load of bliss. Maurice would be happy again. 'Now I want to be good; I want to do something to show my gratitude for giving us to each other. You who are so much higher and nobler must help me.'

'We must help each other,' he replied solemnly. But Janet little knew how her words thrilled him; never before had those proud lips spoken in that childish fashion—'I want to be good!' but some natures are softened more by prosperity than adversity. To-night she really felt it would be easy to be good. Easy to be good! alas! poor misguided woman! when her very happiness was resting on the wrecked hopes of another life.

A new existence had dawned for Mary with her brother's arrival; from this time her busy days hardly knew an unoccupied moment. While Janet devoted herself to her

children's education—and lessons with mamma, with the
beautiful new schoolroom, were far more interesting and
less trying to the patience of teacher and pupils than
they ever had been—or roamed happily with them about
the park and lanes, looking for the first spring flowers,
Mary was devoting all her energies to the reformation of
Brotherton.

When Mrs. Pratt had received her orders for the day,
and Bee had been kissed and played with a little, and there
had been a game of hide-and-seek among the marble pillars
in the hall, Maurice and his sister would sally forth together, and their faces were always set steadily towards
Brotherton. They had begun work on a very humble
scale. While Maurice went from house to house, making
friends with the women, and half reasoning, half coaxing
them into more decent ways, Mary was gathering children
of all ages round her in the low-raftered kitchen behind
Anne Weevil's all-sorts shop, teaching them the rudiments
of learning and needlework, and making elementary efforts
for their personal cleanliness. They had at first made use
of the dilapidated chapel, but Josiah Culpepper had once
borne down upon Mary in his seedy black raiment, and had
carried off three of his lambs at one fell swoop, disregard-
ing their shrill remonstrations—'Us wants to stay and
learn A B C and "Our Fathers in Heavens" with her!'
but Josiah, with wrathful eyes, and darting looks of fire and
brimstone at Mary, had succeeded in dispersing the little
flock; and the next Sunday, when Maurice held a cottage
meeting, he was obliged to content himself with a bedridden old woman and her blind daughter, all the rest of
the Brotherton folks being evenly divided between the alehouse benches and the chapel, where Josiah Culpepper
thundered about the scarlet woman, and Jesuits in petti-
coats, and the seven-hilled abomination, and Antichrist, and
such like hot-spiced subjects, until the agricultural brain—
slightly bovine, and not infrequently muddled by inward
and outward stimulant—became confused. And Anne
Weevil's little grand-daughter, Lizzie, propounded the views
of the whole village when she informed the bewildered

Mary one day 'that Antichrist was come, and was talking to Dan Tucker behind the hedge,' meaning Maurice.

It was uphill work, but somehow Maurice and Mary thrived on it—at least Maurice did. Mary, who was very energetic and sanguine, was rather discouraged after a time by their slow progress; but Maurice only laughed, and quoted his favourite motto, 'Little by little.'

Mary was for constructing an iron church at once, but Maurice answered there was plenty of time for that. His cottage meetings were badly attended; the people were so thick-headed and ignorant, and in spite of Josiah's rantings so utterly sunk in heathenism and vice, that the ordinary well-ordered church service would fail to attract them.

'If it were warmer I would try open-air services,' he said; 'that might draw them. At present when I want the men I have to wait outside Dan Tucker's beer-shop for them, and often they are too muddled to listen to me. I find the best time is when they are eating their dinner under a hedge; they will let me talk to them then. I had a good talk to half a dozen of them the other day sitting on a turned-up wheelbarrow; I began by reading the paper to them, and then it led to other things. Robin Weevil, Lizzie's father, promised me to put on a clean smock-frock and come to our next cottage service. Robin is my first-fruits,' and Maurice's eyes brightened.

'Only Robin, and you have worked so hard for three weeks,' sighed Mary, who was tired with a long morning's teaching in the close, dark kitchen. It was strange, she was so strong, and yet she was often conscious of fatigue now.

'Well, Rome was not built in a day, and Brotherton is not to be reformed in three weeks,' he returned cheerfully. It was astonishing how cheerful Maurice always was now. 'Poor Mary! you are thinking of your iron church: never mind, by and by we will have it and a little schoolhouse for the children, with a resident teacher. It is too far for the girls to come to Crome in the winter; and now we have found out Hilstead'—another straggling, neglected hamlet —'it will be worth while to have it.'

'Oh yes,' returned Mary, shaking off her lassitude with
an effort; 'and I was thinking yesterday what a capital
thing it would be if Susan Fairweather—you know that
nice young widow who lives near the church, and is so
destitute—if we could set her up in a good, useful shop
either at Brotherton or Hilstead.   Anne Weevil is too old
for her business, and really the things she sells to these
poor people are scandalous—mouldy cheese, and rotten
apples, and tainted bacon.   Yesterday she mixed tea and
snuff together by mistake.'   And as Maurice again laughed,
she went on more eagerly : 'She is a good old soul, but
she is getting deaf as well as blind.   Now Susan Fairweather is a strong, capable young woman, and before she
married she kept a little shop with her mother.   I have
been talking to Lady Vendale and Diana about it; Lady
Vendale is quite enthusiastic about it; Susan is such a
favourite of hers.   We would stock the shop with things
likely to be useful to the people, and everything should be
of the best; and if I could only interest our ladies at Crome,
we would have working parties in the winter, and sell
ready-made linen just at the cost price of the material.   I
spoke to Mrs. Fullerton about it, and she approved most
thoroughly; she said it would be such a boon to find
employment for all their idle young ladies—the Rolf Egertons and Mabel Ducie.'

'Our Lady Bountiful means to be a blessing to rich as
well as poor,' observed Maurice, with one of his rare smiles.
They were walking towards Crome ; Mary, who was picking
her way through the muddy lane, came a little closer to
him.

'Oh, Maurice, it is my life; if one can only do a little
good before one dies, and make a few people happier,'
then she paused and went on.   This was her rest, her
reward after her day's labour, this quiet walk and talk with
Maurice.   'I am sure of help from Diana and Emma
Ducie.   Emma actually offered the other day to help me with
the children at Brotherton.   Think what a comfort it would
be to those poor women to be able to buy their husbands'
shirts, and cheap blankets, and every kind of useful gar-

ment for themselves and their children, just at the cost they would give for the material.'

'A capital thought, Aunt Mary ; but why not teach the women to work themselves ? '

'We hope to do that too. I am teaching the children already. When we have the new schools, Maurice, the teacher might live in the rooms over the shop. She would be a nice companion for Susan, whose children are so young.'

'Another good idea ! What a head our Aunt Mary has ! '

'Then when I have a little less to do—for at present I am fully occupied with our elementary school, and cottage visiting at Crome, Hilstead, and Brotherton—not to mention my social duties——'

'Which, by the by, devolve on Janet,' interrupted her brother.

'Oh ! that sort of thing pleases Janet,' returned Mary with an embarrassed laugh. 'What was I saying ? why do you stem the torrent of my parochial eloquence ? Let me see, I was saying when the school is off my hands, Emma and I mean to have working and knitting parties for the women both at Brotherton and Hilstead. They shall bring their babies, and we have some nice interesting books, and Emma thinks we might get up a course of cooking lessons, and have a few sanitary lectures and——'

'My dear Mary, you take my breath away. You certainly are a wonderful woman ; I am getting unduly proud of having such a sister ! We will talk about these things again, for there are Janet and the children coming to meet us. I am bound that she wants us to go down and look how the Rectory repairs are getting on ;' and Maurice quickened his steps to join her, and Brotherton for the moment was forgotten.

CHAPTER XXXIV

IT must not be supposed that all Maurice's and Mary's energies were devoted to Brotherton. At Crome the new vicar, as they persisted in calling him, was decidedly popular.

His earnestness and straightforwardness of purpose recommended him at once to such men as Sir George Vendale and Colonel Fullerton, while his sweetness of manner and his unfailing courtesy won the heart even of Miss Brettingham.

'Mr. St. John is a most gentlemanly man—I may say a very gentlemanly man!' she observed confidentially to her favourite gossip Mrs. Woodyard. 'I think if you could rouse yourself sufficiently to see him, my dear Adelaide, it would do you a world of good. His manners are most charming.'

'He was here yesterday,' returned Mrs. Woodyard languidly, shivering in her luxurious Indian wraps. 'I liked him exceedingly. I had one of my worst headaches, and Lydia was bathing my temples with eau-de-Cologne when he came in; but he spoke so softly that he did me no harm at all. He got up and arranged the blind himself once, because he noticed the light fretted me. I like that in a man; it reminded me of my dear Allan—he was just such a kind thoughtful creature. I hear his wife is a handsome woman, at least Carrie Egerton said so.'

'Handsome! she is superb! I never saw a more beautiful woman,' observed Miss Brettingham with quite a gush of enthusiasm. 'I hear she was one of the Cheetams, and that they never forgave her marrying so much beneath her; though Mr. St. John is a perfectly well-bred man, an exceedingly well-bred man!' repeated Miss Brettingham, who was much given to elegant repetition—'far superior to his dowdy outspoken sister.'

'She is a little brusque, but not exactly unpleasing,' returned her friend, closing her eyes. This was always a hint for dear Arabella to take her departure. When Adelaide was in this mood, there was no prospect of highly-flavoured Indian tea and hot rich cakes; so Miss Brettingham rose reluctantly, and went back to her diminutive parlour and tiny handmaiden, and took her solitary meal in rather a penitential fashion.

There could be no doubt that Janet's beauty took the whole neighbourhood by storm; the Rolf Egertons and Ducies raved about her; Emma Ducie indeed remained staunch to Miss St. John, but Mrs. Ducie and Mabel, and even Jack, were at her feet. Lady Vendale and Mrs. Fullerton, too, pronounced her a very pleasant person, with good manners, but a little distant, not to say haughty; not that Janet was ever distant with them; but there was always a certain queenliness and dignity in her carriage, as though she felt herself superior to her belongings, that not all Maurice's gentle hints could induce her to lay aside; and yet it must be owned that she was perfectly unconscious of it.

'Janet, you walk into a room as though you would say, "Here I am, Mrs. St. John; find my equal or superior if you can!"' observed her husband one day, half jesting and half serious.

'Nonsense, Maurice; how can you be so absurd?'

'Ah! but seriously, love, people will think you are proud.'

'Well, so I am!' with a toss of her head.

'Only a poor curate's wife; consider, my darling!' his voice becoming a little grave; for, with all his fondness, he would tell her of her faults.

'I am proud!' she repeated, and then her voice softened,

as it always did to him. ' I am proud of being your wife;
if I carry my head high, it is because you have crowned
me with your love, because I would not change places with
the Queen on her throne!' and then she pressed closer to
him, and Maurice's rebuke ended in a caress.

Invitations poured in on the new household at Crome
Park—a dinner at the Hall and the Priory and Combe
Lea; an evening gathering, select and musical, at the
Glade; afternoon tea at Crome Cottage; and actually at
St. Norbert's!

The last was the most astonishing feat of all! how Miss
Brettingham's guests ever contrived to seat themselves in
her tiny parlour? Jack Ducie indeed took up his position
on the stairs. How, when they were once successfully
wedged in their places, they ever got out without overturn-
ing the spidery tables with their marvellous assortment of
china was ever an enigma both to Janet and Mary.

The tea, which was of the poorest quality—somehow
Miss Brettingham's water had never been known to boil in
the memory of the oldest inhabitant of Crome—was served
in cups of priceless china without handles. The thinnest
slices of bread and butter, and the tiniest wedges of seed-
cake were offered for the refreshment of the guests. Jack
Ducie, who was an incorrigible young man, once asked, in
what he meant to be a whisper, for a magnifying glass or
microscope to examine the specimens; but his tone had
been audible, and Miss Brettingham had never forgiven the
affront. She always called him afterwards 'that ill-man-
nered disagreeable young man, a perfect cub, my dear,—
between ourselves, a perfect cub!'

The dinner-parties at the Hall and the Priory were
grand affairs. Janet enjoyed them immensely, and only
two things damped her pleasure in the slightest degree:
first she had to waive her right of precedence in favour of
the lady of the manor; and secondly, Mary was incorrigible
in refusing to wear ornaments.

She had consented, however, with some reluctance,
to have two new dresses provided for these festive
occasions; in fact, after a great deal of persuasion on

Janet's part, she had agreed to have her wardrobe properly replenished.

The evening dresses, which she had chosen herself, were black silk and lace. Nothing could be quieter, but as they were well and stylishly made, Janet owned herself satisfied.

'Your mourning is so slight now, that you can wear a pearl necklace, or even your diamond ornaments,' Janet observed, as they separated to their different apartments to dress. Great was her wrath and disappointment, therefore, when, just at the last moment, when the carriage was at the door, Mary entered looking comely and well-dressed in her black silk, but without a single ornament except some white flowers and maidenhair in the front of her dress. Janet, who was also in black silk—her sister-in-law's gift—with scarlet geranium in her hair, threw her entirely into the shade.

'Mary, where are your ornaments? You must wear either the pearls or diamonds; let me fetch them for you, quick!'

'You may fetch them for yourself, Janet. I only wish you would wear them.'

'My dear, a clergyman's wife!' observed Maurice, in a rebuking tone, and then he continued more mildly, 'she looks almost too brilliant as it is. How well these flowers suit you, Janet!'

'It does not matter what I wear,' replied his wife impatiently, for she was fretted at Mary's obstinacy. 'Do speak to her, Maurice; it is too absurd for her to leave her jewels in their cases.'

'It will be no use my interfering, I am afraid,' returned Maurice, after a glance at his sister's face. 'Mary, how pale and tired you look! Brotherton has been too much for you to-day.'

'I wish we were going there to-night,' she returned wearily. 'Don't tease me about the diamonds, Janet. I never mean to wear jewels.' Her tone was just a trifle irritable, and Maurice secretly marvelled at it. It struck him not only that evening, but on the succeeding ones at the Priory and Combe Lea, that Mary was not quite her-

self, that she did not seem in her usual spirits—not half
so bright as she was on the coldest wettest day when
they ploughed their way through the miry lanes to Brotherton; and yet, when he mentioned this afterwards to Janet,
she chid him playfully for his fancy, though she took an
opportunity of lecturing Mary privately for her apparent
want of interest.

'You are so good to the poor, so dear to us all,' she
complained, 'and yet you want to shirk all your social
duties.   You are at Brotherton all the morning, and in and
out of the cottages and schools at Crome all the afternoon,
and leave me to entertain your visitors.   When I am talking to them in the morning-room, sometimes I hear you
come in and slip across the hall to avoid them.'

'It was only the Rolf Egertons and Mabel Ducie, and
I was so wet and tired,' returned Mary, with a flush.   She
hoped Janet had not heard her, but nothing escaped Mrs.
St. John.

'If it had been one of your special favourites—that plain
awkward Miss Ducie, for example, or Diana Vendale—you
would not have complained of fatigue,' replied her sister-in-
law in her most chilling voice.   'You ought not to be so
exclusive in your likes and dislikes.   The Rolf Egertons
are only parvenus and a trifle vulgar, but the girls are good-
natured and harmless, and Mabel Ducie is a sprightly,
charming little creature.'

'She always looks as though she were a specimen young
lady, to be kept carefully under a glass case,' observed
Mary, moved to unusual retort by this sudden attack on her
exclusiveness.   'Emma is worth a dozen of her.'

'Oh, we all know your opinion of Emma,' returned
Janet crossly, for she had conceived a strong dislike to the
elder Miss Ducie; her brusque ways, her prominent teeth,
and irredeemable plainness, and above all, her keen sensible
tongue, were all sources of offence to Mrs. St. John.   'What
can Mary see in that very unattractive young woman!' was
always her interjection of wonder after one of Miss Ducie's
visits.

'Now, Janet, I will not have you talk against my friends,'

began Mary a little hotly; but her sister-in-law interrupted her.

'Oh, it is not Emma with whom I was finding fault; it is you, Mary. Do you know, Maurice is beginning to notice your want of interest; when we came home from the Priory, and again last night from Combe Lea, he noticed that you seemed out of spirits.'

Mary was silent, but a sudden flush crossed her face.

'Maurice has such keen eyes, it is so difficult to deceive him. Indeed, Mary, I am speaking for all our sakes. You do your duty so admirably in all other respects; you make us and the children so happy. But in this one matter you fail. When our friends are round us, and every one looks bright and gay, you seem distraite and almost miserable— well, not miserable exactly, but as though your thoughts and interests were elsewhere.'

'Oh, Janet!' but she could say no more; only the tears rose to her eyes, and she hastily brushed them away. What was the use of her speaking? How could Janet know how heavily those festive hours passed for her? how the lights and the music and the laughter dazzled and made her giddy. All last evening an unbidden guest had stood by her chair,—a tall figure with fair hair shining like a halo, with sorrowful reproachful eyes. Hush! what were they playing? Was that the carillon? 'Good-bye, happy days; golden hours that could be no more.' No; it was his voice speaking: 'It is I who am giving you up, Mary; remember that.' Oh that simple honest tongue! How it had stammered and stumbled, and still the words had been said. 'Bertie! my Bertie! where are you now? What are you doing, away from me so long?'

'Miss St. John, your brother says the carriage has come. May I take you down?' Sir George is talking in her ear with old-fashioned garrulity. How welcome the dark roads and the silence of her own room after those weary hours! 'God bless my Bertie!' Was that always her prayer before she laid her head on her pillow? Could Janet know how often it was steeped with her tears? Cruel Janet!'

'Mary dear! Aunt Mary! I never meant to hurt you!'

exclaimed Janet impetuously, and she rose from her seat and threw her arms round her sister. 'I only thought I ought to warn you and put you on your guard before all those people come on Thursday—your own guests in your own house—you will try to rouse yourself?'

'Yes, yes; I will do my best. Never mind my crying a little; I am tired, and what you said upset me. Don't worry yourself, Janet; I will promise to be bright for Thursday.'

And Mary kept her word nobly.

The evening at Crome Park was pronounced a decided success.

There was a dinner-party for the elders, and afterwards all the young people of the neighbourhood and a bevy of guests from the Priory filled the great drawing-room. Two or three officers from Canterton, who were shooting over the Hall preserves, were brought in the Rolf Egerton train.

'How sweet our Mary looks to-night!' whispered Maurice to his wife. As the heiress in her unobtrusive black dress moved among her guests, there was a little flush on her face, but her manners were very bright and winning.

When at Carrie Egerton's request dancing commenced in the hall, she sat down beside Lady Vendale and watched the dancers. Janet begged her to join, but she only smiled and shook her head.

'You are younger than Sophy or Carrie Egerton; you must not make yourself old before your time,' said Lady Vendale, looking affectionately at the girl.

'I never dance now, and I would rather talk to you,' returned Mary simply. 'How well Diana looks! that ruby velvet suits her superbly; she will make a sensation next season in London.'

'It is her own fault that we do not go to town this May; she has persuaded us to put it off for another year. Of course Sir George is quite willing to listen to her, for he hates London, especially in the season; but I am not sure that the dear child is not sacrificing her own wishes out of consideration for us.'

'She thinks that next year you may be stronger; indeed, dear Lady Vendale, you need not be so anxious. I am sure Diana is perfectly happy; she is so young too, that a little delay will not matter.'

'And we are in no hurry to lose her,' observed the poor mother despondently, who already looked on all mankind as leagued against her to rob her of her only treasure; she even looked with some anxiety on a vapid young officer, with a round boyish face, who was then waltzing with Diana. Mary, who followed her glance, laughed outright.

'When Diana marries, she will choose a sensible man; I am sure of that. I never knew any girl with a more decided opinion of her own, and one less likely to err in her judgment; now I must go and speak to poor Miss Brettingham; she is sitting bolt upright and looking miser-able;' and the young hostess crossed the room in search of the highly-born spinster.

'Mary, you have done admirably; I am proud of my sister!' exclaimed Janet as she followed Mary to her room that night.

'I am glad I satisfied you,' was the quiet answer; and Mary, tired and jaded as she felt, seated herself patiently for the long hour of criticism and eulogiums. It was an astounding fact that Janet actually found no fault with any of the arrangements. Mrs. Pratt was a capital manager. Pratt and his subordinates had waited well; the dinner had been excellent; all the table ornaments and flowers faultless; the impromptu dance in the hall had been thoroughly en-joyable; and last, but not least, all the little girls had looked nice and almost pretty in their white frocks and new sashes.

Here Aunt Mary struck in.

'Lettice was always sweet-looking in my eyes; she is the image of Maurice.'

'Yes, dear old fellow; and how well and happy he looked to-night! Sir George seems devoted to him; and don't you think, Mary, Hatty is rather uncommon-looking?'

'Yes; and Rosie had such a pretty colour to-night.'

'And May is certainly improving; she looks fatter and not so lank; if only Bee had not been asleep!'

'For shame, Janet, you idolise that child!'

'I am afraid I do; but she is such a darling,' replied the proud mother. 'Ah, there is Maurice coming to fetch me; well, good-night, Mary. I was only sorry for one thing, that you would not dance to-night; you used to be so fond of it.'

'Ah, but I am getting old and staid now,' returned Mary with a curious smile; she did not care to tell Janet that the last time she had danced, Bertie had been her partner.

CHAPTER XXXV

'WHAT HAVE YOU BEEN DOING TO AUNT MARY?'

'AND now, Mr. St. John, I want to know what you have all been doing to Aunt Mary?'

The speaker was Dollie, and she was seated on the low window sill outside the morning-room, with her feet on the grass and her straw hat full of roses beside her. Maurice had just joined her; he had crossed the park from the Rectory. The repairs were all finished now, and a week ago they had taken possession of their new home, but the Crome Park motto—'Welcome the coming, speed the parting guest'—had been fully illustrated, for Mary had only returned from the Rectory, where she had been doing the honours of the first family meal, just in time to greet Dollie and her mother.

It was the middle of June when Mary stood smiling in the Rectory porch, while Maurice led his wife and children across the threshold of their new home.

'Love, do you think you will be happy here?' he asked, when Janet had completed her tour of inspection through the rooms; but he was a little touched and surprised when, instead of answering him, she suddenly burst into tears and hid her face on his shoulder.

'Why, Janet, my darling, I expected a different reply to that.'

'Oh, Maurice, it is all so beautiful, and I do not deserve it; Mary has been so good;' and for a long time she could say no more.

Dollie, when she saw it the next day, pronounced it the

ideal of a country rectory; the low bow-windowed drawing-room with its new carpet and cretonne, and china bowls of sweet-smelling roses, looked the very perfection of ease and comfort; so did the old-fashioned dining-room and Maurice's study. Janet's favourite window in her room was shaded with rose-coloured hangings, and fitted up with an easy-chair and table, on which stood an exquisite workbox and writing case; in the wardrobe hung some dresses chosen with a special regard to Janet's fastidious taste.

With regard to the children's rooms, which had to be entirely refurnished, Mary and Maurice had consulted together, and their combined efforts had been eminently successful. Simple, tasteful papers adorned the old walls; the little beds with their pink-and-white hangings, and a plaster angel at the head of each, looked charmingly snug. In Bee's nursery there was a toy cupboard, stocked with all manner of toys; a wonderful baby doll in its bassinette lay beside Bee's bed. In the other rooms there were book-shelves filled with inviting-looking books. All manner of surprises awaited the children. Lettice, who loved birds, found a tame canary hopping over her·pillow; a white Persian kitten was coiled up at the foot of Hatty's bed; a fussy little gray dog, answering to the name of Snap, was discovered shut up in a cupboard in May and Rosie's room, from whence he was indignantly ejected by Boy, and hustled downstairs, where he was found by May after-wards, shivering and whining on the mat, but fussy still.

There was no end to Aunt Mary's thoughtfulness. In every room there was a prayer-desk with each child's Bible laid upon it; a sacred picture hung over each mantelpiece. Outside the Rectory there were other surprises which elicited screams of delight. May's she-ass, white as milk, was discovered in the paddock, feeding beside a rough shaggy pony that was meant for the elder children's use; a hutch of white rabbits with pink cornelian eyes stood under a mossy apple-tree at the bottom of the garden; in the poultry-yard there were marvellous cocks and hens, and some fancy pigeons strutting about; a beautiful Alderney cow looked at them across the paddock paling, with mild brown eyes.

'Mammie, I think we've got to 'eavens and 'omes now,' murmured Bee, as her mother sang her to sleep that night. 'Where is the new dollie baby? you must by-by her too!' and for many a night Bee refused to close her eyes, or to listen to her mother's voice, until the waxen baby occupied Janet's arms as well.

Oh, no wonder that scalding tears fell from Janet's eyes that night as she sang that simple tune! what had she done to deserve such blessings?

Mary missed the children dreadfully; the house felt large and empty when their scurrying footsteps were not scampering all over the place; she missed the daily game of hide-and-seek among the marble pillars; she missed Maurice too and their quiet chat in the study at night. But in some ways their absence was a relief. A strain of which she was unconscious seemed removed when Janet's keen eyes were not always on her. When she came in tired from her daily labours at Hilstead and Brotherton, it was rather a comfort to escape the long chiding which somehow always made her feel irritable.

'What does it matter if I am tired or look tired? what does anything matter now?' she once said when she had felt unusually harassed by these ill-timed remonstrances; but Janet's horrified look had filled her with remorse.

'Mary, how can you be so wicked?'

'I am afraid I am wicked,' returned Mary humbly; 'but you try me past my strength sometimes!' and then she went away, looking stricken and ashamed.

Now, when she returned home, Dollie came running across the grass to meet her, in her pretty white gown, with her hands always full of flowers; she would follow Mary to her room and stick them into her dress and hair, chattering like a little magpie all the time about her day's doings; but somehow her talk never tired Mary.

She had been so happy—she never had been so happy in her life before. She and the children had been ever so far—all the way to Farnborough, Lettice and Hatty and she mounting the pony by turns. Rosie had ridden the donkey. Janet would not let May or Bee join them for fear of being overtired, but Boy and Snap had accompanied them.

They had met Sir George and Diana riding, and Sir George had laughed unmercifully at the donkey; and after that they had encountered Jack Ducie, who had insisted on turning back and helping them to collect wild flowers. Jack was a very handsome fellow; did not Mary think so?

'Yes, very; but she believed that he and his cousin Mabel were half engaged,' was Mary's somewhat dry rejoinder; upon which Dollie pettishly returned that she did not care if he were half or wholly engaged to a dozen Mabels! And what did Mary mean by answering in that tone? if she were going to be disagreeable, she would tell her no more.

'Who is cross now, I should like to know?' returned Mary playfully.

'Why, you, of course!' pouted Dollie, with a penitent hug; 'you dear old thing, how I do love you!' and after this small relief to her feelings Dollie took up her parable again, and a long and animated description followed of their picnic luncheon under a hedge—in which it appeared Mr. Jack Ducie had joined—and how they had passed the Glade on their way home, and Mabel had run down to the gate with a basket of strawberries for the tired children; how they had there and then eaten them under the shady verandah, and Mrs. Ducie had brought her out a cup of tea.

'And we are all invited to tea and tennis on Wednesday,' continued Dollie, with sparkling eyes. 'Every one nice is to be asked—you and Miss Vendale, and your brother and Mrs. St. John; none of the half-and-half gentry —the Egertons, for example. They call it a strawberry feast, and Lettice and Hatty are to come too. Mabel says perhaps we may get up a dance on the lawn, only there are so few gentlemen.'

'Wednesday—did you say Wednesday?' exclaimed Mary suddenly, waking out of a reverie; and then she checked herself and half smiled—no, she would not tell

Dollie that that was the day on which she expected Grey; she had already given Mrs. Maynard a hint to that effect, but the widow had only sighed and looked conscious, and nothing more had been said.

'You will come, Aunt Mary?' continued Dollie coax-ingly. 'I mean to have such fun, and I shall not enjoy it a bit without you! and then Diana will be there,' with a little jealous pout.

'We shall see; perhaps I will look in during the after-noon,' replied Mary evasively. 'I shall be at Brotherton until half-past three; but I can follow you as soon as I am dressed. Now, Dollie, dinner is waiting, and I have been ready for the last half hour; your mother will be wondering what has become of us.'

These summer evenings were very peaceful and pleasant. When dinner was over, and Mrs. Maynard had settled herself in an easy-chair in the morning-room with her book or work, the girls would wander up and down the 'peacocks' promenade,' long after Topaz and Sapphire had gone to roost in the low branches of their favourite silver birch; sometimes, with only a light scarf flung over their heads, they would cross the park in the dusk, and creep round the verandah and tap at the window of the Rectory drawing-room. What a welcome Aunt Mary had then! Maurice would throw down his book and stride to the win-dow; Janet and her girls, who would be grouped cosily round the centre table with their work, would look up smilingly.

'Dollie and I have only looked in to say good-night,' Mary would say, gazing at the family scene with happy eyes. 'What are you reading to them, Maurice? Kingsley's *Water-babies*! don't you love that book, Dollie? it is the very prince of fairy stories, so quaint and wise.'

'I don't think I ever quite understood it,' returned Dollie, when they had bidden the Rectory party good-night, and were crossing the dim park again. 'It was very pretty about Tom, but the latter part is horribly con-fusing.'

'Do you think so? Maurice and I once read it to-gether, and we enjoyed it so. It was Bertie's favourite

book,' replied Mary softly. Dollie started but said
nothing; it was the first time Mary had mentioned his
name, and yet how naturally she spoke it. They were
both quite silent until they reached the house.

The shaded lamps were all lighted in the morning-room.
Pratt had brought in the silver urn and tea equipage. Mrs.
Maynard looked up from her book with a sigh of satisfaction.

'How long you have been, my dears!   I was beginning
to be afraid for you, the dews are so heavy to-night.'

'We crossed the park to the Rectory; the moon was
out, and it was so delicious!' exclaimed Dollie, looking
furtively at Mary's quiet face as she seated herself at the
tea-table. When the little meal was over she went to the
piano and sang some of Mary's favourite songs, one after
another, in her sweet thrilling voice.

Mary sat by the window, looking over the moonlit park;
a broad silvery path seemed to wind upward through the
trees; a heavy shadow brooded near the house. What
was that Dollie was singing? 'Good-bye, happy days!'

Ah! yes, she must sing that too—no, she had broken
off and changed its plaintive melody into something graver,
sweeter, and higher in tone. Surely that was Mary's
favourite hymn she was singing now!

> Father, whate'er of earthly bliss
>   Thy sovereign will denies,
> Accepted at Thy throne of grace
>   Let this petition rise :
> Give me a calm, a thankful heart,
>   From every murmur free ; ·
> The blessing of Thy grace impart,
>   And make me live to Thee.

'Thanks, dearest; now we will ring for Pratt and have
prayers.' There were tears in Mary's eyes as she spoke,
but there was a smile on her lips. When prayers were
ended and the good-nights were said, her hand lingered
caressingly on Dollie's shoulder.

'I am so glad you have come; I like to have you near
me—you always do me good!' she said, looking wistfully
at the girl.

Dollie's cheeks quite flushed with pleasure, but she answered in her quick off-hand way—

'You want some one to do you good!' but Mary only smiled, and went off humming the hymn tune—

> Give me a calm, a thankful heart,
> From every murmur free.

'Ah! Bertie, that is what we want, you and I.'

> The blessing of Thy grace impart,
> And make me live to Thee.

It was on the Wednesday that had been fixed for the garden-party at the Glade that Dollie had put her somewhat startling question to Maurice; and if a thunderbolt had fallen at his feet, he could not have been more astonished.

'And now, Mr. St. John, I want to know what you have all been doing to Aunt Mary?' Dollie's tone was grave and a little indignant as she looked up from her roses.

'What we have been doing to Aunt Mary!' returned Mr. St. John, looking down on her rather awkwardly from his great height, as he stood beside the window twirling his soft felt hat between his fingers. Mrs. Maynard had a headache, and he had crossed the park at Mary's request to fetch Dollie; but there she sat in her white gown leisurely sorting her flowers, and seeming in no hurry for her party. 'Why, nothing at all; what do you suppose we should do to her, except spoil her dreadfully?'

'I don't know about the spoiling!' rejoined Dollie, finally selecting her rose, and adding it to a most bewitching little breast-knot for her own private use. 'I am afraid it does not agree with her much.'

'Why, do you think she looks ill?' returned Maurice, becoming very grave all of a sudden. But his keen penetrating glance so embarrassed Dollie that she got a little confused; perhaps Mary would not like her mentioning her looks to her brother, and yet——

'Well, not ill exactly, Mary is so strong; but she looks different somehow, tired and thin. I think Mrs. St. John is right, and that stupid Brotherton is too much for her; she works so dreadfully hard, don't you think so?' glancing up dubiously into Maurice's face. Dollie was very unhappy about Mary, and could not see how to help her, and yet what was the good of making Mr. St. John vaguely uncomfortable; how would that help Mary?

A shadow crossed his face now, for Maurice's love for his sister was very great, beyond ordinary brother's love; there was something of twinship in its nature and responsive sympathy.

'Well, now you mention it,' he returned, dropping his voice as though he feared to be overheard; 'I have noticed a change in Mary, and have spoken of it once or twice to my wife.'

'Well!' interrupted Dollie eagerly, 'what did she say?'

'Janet thinks with me that she is rather over-burdened and oppressed with the weight of her responsibilities; her life is new to her, and it is rather an anxious one for a young girl. Do you think we are right, Miss Maynard? Janet says I am too fanciful, but once or twice lately I have feared that Mary did not seem quite happy.'

'Oh, she is too good to be unhappy long about anything!' exclaimed Dollie, with an involuntary burst of feeling; 'she is like an angel for goodness. I have never seen her equal, never! Ah! there she is coming between the trees. Don't betray me, Mr. St. John; she never likes people to make a fuss about her, I know. If you could induce her to rest more, or go away for a little change.' Dollie had a vague idea that going abroad always set people right.

'Her walk is different; it is not so elastic and springy,' observed Maurice anxiously; but his query 'Tired, Mary?' was met at once by a prompt denial.

'Not a bit; I have had a most satisfactory afternoon. Mrs. Copeland has yielded at last, and has promised to bring all her five children to be baptized;' and thereupon followed a long and animated account of her afternoon's work.

But for once Maurice lent a divided attention. 'I am

sure you are tired, Mary,' he persisted; 'you are quite flushed and breathless. Miss Maynard—at least, we all think you work too hard. Let me look at you—you are certainly thinner.'

'Nonsense,' returned Mary rather abruptly. 'That is some of your rubbish, Dollie; you are setting Maurice to talk to me, but I will not allow it; I will not be lectured, not even by my great big brother!' shaking her head at him.

'1 was only telling him that mother and I think you work too hard,' returned Dollie demurely.

'You are only bringing an avalanche about my ears,' rejoined Mary, in a comical half-vexed tone. 'You don't know Maurice; he will give me no peace now you have put that into his head; what a little mischief-maker you are!'

But underneath her playfulness Dollie saw that Mary was really disturbed.

'Do you know you are both half an hour late? take her away, Maurice, please, while I go in and get rid of this dust.'

'You are right; she does not look like her old bonnie self,' observed Maurice thoughtfully, as they pursued their winding walk through the trees.

Dollie held her peace; she was a little alarmed at the effect of her own words. She had invoked Maurice's aid, but what could even Maurice do over circumstances that were so uncontrollable? Foolish little Dollie! how perplexed she felt, and at that moment Mary was welcoming Grey.

24

CHAPTER XXXVI

It was a most delightful party !

Every one was making much of Dollie ; Miss Maynard was pronounced piquante, uncommon-looking. For once Mabel Ducie's rosebud prettiness seemed cast into the shade, and Miss Vendale's classical features failed to attract. Dollie's dainty figure, her animation, her laugh, drew all eyes towards her ; Jack Ducie almost wavered in his allegiance to his cousin ; the two young officers from Canterton were at her feet ; and indeed the girl looked a sweet embodiment of health and youth and bright sunny happiness.

What a pleasant world it was, Dollie thought, and how kind every one seemed ! She liked the Ducies exceedingly, and Mr. Jack was certainly a very handsome fellow, almost as good-looking as poor Bertie ; and, talking of Bertie, there was Mary crossing the lawn in her soft black summer dress, with some cream-coloured roses nestling in her lace fichu, looking very nice and ladylike ; and who was that slim dark young man beside her?

Dollie could not see his face, for they had stopped, and Mary was introducing him to Miss Vendale ; the next moment her cheeks were flaming, and she almost turned her back on her partner.

'Fourteen — love — the Fates are propitious, Miss Maynard ; the game is in our hands !' exclaimed Captain Thompson enthusiastically.

'Oh, I am so hot, and the sun is shining full on our

court,' returned Dollie, dropping her racket. 'How nice and cool it looks under these trees.'

'I shall be at your service in a minute,' returned her partner, hitting the ball cunningly over the net. 'There, we have won! Miss Ducie and Jack are nowhere. Now let us take a turn and cool ourselves.'

'Not there! not that way!' returned Dollie imploringly; for Captain Thompson, flushed with victory and budding admiration for the little white-gowned figure beside him, was leading the way towards the group she wished to avoid. What did Mary mean by bringing him upon her in this way? Why had she not given her a hint that he was expected, that she might prepare her weapons of defence?

Poor Dollie was flushing with embarrassment to her very finger ends; but she need not have disturbed herself. Grey met her very coolly; he just lifted his hat and shook hands with her quietly. 'How do you do, Miss Maynard? what lovely weather you are having here!' and then he drew back and let her pass on with her companion.

When Dollie returned from her saunter half an hour later, she found him playing at tennis with Miss Vendale for his partner. The unfortunate Jack was scoring now; Grey was losing ground rapidly.

Diana was doing her best to retrieve their misfortunes; she moved across the lawn with the grace and agility of a young fawn. When she raised her racket, the poise of her head and arm were perfect. Captain Thompson stood still to watch them, but Dollie slipped away. Later on he discovered her behind a belt of laurels with Lieutenant Parkington beside her, looking very demure.

When tennis was over, dancing began. In spite of the few gentlemen, Dollie had plenty of partners; but, both to her own and Mary's secret astonishment, Grey was not one of them. He danced with Miss Vendale twice, and when Mabel was obliged to refuse him, he went and sat down by Mary, and let Captain Thompson carry off Dollie before his eyes. The fact was, Grey had come down to Crome in a very high and mighty frame of mind; Mary, who knew nothing of the state of affairs, was full of chagrin and disappointment. He was in love with Dollie, and yet he paid her no attention; he was engrossed with Diana, who was looking very handsome and animated, and never seemed to notice Dollie at all. And Dollie, on her side, was flirting most audaciously with those young officers. Lieutenant Parkington, who was the heir to a large estate, seemed to think it an honour to fan her; and Captain Thompson would have no other partner, and made himself quite conspicuous hovering about her. But then every one knew Captain Thompson had a fresh flirtation every three months—his 'quarterlies,' as Carrie Egerton termed them.

The truth was, Grey had been much hurt and displeased by Dollie's behaviour. He had called at Abercrombie Road several times. On the first occasion Dollie had been shy, but had not repelled him; the second time her manner had changed and been more distant; but on his succeeding visits he had failed to understand her. There had been a flightiness, a caprice, and a stand-offishness that had almost affronted him.

After that he had called again, and had been told they were at the seaside. No message or address had been left for him, and yet his weekly visit must have been expected; and Grey's feelings had been much wounded. For the first time he felt himself angry and offended with the girl; she was playing with him, or else her heart was not to be won by him. As far as her mother was concerned, his courtship had been highly successful. Mrs. Maynard already liked him very much; but to all her eulogiums Dollie had turned a deaf ear.

'What a pity you cannot marry him yourself! you are still very young and nice-looking,' she said one day, to her mother's intense horror.

Grey was losing heart; but he little knew that what he imagined caprice on Dollie's part was really a despairing flight. After his first visit, Dollie felt that she could no longer be sure of herself. At Lesponts he had not been formidable; she had rather looked down on him there as a very good but slightly uninteresting young man; and on the whole she had rather envied Mary her Adonis.

In Abercrombie Road he had appeared altogether different. When he had entered their little parlour, holding out his hand, and looking at her with a kind smile, something seemed to take her speech away, and she had grown very shy and pale. It was pleasant to have him there watching her about the room as he pretended to talk to her mother. How kind and thoughtful he was! he seemed to anticipate her little wants, and almost to read her thoughts. Sometimes he brought her flowers, sometimes a book; he did not harrass her with his attentions, but seemed content merely to be in her presence. When she turned capricious and plagued him, he looked sad and thoughtful, but never reproached her even by a look. The last time she had seen him he had been so gentle with her that she felt herself on the point of yielding. Then she had packed up her box and fled; and by her contrivance Susan was kept in ignorance of their address until after Grey's visit.

Now he had followed her here, but to-night his manner had wholly changed. Had she hurt him? was he really offended with her? she wondered. Nothing could be colder and more distant than his behaviour to her. She remembered his loose grasp of her hand with feelings of absolute dismay; he had looked at her as though she were a stranger—'How do you do, Miss Maynard? what lovely weather!'—something to that effect; and then he had gone on talking to Miss Vendale. And as far as she could see—and Dollie took all manner of furtive glances—he had not looked at her again!

And this was the man who told her that he must go on doing it—doing what?—and then Dollie blushed again still more angrily, and answered Captain Thompson almost crossly when that troublesome individual implored to be allowed to escort her to Crome Park.

'Are we to walk home? We shall be a large party, and there is no fear of tramps. Very well, if you will, Captain Thompson,' returned Dollie quite ungraciously.

She began to think she disliked Captain Thompson.   He
was good-looking, but his moustache and whiskers were
red—not auburn, whatever Mabel might say.   And he was
so tiresome, too, loitering to listen to the nightingales, and
to watch moonlight effects, when she wanted to know what
Mr. Lyndhurst and Mary were saying to each other, they
were walking so close together, and seemed so wrapt up · in
their talk.   Moonlight effects ! what rubbish ! and then
Captain Thompson lisped ! and that was always so tiresome and affected.   She could not bear young men who
lisped !

When they came up with them at last, and Captain
Thompson consented to hold his tongue for a moment,
they were evidently talking about Diana.

' I think her face is almost perfect,' observed Grey; and,
as though by contrast with the unlucky Captain, his voice
sounded clear and concise.   ' The features are quite beautiful in repose, but when she grows animated she is certainly
most striking-looking.'

' And her face is such a clear index to her mind !'
returned Mary, pleased with this encomium on her friend.
' Diana is so simple and transparent ; she has plenty of
intellect and a large heart ; and she is so absolutely truthful that she allows her feelings to be easily read.   I am
very fond of her.'

' No wonder; she is just one of your sort !' replied
Grey pleasantly.   ' I liked her father too ; he is a thorough
specimen of an English squire.   Do you know, he found
out my love of riding.   He asked me to accompany him
and his daughter for some of their country rides : he
actually offered to mount me.'

' Oh, there is no need of that; Brown Peter would
carry you famously; you are quite welcome to him.   You
are looking thin and fagged, Grey; a few rides would set
you up.'

' Thanks, we will see about it,' returned Grey ; but his
voice sounded well pleased.   ' Some of you might accompany us, and then the party would be complete.'

' I am afraid our education is rather deficient; neither

Dollie nor I know much about riding; thank you all the same,' was Mary's laughing answer; and then she pressed Grey to go round the next morning and look at Brown Peter in his stall.

'He is a handsome animal, and as gentle as a lamb,' she finished. By that time they reached the hall-door, and Janet and Maurice said good-night and struck off across the park, followed by Lettice; and Captain Thompson reluctantly took leave.

'Well, Dollie, have you had a pleasant evening?' asked Mary.

'Oh yes, a delightful evening!' returned Dollie, in a slightly fatigued voice. 'Every one was kind, but dancing on the grass tires one dreadfully;' and then she gave a little yawn. 'Well, good-night, I must go and see how mother is, and if she has lost her headache!' and Dollie shook hands with Grey without looking at him, and ran off to her room and locked herself in.

And if her cheeks glowed in the darkness, no one was the wiser.

'What does he mean by coming down here if he has left off doing it?' she said to herself, as she sat at the open window trying to cool her burning face. 'He is angry with me—he has not looked at me nor spoken to me to-night; he thinks I am a silly little thing, and not worth so much trouble after all!' and then there was something wet on her cheek, and she brushed it angrily away.

'What do I care what he thinks, or if he pay attention to Miss Vendale or not? I suppose he thinks I behaved badly running away like that without a word—as though I must ask his leave!' and here Dollie began to work herself up into impotent wrath. 'Why could he not have stayed away, and not come down just now to spoil my visit? nobody wanted him!' and then again the suspicious moisture made itself felt. Poor Grey! if he had only known!

The next morning things were no better. Grey was undeniably stiff and constrained in his behaviour to Dollie and her mother; even poor Mrs. Maynard came in for a share of his displeasure.

'Mr. Lyndhurst, I feel we owe you some apology for our carelessness,' she said to him in her softest voice, when they met at the breakfast-table. 'When Susan told us you called, I was afraid you would think us very remiss.'

'Oh no, not at all!' returned Grey stiffly. 'I only brought the books I promised to Miss Maynard; of course it was no consequence, and I took them back to Mudie on my way home. I hope you had finer weather than we poor Londoners enjoyed.'

Then Mrs. Maynard understood that the sin of omission had been a heinous one in his eyes, and that only the most abject submission on Dollie's part could wipe it from his memory.

'I am so sorry,' she faltered, and then she looked help-lessly at her daughter. But Dollie took no notice; she was rattling on in her liveliest manner to Mary about the events of last evening. What pleasant people the Ducies were! Mr. Jack was very witty and agreeable, did not Mary think so? She would not be surprised if Mabel sent a note round that morning. Captain Thompson and Lieutenant Parkington were not returning to Canterton that night, and they talked of a game of tennis for the afternoon.

'Mary, if we have finished breakfast, we might as well go and look at Brown Peter,' observed Grey rather abruptly, when the tennis party had been fully discussed. He had made a good meal, but had hardly delivered himself of half a dozen sentences, and these had been directed chiefly to Mrs. Maynard. Perhaps the widow's gentleness, and a certain softness of appeal in her eyes, had disarmed his wrath; for his manner relaxed a little as he addressed her.

'Very well,' returned Mary cheerfully. 'Will you come, Dollie?' But Dollie declined. When the stables had been inspected, and Mary had trudged over to Brotherton, Grey strolled across the park and paid a lengthy visit to the Rectory, returning late for luncheon.

There was plenty of business discussed at that meal. The note had come round for Dollie, and Captain Thompson had brought it; and the greater part of the morning had been spent by that gallant officer in loitering about the Crome grounds.

Dollie, who found herself a little ennuyé that morning, had been tolerably gracious to him, and had even picked a flower for his button-hole. As she came down after luncheon, prepared for her game, Grey passed through the hall ready equipped for riding. He stole a swift downward glance at the dainty dress and broad-brimmed hat, and then turned to mount Brown Peter.

'I hope you will have a pleasant game; we are going to ride over to Canterton,' he said coolly.

Dollie nodded him a curt reply—of course she would enjoy her game. And yet what a long afternoon it was! She wondered once or twice if he would have afternoon-tea at the Hall. Diana would make it in her riding-habit; she would come to him across the shining oak floor holding up her long skirt, and looking at him with large serious eyes. 'Is it our turn? Oh, how hot it is! and one cannot play when the sun is in one's eyes. I think I am tired, Captain Thompson. Will you play with Miss Ducie, and I will sit in the verandah a little;' and Dollie sat down on the steps and pulled the rose to pieces that Captain Thompson had just given to her, and thought how well Mr. Lyndhurst looked on horseback.

After a few days Mary began to get puzzled. She could not understand her visitors' behaviour at all; ever since Grey had arrived an element of discord seemed introduced into her household; nothing seemed to go smoothly or well.

In the first place, Dollie was so tiresome; her conduct was enough to provoke any lover. She seemed quite to ignore Grey's existence. When he talked to her, which was rarely, and only on the most general subjects, she answered him in the coolest briefest manner; when he turned over her music for her in the evenings, she scarcely thanked him; his favourite songs were left disregarded in their cases; when he approached her seat, she generally made a pretext to leave it. Never was there a more capricious, tiresome Dollie! Then she had taken such an

absurd fancy for the Ducies—morning, noon, and night
she was haunting the Glade.   She and Mabel must practise
their duets together; Mabel was going to teach her painting
on china; she had promised to help Mrs. Ducie with her
crewel work; they wanted a fourth at tennis;—excuses
were never wanting.   Mary protested, but in vain.

Nor was Grey more satisfactory.

His manner was less constrained, but he was still very
grave and quiet.   He watched Dollie incessantly, but he
paid her no special attention; he never offered to escort
her to the Glade, or contrived errands for waylaying her;
as far as he was concerned, she had perfect freedom of
action; it was only Mary and her mother who remonstrated.

But his rides became a daily occurrence.   Sir George
had taken a fancy to him, and was always asking him to
the Hall.   Once he dined there; another time he went up
to luncheon.   It became a matter of course to fall in with
Diana and her father somewhere in the course of their
afternoon rides.

Dollie, coming down the village, would often see the
three returning slowly homewards.   How the sun shone
on Diana's brown hair, bringing ruddy gleams into it under
her hat!   Grey would be leaning towards her talking
eagerly, and patting Brown Peter's neck.   How brightly
she seemed to answer him!   None of them saw Dollie
looking after them.   Dollie would droop her head and
grow a little pale, as she turned in at the Park gates.   But
she was always very lively at dinner.   No wonder Mary
felt perplexed; and she took them both to task after a time.

'Dollie, have you and Grey quarrelled?' she said one day
very suddenly, when they were alone together.   Grey was
not at the Hall; he was writing letters in the library.
Dollie, who was painting, went on very carefully with the
petals of a flower; but Mary noticed her hand shook.

'What has put such an absurd idea into your head?'
she said at last, trying to speak in her usual voice.   .

'Oh, lots of things.   You are both so strange and
constrained in manner, and at Lesponts you used to be
such good friends, always together and——'

'Oh, Lesponts! that was an age ago,' replied Dollie, with a little shrug. 'Mr. Lyndhurst has other friends now. You must be glad you have given him so good an introduction; he and Diana seem to get on famously.'

'Diana!' burst out Mary indignantly, and then she stopped and smiled to herself, for just a little bit of Dollie's cheek and one ear were turning rosy. Here was the solution of the mystery. She dropped the subject abruptly, and soon found an opportunity of speaking to Grey; in fact she disturbed him at his letters.

He looked at her a little gloomily as she entered.

'Am I interrupting you? I only wanted to know if you were going to ride this afternoon,' she began, with a little feminine diplomacy.

'Yes, I suppose so; there is nothing else to be done,' he returned somewhat moodily. 'Sir George asked me up to dinner, but I hardly know if I shall go.'

'Oh, not to-night,' she returned quickly; 'you go there rather too often, Grey, and I fancy some one is beginning to think so.'

'Who do you mean?' he exclaimed; but his whole manner changed and brightened, and he looked eagerly at Mary; but she went on in a very matter-of-fact way.

'You know Mabel Ducie is coming over about Canterton to-morrow. Mrs. Maynard and Dollie want to see the cathedral, and neither Janet nor I can be of the party. You must promise to go, Grey.'

'I will go if you wish it,' he returned ungraciously; 'but I should think Mr. Jack Ducie and Captain Thompson are sufficient escort; I don't suppose my absence would be noticed.'

'Nonsense!' returned Mary decidedly. 'You are taking a girl's caprice too seriously, Grey. If you ride with Diana and her father every day, and are always up at the Hall, you have no right to complain if other people amuse themselves with Captain Thompson. You are no better than other young men; you play with edged tools, and then wonder that any one is hurt. I am ashamed of you!' and with this enigmatical and highly-incomprehensible speech, Mary playfully ran off, leaving Grey mystified but radiant.

Was Dollie jealous? was that what she meant? Had his careless attentions to Diana really given her uneasiness? was this the reason of her flightiness, her absurd predilection for those Ducies? And then Grey glowed and got hot over his own conceit. He was not a vain man, and he hardly knew how to believe it. Dollie jealous of his friendship for Miss Vendale! and he certainly did like and respect the girl—why, the very idea was rapture!

The young man's pulses beat as though there was new life in his veins; his countenance softened strangely although he was alone.

'I will watch her; I will see if Mary be right—if this be true,' he said to himself, as he pushed aside his papers impatiently. When the gong sounded for luncheon, he entered the room with an aspect so changed and alert that Dollie secretly trembled and wondered what was coming. Had he really changed to her? Could he indeed have fallen in love with Diana? And somehow the thought made her feel so chill and numb that she scarcely spoke or lifted her eyes during the meal; had she done so, she must have read the secret meaning shining out of Grey's eyes as he looked at her.

CHAPTER XXXVII

AFTER all, Mary's little plan failed, and Grey did not join the party to Canterton. Some important papers had arrived by the morning post, and instead of sightseeing and acting as Squire of Dames the young barrister found himself condemned to an afternoon's dry labour. But it was not in his nature to complain over small contrarieties—so he merely said after he had informed them of his disappointment in a certain cut-and-dried manner that provoked one of his listeners,

'I am very sorry, Mary, but business is business, and a working man cannot be his own master. The worst of it is, my visit may have to be curtailed; I am afraid I dare not reckon on a day after Friday.'

'Friday!' exclaimed Mary in a tone of strong remonstrance, 'and this is Tuesday; and how about my garden-party, or rather my fête-champêtre, as Dollie persists in calling it; and not a note written, or an invitation sent out!'

'Could you not manage it for Thursday?' asked Dollie in a low voice, and then she coloured. Perhaps Mr. Lyndhurst would think she was taking too much interest in his movements.

'It would be rather an impromptu affair; Janet would be shocked,' hesitated Mary. 'She wanted rather a grand fête, a band from Canterton, and——'

'Oh, we will do without the band,' returned Dollie hastily. 'Just ask the people to tea and tennis. You

know a grand affair such as Mrs. St. John is always worrying
you about would only make you miserable. Why should
you put yourself out for your neighbours in that way?
You are too yielding, Mary; you should think of yourself
sometimes.'

'If only Janet would not be disappointed,' sighed her
friend. 'What do you think, Grey?'

'Impromptu affairs are by far the pleasantest,' he returned decidedly. 'If Mrs. St. John wants a party there is
plenty of room in the Rectory garden. Just assemble your
friends round you—the Vendales and Ducies, et cetera—
and make them comfortable in your own way; I will be
bound they will enjoy themselves. As to details, you must
settle them by yourselves, for I am off to the library;' and
Grey crumpled up his papers and nodded good-humouredly
to the party as he left the breakfast-table. He was too
busy to appear at luncheon. When the party drove up to
fetch Dollie, she had not seen him again.

Now what possessed Dollie that she should not enjoy
herself a bit that afternoon?

The weather was lovely; the cathedral far beyond her
expectation. Captain Thompson was almost too devoted
in his allegiance, while Mr. Jack Ducie divided his attentions equally between Miss Maynard and his cousin.

Mrs. Ducie was most amiable, and Mabel laughed and
talked incessantly; and they both petted Dollie, and made
much of her in a pleasant feminine fashion. And yet
the ungrateful little thing felt secretly bored and tired to
death. Nothing pleased her; the sun was hot, and the
roads dusty. Mabel's remarks were vapid, and she thought
she and her mother talked a great deal of unmeaning
nonsense. Mr. Jack Ducie was decidedly officious; and as
for Captain Thompson, she quite hated the sight of his red
moustache. How tiresome they all were when they went
into the cathedral, and Dollie wanted to be quiet!

'Hush! you must not talk so loud,' she said once or
twice in a reproving whisper to Jack. When Mabel
laughed a giddy little laugh, she turned on her with a
frown, 'We are in church now, Mabel!' She grew quite

irritable at last, and refused to answer Captain Thompson.
Oh, if they would all go and leave her alone in this great
beautiful place, with just her own thoughts for company !
She wanted to think, to sit quiet, perhaps to cry a little !
Half unconsciously her thoughts strayed away to another
scene. This was a cathedral too. There were dimly-
burning lights, a strange smell of incense, a few scattered
worshippers. In a little side chapel a girl sat looking before
her with vague wistful eyes ; there was the workshop at
Nazareth, a St. Joseph, with the infant Christ in his arms.

'Are you ready now ? Shall we go home, Miss Maynard ? ' How quietly he had stood beside her, watching her
with a young man's half-understanding reverence, and yet
respecting this mood of hers ! How patient he had been
with her long silence ! She turned almost fiercely upon
Captain Thompson when he came up to her with one of
his flippant remarks, 'Awfully nice, don't you think so, Miss
Maynard ? ' and he pointed with his cane to the glorious
perspective of arches.

By and by they all went outside in search of some
gardens that lay near, and how it happened no one knew,
but when they looked round, Miss Maynard was not with
them !

There was a little crowd of sightseers in the porch ;
Captain Thompson was piloting a way through them ; he
thought Dollie was following him. When he turned round,
the gray dress and broad-brimmed hat were not visible.
'Jack must have carried her off,' he said to himself ; and
then he invoked something under his breath that was not
exactly a blessing upon that young man. 'Confound him !
what does he want with two of them ? ' muttered the
aggrieved Captain, and then a casual acquaintance waylaid
him ; and when he came up at last with the others, Miss
Maynard was not with them !

'Good heavens, Thompson ! how could you be so careless ? ' exclaimed Jack in his gruffest voice, for he was
secretly jealous of his friend's monopoly of Miss Maynard.
'The poor little thing will be frightened to death in this
strange place ! '

'Nonsense, Jack!' returned Mabel sharply, for she was not quite pleased at her cousin's tone. And why should he call Miss Maynard a poor little thing! 'Dollie is not such a baby; she will go to the "Green Man" where the wagonette is put up, and wait there until we come.'

'That is not a bad idea, Miss Ducie,' observed Captain Thompson, who felt horribly guilty, and yet half inclined to resent Jack's snubbing speech. 'I vote we all go to the "Green Man" first;' and then they turned back a somewhat dispirited little party, rather inclined to find fault with each other, and at last even with Dollie for spoiling their pleasure by being lost.

As for Dollie, that wicked little person had wholly forgotten all about them; and indeed a most strange thing had befallen her. 'I begin to think something is always happening to me in cathedrals,' as she said to herself afterwards.

She was following Captain Thompson rather slowly and absently, and thinking how glaring the sunlight was after the cool shadow of the arches, when some one caught her sleeve, and an agitated voice said, 'Miss Maynard!' and, looking up, there was Bertie's ghost, lurking in a dark corner underneath the gargoyles!

At least Dollie afterwards declared to her mother that she really thought for a moment that it was Mr. Bertie's ghost. The corner was dark, and his face was pale, and his gray coat looked colourless and indistinct. 'And of course ghosts in the nineteenth century are dressed like other people, and are not like stupid ghosts in white sheets and all that nonsense,' finished Dollie. But there was the grasp on her sleeve, and a very strong, sinewy grasp it was.

'Mr. Bertie—oh!' and Dollie got very pale with surprise.

'Oh, don't go; come back with me here. I want to speak to you; I have been watching you ever so long, but I was afraid the others might see us and tell of me. Come back with me; what does it matter? Let that idiot with the red moustache go on without you.' And though Dollie hesitated, and gave one dubious glance at Captain Thompson's retreating figure, she let herself be persuaded, and actually followed Bertie back into the cathedral, where they soon hid themselves behind the pillars.

'They will be so frightened; they will think they have lost me!' exclaimed Dollie, with a nervous little laugh.

'What does it matter what they think?—they are only strangers,' returned Bertie scornfully. 'Do you think I could let you pass me like that?—when I am famishing for the sight of a friend's face. It does me good to look at you, Miss Maynard;' and the poor fellow almost pushed Dollie into a seat, and took up his station near her. As for Dollie, she was so pleased and touched and frightened by this sudden encounter that she hardly knew what to say to him. She only gave another nervous little laugh.

'I thought it was your ghost, not you, Mr. Bertie,' she said; and then she remembered that some one had told her that he had been ill, and she looked at him again more carefully.

He did not look very well, she thought. He was sunburnt, and yet pale, and there was a heaviness in his eyes, and indeed in his whole aspect, as of a man who had had some heavy trouble. His hair was a little longer, as though he had grown careless of his appearance; and when he pushed his fingers through it in his usual fashion it was more of a halo than ever. And yet, in spite of this, in spite of his heaviness and want of animation, how beautiful he was!

'He is Adonis still. I have never seen any one half so handsome;' and then as she looked at him she thought of Mary, and her heart became very pitiful.

'You are not well. Are you not well?' she asked, correcting herself.

'Oh yes,' he said, astonished at the question. 'I am as strong as a horse. Nothing ever ails me.'

'But you were ill in the winter?' she persisted.

'Ill! Nonsense! Who says so?' he returned, colouring a little. 'It was a mere nothing. Grey is such an old woman, and mollycoddles one so. We have been abroad for the last three months, Ralph and I. Ralph's chest is delicate, and there is some talk of Mentone next winter. We are going to Scotland now.'

'You have plenty of change, then?'

'Oh yes,' he returned indifferently. 'And there is some idea of Switzerland later on. Lady Howard is making up a party for the Engadine, and wants us to join her. You see the doctors do not wish Ralph to study much. He is to travel and be amused, and all that sort of thing; so we are never long in one place. It rather suits me to be always moving on, so every one is pleased; and my berth is not a bad one after all.' And Bertie spoke in a would-be cheerful tone that did not deceive Dollie in the least.

'And how came you here?' she asked in a matter-of-fact way. But to her surprise Bertie got suddenly confused.

'Ralph has gone to stay with his aunt, Lady Combermere, and I had a couple of days on my hands,' he stammered. 'I had never seen the cathedral at Canterton, and I thought I would just take the train and have a look at things;' and then he stopped and looked at Dollie, and something in her face moved him, and he gave a fierce pull to his moustache.

'I came because I was a fool—a poor weak fool,' he burst out. 'Don't tell of me, Miss Maynard; don't let her know you have seen me.'

'Oh, Mr. Bertie!'

'I thought I should get news of her before I went away. I never hoped for this, you know,' sitting down beside her. 'It is so nice to see you, Miss Maynard—ever so nice. Don't you recollect that evening at the Chateau de St. Aubert when you catered for me and I called you Hebe? How good you were to me then!'

'I should like to be good to you now,' returned Dollie, with the tears starting to her eyes. And then she added, somewhat incautiously it must be owned, 'I should like to do something to help you and Mary.'

He gave a great start at that.

'Why! What do you mean, Miss Maynard? Is not

Mary happy? Has she not forgotten me—at least not forgotten, God bless her! she will never do that; but is she not well and cheerful? How does she look? Oh! if you only knew how I long for a crumb of comfort, a word of news,' went on the poor fellow. ' Grey never says anything. He is so wise; he thinks it better not.'

'Perhaps he is right,' observed Dollie in a low voice, but Bertie interrupted her half angrily.

'Why, it can hurt no one but me; and I have left off caring what happens to myself. Is it not hard, Miss Maynard, to have to go on living without a definite aim or purpose, just to kill time, and do one's daily work, and go on living, not caring very much about anything?'

'Oh, but that is wrong,' reproved Dollie, with a girl's precocious wisdom. ' Mary is not like that.'

'What is she like?' he asked cunningly. And Dollie, absorbed in her subject, fell at once into the trap.

'She does not think about herself at all, whether she is happy or unhappy. She says the future is not ours, that we are robbing God, stealing mysteries out of His treasury when we meddle with that. It is only the present and the past that are ours. She thinks it a duty to be cheerful,' went on Dollie still more eagerly, 'and so she never lets people see that she is depressed or low about things, or that she finds her life uncongenial. I have often heard her say "that a bright hearth and cheerful looks make up a home," and that people ought not to burden others with their private troubles.'

'That is just like her,' he returned, shading his face with his hand. ' Go on, Miss Maynard.'

'Oh, but I have nothing more to say,' replied Dollie, becoming rather frightened. Ought she to be talking to him at all about Mary? What would her mother and Mr. Lyndhurst think of her imprudence?

'But how does she look?' he persisted. 'Oh, Miss Maynard, you were so good to me once. Please tell me a little, just a little more,' and Bertie's eyes looked appealingly at her.

'She does not look very well,' faltered Dollie. ' At

least nothing ails her; but her eyes have a tired look, and I think she is a little thinner. She does not seem to care for her grand house and fine things, but spends all her time amongst the poor people at Brotherton. Sometimes she comes back looking so fagged and weary that she makes my heart ache. But she never complains, and there is always a smile upon her face—always.'

'God bless her!' groaned Bertie; and then his head dropped again between his hands. Presently he spoke in a sort of muffled voice—

'I must go away now. Thank you, Miss Maynard; you have always been awfully good to me. I wish I could do something for you in return.'

'Oh, Mr. Bertie, must you go?'

'I dare not stay,' he returned quickly. 'Some one might see me and tell her, and then she would be troubled. She would think I was unhappy and restless. Do you know what a fool I was once?' he went on in an odd, choked sort of voice. 'Grey would call me daft, and perhaps I was. It was in the winter, just before Ralph and I went away. I got a strange sort of longing just to see the place where she was to live. I thought no one was there, but just as I was turning in at the Park gates a carriage passed me in the dusk, and I knew she was inside.'

'Well?' interrogated Dollie breathlessly. No romance she had ever read thrilled her like this narrative that Bertie's sad tones were telling. Oh, how unhappy he was! and yet what could she say to comfort him?

'I waited a little while, and then I climbed the palings and followed. The snow was on the ground, and I tried to keep to the horses' track. There were no lights in the front of the house, and I went wandering round it like a lost spirit. Presently I came all at once to an uncurtained window; the blind was raised, and I could see the room. Such a pretty room; bright with firelight and lamplight, and she was sitting by the hearth alone. She raised her head once,' went on Bertie, 'and I could see her as plainly as I can see you. .There was a smile on her face, and it seemed to me that I knew what she was thinking.'

'Oh, what a fool I am!' suddenly rising and standing before Dollie. 'I have carried away that picture in my mind ever since. Now I must go; they will be looking for you now, Miss Maynard, and they must not find us together. Thank you, thank you for being so good to me,' and Bertie held out his hand with a grasp that told volumes.

'Good-bye, Mr. Bertie,' returned Dollie. She watched him sorrowfully as he went striding underneath the arches. Once he turned round and waved his hand to her. Some people who were leaving the cathedral looked curiously at the young man in the gray coat with the fair dishevelled hair, and then they looked at Dollie sitting disconsolately on her bench.

When Dollie noticed them she got up and walked away rather proudly; and then she began to ask herself what she must do.

It was growing late now, and all the people were leaving the cathedral. The old gray-headed verger hobbled up to her as she stood hesitating.

'There's a party asking for a young lady. Maybe it is you, miss?' he said, peering up in Dollie's face with his small weak eyes, and just then Bertie sauntered past. As he did so he motioned with his hand and lips. 'Outside,' was what he seemed to say. Dollie nodded, and went on talking to the verger. By and by she stepped out boldly into the sunlight, and into the midst of the little frightened group who were holding council together.

Jack was scolding, Mabel half crying with vexation and fatigue, Captain Thompson pulling at his moustache, and Mrs. Ducie fanning her pink cheeks, that were becoming pinker every moment with worry and heat.

'Well, what have you got to say for yourselves?' asked Dollie, looking very cool and haughty. She was quite fresh and undaunted. She came out of the dark old porch in her little gray gown, looking perfectly demure and innocent. 'Thank you, Captain Thompson, for taking so much care of me. What a capital escort you are! Do you often lose young ladies? Some one asked me a

question, and I went back into the cathedral. I was not
at all frightened. I was sure you would turn up after a
time, and so I sat down and waited. How hot and tired
you all look! Have you ordered the wagonette, Mr.
Jack?' and Dollie patted her hair with her gray glove, and
listened with wonderful magnanimity to Captain Thompson's
excuses.

'Well, it could not be helped. Supposing we say no
more about it,' said Dollie carelessly, when they had nearly
overwhelmed her with their expressions of contrition and
pity. 'The cathedral was very cool, and I am quite rested
and comfortable.' As the wagonette drove rapidly from
the door of the 'Green Man,' no one noticed a tall young
man in a gray coat who looked after them eagerly and half
raised his hat. If Dollie waved her hand it must have
been to the old towers of Canterton Cathedral, over which
the rooks were circling. When she grew quiet by and by
Mrs. Ducie petted her, and said the darling girl was tired.

Dollie let them think so. She sat bright-eyed and
silent in her corner, while Mabel and Jack rattled on.
She was very affectionate to Mary all that evening, waiting
on her and speaking to her with the utmost tenderness,
while to Grey she was so very gentle that he looked at her
in some anxiety to know what ailed the girl.

CHAPTER XXXVIII

DOLLIE told her mother all before she slept that night; but Mrs. Maynard said very little in reply.

'Poor fellow! it is very hard for him,' she exclaimed with a sigh when Dollie had finished. But she hardly mentioned Mary. She would not harass Dollie by telling her how the girl's careworn face began to haunt her. In spite of her gentleness, in spite of the smiles that were never wanting, there was a deep-seated sadness that went to the widow's heart.

'Even Dollie thinks she will get over it some day,' she said to herself. 'Poor child, it makes her happier to think so. She is so brave and cheerful that no one guesses how she suffers except the good God who knows a woman's heart;' and Mrs. Maynard was right. Mary hid her sorrow bravely, but none the less did she own it to be a sorrow.

Dollie dreamt of poor Bertie's sad face all night; but the next day Mary kept her so hard at work that she had not a moment to think.

In spite of Janet's disapproving face the garden party had been fixed for Thursday. Before Dollie returned from Canterton the notes had been sent out, and as every one accepted, Mary hoped that the evening would be successful.

Dollie threw herself heart and soul into the preparations. She was unhappy and restless, and the occupation suited her. She was hurt because Mr. Lyndhurst went up to the Hall to dine. It was his last evening but one, and she thought he might have spent it with them. He had ridden

with Diana and her father all that afternoon, too. She
little knew what a struggle it had cost Grey to go, and how
willingly he would have declined the invitation. But Sir
George was pressing. He had some business on which he
wished to consult Mr. Lyndhurst, and Grey was obliged to
yield.

He thought of telling Dollie all this, but she had shut
herself up in her own room to avoid him. Poor little soul!
her heart was strangely heavy that night. She had counted
on that last quiet evening; she would be so good to him;
she thought she would sing all his favourite songs without
his even asking her; she would not contradict him once,
and if he asked her to come out into the garden with him,
as he had done once, and she had refused, she would go
with him. Yes, though her heart beat, and she trembled
at the thought of being alone with him, she thought she
would go.

And now all her good resolutions were made in vain.
Mr. Lyndhurst preferred to spend his last quiet evening
with Miss Vendale. Oh! how blind and foolish she had
been. She had failed to appreciate him; she had humbled
and tyrannised over his true heart, and now he had left
her. Poor little Dollie! Never to the last day of her life
did she forget the mingled pain and bitterness of that
evening.

Grey thought her very cold and constrained when they
met the next morning. She had avoided him a good deal
of late, but this time it seemed as though she were unwilling to meet his eyes. When he spoke to her she
answered him with downcast looks, and he noticed that
her lip trembled. Strange to say Grey's eyes brightened,
and his voice became more cheerful. He did not seem
put out or discomposed when, shortly afterwards, she disappeared, and for all his search he failed to find her.
'There is plenty of time,' he muttered, 'I shall catch my
wild bird yet;' and the young man's heart throbbed with
a great pulse of excitement and happiness. Dollie would
not have cried last night if she had known how truly the
meaning of those tears had been read.

'Has any one seen Dollie?' asked Mary, rather puzzled, as the Vendales' carriage drove up from the lodge. 'Oh yes,' for as she spoke there was Dollie herself, in her fresh white gown, with her yellow hair shining under her little straw hat. She had some crimson roses in her hand, which she began to fasten with trembling fingers into Mary's dress. One of them fell, and Grey picked it up, and put it into his button-hole.

'Where is your racket, Miss Maynard? I hoped you would be my partner in the first game?' asked Grey, coming up to her and speaking in a low voice.

'I have promised Captain Thompson, and after that I am to play a set with Mr. Ducie,' returned Dollie, moving away hurriedly. 'There is Miss Vendale coming up the lawn; you had better ask her.' Poor little Dollie! how her heart ached! but she could not avoid this Parthian thrust. It was a pity she could not see Grey's amused smile in answer; but one cannot see unless one looks. After all, Grey had Miss Vendale for his partner.

Dollie saw them coming between the trees, and began to play fast and furiously. How the balls flew, and her head ached! she played so badly that her partners, Captain Thompson and Jack Ducie, looked at her in dismay.

'That is the second game we have lost this afternoon,' said Jack rather sulkily, for his cousin Mabel was looking on amused and triumphant.

'Oh, I don't pretend to play well,' returned Dollie indifferently. She was too secretly exasperated to say pleasant things to her admirers. 'Why don't you ask Miss Vendale? she wins every game.'

'So I would, only that fellow Lyndhurst has been monopolising her. They have been playing splendidly three sets, and winning every game. One sees what's up in that quarter,' finished Jack, with a quizzing smile.

This was too much for Dollie. Other people noticed them; even comparative strangers like Jack commented on his admiration for Miss Vendale. 'I think I will go and sit down; I am tired,' faltered the poor child! Her lips trembled; she would have liked to have burst into

tears ; but instead of that, she walked away from Jack with
her little head erect, picking her steps daintily over the
grass.   Grey saw her as he played his last winning game.
All through the afternoon he had watched her afar off;
even as he dealt his vigorous strokes he felt as though he
lost none of her movements.   People were envying him
his partner, but he scarcely noticed her.   Diana's beautiful face, her fawn-like step, and splendid play, were all
thrown away upon the infatuated young man.   His eyes
were following a little figure in a white gown, with some
roses fastened coquettishly in it.   Dollie's yellow hair
seemed to absorb all his sunshine.   Why had she left Jack
so suddenly ?   She was sitting now alone near one of the
little tea-tables ; he wished his game were finished that he
might follow her.

Poor Dollie ! she felt forlorn and miserable enough as
she crept into the seat under the shade of a low willow.
Two ladies were talking busily at the tea-table near ; they
were Mrs. Fullerton and Miss Brettingham.   They did not
see Dollie, but she could hear every word they were saying.
She listened languidly at first, until her attention was suddenly arrested by hearing Mr. Lyndhurst's name.

'A very nice young man, well bred and clever, and with
such pleasing manners,' observed Mrs. Fullerton in a
gentle gossiping voice.

'Very so, indeed, my dear,' returned Miss Brettingham.
'That is exactly what I said to Adelaide, a very well-bred,
pleasant young man, but not a match for Diana.   Why,'
continued Miss Brettingham, shaking the crumbs from her
well-preserved satin gown, 'Sir George must be out of his
senses to countenance such a thing.   A briefless barrister,
with no pedigree ! with perhaps a grandfather in trade !
and Diana, who would be the beauty of a London season
—monstrous, my dear, monstrous !'

'But he is a very rising young man,' returned Mrs.
Fullerton mildly; 'the Colonel was only saying so this
morning.   "He is made of the right stuff, and may end
with the woolsack," that is what Reginald said.   And if
they are fond of each other, I think Sir George is right to

give Diana her way. She has money enough for both, and, after all, mutual sympathy is the first thing to be considered.' But here the Brettingham hands were uplifted in pious horror !

'Fie, my dear ! what heresy ! Noblesse oblige ! have you forgotten that ? Diana owes a duty to herself, to her parents, to her long line of ancestors. Mutual sympathy ! pshaw ! A Vendale must marry rank. Mr. Lyndhurst is a very proper young man as far as young men go, but he is not fit for Sir George's son-in-law. The idea is monstrous —monstrous !' and Miss Brettingham shook her aristocratic head with an air of profound sorrow.

'Depend upon it, the young people will talk him round ; Sir George is so soft he would not deny Diana anything,' returned Mrs. Fullerton with mild persistency. But Dollie slipped away ; she could bear no more. They were talking of it as a settled thing ! Sir George's son-in-law—Diana's husband. It was all over, then ; she had lost him ! Oh, it was hard, hard !

'And I wanted him so ; I had grown so fond of him,' groaned Dollie, as she almost rushed away. Where could she go ? she must be alone a little. The park was full of sauntering groups ; then she bethought herself of the peacocks' promenade—it would be quiet there. In another moment she had unlatched the little gate. There was the long terrace-walk and the arbour ; on the sunny wall peaches were ripening. Topaz was trailing his draggled glories in the dust with Sapphire beside him ; the old sun-dial looked mossy and gray. 'I watch the hand of Time '—as Dollie stood beside it, trying to decipher the half-obliterated words, her tears came dripping down on her white dress ! 'Oh, I want him so ; I can't bear to be all my life without him, and all because of my own fault,' sobbed the poor little thing ! feeling all at once as though life were gray and waste around her. And then there came over her a certain sharp memory of an autumn evening. They were on the bridge by the Béguinage— there was the old archway, the broad sweep of the silvery canal, the low alders, the willows coming down to the water. There was a low voice pleading with her. 'You must not go on doing it if I tell you not!' that was how she had answered him, half petulantly, half childishly. Well, he had taken her at her word, that was all. He had turned from her with a pale face and compressed lips, trying to hide his pain. And now he was comforted, and she was standing here with her tears dripping on the old sun-dial, and Topaz and Sapphire strutting beside her in the vain expectation of being noticed.

By and by another hand unlatched the little gate; but Dollie, overwhelmed with her remorseful thoughts, did not hear the footsteps until they paused beside her.

'Miss Maynard, I have been looking for you everywhere. Good heavens! you are crying!' The sudden change in Grey's voice was as though a thunderbolt had burst under his feet. 'You are crying!' he said in a tone so appalled and conscience-stricken that at another time Dollie would have laughed.

She would have given worlds to be able to check the flow of her tears. This was the climax of her sorrow, her humiliation—that he should find her like this, actually crying! that he—but no, it was of no use—the pent-up agony of the last few hours had been too excessive. Something had opened the flood-gates, and the tears must have their way. There was Grey looking at her with terrified eyes, and Dollie hiding her face in her little hands, sobbing as though her heart would break!

And then all at once a light that was almost inspiration dawned on the young man, as he stood helpless and bewildered. Love has these moments of inspiration, and he went up to her and touched her softly—'Come and sit down, darling,' he said, 'I want to talk to you;' and before Dollie knew how it happened she was sitting on the little bench in the dark arbour with Grey beside her, with one of her hands held firmly in his. And what he said to her she hardly knew, nor what she answered; but all at once the sun was shining so brightly as though it would blind her, and the tears were flowing far more quietly now, and something was making Dollie's cheeks burn, and her head drooped until her yellow hair nearly touched a certain coat sleeve.

And when she woke up—which was not for a long time —there was Grey saying softly over and over to himself seemingly, 'My own at last, my own Dollie!' in a voice as tender and caressing as though he were speaking to a child. And then he added remorsefully, 'But I ought not to have made my darling so unhappy.' That roused her.

'How could you? To make me believe that you were in love with Diana! Oh, it was cruel, cruel! And all the people noticing and talking about it too.'

'Miss Vendale never thought so,' he replied quietly, 'nor Sir George either. I think Mary gave them a hint, for Miss Vendale was always speaking to me about you.

'It was wrong perhaps,' continued Grey, feeling a contraction of heart at the thought of all Dollie's misery, 'but, my dear, why were you so hard to me? I was driven to despair, and then when I guessed how it was, I could not resist the temptation to watch you. Why, you were never out of my thoughts a moment, not even when I seemed most occupied with her.'

'It was very cruel,' repeated Dollie; but her tone was so gentle that Grey knew he was forgiven. What was there that she would not have forgiven him who was now her dear, her dearest? Long after Topaz and Sapphire had retired to their couch in the willow, long after the sun had set behind the house, did they pace the terrace-walk, or pause hand in hand beside the sun-dial.

Dollie told him all in her sweet candid way—how her heart had softened to him, and how from only thinking him a very good and rather uninteresting young man she had grown to love his coming, and to cherish every word he said.

'I ran away because I was afraid of you, and yet I wanted you all the time,' she whispered, pressing closer to him in the gloaming. 'When I saw you crossing the lawn that afternoon with Mary, and knew you had followed me down here, I was so terrified and yet so happy I could scarcely speak; and yet my only longing was to go away and hide myself.'

'My poor little startled bird! How proud and shy you have been with me. But you are not afraid of me now, are you, Dollie?'

'Oh no, not now,' and Dollie looked up in his face with eyes so full of innocent affection that Grey thrilled all over with the gratitude and joy of winning this pure heart. Had she ever thought him plain, she wondered? She had called him angular and dark once, but now his face was more beautiful to her than Bertie's perfect features. Plain, with those dark eyes glowing with proud tenderness, and all because he had won her, his foolish little Dollie!

'Well, what now?' he asked her, smiling. 'May I share that thought, Dollie?'

'Oh, it was nothing,' she answered, blushing slightly. 'I am only a silly little thing, and my thoughts are not worth much. I wish I was clever and sensible for your sake, Grey,' the name dropping unconsciously from her lips —she had called him Grey so often to herself.

'You are too good for me,' returned the young man humbly, and again that thrill passed over him. 'Heaven is giving me more than my deserts. I do not deserve such a blessing;' and he kissed her little hand with such reverence that Dollie was abashed.

They went in after that; but Dollie, scared with her great happiness, fled for a little time to the safe refuge of her own room, while Grey went in search of Mrs. Maynard. He found her sitting alone in a corner of the crowded drawing-room. She was watching the door anxiously.

'Where is Dollie?' she asked, looking up into the young man's face rather scrutinisingly.

'Will you go to her?' was all he answered, but his look and tone were sufficient. The widow's thin face flushed as she rose and went away tremulously.

Dollie whispered her whole story on her mother's bosom. How the widow blessed and hung over her child! 'He is robbing me of my all, Dollie,' she half sobbed.

'Oh, mother!' exclaimed the girl, somewhat awed by this view of the case, and touched by the pathos in her mother's voice. And then she said pleadingly,

'But you will love him a little for my sake, won't you, dear?'

'Yes, and for his own too,' returned Mrs. Maynard, drying her eyes. 'He is so good and wise. He is worthy of my Dollie. I always liked him—always, even when I knew he wanted my treasure,' and she looked sadly and proudly at her girl.

They came downstairs clinging together. Grey, who was waiting for them, stepped forward to meet them, and took the mother's cold hand into his warm grasp.

'You have a son now as well as a daughter,' he said, looking straight in her face with his honest eyes. 'I am not robbing you. I am only adding to your little store,' and somehow the kindliness of that speech comforted her more than all her child's caresses. He would not take Dollie from her, that was what he meant; and Mrs. Maynard said, 'God bless him!' as he led Dollie away.

The remainder of the evening passed rapidly away. When it was all over Mary came quickly up to Dollie and kissed her.

'I wish you joy, dear,' she said, putting her hands on the girl's shoulders. 'Grey has just told me. Oh, how good he is! How happy you will both be!'

'Oh, if you could only be happy too!' sighed Dollie, throwing her arms round Mary's neck. A sort of nervous twitching passed over Mary's pale face. She caught her breath suddenly.

'I cannot half enjoy it unless you are too,' persisted the warm-hearted girl impulsively.

'All is as it should be, and we are in God's hands,' replied Mary gently. She was tired out with the fatigue of the evening, and this sudden appeal to her sympathy tried her worn spirits too much.

When she had answered Dollie she went away quietly to the solitude of her own room. She was more lonely in a crowd than there; all sorts of waiting angels tarried for her on the threshold—invisible figures of Faith and Resignation and Patience took her by the hand and led her softly in.

There she could pray for him, and for herself too

There she could love him without sin, and meet him in most guileless communion. There she replenished her cruse and gathered up her barrel of meal; there her wasted strength recruited itself, and hope for the morrow grew stronger; and long after Dollie had slept, and was dreaming happily of her lover, Mary sat tranquilly in the darkness with a peace that was not of earth stealing into her tired heart.

CHAPTER XXXIX

GREY did not leave the next morning. When the early post came in he found he had a three days' reprieve.

What a wonderful time that was to them both!—wonderful to Grey, who bore his new happiness with all a young man's gravity and importance; and wonderful to Dollie, who grew so sweet and bright under her lover's eyes that Grey fell more in love with her every day.

He and the mother used to exchange looks sometimes—silent looks—in which there was a world of confidence, of overflowing pride. The girl was so artless with him, so thoroughly natural. As she grew more used to him she brought out a store of old-fashioned wisdom, airing it so prettily and yet so quaintly that not for worlds would Grey have silenced her by any cut-and-dried sophistry. How innocent she was, how loving! 'How am I ever to fit myself to watch over this pure heart?' he thought; and he felt as though he must stand for ever bareheaded and reverent before the holy ground of one simple girlish nature. True love has these moods of humility, of self-abasement; the affection of a good man has something akin to worship in it. Woe to the lover who finds the excellences of the beloved object crumbling into dust before his eyes, when pure gold is found to be dross and tinsel, and under the freshest roses glides the canker worm!

Nor was Dollie without her sweet surprises. Every day, every hour, she discovered some fresh trait to admire in her lover. Oh, how good he was, how unselfish, how full of

26

thought for others! She had never known him to be witty, and yet alone with her he was as light-hearted as a boy, and indulged in the most playful sallies. In fact, as Mary told Dollie one day, 'They were orthodox lovers; everything that Grey said or did, in Dollie's eyes, was right, and nothing she could do was wrong in his.'

To be sure Grey was a little impetuous in his wooing. Before twenty-four hours were over, Dollie found to her dismay that her freedom was to be speedily curtailed; that he had talked her mother over to consent to an early marriage, after which all Dollie's blushing objections availed nothing. Now it was that she found that he had a will of his own.

Grey was poor, and his prospects uncertain. This was a drawback certainly in a worldly point of view; but as he had no intention of separating Dollie from her mother, and would have thought it the height of cruelty to rob the widow of her only comfort, it was Mrs. Maynard who herself suggested that the three slender incomes should be united.

'There will be enough and to spare while I live,' she said, looking affectionately at the young man who was so generous, so forbearing with her even in the first flush of his gratified hopes. 'Dollie hates Abercrombie Road, but you might find a prettier cottage elsewhere. If Heaven spares me for a few years, we shall do well; and by that time you will have risen in your profession.'

'I could take pupils now. Dollie is not extravagant; we should neither of us be afraid of poverty. I am only afraid of loneliness, and of being without Dollie,' exclaimed Grey, kissing the mother's hand as he spoke. 'You must talk to her; you must make her see how happy she will make us. What does it matter how humble our home is, if I can only see my wife's face in it?' finished the young man with a flush.

But Dollie had her own little protest to make against this arrangement. She had stopped her ears and run away while Grey was talking to her mother; but that evening she came to him very shyly, and accosted him almost with timidity.

'Grey, I do want you to be patient a little about—about—you know what!' stammering and blushing.

'And if I cannot be patient?' he repeated, drawing her forward that he might look at her. 'Dollie, your mother is quite of my mind; there is no reason in the world for delay.'

'Oh! but there is,' she replied softly; 'I cannot leave Mary yet—you must not ask it, Grey; we have only been engaged three days, and there is no need to settle anything before you go. I must stay a little longer with Mary.'

'Oh, if you wish it,' he returned a little stiffly, for he did not like this at all. Grey was a trifle arbitrary in his disposition in spite of his gentleness. 'If you wish me to go back to my London chambers and work on alone with you down here; remember I could not run down more than once a month just for a day, so we should be quite separated; but if you would rather be with Mary!' Oh, the jealousy of even such lovers as Grey!

Dollie's eyes opened widely at this outburst, but she bore it very sweetly.

'How naughty you are!' she said, stroking his coat sleeve with her little white hand; 'as though I wished you to be lonely and dull in those horrid chambers. I shall want you dreadfully, Grey; oh, dear! don't you know how dreadfully I shall want you when you are gone?' and her voice grew rather pitiful.

'We can write; of course we can write,' returned the deceitful young man, speaking in his most matter-of-fact voice, but secretly pleased at the manifestation of feeling he had called forth; 'I daresay I shall not often be too busy.'

'You will write to me every day—no, every other day if you are too hard worked,' returned Dollie, frightened at this coolness. It was not light enough to see the mischievous gleam in Grey's eyes, and his voice was always well under his command. And then she came closer to him, and said in a little tremulous voice—

'Don't make it too hard for me, Grey, because I think

I owe poor Mary a duty. I always want to do as you wish—I will do everything you wish, dear, if you will only give me my way in this.'

'My darling, how can I? Just consider,' began Grey. But she stopped him.

'We are so happy that we ought not to be selfish,' she went on; and there were tears in her voice as she spoke, for she was very earnest with him about this. 'When you talk about being lonely and dull without me, you make me miserable, and yet I feel I dare not leave Mary.'

'But her claims are nothing to mine,' returned Grey half sullenly; 'she has other friends, and I have no one— no one but my Dollie.'

'Oh, but you have me!' she returned eagerly. 'I shall always be thinking of you, and longing to see you— no, be quiet, Grey, I want to finish what I am saying.

'Poor Mary! she is so lonely, and I do not think Mrs. St. John is always kind to her; and we have promised to stay with her all the summer, and it seems so hard to disappoint her, and just to go away and be happy! A little separation will not hurt us, dear, though it will try us dreadfully. Oh, how difficult it is to do just what is right!' cried poor Dollie, finding it hard to adjust these nicely-balanced claims, and feeling she must choose between duty and inclination.

But here Grey's magnanimity stepped in to help her. He was not a bit convinced in his own mind, and thought Dollie's scruples could easily be overcome. She was sacrificing his interests and her own to her friend. But Grey could be generous too. Her poor little conscience was uneasy—she was troubled at her own overplus of happiness and Mary's dearth of it. Well, she should make herself uncomfortable and him too if she liked.

'Have it your own way, darling,' he said at last, but not at all grudgingly, or as if he were annoyed. 'Of course I am disappointed. I had half hoped we should have been married in July, but don't worry about it. I will run down in a month or five weeks just to see how my Dollie looks, and we will have another talk about it.' And as Dollie thanked him with a little gush of gratitude for being so good and patient, Grey was slily thinking how he would hunt out all the desirable cottages within reasonable distance of Lincoln's Inn, and how he would come to Crome in July, armed with all manner of new arguments, and if need be enlist Mary on his side.

Dollie half repented when she saw him go off the next morning. How empty the great house felt without him! She sat by her mother's side working or pretending to work, looking very sad and subdued. Mrs. Maynard was thankful when Mabel Ducie rushed in and carried her off to the Glade for a game of tennis.

Dollie's first letter was begun that very evening. Before the first week was over, she had covered sheetfuls of paper. If Grey's letters were not quite so lengthy, they were sufficiently satisfactory to judge from Dollie's looks, she dimpled and blushed so over them!

She was writing her second letter to Grey one afternoon, when Mary came into the room in her old straw hat to tell Dollie that she was going over to the Rectory.

'Oh, Mary, and you have been at Brotherton all the morning, and at the schools since luncheon, and you are so dreadfully tired!' protested Dollie, looking up from her letter with happy, rather absent, eyes.

'What does that matter?' she returned cheerfully; 'it is all in the day's work. If you are writing to Grey, you may give him my love, and tell him Sir George misses him dreadfully;' and then a sudden thought struck her, and she came a little closer. 'Does Grey ever speak, does he mention Bertie?' she asked, leaning a little heavily on the table.

'Not often; he—I do not ask!' returned Dollie, feeling very guilty. Oh, if Mary had only known of that talk in Canterton Cathedral! 'I believe—that is, some one told me—that he was going to Scotland.'

'Some one! that must have been Grey,' rejoined Mary; and Dollie got suddenly red. The pink colour spreading over her face and neck arrested Mary's attention, and she looked at her narrowly.

'Have you seen him?' she asked at last, very abruptly.

Poor Dollie jumped up from her chair in a little flurry. 'Don't ask me,' she implored; 'he wanted me not to tell; he was so earnest about it. Dear, dear Mary, don't make me disobey him!' and Mary was silent; only a white, almost a gray, look came over her face. She looked quite worn and old.

'I will tell you all I can,' went on Dollie, who could not bear to see that look. 'He is quite well, at least he says so; and they have plenty of change, he and Ralph. They are in Scotland now—he was going there—I mean he will be there by this time. And afterwards they are to join Lady Howard at the Engadine, and they are talking about Mentone for the winter, because of Ralph's delicate chest.'

'Thank you, that will do,' returned Mary faintly. 'He is quite well, you say?' and then she moved to the door slowly; but as she opened it she said in her usual voice, 'I ought not to have disturbed you; I am so sorry, Dollie, dear. Now I must go to Janet; she wants to see me about two or three things. Rosie and May are not quite well; they have headaches, she says. Perhaps I shall stay and have tea with them; don't let your mother wait.'

'Mary, I wish you would not wear that dowdy old hat; it makes you look quite plain and old!' was Janet's unpromising greeting, as Mary entered the cool Rectory drawing-room, with rather a languid step.

'Oh, it is only my garden hat,' returned Mary, tossing it off with good-humoured compliance. She was too much accustomed to be taken to task by Janet to mind it much. Mary's indifference to appearances was always a bone of contention between them; but this afternoon she was not disposed to wrangle over trifles. 'But you look smart enough for both,' she continued, eyeing her sister-in-law's rich silk and beautiful lace, with some little surprise. True, both were Mary's gifts, but it seemed strange that she should be wearing them this warm afternoon.

'You know I told you that we had to dine at the Fullertons' this evening, to meet the Dean and Mrs.

Grantham,' returned Janet rather peevishly—Mary was always forgetting these little arrangements of hers. 'It is so tiresome, for it is such a warm evening, and Maurice is not inclined for it; and then neither Rosie nor May seem quite the thing.'

'Shall I stay with them?' asked Aunt Mary briskly; there was nothing she would like better — nothing that would suit her half so much as a quiet evening with her darlings, to have them all to herself without the mother. 'Do let me, Janet; I have seen so little of them lately, and Dollie and Mrs. Maynard will spare me, I know.'

'That was just what I wanted, only I was afraid you would not offer,' was Mrs. St. John's reply, in rather a grudging tone. 'You have been so taken up with the Maynards and your own affairs and that tiresome Brotherton, that the poor children never get you now!'

'Whose fault is that?' returned Mary reproachfully; for this innuendo was more than she was disposed to bear. The children were Aunt Mary's weak point; no one in their senses could accuse her of neglect of them. 'How many times I have asked you to send Lettice and Hatty up for the evening! I could not leave my guests, and yet I was missing them.'

'To tell you the truth, they have none of them seemed quite the thing lately, and I thought it better to keep them quiet,' replied Janet, changing her tone skilfully at Mary's somewhat displeased remonstrance. When Mary took high ground, Janet always grew mild at once. 'I thought nothing would ever ail them now we live in the country, but Rosie and May seem both as poorly as possible.'

'Very well, I will stay with them until you come back,' was Mary's ready answer; and then she left Janet and went upstairs. She turned a deaf ear when Janet protested that there was no hurry, that they were not going yet, and that she had several things that she wanted to talk over with Mary. The old irritability awoke at the first sound of her sister-in-law's querulous voice; and she was too languid and weary this hot evening to combat it as successfully as usual.

Maurice came out of his dressing-room as she passed, and his face brightened at the sight of her.

'That is just like our dear Aunt Mary,' he said gratefully. 'Now Janet and I can leave more happily. This dinner is such a bore, and Janet was troubled about Rosie and May; not that there is much the matter with them, but mothers will be anxious;' and Mary, as she followed him into the room, felt a little prick of conscience. Perhaps Janet's uneasiness was making her tiresome; she half wished she had been more patient with her.

The little girls were all together in Rosie's room. Rosie and May were lying side by side in their little frilled dressing-gowns on one of the white beds; the little gray dog Snap lay between them; Bee was coiled up at their feet with a Noah's Ark. Lettice and Hatty were reading quietly at the window; the canary was singing loudly in its cage; the roses were climbing in through the open lattice. Outside the evening sunshine was streaming on the quiet Rectory garden; the children's pigeons were fluttering and circling in the orchard; through the low apple-trees one had a vista of green meadow grass swaying softly in the breeze. Never to her dying day did Aunt Mary forget the mingled sweetness and tranquillity of the scene.

There was a joyous exclamation when their father entered with Aunt Mary! Bee clapped her hands, Snap barked, the animals came pell-mell out of Bee's pinafore, dropping everywhere, on the coverlet, the carpet, and into Mary's dress. Snap got hold of an elephant and zebra, and privately licked all the paint off. Days afterwards Mary found a camel and hippopotamus in the pocket of the dress she wore that night.

'Children, I have come to stay with you; we will have one of our old delicious evenings,' cried Aunt Mary cheerfully, as she kissed them all. How hot and weak May looked as she raised herself from the pillow! Rosie's cheeks were pale, and her eyes were heavy; but she gave a little contented smile as she slid a burning little hand into Mary's.

'Oh, that is nice,' she sighed; 'Bee is making such a

noise, and will not let Hatty read to us, and it makes my head bad.'

'Stupid 'Oosie!' cried Bee, with profound scorn. 'I was only crowing like all the cocks, father; when the little pig comes out of the Ark it must squeak, you know!'

'Yes, and then Snap barked,' groaned Rosie, 'and Hatty began to laugh, and then the canary went on singing, singing!'

'My poor little girl!' exclaimed sympathising Aunt Mary, laying her hand gently on the child's throbbing forehead. 'Maurice, don't you think the canary might go into Lettice's room? and perhaps Snap would be the better for a run in the orchard.' And as Maurice acted on this suggestion, she continued rather solemnly: 'Now, Bee, you must be very quiet, or Biddy must carry you off too;' for faithful Biddy had followed them to the Rectory.

Bee looked injured. 'Must not the bulls bellow at all, Aunt Mary—the poor bulls?'

'Certainly not, Bee.'

'Or the lions roar?' in a shrill voice of protest.

'Of course not. The sun is setting, and it is time for all good children and animals to be asleep,' replied inexorable Aunt Mary; upon which decided hint Bee suddenly subsided into a little mouse, and moved her menagerie in profound silence in and out of their wooden refuge.

Maurice looked round the room well pleased when he returned, and seemed hardly disposed to tear himself away. 'There, you are better now, darling,' he said anxiously, as he watched Rosie. Somehow it struck him suddenly that she looked dwindled and weak.

'I am always better when I have dear Aunt Mary,' returned Rosie, drawing Mary's hand down and kissing it. The little scene seemed to touch Maurice strangely.

'Well, God bless you all, my darlings!' he said, as his wife's voice called him. He looked back once again as he left the room. Bee had crawled noiselessly into Mary's lap; Rosie was still stroking her hand; Hatty had brought a low stool to her feet, and Lettice was standing beside her. 'God bless them all, and her too!' whispered Maurice as he closed the door.

CHAPTER XL

MARY was still at her post when they returned that night. As the hall-door opened, she came softly downstairs, and followed them into Maurice's study. Janet, who looked fagged and dispirited, had thrown herself into an easy-chair. The evening had been oppressive; there was a storm brewing. The Dean had been fussy and a little deaf; the dinner had been long and tiresome; Janet had not enjoyed herself at all; she had wanted to be at home. She was fidgeting about the children.

'We had a very quiet evening,' began Mary, in a hesitating voice. 'We sang all our favourite hymns—at least Lettice and Hatty and I—and then I read to them, and we talked a little. Rosie seemed better and disposed to sleep, but just now she is poorly again, and has been very sick!'

Janet started nervously from her chair. All her fatigue was forgotten; her forehead was furrowed with anxiety.

'Oh, Maurice, do please send for the doctor!' she implored. 'I had such a miserable feeling all the evening, just as though something were going to happen. Rosie has never been like this;' and Janet's eyes filled with tears.

'Nonsense, love!' returned her husband gently; 'you are overtired and fanciful;' but all the same Mary noticed he looked a little grave. 'Let us go upstairs and look at her. Unless it is quite necessary, I should not like to disturb Dr. Radley at this hour;' and then they followed Mary.

May was lying half asleep. She said, 'Good-night, dear mamma,' as Janet passed her; but Rosie was tossing restlessly on her little bed. She was flushed and feverish; her eyes had a strange look as she glanced up at them.

'Who was it wanted a drink of cold water to cool his tongue, Aunt Mary?' she asked, as her aunt raised her a little on her pillow. 'I keep thinking and thinking, and I don't remember; some one in the Bible?'

'Would you like some water?' asked Mary tenderly, and Janet looked at her husband in affright. 'Oh she is ill, very ill!' she exclaimed, forgetting Rosie would hear her. And Maurice said, 'Hush!' rather sternly; but a minute after he whispered to Mary that he should go for Dr. Radley.

But their anxiety was not to be allayed that night. Dr. Radley had been called away to a distant village, and would not return before morning. Janet fretted sadly over this delay.

'What are we to do if she gets worse, and we have no doctor?' she exclaimed; 'and we do not know what to do for her.'

'Dr. Radley will be better able to judge to-morrow,' returned Maurice very gravely, for both he and Mary feared the child was sickening for a fever. Mary was sure of it; she could not mistake the symptoms, but she would not disturb the poor mother with her fears. She tried to question Janet a little about the past week, during which she said the children had been ailing, but Janet got alarmed at once.

'Oh, I am sure you think she is very ill, that she is sickening for something! I ought not to have left her; I ought to have sent for Dr. Radley before, but I thought it was only a bilious attack, and Maurice did not seem to think much about it.'

'Neither did I, until about an hour ago,' returned Mary quietly; 'and then I sent a note to Dollie, and told her that I should remain for the night. Now, Janet, I want you to be reasonable; I want you to go to bed, and let me sit up with Rosie. Remember you are tired out;

that if the child be really ill you will want all your strength for the next few days;' but though Mary reasoned and Maurice coaxed, Janet could not be persuaded to leave the room. The utmost she would do to please them was to put on her dressing-gown, and lie down on the couch at the foot of May's bed.

When Maurice withdrew, feeling terribly anxious, she lay with wide-open aching eyes, watching Mary as she sat beside Rosie.

Rosie was very restless, but patient. Her throat was sore, she said, and she felt hot and thirsty; and did poor mamma think she was very ill? and why did she lie there if she were so tired? Aunt Mary would stay with her—dear Aunt Mary—and tell her about all those little children she nursed in Sloane Court, and the humpbacked boy who died.

'Oh no, dear Rosie!' exclaimed Mary, with a sudden pang when the child said this, for the case had been a terrible one. The fever had decimated the foul alley like a plague, and had carried off eleven children. She had worked amongst them night and day, keeping quarantine long afterwards in a miserable little whitewashed room, scantily furnished, that Maurice had found for her. It had seemed to Mary as if those weeks were a hideous nightmare; as though she had spent months in laying out dead children, and straightening their thin limbs in their coffins.

'Another happy little child,' she used to say to herself, as she shut out the still face from view. It seemed to her excited, half-dreaming fancy sometimes as though she heard the fanning of wings above the oaths and the curses and the hideous sights and sounds of that reeking alley. 'He has gathered the lambs with His arms!' she used to say as she saw the maudlin tears of the wretched mothers. Neither she nor Maurice ever grieved when the children died, but now——

'No, Rosie, dear,' she whispered softly; 'we must not disturb poor mamma! You must try and sleep a little;' and Rosie, with sweet obedience, tried hard to lie still.

The next interruption came from May's bed. A

lamentable little voice broke the stillness: 'Oh, Aunt Mary, is it nearly morning? I do feel so sick!' and Mary, with cheerful looks but a sinking heart, hurried to the child's side.

May had waked tearful and frightened, and Rosie set herself to console her sister, but her voice was a little thick and indistinct.

'Don't cry, May, darling; it is not nice to feel sick, and it worries poor mamma so. The good children in books never cry when they are ill.'

'But I do not want to be ill,' returned the poor little girl, sitting up in bed, and looking unutterably miserable. 'It was all Bee's cocks that crowed so loudly, and made my head ache. Is your head bad, Rosie, and don't you feel hot?'

'Yes, very hot,' returned Rosie in a patient voice. 'I don't think Shadrach, Meshach, and Abednego ever felt hotter,' and Rosie flung herself despairingly on her pillow.

'Oh, Rosie is burnt! poor Rosie is burnt!' exclaimed May in a terrified voice.

'Oh no, not burnt, only burning,' returned Rosie in an old-fashioned way. She was a most quaint child. 'Shadrach, Meshach, and Abednego had Some One with them, you know, May, so I need not be afraid;' and then she lay back and closed her eyes. And Mary heard her say something about the Good Shepherd, and the green pastures, and the still waters that went trickling and trickling on for ever. But this talk only frightened May more.

'Oh, Rosie, are you going to die? oh, dear Rosie, don't go and die!' she implored, trying to peep round her pillow at her sister.

'I won't if I can help it,' returned Rosie more faintly, for her throat was sore, very sore. 'Don't cry any more, May; you shall die too, if you like. I will ask the Lord Jesus to take us together.'

'Oh, my darlings, hush! think of your poor mother, and hush!' exclaimed Janet, rising from her couch with the tears streaming down her face. Mary went to Maurice, and roused him.

'The children are very ill; I think you must send Denis on horseback for Dr. Radley,' she said. 'In a case like this there is no time to be lost;' and then she went back to her watch.

The next morning, as Dollie was dressing herself, her mother came into her room with a very grave face.

'I have just had a message from the Rectory,' she said. 'Poor little Rosie and May are very ill. Dr. Radley has just been there, and pronounced it scarlet fever; they say Rosie is the worst, her throat is so bad. They have decided to move the other children to Mrs. Crowder's; it is just by; and she has two empty rooms. They can see the cottage from the Rectory windows, so Mrs. St. John will not feel they are far from her.'

'Oh, mother, poor Aunt Mary!' exclaimed Dollie, aghast at this intelligence. Here was a sad prospect for all of them. It was bad for the parents of course, but she could not help thinking first of her friend.

'Yes, indeed,' sighed Mrs. Maynard, 'she has her work cut out for her, nursing those poor children. Denis told me Mrs. St. John is terribly upset, and looks very ill. Mary could not write, but she sent her love, and hoped that we should not be anxious. Emma Ducie has promised to look after the other children; she has had the fever, and is not at all afraid of it. She met Mr. St. John in the village, and went back with him at once.'

'I wish I could help Mary,' returned Dollie plaintively, 'but I must think of Grey, must I not, mother?' And when breakfast was over, she consoled herself a little by writing four closely-written pages to her lover. There was no danger of infection, none at all, she assured him; but Grey nevertheless worked himself up to such a pitch of anxiety that he actually took an early train and arrived one morning at breakfast, startling the roses out of Dollie's cheeks with the sudden surprise and pleasure. He had to return to town that evening, but he and Dollie had some happy hours together.

'I wish I could carry you both off with me,' he said disconsolately, as he prepared to take leave. Dollie was gathering a rose for him; she looked up with sweet rebuke in her eyes.

'We cannot leave poor Mary now; she likes to think we are here taking care of things. Do you know, I actually take her class at Brotherton; Diana and I work together. We like to feel we are helping her a little.'

'You are an angel!' returned Grey, as he took the rose; a compliment that Dollie received with a grain of salt.

'But was it not nice of him to come and look after us, mother?' she said, with a little glow of exultation and pleasure, when he had gone. 'Poor fellow! I am afraid he is very dull;' and she sighed.

Grey had obtained something by this impromptu visit. Dollie had promised that directly Mary could spare her she would get ready for her wedding; and she listened quite reasonably to the account of a cottage Grey had seen in Brompton, and which he thought would suit them admirably. She even consented to come up to town with her mother and look at it, when Grey should be at leisure to take them.

Meanwhile things were progressing very sadly at the Rectory. The very next day a fresh trial awaited the unhappy mother; for just as the other children were being removed, under Miss Ducie's care, Hatty was discovered to have a headache; and when Dr. Radley looked at her and felt her pulse, he forbade her removal.

Alas! before morning other symptoms followed, and she lay in her own and Lettice's room, which opened out of Rosie's, with her long fair hair cut off, in a high fever and delirious, talking loudly of the sunshine and the flowers, which she and her sisters were for ever gathering—daisy chains and cowslip balls and baskets of yellow primroses, happy childish fancies beguiling her pain.

When the first shock of her terror was over, Janet rose nobly to the emergency. True, she would not spare herself or listen to her husband's almost agonised entreaties to rest, to lie down to recruit her exhausted strength.

'There will be plenty of time by and by, when Rosie is better,' she would say quite calmly, returning to her seat by the child's bedside. Rosie never woke from her brief delirious sleep without seeing her mother's beautiful face bending over her pillow; the tenderest arms used to raise the weary child from her cramped restless position.

'Love, let Mary hold her now for a little,' Maurice would say, when he noticed her face was drawn and contracted with fatigue. But she never seemed to hear him or listen; her whole soul was with her suffering children.

Once, but only once, she sought him of her own accord, and stood by his side with dry eyes for a moment. 'Maurice, you must pray—you must pray for both—for all of us!' she said; 'I cannot; the words die on my lips!' and then as he looked at her sorrowfully, she brushed back the hair from his forehead. 'Take care of yourself, husband,' she whispered, 'for I cannot take care of you just now;' and when he held her closely to him, seeking to detain her—for he needed the comfort of her presence— she broke away hurriedly from him, saying she must go back to Rosie.

But after all it was Aunt Mary who was the child's best comfort, though she loved her father's prayers, and always stroked his face with her feeble fingers, as he knelt beside her.

It was Aunt Mary who repeated Rosie's favourite texts, who sang or said those sweet hymns that Rosie so dearly loved.

'Once again, Aunt Mary,' Rosie would gasp; for the poor throat was getting more swollen now, and Mary's clear tones would sing—

> He will be our Shepherd
> After as before,
> By still heavenly waters
> Lead us evermore,
> Make us lie in pastures
> Beautiful and green,
> Where none thirst or hunger
> And no tears are seen.

'No more thirst,' sighed Rosie; 'that will be nice.'

Hatty used to hear the singing in her intervals of heavy stupor. When Mary went to her there would be a faint smile on her face. 'I am tired; I seem to like the other verse best.' She paused, and Mary would sing it softly over again—

> There it was they laid us
> In those tender arms,
> Where the lambs are carried
> Safe from all alarms.
> If we trust His promise
> He will let us rest
> In His arms, for ever
> Leaning on His breast.

'Oh yes, I like that best,' repeated poor Hatty. 'Don't tell mamma that I feel so very tired,' as Mary, alarmed at her exhausted looks, gave her a little champagne and water. Strange to say, Janet seemed so wrapt up with Rosie that she hardly recognised the sad ravages the fever was making in Hatty. And the little girl was so good and patient, always sending her love to her dear sisters, and telling them they would be better soon.

But, alas! there was no better for Rosie; slowly but surely the disease had its way. Other advice was sought from Canterton; every remedy was tried, but in vain. The sponging, the vapour bath, brought no moisture to the dry, burning skin. Rosie lay with flushed face and bright eyes, talking in gasps of green beautiful pastures. By and by she ceased to talk; only she put up her dry lips and kissed first her mother, then her father, and then motioned Mary to come closer.

'Good-bye,' she said faintly; 'tell May not to be long!' Slowly the little burning hands grew cold in Janet's; the child's difficult breathing grew quiet, and then stopped!

'"The Lord gave, and the Lord hath taken away, blessed be the name of the Lord!' cried Maurice loudly, as he unclasped the mother's hand from the child's, while Mary closed her eyes.

The weeping was not from Janet, as her husband led her away.

'Miss St. John, come here a moment; I want to speak to you,' said Dr. Radley in a grave voice, as he beckoned Mary from the room. 'I want you to break the news gently to Mrs. St. John; but the eldest girl, Lettice, has the fever; they are moving her here now.'

CHAPTER XLI

'OH no, not Lettice; I could not bear that,' exclaimed Mary as the name passed Dr. Radley's lips. The tears were still running down her face at the thought of her little dead Rosie, and now this fresh trial awaited them all. The children were all dear to Aunt Mary, but none so dear as Lettice.

'You must not give way like this,' returned Dr. Radley kindly. He was a white-haired man with children and grandchildren of his own, and he had taken a fancy to this brave, self-reliant girl. 'As far as we can judge, she seems to have the fever very mildly. It is Hatty about whom Dr. Morton and I feel most anxious, and we cannot deny that May is in a very unsatisfactory condition.'

Mary wrung her hands without speaking. Would Dr. Radley tell her this if he had any hope. But there would be time enough, plenty of time, for grief afterwards.

'Come, let us go to her,' she said resolutely, drying her tears. 'Biddy is with the others. I can leave them a little;' and she followed Dr. Radley into the children's nursery, where Biddy had hastily made up a bed under the doctor's direction. Lettice lay with her face to the window. She looked round languidly as they entered the room.

'Oh, I am so glad to be here; to be near you all and my poor little sisters,' she said, with a smile. 'I don't mind having the fever at all if you will only nurse me, Aunt Mary;' and then as she caught sight of Mary's face, 'but you have been crying, dear Aunt Mary! Is poor Rosie worse?'

'Oh no, she is better. She will never suffer any more,' returned Mary gently, for she knew the truth could not be hidden long.

'Then she is dead?' returned Lettice, and her lips trembled slightly. 'My poor little Rosie is dead! Oh, Aunt Mary, how sorry father will be, and poor mamma too! I don't feel like crying somehow, but I am so sorry. Oh, how we shall miss her! On Hospital Saturdays and Sunday Populars, and all our nice times!' and Lettice's eyes grew sad as she thought of that first break, and of the loss of that most sweet sister.

'Dear Lettice, it is better, far better, as it is.'

'Yes, I know, and Rosie always wanted to die. She used to pick out the hymns about death, and she was so fond of that chapter in Corinthians. Do you think father would come to me?' for Lettice's loving heart yearned to comfort her parents.

'I will bring him, darling! and now you will lie quietly while I speak to Dr. Radley.'

'Oh yes, I have a great deal to think about,' returned Lettice, turning her face to the window. The roses were climbing in at the nursery window; one of her tame pigeons was cooing and strutting on the window-sill; down in the Rectory garden the bees were humming, and a thrush was singing loudly. Only a week since the five sisters were gathered round this very window—and now Rosie was far away. Lettice had plenty to think about as she lay looking out at the blue sky. She was trying to follow Rosie in that solemn journey of hers. Had the angels met her? she wondered. Had they come into that very next room that she might not be alone a moment? Rosie was very timid. She would like them to come and carry her through the clouds, as they carried St. Catherine.

'Dear little Rosie! I hope she will not feel strange without us,' she thought, and all sorts of quaint fancies haunted her. A vision of the green pastures and still waters came over her. Was that Rosie led by some solemn beautiful angel into the paradise of God? Whose was that figure—diviner, grander far—who came to meet them, who held out a hand with a pierced palm?

'Welcome, faithful little child, whom I lov̇ed, and who loved me!' Was that what the voice said? Lettice seemed to see, to hear it all. The golden valves of the Holy of Holies opened before her. 'Blessed are the pure in heart, for they shall see God,' said the Redeemer of children and of men.

Mary had certain sad offices to fulfil, and she went her rounds carefully. After that she sought Maurice, and found him standing looking down at his dead child.

'Where is Janet?' she asked softly, for he seemed so rapt in his contemplation that she hardly liked to disturb him; and yet he must be told about Lettice.

'She is lying down,' he replied. 'For the present she seems utterly spent. I wish she could cry, Mary; there is something so unnatural in this forced calm of hers. I have been talking to her, praying with her, but nothing seems to move her. It is the first child we have lost, and I fear her heart is broken over it.'

'Oh no,' returned Mary quickly, 'she is stunned just now. By and by she will cry, and then she will be better. Maurice, dear brother, I must tell you something more to grieve you. Hatty seems worse this evening, and they have brought Lettice here;' and then she added, 'Dr. Radley thinks she has the fever too.'

Such a stricken look came over Maurice's white face as she said this! 'Oh no, Mary, not Lettice, not my first-born!' he cried, and his lifted hand dropped heavily on her shoulder.

'She is not very ill, and she looks so sweet,' she returned softly. 'They have put her into the nursery, it is so spacious and airy. Come and look at her, dear. She is asking for you, and she seems just the same as ever. I have not cut her hair off yet,' faltered Mary, feeling this sad duty would soon have to be done. 'I wanted you to see her first.' And Maurice, with a dumb look of anguish, hurried from the room.

'Oh father dear father!' exclaimed Lettice lovingly, as

she opened her arms to receive him. 'Father is crying too,' she said, after a moment, as Maurice, utterly unmanned by this fresh blow, knelt down by the bedside and hid his face in the pillow. He had given up one child, and now he might be called upon to give another. 'Oh, it is hard, hard!' he murmured, hardly knowing what he said, but feeling at this supreme moment as though the father's heart was breaking within him.

'He is so sorry about dear little Rosie,' whispered Mary.

'Yes, poor father! He loved Rosie so. But God loved her too, or He would not have taken her.' And then Lettice drew her father's head closer to her, and tried to stroke his face with her weak hand. 'Father, shall you mind much if Aunt Mary cuts off all this long hair, my head feels so hot; and it is so much in the way, and tangles so.'

'No, darling, no, if it will give you comfort,' returned Maurice, with a groan. He was feeling stronger now; the first moment of his weakness had passed, and the black cloud was passing from his soul. He was even glad— with his old unselfishness—that Janet was not there to see those beautiful fair locks lying beside him.

'I look like a little shorn sheep now,' said Lettice quaintly. 'Rosie is the folded lamb. Thank you, dear Aunt Mary; that feels more comfortable. Now, father will read the evening psalms with me. Won't you, father?'

'I will go to Janet,' whispered Mary. She could leave them more happily now. Lettice was not so very ill. Perhaps, after all, Dr. Radley might be right, and this was a milder form of the disease. 'We must hope for the best,' she said to herself as she hastened to Janet's room.

She was lying outside the bed where her husband had placed her. She looked round with dry miserable eyes as Mary entered. A worn, childishly-fingered hymn-book dropped from her hand.

'I can't find it. Which was the verse?' she said fretfully—'the one you were always singing?' and Mary repeated the lines softly.

He will be our Shepherd
After as before ;
By still heavenly waters
Lead us evermore.
Make us lie in pastures,
Beautiful and green ;
Where none thirst or hunger,
And no tears are seen !

'Yes, that is it,' returned Janet, closing her eyes with a more satisfied expression.   Perhaps that perpetual surging in her head would cease now, and she would be able to rest; but no, Mary's next words dispelled that hope.

'Lettice here, Lettice ill! oh, my poor Maurice!' and Janet sat erect, and spoke in her natural tone—the wife was thinking now of her husband.   Janet loved all her children, but Bee was her Benjamin, her heart's delight; it was the father who gloried in his firstborn.

'He is with her now; I have left them quite comfortable; you need not disturb yourself yet.'   But Janet looked at her and spoke with her old sharpness, as she put her feet down and smoothed her dishevelled hair.

'How you talk, Mary! am I not the mother, Lettice's mother?   I must nurse her.   I must devote myself to her. We must have fresh advice—we must save her for Maurice's sake.'

'And for her own too,' thought Mary, with an aching heart, as she followed Janet.   No, she and Maurice could ill spare their darling; and the fervent prayer rose from her lips that God would spare this one—that if Hatty must die and May too, at least this one precious life might be spared.

Lettice welcomed her mother with a sweet smile. 'Here is my own dear mamma!' she said ; and Maurice looked up anxiously at his wife.

Her perfect calmness reassured him.   Janet kissed her child, and felt her forehead and pulse, and then laid her hand on the cropped head.   'I am glad you have cut off her hair, Mary,' she said in quite a matter-of-fact way, turning to Mary.

'Don't I look like a little shorn sheep?' repeated Lettice

with a little laugh. 'Are you going to stop with me, mamma? won't Hatty and May want you?'

'Aunt Mary is going to them. I will sit with you a little, dear,' returned Janet, with a loving look; and the child seemed more than satisfied.

Maurice gave a sigh of relief as he followed Mary into the next room.

Janet's wifely instinct, always so strong within her, was absorbing all her energies now in trying to save this one for Maurice. She hardly noticed the others leave the room, she was so engrossed.

When Dr. Radley paid his last visit that night, he found her alert and useful—making all sorts of necessary changes in the nursery—while Lettice lay still and watched her with satisfied eyes. She was quite brisk and active, but not all his hints as to Hatty's danger seemed to reach her.

'How is Lettice? She is feverish of course, but she does not complain much of her throat,' she said, pushing back her hair from her face, and looking at him anxiously.

'Oh, Lettice is doing famously,' he returned cheerfully; 'she is a good little woman, and does not mean to give us any trouble. But, Mrs. St. John'—dropping his voice cautiously—'I ought to tell you that Dr. Morton and I are not quite satisfied about Hatty. There is a weakness, a lassitude, a prostration that makes us anxious.'

'Yes, Hatty was always a weak child,' returned Janet; she had not half understood the implied meaning of Dr. Radley's words. 'Then you think I am doing right by Lettice?' she returned, going back to the one engrossing subject of her thoughts. Rosie was dead, her precious little Rosie; but this one must be saved for Maurice!

Meanwhile Maurice was keeping watch beside his dying child.

'This night must be the turning-point,' Dr. Morton had said to them; 'give her wine if she can swallow it; rouse her if necessary, but I fear we can do little.'

Poor little girl! she lay with feeble pulse and dry tremulous tongue, trying obediently to take what they offered, but almost too prostrate and weak to speak.

'Does my darling know her father?' asked Maurice
once, and Hatty's heavy eyelids quivered.

'Dear father,' she whispered, and a moment afterwards
she added, 'Dear mamma too!'

'Go and fetch her,' motioned Maurice. Hatty was
always a patient undemonstrative child, seldom expressing
her feelings, which were nevertheless very strong and deep;
and he could not bear that she should be deprived of the
comfort of her mother's presence.

Mary rose reluctantly; she was absent several minutes,
but when she returned Janet was not with her.

'I cannot make her understand,' she said, with a pained
contraction of brow. 'She is singing Lettice to sleep, she
says, and will not leave off to listen. I wish you would go,
Maurice, it does seem so dreadful for her not to know!'
and Mary stooped over Hatty and moistened her lips again,
for she had ceased to swallow.

Maurice hesitated, he was reluctant to leave; and yet
the mother ought to be here. 'Very well, I will bring her,'
he said at last.

'Hush! Maurice, she is asleep,' whispered Janet, advancing to the door as she heard his footstep. Have you
come to fetch me to Hatty? Is she worse? Wait one
moment.'

'No, not an instant!' he said, clutching her arm; for
this strange perversity, as he thought it, tried him. 'Do
you know, Janet, our child is dying? our poor little Hatty;
she cannot swallow, and she is sinking fast!'

Janet looked at him with half aroused faculties, and then
threw a glance at Lettice, who was sleeping peacefully; but
her husband's grasp was too strong, and she submitted to
be half dragged from the room.

When she saw Hatty her mood changed. 'Oh, why did
you not tell me?' she said, looking up reproachfully in
Mary's face, as she made room for her; and then she
went on in inexpressibly tender tones, 'My little Hatty,
mamma is here!' but alas! not even a flicker of an eyelid
answered her.

'She is going fast!' whispered Mary; and Maurice, for

the second time in twenty-four hours, knelt down and commended his child to God. Eleven years before he had held Hatty a feeble babe in his arms, and had signed her with the sign of the cross, dedicating her most solemnly to her Heavenly Father. Now she had passed the waves of this troublesome world ; now she was enjoying the bene- diction of the heavenly washing ; now the folded lamb was carried in the arms of the Good Shepherd ; and Maurice's stricken heart could yet say, ' that it was well with the child.'

As for Janet, she just touched the cold forehead with lips that were almost as chill and white. A dim blankness seemed over her sight as she rose and stumbled from the room back to Lettice.

Maurice could pray. His soul, triumphant even in this tremendous conflict of flesh and blood, could still bow and submit to the strokes that seemed to paralyse her ; but her soul was dark, hidden under a cloud of hideous blackness. Was it for her sins God was smiting them ? was her innocent well-beloved husband suffering for her sake ? were these children the scapegoats of their mother's sin ? In a numb unconscious sort of way she took herself to task. How hard, how discontented, how bitter she had been ! how she had set herself against her husband's work, God's work ! how jealously she had guarded her privileges, her wifely pre- rogatives ! how obstinately she had refused to sacrifice herself or her children in the smallest degree !

She had robbed God ; and now he was taking all her treasures from her. One by one the ruthless Angel of Death was taking them out of her shrinking arms. ' What has my fault been ? ' she seemed to cry aloud in her heart, as she stole in the summer dawn to Lettice's bedside. ' I have only loved them too well. I have desired nothing for myself, but to see them well and happy.' And a voice seemed to answer her : ' You have loved them as heathen mothers love ; your devotion has been idolatry ; you have given them all your heart, and have grudged the smallest service to Christ's poor ; now the hour of retribution has come, and you are feeling the anger of a jealous God.'

Miserable creed ! one of hideous fear and observance ;

and yet it was all that seemed to belong to Janet now. Meanwhile Maurice was praying with streaming eyes, ' Not my will : help me to say it. Thou who chastenest in mercy, who blessest and smitest together, are we not all Thine— I and the children whom Thou hast given me ? ' And when he had said this prayer he went in search of Janet. He found her dry-eyed and busy. Lettice had woke suffering, and she was moaning with discomfort; Janet was soothing her.

' I wish I could be patient,' she sighed, as her mother gave her a cooling draught, and turned her hot pillows. ' Dear mamma, how I trouble you, and you look so tired and your face is so white ! Do go and lie down.'

' By and by, darling.'

' Is Hatty better, mamma ? father seemed so anxious about her ? '

' Yes, dear, she is better,' returned Janet calmly, looking at her husband. Maurice watched her with a sore heart. Where did she derive this fictitious strength ? why were her eyes so heavy and yet so tearless ? how could she speak and move so naturally while they were digging the little grave under the chestnuts for Rosie, and Hatty lay in her last sleep, with her pale hands crossed on her bosom ?

' Love,' he said most tenderly, ' will you not let me relieve you a little, while you go and rest ? '

' I cannot rest,' she said almost sharply, and a sort of spasm crossed her face. ' Let me alone, Maurice ; you are more tired than I, and Mary too ; ' and she turned again to Lettice, and Maurice, with a sigh, left the room.

CHAPTER XLII

'SHE WILL DO NOW!'

JANET remained in this strange state for days.

'She is stunned; the brain is partially and temporarily clouded,' observed Dr. Radley, to whom Maurice had mentioned his anxiety. 'In some sense she is in a comatose state; she feels and yet does not feel; that is to say, she does not perfectly realise things.'

'And when she does?' asked Maurice rather bitterly.

'Ah, then the sudden revulsion will be excessive; one has to fear a break-down in these sort of cases. We cannot guarantee that she will not suffer, but with care and her splendid constitution, things will soon right themselves. She may be hysterical—you must be prepared for that—but you have no other cause for alarm.'

'But she does not sleep except by snatches; she will not rest. The best constitution in the world cannot resist such wear and tear.'

'Leave her alone; when the child is better she will sleep fast enough. At present her thoughts are so absorbed that it will only irritate her to try and turn them. Lettice is doing well under her care; one must be thankful for that.'

'And May?' But Dr. Radley shook his head, and turned aside sorrowfully, for he knew another little life was ebbing slowly away. The children had not inherited the mother's constitution, and not all that skill or care could do could save the child.

Mary never left her except to take necessary rest, and

then Maurice relieved her. Janet came once or twice in the twenty-four hours to stand beside her child and say a loving word or two, but she was always restless to get back to Lettice. 'I can trust her to you, Mary,' she would say quietly, 'but Lettice cannot do without me;' and then she would resume her nursing. Once, as she crossed her own room to fetch something Lettice wanted, her attention was arrested by a little group under the horse chestnuts. There were Dollie and her mother surely, and they both wore black dresses, and Dollie was crying; and there was Maurice standing bareheaded in the hot sunshine; and a gray-haired clergyman in a white surplice was reading out loud. It was some minutes before Janet realised that it was Hatty in her little coffin they were lowering into the grave, where Rosie already lay. 'He cometh up, and is cut down like a flower!' why did the next clause ring with a hollow sound through Janet's heart: 'In the midst of life we are in death: of whom may we seek for succour but of Thee, O Lord, who for our sins art justly displeased?' 'For our sins—for mine,' thought Janet, as she went back to Lettice.

'Dear mamma, are you sure Hatty is better?' asked Lettice, feeling there was something in her mother's face she could not understand.

'Quite sure, darling,' returned Janet in the same passive voice.

'I had such a strange dream about her,' went on Lettice; 'that is why I asked. I thought she came in to me to show me her dress, and when I looked at it, it was all white and glistening like an angel's; and then she had such beautiful curls, and Aunt Mary told me she had cut them off;' and Lettice looked anxious and unsatisfied.

'Never mind Hatty, darling. Are you not going to eat the peach May sent you?' but Lettice turned away. A faint distrust of her mother's words began to steal over her. Was Hatty really better? and why had mamma turned her face away? And then she lay and watched for Aunt Mary.

Janet had gone to her husband a moment; she was anxious about his standing in the hot sun. Mary thought

Lettice looked unusually feverish, and her eyes had a disturbed expression.

'Well, what now, little woman?' asked Mary, summoning up a smile for the benefit of her favourite.

'Aunt Mary, I wanted to ask you something. Mamma puts me off so, and will not talk about Hatty. She says she is better, and yet she will not speak about her?'

Mary looked troubled. Janet was not dealing wisely with the child. Suspense would be worse for her than fretting; and yet if it should be a risk; but her hesitation and pained look were sufficient for Lettice.

'You need not tell me; I know,' she whispered, turning very pale. 'Hatty is with Rosie; they are both gone!' She lay still for a long time in awe-struck silence, while Mary petted and fondled her. 'That was what poor mamma meant when she said she was better. Of course she is better—quite well now!'

Mary quoted the words, 'They shall suffer no more, neither thirst any more;' but Lettice interrupted her.

'She came to say good-bye to me, dear Hatty, and to show me her white dress! How beautiful she looked, and she had her curls too—her own curls! Was mamma with her when she died?'

'Yes, dear; and father and I.'

'Ah, you have seen so many children die,' returned Lettice in her wise, old-fashioned way. 'You must be quite used to it. I am glad poor mamma was there! Hatty was so fond of her, and now Rosie has her. Ask father to put that beautiful verse over them;' and Lettice repeated in her weak voice—'They were lovely and pleasant in their lives, and in death they were not divided.'

'She knows, Janet,' said Mary, when her sister-in-law re-entered the room.

'Oh yes, I know, mamma,' returned Lettice, taking her mother's hand. 'You have only May and Bee and me now; poor, poor mamma!' and Janet shivered and turned away, for was not May dying?

May was very good and quiet; her mind did not wander much, but she suffered more than Hatty and Rosie.

The pulse continued very high, and no moisture came upon the dry skin; now and then she got excited, and talked incessantly when she wandered. Her talk was principally of that evening when she and Rosie lay side by side in their little frilled dressing-gowns, and Bee had paraded her menagerie in and out the ark.

'The cocks crowed so terribly loud, Aunt Mary,' she would say; 'and then Snap barked; and the little wooden dogs barked too—and, oh dear, how my head ached, and Rosie's too! Poor Hatty couldn't go on with *Scamp and I* at all; she had to put it down at the most interesting part, and then you came in, Aunt Mary, and father carried off Snap and the canary!'

'Yes, dear, I remember.'

'I wish Bee would come and sit on my bed now,' sighed May, who missed her dear merry little playfellow; and then she added, 'But I must not be naughty or want anything!' for the children were so sweet and docile and well-trained that they yielded all their childish wishes at a word.

'Shall mamma come and sit with you?' asked Mary, who could not bear to see the clouding of the patient little face.

May had been fretful at first, but now she was very quiet—far too quiet, and far too good for restless little May. But, as she brightened at the question, Mary brought Janet, and insisted on her taking her place for a little.

Janet yielded passively, and was very gentle with her child. May crept up to her and laid her hot little head on her shoulder. 'That is nice,' she said, 'dear mamma!' They were her last sensible words. There were hours of intense suffering, and the end came gradually near. Janet did not remain entirely with her; she went backwards and forwards between the two rooms, seeming as though she could not remain long in either. As May breathed her last, she stooped and leaned heavily upon her husband's shoulder as he knelt.

Mary feared she would fall, and motioned to Maurice,

who rose quickly to support her. 'Another taken!' was all that Janet said between her dry lips; but this time she did not refuse her husband's help.

But the cup was not yet filled to the brim.

That evening, when the last sad offices were finished, and Mary, worn out and exhausted, sat half dozing by Lettice's side, with the child's hand locked in hers, Biddy brought her a message—there was some one downstairs wanting to see her.

'Who is it?' asked Mary drowsily, for she felt as though her inert limbs would never move freely again, and her head was throbbing with grief and fatigue.

'It is Miss Ducie,' answered Biddy shortly; but Mary noticed the girl's face had a frightened look. If Bee should have sickened! and yet would not the fever have shown itself before this? She shook so with sudden terror that she was obliged to hold the balustrade for support. She entered the room quite unsteadily, where Miss Ducie was standing with her face to the window.

'Oh, what is it?' she cried, almost beside herself. 'May is gone, and now something has happened to Bee!'

Emma Ducie burst into tears. For some time she could not speak for sobbing; presently she gasped it out, while Mary listened, pale with horror. Bee, their own bright busy Bee, was dead!

The walls seemed to reel before Mary's eyes. For some minutes she was utterly incapable of grasping the truth. If Bee died, Janet would die too, she was so bound up in the child. They were all dying, one by one; the house would be empty soon, and Mary gave a little convulsive laugh at the notion!

'Don't do that, my dear!' said Emma, horrified at the sound; 'cry as much as you will;' and indeed the tears were rolling down Emma's plain harsh-featured face. 'When I think of that dear little child, I could almost break my heart.'

'But, Emma, how has it happened? do try to make me understand!' and Mary made a strong effort to compose herself.

'It was the fever, only it attacked the brain,' returned Miss Ducie sorrowfully. 'Do let me tell you all from the beginning. She was quite well, the dear pet, as happy and merry as possible; even after Lettice sickened she looked so blooming, I had not a moment's uneasiness on her account.

'She used to play in the garden all day, making up her little nosegays, and bringing them to me—this one for dear mamma, and this for Hatty and Lettice, and so on. And once or twice she crept through the paling, and ran into the next garden shouting with laughter, and calling out to little Dick Faucit to come and catch her.

'I hurried after her and brought her back; but she ran away from Mrs. Crowder in just the same way, and hid for a long time. Mary, we none of us knew that there was scarlet fever there too. They never told us what ailed little Nanny, until Dick sickened; and then they sent for Dr. Radley, and he came and told me about it.'

'But you moved her surely?'

'Yes, I moved at once. Dr. Radley found me some rooms a little higher up the village, but the mischief was already done. Dr. Radley would not hear of my telling you; you were too overburdened and troubled at the Rectory; we could but do the best under the circumstances, and trust to Providence.'

Mary groaned, but she would not interrupt.

'The fever was raging in Crome,' went on Emma; 'many of the cottages had it. There was a child in your own lodge down with it, and it was devastating the Rectory.

'I noticed nothing until yesterday, when Mrs. Crowder told me Bee had been sick and did not seem very well. I did not quite like her appearance, and sent for Dr. Radley at once. He examined her rather gravely, but said little, except that he would not have the Rectory disturbed. May was dying, and Mrs. St. John looked very strange and worn, and he would not answer for the consequence of another shock. After all, it might not be the fever; the weather was hot and thundery, and this might be some childish ailment.

28

He would come round early in the morning, and then he would be better able to judge.

'Oh, Mary, the night of anxiety that I passed! The darling slept very fairly, but was now and then restless, and complained of being thirsty; and once in the night she woke up and began to cry because "mammie" was not there to sing her "'eavens and 'omes." I could not make out what she meant, and presently she began crooning out to herself in such a baby voice—

> 'There's a crown for little children,
> Above the bright blue sky.

And then she interrupted herself, and said, "Such nice beautiful 'omes and 'eavens for Hatty and 'Oosie and May, and for Bee too!" nodding her little head and looking so satisfied.

'"And for Lettice, darling, surely for Lettice!" but she only nodded her little head again and repeated, "for Hatty and 'Oosie and May and little Bee too."

'She got nicely drowsy after this, but woke up once and asked where "auntie" was, and towards morning I heard her talking quietly to herself. "Mammie, I loves 'oo; I loves 'oo very much!" she kept repeating in such a dear little voice.'

Mary covered her face with her hands with a choking sob, and for a little while Emma could not finish her sad narrative. Oh, for Janet's darling, her beauty bright!

'Dr. Radley came round early,' continued Miss Ducie presently, when Mary was a little more composed. 'He said he was afraid she was going to have the fever, but still he could not be sure; he would look in again in two or three hours, and perhaps he would bring her father with him. He came again at noon, but he was alone. Mr. St. John was with May, who was rapidly sinking; and he hoped to carry back a good report of the child.

'She seemed really doing very nicely, though she was a little quiet and heavy. She had her doll beside her, and she asked Dr. Radley to give it some medicine too; but she did not talk much.

'He had only left the house a minute when he was

summoned back. I had gone downstairs with him, and was just standing at the door looking after him, when Mrs. Crowder called out to me in a frightened voice to bring him back. We ran upstairs. Oh, Mary, Mary, the darling was in a fit!

'We put her in a bath; we did all we could, and Dr. Radley never left the house again all those hours. Mrs. Crowder went up to the Rectory once to speak to you or Mr. St. John, but she came back saying that every one was shut up in May's room, and that she was actually dying.

'Dr. Radley and I consulted together, but what could we do? we both thought it was better that the parents should be spared this agonising sight. The sweet pet did not come to herself at all; sometimes she lay quite stiff with her eyes open, but not seeing or recognising us.'

'And when did she go?' asked Mary, unable to bear any more of these details.

'Not an hour ago. I wanted Dr. Radley to come up without me, but he thought I had better accompany him.'

'Is Dr. Radley here?'

'Yes, he is with Mr. St. John in his study. Mr. St. John came out to meet us, and when he saw our faces he beckoned to Dr. Radley, and they went into the study and shut the door behind them.'

'And I shall not have to tell Maurice,' thought Mary. And the first feeling of relief crossed her mind; but a moment afterwards she started up nervously, for the study-door was opening.

'I must go to him,' she exclaimed; but on the threshold she encountered them both coming in search of her.

'I was just looking for you, my dear! Will you come with us?' Oh, the haggard weariness of Maurice's face as he spoke, and the coldness of the hand he held out to Mary! None of them noticed except Emma that Mary was bareheaded as she stepped out into the summer dusk and walked up the village street. Emma threw a light shawl over her, taking it from her own shoulders. They had to pass St. Norbert, and Miss Brettingham looked out, half frightened, half scandalised, at the little procession—

Mary, with Emma's shawl drawn over her hair, holding
Maurice's hand, and walking between him and Dr. Radley.

The others lingered in the little parlour, while Maurice
and his sister went upstairs.   The dear little child lay
peacefully smiling in her sleep, with her baby doll still
beside her.   Some of the golden curls had been cut off,
but the little fair rings still clustered round the temples.

'And her mother and I could not give her one kiss.
Oh, my little Bee ! my bright busy Bee !' and the unhappy
father groaned in anguish.   What task was this that lay
before him, and which was daunting his brave spirit ?—
the task of telling the bereaved mother that her Benjamin
was gone.

No wonder Maurice felt his heart die within him as he
kissed the soft rings of hair and the waxen brow, but he
would not linger to unman himself.   'Come, Mary, the
bitterest part remains,' he said in a sad voice.   'Do not leave
me.   Let us go to her together.'   And Mary, still holding
fast to him in her mute sympathy, walked back with him
through the dark village, and into the room where Janet lay
quiescent and open-eyed, in a state that was almost lethargy.

She struggled up into a sitting posture when she saw
them, as though she were reminded of some half-forgotten
duty, and indeed the poor soul was half-dazed with grief.

'I am going to Lettice,' she said, striving to stand upright, but swaying a little as though from weakness.   Never
once had she asked after Bee since Hatty died.

'No, love, you must stop with me,' returned her husband.   'Let Mary sit with Lettice. · She is doing so well.
God is merciful.   He is sparing our firstborn.'

'Yes, yes.   I wanted to save her for your sake, Maurice,'
looking up at him with dim lustreless eyes.

'We must love and cherish her, dearest.   We must
make up to her for the loss of her little sisters !' and then
his voice shook.   'Oh, my wife, try and bear it for my sake.
Am I not better to thee than ten sons ?   Bee—our baby
—oh, Mary, I cannot tell her !' suddenly breaking down.

There was no need to tell her.   For as the name—the
beloved name—crossed his lips, she uttered a cry that was

almost a scream, and her arms went up wildly above her head. Had not Maurice's arms been round her she would have swayed and fallen at his feet; but he held her fast, weeping over her, and Mary helped him to lay her down. Dr. Radley was still in the house, and came at once. It was hysteria, he told Maurice, a state of mental and bodily collapse from the successive shocks she had received. Sedatives must be administered, and the utmost care and quietness enjoined. 'Had she understood that the child was dead?' asked Maurice.

'Yes,' Dr. Radley assured him. He had little doubt from the cry he heard that she had grasped the truth instantaneously. She would have guessed it from her husband's face.

Lettice was left in Biddy's charge that night, and indeed the child had taken the disease so favourably that the doctors had never felt the least uneasiness in her case.

The sedatives had taken effect, and Janet slept heavily. Mary lay down by her side, with her arm over her that she might feel the least movement, and soon fell into an exhausted slumber.

Maurice was trying to court rest in his dressing-room. He was ill himself from anxiety, and Dr. Radley had begged him to leave Mrs. St. John to his sister's care.

'My dear sir, the human frame is not capable of sustaining such prolonged effort,' he said. 'You must give up a little, or we shall have you on our hands too. To-morrow, when your wife wakes, she will need you more than she does now. What would be the good of your watching her?' And Maurice, who felt himself strangely ill, yielded. But he passed a miserable night, and his snatches of sleep tortured him. For first Bee with her merry laugh, and then May and Hatty and Rosie with sweet pale faces, seemed to stand beside him. Little hands pulled him hither and thither; childish voices calling 'Father, father!' sounded in his ears.

It was a relief when in the gray dawn he felt a light touch, and looking up, saw Mary standing beside him.

'Dear Maurice, you called out, and so I came to you,'

she said softly. 'How uneasily you are resting! Let me put your head more comfortable. Janet is still asleep, and Lettice too,' and she smiled at him and left him somewhat comforted.

The sleep that followed strengthened him a little, and he was able to rise at his usual hour; and by and by, when his other duties were done—and there were many arrangements necessary—he went to Lettice.

She was looking better, but her eyes filled when she saw him. 'Oh, my poor father,' she said, 'my dear, dear little sisters!' for she had heard her mother's agonised cry, and Biddy had not been able to keep the truth from her. Dr. Radley had himself spoken to the child, but so wisely and carefully that no harm had been done. Lettice was so unselfish even in her grief that her first thought was for her parents.

'Dear Lettice, we have only you left,' exclaimed Maurice, with deep sadness in his voice.

'Yes, and I must love you more than I have ever done;' and then she added timidly, 'I have not said my prayers, dear father; shall we say them together?' And perhaps nothing could have soothed Maurice so much. It seemed to strengthen him a little for those weary hours that followed.

Janet lay in this strange state for days, sleeping a great deal, and taking any light nourishment that was offered her, —for she could not eat,—but not speaking or showing the slightest interest in what was going on.

When Maurice went out to his children's funeral, and Mary asked her if she could spare her a little, she looked at her listlessly without answering. Little Bee lay with her sisters under the horse-chestnut tree before Janet's numb faculties stirred themselves to ask particulars.

To all Mary's cheering accounts of Lettice's progress she listened quite silently. In the same passive manner she took all her husband's caresses. When Maurice prayed with her, pouring out his strong heart in supplication for his afflicted wife, she lay watching him with dark clouded eyes. What were her thoughts? Mary wondered. When would the dumb grief that was closing her lips find voice and utterance?

'Let her alone. Nature will recover itself gradually,' Dr. Radley said in his daily visits.

Lettice lay outside her bed, now watched over by the faithful Biddy, and nursed by Emma, who came to sit with her for hours every day.

Maurice was beginning to go about his parish now into other infected houses. It seemed to rouse him and do him good as nothing else did. He was looking ill and hollow-eyed, and he missed the comfort of his wife's care.

The first thing that roused Janet was seeing some gray hairs in Maurice's head as he knelt beside her, and she pointed them out without speaking to Mary.

That night, after a brief consultation with Dr. Radley, they tried something else, and Mary carried Lettice in and laid her in her mother's arms.

When Janet felt her child clinging to her, the frozen brain seemed to thaw. 'Dear mamma, my poor mamma!' cried Lettice, creeping up to her and kissing her pale face. To their delight, Janet began to return her kisses, and then she suddenly shivered and burst into tears.

'Cry, dearest, it will do you good,' said Mary, clasping her. 'Thank God you can cry, Janet!' and the weeping so long deferred became so uncontrollable that they were obliged to remove Lettice.

'Don't be afraid, little woman; you have done mamma a world of good,' said Dr. Radley cheerily, as Lettice looked up at him with scared eyes, and to Maurice and Mary he said quite brightly, 'My patient will do now!'

CHAPTER XLIII

THE next morning Janet rose and dressed herself—very feebly and by slow degrees, but refusing all efforts of assistance from Mary. Then she seated herself by the window, looking out on the corner of the churchyard where the horse chestnuts spread their foliage over her children's grave, and Lettice crept in and lay on the little couch beside her, and so the day passed on.

But the next evening she asked for Emma, and sat motionless in the summer twilight listening to the sad account of her darling's strange seizure and end; once only she seemed moved out of her rigid calm, when she took Emma's hand suddenly and kissed it. 'Let me do it,' she said in a low passionate voice, 'for it has touched my darling!'

But when Maurice came to her, fearing the effect of this excitement, she clung to him and would not let him go, and they could hear her sobbing convulsively in the darkness.

Poor Maurice! how his sister's heart ached for him, and yet how little she could do to comfort the broken-hearted father!

Maurice crept about the parish, looking old and bowed. There were houses of mourning for him to enter—other parents who were weeping for their children, for the fever had raged like a plague through Crome. When he came home he would go to his study and sit there with his open Bible beside him. Upstairs was the empty nursery—the four little vacant beds. His wife, who ought to have been beside him, sat looking out on the graves like a pale image of woe, and Lettice, by some strange instinct, stayed with her mother, feeling as though she dare not leave her. And indeed the little thin hand stealing into Janet's, the sweet childish voice repeating hymns and psalms, were her greatest comfort. Maurice knew this; knew too by some mysterious prevision that his wife was uneasy in his presence, and so he left mother and child to minister to each other, and remained sad and solitary in his study.

Dr. Radley had strongly urged change of scene for Mrs. St. John, while the Rectory should be cleaned and fumigated, but Janet would not hear of such a thing. Mary, who was for rousing her at all costs, wanted her to visit the children's grave, and to help her plant some flowers, but Janet shivered and shook her head. 'Not yet, I am not worthy,' she said. 'I have something else to do first.' But though Mary marvelled over her words, she would not explain herself.

But one evening when Mary was helping Lettice to get ready for bed, Maurice heard a slow footstep outside the study door—a footstep so changed and faltering that he could not recognise it for his wife's, and when he looked up and saw her beside him he absolutely started.

'My darling! you have come to me at last,' in a tone that must have told her all—his longing for her, his unutterable desolation; but she almost pushed him from her with her cold feeble hand.

'Don't, Maurice; stay where you are. I want to speak to you. I must speak to you, for fear I go mad!' And as he saw the wildness of her wan face he subdued the pain he felt at her repulse, and seated himself again, and said gently, as though he were speaking to some troubled penitent, 'Tell me all, my poor child! Ease your sore heart! Tell all to your husband, Janet.'

But her next words made him thrill with horror; for the moment he verily believed sorrow had crazed her brain.

'I don't want you to touch me, Maurice; you would not if you knew. I have murdered your children! I, and not the fever, have been their murderer.'

If he had shrunk from her it would have been worse for
them both ; but at this awful moment love taught him its
divinest lesson.   He opened his arms to her, and said in a
perfectly quiet voice, ' Well, if you have, Janet, you are still
my wife, and I am still your husband.   And " there is forgiveness in heaven over one sinner that repenteth ! " '   For
how could he tell if trouble had driven her mad, or if some
sin pressed heavily on her conscience ?—in either case was
he not her husband ?

Then in another moment she was on her knees beside
him, and the tears were streaming from her hot eyes, and
she was telling him all the pent-up misery of her life.

Oh, what a story of an undisciplined woman's heart !
What she had been his beloved, the one woman in the
world to him, and she had suffered and borne all this for
his sake !

Now he knew what he had always dimly surmised—the
secret of her restlessness and want of peace, the inward
revolt of her will against his, the jealousy of his work, the
fixed rebellion against the sordid condition of her life, the
hideous guise that poverty had worn for her, the pride,
the ambition of her worldly nature.

How had she masked all this pain from him ? dressing
her face with smiles whenever he looked at her, and per-
forming all her household labours with no word of complaint to him.

Out of her very love had risen her temptation.   Maurice
spoke no word when Janet came to this part of her confession.   He listened with absolute dumbness, when she
narrated without reserve every detail and almost every word
of what passed between her and Mary on that fatal night
at the Chateau de St. Aubert.   ' I clung to her dress.   I
prayed her to have pity on us all,—not to sacrifice you and
our children to that young man.   " What is your love compared with mine, who have loved Maurice all these years ? "
That is what I said to her,' went on Janet, humbling herself
ruthlessly in the dust.

Maurice pressed her hand, but he said nothing.   If
Janet had only known that terrible sinking at his heart !

What was his children's death compared with this—his white folded lambs as he often called them? So strangely and nobly was this man's nature fashioned, that this knowledge of his wife's crooked dealings inflicted the keenest agony of all.

He had known her not to be a Christian when he married her—she was too worldly-minded for that; but he had ever admired the uprightness and a certain loftiness in her character. Now she had humbled herself and him too in the dust. True, she had not lied to him with any actual falsehood—she could not have stooped to that; but she had evaded.and deceived him; her whole course for months past had been one of duplicity and double-dealing. She had accepted Mary's sacrifice—had in fact demanded it as a right—and had blinded him into the belief that Mary was happy. She had taken these rich gifts for him and for her children—not for herself, for she was not selfish —and had enjoyed them, knowing them to be at the expense of another woman's happiness. Now he knew the meaning of Mary's worn face, her sweet sad looks, her restless desire for work, and yet more work; and then, in spite of his self-restraint, he groaned aloud.

'Maurice, forgive me,' as she heard the groan.

'Nay, Janet, I am your husband and not your Judge. It is for us to ask forgiveness together.'

'No, no, not you. You have not sinned,' she returned, for she misunderstood him. 'You are good, blameless. You have done no wrong. Oh, how bitterly you must be disappointed in your wife!'

'Yes,' for he was perfectly truthful with her; 'but she is still my wife.'

'Then you do not hate me?' she whispered, coming a little closer. 'You have not turned against me? I did not dare come near you until I was strong enough to tell you this. Oh, Maurice, if you are miserable, what must I be? But for me my darlings would be living now; I should not have brought them to this fever-stricken place. God has done well to punish me. But why has He punished the innocent with the guilty?'

'My poor child, He has not punished you;' and then at the sight of her misery his heart melted, and his brief coldness vanished. Was he to speak harshly to this bruised reed, this desolate creature who had lost so much?

'Oh, you poor mother!' he cried. 'God has taken your children because He loved them, and because He loved their mother too!'

'Loved me?'—incredulously. Here was strange doctrine to one who believed in the thunderbolts of vengeance.

'Yes, you, who have so sinned against His mercy; the very severity of His strokes proves that. Oh, why are you so hard, Janet? Can you fight against love like this, when He will have your heart? When He is removing your idols one by one, will you still resist? Oh, Janet, be silent; humble yourself in the dust, and kiss the feet that were pierced for you, for it is not vengeance but love that hath allured you, and brought you into the wilderness to suffer!' And then he took her to his heart and comforted her.

And when she was a little calmer he said to her quietly—

'Janet, we must bring forth fruits meet for repentance. You will not be afraid of poverty now?'

'Oh no,' she answered wearily. Her face was pale as ashes, and her eyes swollen, but there was a look of peace on her face that it had never worn before.

'And I may speak to Mary?'

'Yes, yes. Do all you think right. Only make me worthy of seeing those little angels again;' and she burst into tears, and so great was her exhaustion that for some hours Maurice feared to leave her.

He had a sleepless night. Alas! sleep had grown coy with him of late, but Janet slumbered peacefully, and something in her face seemed to touch him as he stood by her side and looked at her.

'My poor Janet! But He is bringing her home; He is bringing this tired wanderer home,' he said as he kissed her hair softly. Alas! there were gray streaks there now.

'Mary, my dear, I want to speak to you,' he said, when they had risen from the breakfast-table. He had been very silent through the meal, and Mary had looked at him anxiously once or twice. How ill he looked, how bowed and shaken !

'Very well,' she answered cheerfully, jingling her basket of keys; 'but you must be quick, for Janet will be awake soon, and there are the orders, and Dollie and Mrs. Maynard will be back to-day, and I must write to them.' For Dollie and her mother had yielded to Grey's persuasions, and had betaken themselves to Abercrombie Road for the last week, where Dollie had been taken to see the loveliest cottage—a perfect little bijou of a place, with dear little low rooms opening on a verandah and a garden, and a tiny greenhouse, and all for a surprisingly low rent, and Grey had actually taken it the next day, and was bent on furnishing it.

'You must not be in a hurry,' returned Maurice gently. 'Mary, my dear sister ! Janet and I want to ask your forgiveness.'

Then she stood and stared at him, and her basket of keys slid from her arm to the table, for he was taking her hand, and his face was very pale.

'She is truly penitent. Oh, Mary, how generous you have been. But I cannot talk of that,' and the tears came into his eyes. 'Ah, you good woman, you true sister, the best friend my darlings ever had ! But you must not think hardly of her. She was cruel, cruel, but she did it out of her despair and love for us. Try to think well of her, dear, for my sake ! '

'Oh, Maurice !' but she could say no more. She was so overwhelmed with the suddenness of all this. Janet had told him, then. 'You are not angry ?' she asked at last—almost timidly.

'No, I was not angry, not even at first. I was too hurt, too wounded with her that she should pain you so— that we should both pain you; that the spoiling of your life should come from us who love you so ! '

'Oh, it is not spoiled,' she assured him eagerly; and now the colour came into her face. 'Maurice, I gloried in the sacrifice. It was for you and the children. If it were to come over again I would do it—ay, and gladly too.'

'The children are gone,' he answered calmly, 'and I do
not think God has blessed a self-sacrifice that involved the
happiness of another.   I do not know, but it seems to me
as though we are left sometimes to reap the consequences
of our own mistakes.'

'This was not a mistake,' she answered steadily.

'Was it not?' he returned, with a sad smile.   'Do you
think so little of yourself as that?   Have you quite forgotten Cuthbert Lyndhurst?'

Then she flushed all over her sweet face, for Maurice's
eyes were very penetrating.   'I do not forget him.   I
never shall,' she answered in the lowest possible voice.
'But if it were to come over again I would do the same!'

'I do not doubt it,' he answered, smiling.   'What a
brave woman you are! the bravest woman I know;' and
then he sighed as he thought of his wife's shortcomings.
'Now, my dear, I have little more to say.   Bertie must do
the rest.'

'Bertie!'   Then she turned pale and trembled.   'Oh,
why do you mention his name?   What has he to do with
it?   Maurice, you must not try me so, for we have all
gone through so much, and I am not as strong as I was,
and I am doing the best I can.'

'Mary, my dear, dear sister!' and then he made her
sit down, for she was trembling so she could hardly stand.

'I mentioned his name because it is the name of the
man you love, and who loves you, and for whose sake I
know you would gladly give up all this wealth.'

'Oh no, Maurice, I cannot,' and now the tears were
stealing through her fingers, as she covered her face.

'Not give up Crome for Bertie!   Why, Mary, how can
you tell me such a thing, when you hate playing the fine
lady, and will not put on a single jewel—when no char-
woman works harder than the mistress of Crome—when you
deny yourself every luxury and every self-indulgence, no
doubt because Bertie cannot share them with you!'

'Maurice, how can you know?' with a violent blush.

'Because I am no longer blinded; because I can read
my sister's heart.   I know you would rather share the

humblest home with the man you love than live in all this grandeur. Answer me truly, Mary. Have you grown afraid of poverty?'

'No, indeed, but why do you ask?'

'Neither have I. God bless you, dear, for all you have done for us! The last months of my children's life were made happy by you, you devoted aunt. How they loved the garden and the pony and the orchard! and there was May's "she-ass," and Snap, and the birds.' He paused, and then he recovered himself.

'Well, they are revelling in the flowers of paradise now, my four treasures. They want nothing more from Aunt Mary but a few spring blossoms for their grave. As for Janet and me, we have resolved—and thank God my wife agrees with me—that we will take no more bounties from our sister's hand.'

'Maurice, how can you be so unkind? Think of Lettice!'

'I do think of her. We have enough for one child. We can live with some little contrivance on what the vicar allows me. When he returns, there are plenty of curacies open to me, for I never mean to return to the East End of London.'

'I am thankful for that,' answered Mary.

'No, never,' he repeated, with a shudder as he thought of his wife's concealed sufferings. 'Oh, if we could only stay here within sight of our children's grave, how thankful I would be! And yet how reluctant I was to come here! It must have been a presentiment. Truly "He leads us by paths that we have not known,"' and he sighed.

'Maurice, are you sure, quite sure, it will be right to do this?' but though she stopped and hesitated, her brother understood the unspoken question, and indeed the appealing look in those clear eyes was not difficult to read. They seemed to say, 'Is it possible, am I really to be happy?'

'Yes, Mary, it were a sin to do otherwise,' he answered, stooping and kissing her forehead. 'To-morrow I shall write to Bertie, and then we shall see what he says.'

'Do not bring him until it is quite safe,' she returned; and then she left her brother, and went up into her room. Who can tell the thoughts that agitated this pure soul? Regret for fruitless pain and self-sacrifice; relief as she felt the burden of her unloved wealth rolling from her; happiness that almost stunned her at the thought of seeing one dear face again!

Now he would no longer be solitary and sad in other men's homes; wandering from place to place as he was bidden, and trying to find solace in change. At the first word, the first gleam of hope, he would fly back to her as an arrow from the bow. Yes, were he even at the ends of the earth he would come to her!

She roused herself at last with an effort, and went to Janet.

'Oh, Mary, I hoped you would come to me,' she said, lifting her cheek from the pillow to be kissed. 'Maurice has been with me. Oh, there is such a weight taken off my heart! Mary, do you think you can ever forgive me? Maurice has, and my darlings have, I know, but I want your forgiveness too.'

'Dear Janet, I have nothing to forgive. You are my own dear sister, and I love you. You must get well now, and help us to be happy.'

'You will be happy, Mary'—and Janet's sad beautiful eyes rested on her with a new softness—'and I will try to be good for all your sakes.' And then she drew Mary's face down beside her, and whispered, 'Ask Bertie to forgive me too!'

'He will be sure to do that. Bertie never bore a grudge against any one in his life,' and then she smiled to herself happily as she thought of Bertie's exceeding sweetness of nature, and how hard it was for him to retain anger against any one.

CHAPTER XLIV

'MY BONNIE MARY!'

BERTIE was in the Engadine when he received Maurice's letter. He was sitting at table d'hôte when the waiter, with many voluble excuses, laid the blue envelope beside him. 'Monsieur must pardon—it had been delayed—some error of direction—it had miscarried for days—the mistake was not with the authorities,' and so on with many flourishes.

Bertie broke the seal a little nervously. Why should Mr. St. John write to him? he thought; and then he grew grave, and the food lay untasted on his plate. Scarlet fever, four of the children dead, and Mary nursing them—good heavens! at the risk of her own life. And Bertie pushed aside his chair, and rose from the table with a muttered excuse to his neighbour, who pouted and looked disconcerted at the loss of her handsome companion.

Meanwhile the young man strode with agitated step through the little group of waiters. Something lay behind; something had happened. He must take refuge in his own room, and read it quietly there. There was a balcony outside his window, with a sort of alcove formed by the jutting roof, and here he set himself to peruse Maurice's lengthy document. He was a man, and whatever happened he would grin and bear it. That was what he told himself; but his brown cheek had turned pale, and his hands were shaking like a girl's. Was Mary, his own Mary, dead? Then the world would be as nothing to him, and he would never return to England. He would go out to

29

the Melanesian Islands, and help some of those fellows in their work; or if he were not good enough for that, he could volunteer into some service that was tolerably hard and risky,—anything that was exciting, and that would prevent him eating his heart out. But go on teaching Ralph,—never. And the boy was fond of him, and he was sorry; but it could not be done.

'Ah!' Now what made this very excitable young man suddenly jump up from his seat as though he were shot, and commence perambulating the balcony with quick, uneven steps?

His third turn brought him face to face with Ralph. The boy limped up to him—he was slightly lame—and touched him on the arm.

'I hope it is not bad news, Mr. Lyndhurst? Papa was afraid, and sent me after you. You don't look as though it were bad news, sir,' regarding his tutor's flushed face rather dubiously.

'No, no, boy, it is good news. At least as far as it concerns me,' as Bertie suddenly remembered the loss of the children.

'Look here, Ralph, where is your father? I must speak to him. I shall have to leave you, and return to England.' And as the lad's face fell, he added kindly, 'You must make up your mind to do without me, for my whole future happiness is involved in this.'

Sir Charles was very reasonable and good-natured, and he was much attached to Bertie, but his face clouded a little with disappointment as he listened to the young man's story. 'I see Ralph will lose you. I am afraid the boy will fret at first; but there, we must not be selfish and stand in your way, and you have been very down and half-hearted lately. Lady Emily has been quite in a way about you. There, go and pack your portmanteau, and have it out with Ralph. When we come back to England next month we must see what is to be done.' And then he patted Bertie's broad shoulder as though he were his son, and went off to tell his wife.

And Bertie packed his portmanteau, and whistled and

talked cheerily to Ralph, who looked on with grieved eyes
at the preparations, and Lady Emily came in and said a
few motherly words; and when he was left alone Bertie
wrote a short concise note to Maurice—

Your letter has been delayed for nearly a week (he said), but I
packed within two hours of its receipt, and shall start for England at
once. I hope to be with you at the Rectory at such and such a time.

And then followed a few lines of condolence—

I will not answer your letter now, as I think we can talk over
things more comfortably; but give my love to Mary, please. She has
had it ever since I can remember.

And it was this last clause which made Mary declare
Bertie's letter was perfect. Maurice brought it to her at
once, for she had gone back to the Park to be with Dollie
a little. Dollie's marriage was fixed for October, and Grey
was coming down in a day or two for a brief visit, and to
escort his fiancée and her mother to London. The cottage
had to be furnished, and there were wedding clothes to
provide; and in short Grey could not do without them
any longer. And as Dollie was now quite satisfied with
Mary's looks, she yielded to his entreaties, only stipulating
that Grey should stop to congratulate his brother.

'Let me see. I think we may expect him to-morrow
evening,' observed Maurice, twirling his felt hat in his
usual way, as he looked down at his sister's happy face.

'Yes, and Grey will be here; and oh, Maurice, how
tiresome! you have appointed Mr. Langley to come down
about the will;' for Mrs. Reid's old lawyer had died suddenly, and his successor, Mr. Langley, was now in active
correspondence with Maurice.

'Why, Mary, what are you thinking about?' remonstrated her brother. 'Of course I timed Mr. Langley's
visit to coincide with Bertie's arrival. I daresay you and
Bertie will be too much occupied to give your attention to
business the first evening, but the next morning there must
be a house committee; and the disobedient heiress must
resign her rights and receive her pittance, and then the
codicil will be read.'

'I wish he could be spared all this, it will distress him so,' sighed Mary. 'I should have liked to have given it all up, and had everything settled before he came. I would rather have met him in London or anywhere else but here;' for she felt that though Bertie would not refuse the sacrifice that was no sacrifice, still it would pain him to see the actual deprivation; and she would have welcomed him more happily in the little parlour in Abercrombie Road.

But Maurice did not see this at all; he only said, 'Nonsense, what does it matter? it is only a matter of form, and will soon be over.' And then he changed the subject—for he saw Mary was a little too agitated—and told her how Janet and Lettice had been out in the pony carriage, and how well Janet seemed, and how she walked with him every evening in the churchyard, when Lettice had gone to bed.

'She is better since you left us, Mary,' he said; 'she seems to think she must rouse herself now to look after things. She actually proposed to-day that I should take her and Lettice to the seaside for a few weeks. She is thinking of us, and what Dr. Radley said about Lettice's growing so fast; for she cannot bear the thought for herself.'

'I think I should do it,' rejoined Mary thoughtfully; 'she is returning to her old self, and is beginning to plan for your good. Oh, how changed she is, Maurice, even in these few weeks! I sometimes can hardly believe when she talks to me that it is Janet.'

'It is a truer, sweeter Janet,' he returned with some emotion; but not even to this faithful sister could he speak much of his wife. The beautiful discontented woman, who had been his pride and his pain, was now humble and teachable as a little child.

'Help me to be good, Maurice; let me learn of you!' was her daily cry; and ever she strove with meekness to lay his lightest word to her heart. 'You do not love me less for all I have told you!' she said to him once, with sad astonishment in her voice.

Love her less! Never had his heart gone out to her

more than when he saw her grave listening face as she sat in her place in church with Lettice beside her, as she sat working by his side in her heavy mourning dress; and he thought how the mother's ears were missing the pattering of little feet in the nursery overhead, and still no complaint crossed her lips, though the tears would fall sometimes into her lap. He would suddenly clasp her to him with a fond movement.

'You are not unhappy, wife? you can wait a little while until we go to the children?'

'Yes, Maurice, I can wait with you!' she would answer patiently, and then Lettice would steal noiselessly across the room and lay her head in her lap.

'Mother, will my sisters be big when I see them again?' for Lettice always called her mother now; and then Maurice would talk to them both gently of that quiet resting-place, where those they loved were dwelling.

'What does it matter if they be changed, or under what new conditions we shall meet them, so that we see them coming to greet us when our life journey is over!' And then Lettice quoted a line that her mother especially loved—

> And oh the joy upon that shore
> To tell our shipwrecked wanderings o'er.

For she was growing fast her parents' comforter—'their daughter of consolation,' as Maurice often called her.

Bertie arrived at the Rectory at the time Maurice expected him. Maurice met him cordially, and took him into his study, and for a long time they were closeted together.

Mr. St. John was very favourably impressed by this interview. He had always regarded Bertie as an honest, kindly young fellow, but with hardly sufficient manliness of purpose. Now, as he stood before him, dusty and travel-stained—for he had hardly given himself rest night or day, so eager was he to reach his destination—there was something so winning in his boyish impulsiveness, in his freedom from selfishness, in his shyly-expressed love for Mary, that Maurice no longer marvelled at his sister's choice.

'He is as beautiful and lovable as a young David!' he said afterwards to his wife; 'his only fault is that he seems rather young for her; but that will mend with time.'

Bertie's first action, when they got into the study, was to wring Maurice's hand till he winced and reddened with pain.

'I am so sorry, so awfully sorry, you know!' blurted out Bertie; and Maurice's sallow cheek flushed a little.   ·

'Thank you,' he answered in a subdued voice; 'it has been a sad time for us—my poor wife especially; but God has brought us through it. I think I may say that Mary has been our greatest help and comfort through it all.'

'I knew she would be; there is no one like her, no one!' with a little burst of enthusiasm that made her brother smile.

'Now, we must talk about your own affairs;' but Bertie interrupted him.

'Look here, Mr. St. John,' he said in a shamefaced way; 'of course I understood your letter, and what it meant, and all that—that Mary is willing to have me—and will give up everything—God bless her! What is there she would not do for me?' continued the young man, faltering a little as he thought of the great blessing that awaited him. 'But the question is, what is best for her? I want you to tell me that.'

'I think Mary would be the better judge of what concerns her own happiness so closely;' but Maurice looked very kindly at him. 'She has never cared much for any of her possessions, and I do not think it will cost her a moment's pang to resign them; not a tithe of what she suffered when for our sakes she gave you up.'

'It was I who gave her up,' returned Bertie eagerly; 'Mrs. St. John is my witness that I spared her that at least; it was I who gave her up—who went away, that she should not be harassed or fretted at the notion that she had been unkind.'

'Yes, indeed, Janet told me how generous you had been.'

'It was for me to spare her, you know. What is the

use of being a man, if one cannot shield the girl one loves from annoyance? And now it is for you and me to consider what is best for her,' continued Bertie, pulling his moustache furiously; for all this speech was difficult to him.

'My dear fellow!' Maurice was so much touched and surprised at the young man's loyalty and unselfishness that he hardly knew what to reply. Instead of grasping at his prize, instead of demanding to see Mary instantly, here he was pausing to think what was best for her, and looking so tired and yet so eager that Maurice was quite sorry for him.

'I have been thinking about it all these days and nights,' went on Bertie; 'one cannot sleep much in the trains. I came at once, as I should have come from the end of the earth if she had held up her little finger to beckon me; but if you think it best—that it will not be for her happiness to marry me—I will go away again without seeing her if you wish it, though I confess it will half break my heart!' finished the poor fellow with a sort of gasp.

'You shall do nothing of the kind, returned Maurice putting his hand on the young man's broad shoulder. 'You shall wash off some of that dust, and we will walk over to the Park together, and you shall see Mary at once. Why, my dear fellow, she is looking for us now, and is wondering why you are not with her.'

'And you really think it would be best?' and a change passed over Bertie's downcast face.

'Yes, indeed, it is best; I think it is altogether right that two people who love each other, and do not fear poverty for their own or for the other's sake, should take each other for better or worse—not dreading consequences or being scared by any amount of self-sacrifice. What matters the loss of Mary's fortune, when you give her back her cheerfulness and peace of mind, of which we have robbed her!' and Maurice's voice grew agitated.

'If I were only more worthy of her,' observed Bertie humbly.

'Oh, we may all of us say that; but love is blind, and

it seems Mary has not found any special flaw in you.
Come, we will not delay any longer for her sake;' and
Maurice took Bertie's arm gently and led him away.

But as they were crossing the hall, they came upon
Janet. She was sweeping past them in her heavy black
draperies when she saw Bertie and stopped, and timidly
offered her hand.

'Mr. Bertie,' she said, 'will you take it? do you think
you can forgive me so far as that?'

'Nonsense, what is there to forgive?' returned Bertie
abruptly, shaking her hand violently. If she had been his
enemy, he had forgotten it all now; but he looked at her
curiously as she stood saying a few quiet words to them
both. Could this be Mrs. St. John, he thought, the woman
he had always secretly disliked, whose handsome face and
harsh vibrating voice and smooth sarcasms he had alike
detested? was it the blackness of her mourning dress that
made her face so white? and then her voice was altered,
and there were gray streaks in her hair!

'Don't let us keep you from Mary.' And she looked at
him so kindly and yet so sadly that Bertie felt quite an odd
choking sensation. When a tall slim girl with closely-
cropped fair hair and large spiritual eyes came gliding up
to them in the dark passage, he hardly recognised her for
Lettice, until she held out her hand to him and smiled.
Bertie had not realised before the terrible change that had
passed over the Rectory!

It had been a trying day for Mary. In spite of her
efforts to occupy herself and to appear unconcerned and
as though nothing were expected to happen, she was rest·
less and distraite. The morning had passed heavily for her
at Brotherton—never had teaching seemed so irksome, or
the room so oppressive and confined; and she appeared
at luncheon with such pale cheeks that Dollie was
alarmed.

'Mary, you must go and lie down,' she said very per-
emptorily, 'or you will not feel fit for Grey and Mr.
Langley this evening.' She did not dare add Bertie's

name, for how could they tell whether he would arrive to-day or not.

'I wish Mr. Langley were not coming,' returned Mary wearily; but in spite of Dollie's peremptoriness, she would not hear of lying down. She dressed herself carefully in her thin black dress, being very particular about the fineness of her ruffles and the smoothness of her brown hair ; and then she took her work and repaired to the 'peacocks' promenade.'

Grey and Dollie found her there as they came strolling down the walk hand-in-hand. It was always the first place Grey visited when he came down to Crome, and it was there that he and Dollie generally took their parting walk ; for since the evening that he had found Dollie crying by the sun-dial the place had been sacred to them both.

Mary looked up and greeted the young man kindly. Grey thought she looked thin and worn, and told her so.

'Oh, it is nothing,' she said hastily; 'I shall get up my strength by and by when I am rested;' for this was the first time they had met since the fever, and there was crape on Mary's dress, and others beside Grey noticed she was altered.

But she would not listen to Dollie's suggestion that they should bring her out her tea. She would go in and make it for them, she said ; and when Mr. Langley arrived, she welcomed him most cordially, and talked to him all through the long dinner. But only Grey, who sat next to her, noticed how nervously she started at every sound, and how her face flushed at any opening door.

'Do you think you can do without me a little ?' she whispered to Dollie, as they left the dining-room.

Dollie nodded, and ran after her mother; and Mary went to the morning-room. It was cool there, and all the windows were open, and she would be quiet, and not have to join in all that light jargon of talk ; and surely that was the hall-door opening and Maurice's voice speaking to some one, perhaps to Pratt.

'You will find her in the morning-room ;' that was what Maurice said, but he could not be talking to Pratt. Mary rose from her chair, but her limbs trembled so that she could not advance a step.

For the door was open, and between the marble pillars she could see a broad-shouldered figure in a gray tweed travelling suit, walking swiftly towards her, and a face that she had only seen lately in her dreams with a halo of rumpled fair hair.

'Bertie!' she exclaimed faintly, but she could not move a step.

'Yes, Mary, I am here; oh, Mary, Mary!' and before another moment he had his arms round her, and she was sobbing as though her heart would break, with her face hidden against the gray coat.

But only for gladness—so she told him afterwards—for this reception rather frightened him. He had never seen Mary cry before; but she had suffered and wanted him so, she whispered, and did he know what it had cost her to give him up? and could he forgive her for being so unkind? and so on; while all the time he was petting and making much of her.

'But, you know, you never gave me up—it was I who did it!' returned Bertie, manfully sticking to his point. 'It was I who went away and left you, and who have to be forgiven, you know;' and then she laughed and grew calmer. But her lip trembled when he took her to the window to have a good look at her, as he said, for the light was fading.

'Oh, Mary, my bonnie Mary, what have they been doing to you?' he said in a grieved voice. 'You have lost your freshness and roundness; your cheek is quite thin and sharp!' touching it gently with his hand.

'You must remember what I have been through with the children; and then I could not help being very unhappy sometimes when I thought of you, Bertie,' looking up in his face with undisguised fondness. How sunburnt he looked! how broad and manly he had grown, and how wildly he had rumpled his hair! and could there be any face in the world so perfect? It gave her quite a pang that she should be so changed and worn in his eyes, while he was as handsome as ever. 'I am afraid you do not like the look of me, Bertie,' she said a little sadly.

Then he laughed a boyish laugh that was delicious to hear, but his answer was so embarrassing that Mary called him to order at last.

'Bertie, you must behave yourself!'

'Well, then, promise you will never talk such nonsense to me again. Not like the look of you—when it is the dearest, sweetest face I have ever seen!' and then he laughed again, this time for pure happiness, and some of Mary's old dimples woke up with her blushes.

By and by another thought struck him.

'I suppose it is all right, Mary. We are regularly engaged?'

'I suppose so,' rather doubtfully, for she could not quite remember when it was Bertie proposed to her, for the very reason that he never had; but it was all understood between them.

'All right,' he returned, quite contentedly. 'I got you the ring coming along. I thought if things went smoothly I should like to make sure of you, and put it on; and if Mr. St. John—at least,' interrupting himself, 'if affairs worked crookedly, I should only heave it into the canal and myself after it.'

'Oh, Bertie!' exclaimed Mary, shocked; and then her face glowed, for he was actually fumbling in his pocket.

'It is only a simple little thing,' he said. 'You know you are going to be a poor man's wife, Mary.'

'Oh, it is lovely!' she replied. It was a broad gold keeper, very plain and massive, with a small diamond sunk in the centre.

'It looks what it is meant for—to keep the other one on,' observed Bertie, with a look of intense satisfaction. And then he added with deeper feeling, 'Mary, when I think of what you are giving up for me, I hardly feel as though I ought to accept such a sacrifice. Fancy the poor home to which I must take you after this!' looking round the luxurious room rather disconsolately.

'Never mind how poor, so that it is the home you have

got ready for me,' she whispered, stealing her hand into his, and as Bertie looked at her a sort of mist came before his eyes.

'Oh, thank God!' exclaimed the young man in a low voice, as he drew her towards him. And he was right, for such gifts come from Heaven.

CHAPTER XLV

It was quite late before Mary bethought herself of her guests and Maurice.

'What are we to do? He will be waiting for you, Bertie.' For Bertie had left his bag at the Rectory, and was going back to fetch it, for neither she nor Maurice were willing that the least risk should be run.

'His brother will be here,' she thought. 'He may as well take up his quarters at the Park for a day or two until Grey goes back to town, and then there are very good rooms at the "Rising Sun"; Mrs. Piper would make him very comfortable.' For Mrs. Piper was the landlady of the 'Rising Sun,' the snuggest, cleanest, and best-managed of village inns, as many a young officer from Canterton testified, who had slept between those lavender-scented sheets, and had dined off salmon steaks and cutlets in Mrs. Piper's best parlour.

But as Mary mentioned his name there was her brother's tall form crossing the grass, and they went out to meet him. 'Oh, there you are at last,' he said, looking very much pleased as Mary put up her face to be kissed. 'And so it is all right, is it, Aunt Mary? And you and Bertie have settled it between you?'

'We had not much to settle,' returned Bertie frankly. 'I think we had made up our minds before we saw each other; but I am awfully happy, as you may suppose.'

'And Mary is too,' trying to see her face in the moonlight before they reached the shadow of the trees. 'Well,

I wish you joy, both of you.   I won't deny you are in luck, Bertie ; and this sister of mine is worth a king's ransom.'

' Oh, Maurice ! '

' So you are ; she is " the woman far above rubies," Bertie, and I am sure her husband's heart will safely trust in her.   Are you coming with me, my dear, to see Janet ? '   And as Mary answered ' Yes,' they went on together.

Janet's congratulations were tearful and heartfelt, but she could not say much ; but Mary understood her and was satisfied, and afterwards she went up to kiss Lettice.

What a walk they had back in the moonlight ! Bertie told Mary how he had wandered that night like an unquiet spirit round the house, leaving footsteps in the snow ; and how he had stood outside the window and watched her ; and then how he had met Dollie in the cathedral at Canterton, and what they had said to each other ; and they were both sorry when the house was reached, and they must go into the drawing-room with their apologies.

But Mr. Langley was not there to receive them, to Mary's great relief ; he had betaken himself and his blue bag to his own room.   Mrs. Maynard was knitting drowsily in her chair, and Dollie and Grey were whispering in one of the windows.

Dollie sprang up when she saw them, and came flying across the room, with her white gown flowing behind her wildly.   And she not only kissed Mary, but she looked most kindly at Bertie as she took his hand.

' For you are as good as my brother now,' she said in an innocent, confiding way.   Bertie reddened and laughed, and then he recollected what she meant, and he went up to his brother and wrung his hand.

' I think we are both to be congratulated, old fellow ! '

And Grey returned in his quiet way, ' You are right there, Bertie.'

After this it was suddenly discovered that Bertie had had nothing to eat.   It was Dollie who found it out, to Mary's infinite confusion.   No one had remembered the fact, not even Bertie, who frankly confessed that it was the first time in his life that he had ever forgotten to provide himself with a meal.

'Oh, and he is starving!' cried Mary, full of compunction at her omission.

'Do let me go and fetch him something!' cried Dollie eagerly. She was so fond of Bertie, and now he was going to be her own brother; and, as Mary smiled indulgently, she darted out of the room.

She was a long time absent; poor Bertie began to look quite pale and fagged with his long fast before they heard her returning footsteps.

'I am afraid I have been rather long,' cried Dollie merrily. She was holding a silver salver with a chocolate-pot upon it. Pratt followed her with a napkin-covered tray full of tempting viands.

'Why, it is Hebe in her white gown!' cried Bertie, starting up with a full recollection of that evening in the Chateau de St. Aubert. He could see the old kitchen with its rafters and red brick floor, and the brasses shining on the wall.

'Yes, it is Hebe coming to minister to Adonis!' returned Dollie, with a little laugh.

'That will do, Pratt; you may put down the tray there.' It was Dollie who poured out the foaming chocolate, who fed with the daintiest morsels the famished young man; while Mary and Grey looked on with amused eyes.

'Why does she call me Adonis?' asked Bertie once in a puzzled sort of way. 'You will never lose your name of Hebe now, Miss Maynard.'

'Oh, I am not Miss Maynard,' she answered pouting; 'you may call me Hebe or Dollie, whichever you like. Bertie is my own brother now; is he not, Grey?' in a little shy whisper that only Grey heard.

Oh, how happy they were! How Dollie laughed as she glided about with swift bird-like movement, while Bertie looked at her and Mary with a half-dazed expression in his gray eyes.

'I feel as though I were dreaming!' he said at last. 'Is it all true, Mary? Shall I really wake up and find myself here in the morning?'

'Oh yes, it is all true,' she answered softly; 'but you are
so tired, Bertie, and you have travelled night and day to
come to me.   After a night's rest you will understand
things better.' And then she called Dollie to her, and Mrs.
Maynard put down her knitting, and the brothers were left
alone together.

The next morning there was only the most general conversation.   Mr. Langley was at the breakfast-table, and his
clean shaven face and starched manners, for he was a prim
bachelor of uncertain age, kept even Dollie's spirits in
order.

Bertie had overslept himself, and came down late.   Mary
looked up and smiled at him from behind her silver urn;
but beyond that mutual look they took no notice of each
other.   Grey had his paper, and Dollie amused herself
peeping at the columns over his shoulder; while Mary
talked to her guests.

It was rather a relief to them all when Maurice came in
at the open window, and proposed their adjourning to the
library—'for the sooner we get this little bit of business
over the better;' and as Mr. Langley said, 'Certainly, Mr.
St. John, and then I shall be able to take the two o'clock
train to London,' they all followed Maurice into the room
he had once used as his study.

Mary was the last to enter—Bertie had detained her
a moment.

'Are you sure you do not repent?' he asked, taking the
hand with the ring upon it, and looking at her anxiously.

'Oh, Bertie, what a question!' and Mary's eyes were
full of reproachful sweetness; but Bertie's face was a little
flushed and troubled.

'All the same I wish it were over,' he said, with an
impatient sigh, and then he followed her into the room.

It was not a very pleasant business, certainly; but no
one looking at Mary's happy face could doubt that she was
doing the right thing; even Bertie's cloudy brow smoothed.
after the first few minutes.   How could he remain downcast when her eyes rested so tenderly on him? 'What does
it matter how poor our home,' they seemed to say, 'if it be

the home you have prepared for me!' and as he thought of
this pure love that was to bless his life, wealth and luxury
seemed to dwindle into nothingness before him; and he
bowed his head and said, 'Thank God!' again under his
breath.

After all, there was very little to do or say, though Mr.
Langley cleared his throat and seemed to make an unnecessarily long speech over everything.

Maurice spoke a few concise words first, explaining
everything. His sister had broken the condition of the
will, he said, in marrying Mr. Cuthbert Lyndhurst; she had
forfeited her claim to everything but a hundred a year.
'She is not married yet,' he added, turning with a smile to
the young people; 'indeed they have not been engaged
many hours, but all the same she felt bound to resign
Crome Park from the moment her decision was made.'

'Very right, very honourable indeed,' returned Mr. Langley, with a profound bow to the ci-devant heiress. He
thought her in his own mind an exceedingly foolish young
woman, but it was none of his business. 'Then we will
proceed to read the codicil, which is very brief;' and then
he cleared his throat again and began.

They were all a little curious, for they wondered what
hospitals Mrs. Reid would endow, etc.—would she sell
Crome, or turn it into some charitable institution? There
was dead silence, and only Bertie fidgeted a little; and
then a simultaneous murmur and buzz of astonishment.

'Oh no, you must be reading it wrongly!' cried Dollie,
jumping up from her seat with burning cheeks. 'He must
be wrong!' appealing to Grey with piteous looks of astonishment and dismay; 'it cannot be all mine.'

But it was. On the event of Mary's marriage with
Cuthbert Lyndhurst the estate was transferred wholly and
entirely to Dorothy Maynard and her heirs and assigns for
ever. The codicil was brief but decisive; Mary had
Dollie's hundred a year, and Dollie was mistress of
Crome!

'Miss Maynard, we congratulate you!' said Maurice
cheerfully. 'I am quite relieved to hear Crome is not to

be turned into a convalescent home. Mrs. Maynard, we must wish you joy too on your daughter's account.'

Mrs. Maynard clasped her hands, and looked at her child. 'Dollie, my dear!' she said timidly, and Dollie turned to her at once.

'Oh, mother, tell them not to do it. I will not rob Mary; what do Grey and I want with this great place when we have the cottage? Mary, you must have half; I am not going to take your place like this.'

But Mr. Langley interrupted her a little stiffly. 'The estate could not be divided,' he said; 'it was Miss St. John's own pleasure to deprive herself of it, and she had no one but herself to blame.'

'Certainly not. Mr. Langley is quite right,' put in Mary; 'I have done it all of my own accord, and you are heartily welcome to it, my dear!' and Mary gave Bertie a reassuring smile, which cheered him mightily.

'And I must keep it!' exclaimed Dollie quite piteously. 'Oh dear, oh dear, what a rich woman I shall be! Are you glad about it, Grey?' looking anxiously at him as he sat a little gloomily in his corner.

Now what ailed Grey that he scarcely looked up or answered her when the others gathered round Dollie, laughing with her and joking her on her fright at finding herself an heiress? and Mary kissing and comforting her with the assurance that she was so pleased, that she never had been more pleased in her life. Grey held aloof, and never came near her, though Dollie kept peeping at him over Mr. Langley's shoulder.

There was not much more business to transact. Mr. Langley put up his papers in his blue bag, and shook hands with them all in his dry formal way. Mr. St. John left the room with him, and Bertie and Mary followed them.

'Oh, Grey, what is the matter? Why won't you speak to me?' asked the poor little heiress when she was left alone with him and her mother.

'I want to speak to your mother first, Dollie,' he said, putting her aside somewhat unceremoniously, and going up to Mrs. Maynard. He looked pale and disturbed, and his mouth twitched nervously.

'Mrs. Maynard,' he said in a hard dry voice, 'your daughter is free. I could not think of holding her to an engagement under these altered circumstances. Dollie is rich, far too rich for a briefless barrister. She is so young too. It would not be honourable. She could marry a nobleman.'

'My dear Grey,' faltered Mrs. Maynard in a grieved voice, for she loved him as a son, and this was utterly unexpected; but Dollie suddenly interposed.

'Why do you address yourself to my mother? why do you not speak to me?' she said in her clear young voice, and Grey turned and looked at her sadly. 'I am not a child that you and my mother should settle everything between you.'

'Very well, Dollie, I will speak to you if you will. I am giving you back your liberty, dear!'

'And why?' she asked still more shrilly, and then she stamped her foot, and her face grew crimson. 'Oh, you coward,' she said, and when she had launched that fiery arrow at him she turned her back upon him and burst into tears.

Of course he followed her.

'You must not call me that,' he said gently; 'it is hardly a coward's action to give you up, Dollie,' and then his face grew white.

'I call you a coward,' she sobbed, 'because you are afraid of being rich, because you—a great strong man—want to leave a poor little thing like me to bear the whole burden alone. Oh, Grey, how can you be so cruel?' and then she peeped between her wet fingers, and saw his face looking quite fixed and pale.

'I won't be free!' she said, suddenly changing her mood, and flinging her arms round him. 'You have got to take me, Grey, and all the money beside;' and then she laughed and stroked his sleeves. 'Never mind about the cottage. I daresay it would have been damp, and I am sure I heard mice scampering behind the wainscot. We shall be just as happy here.'

How could he put her away when she was nestling up to him and cooing in his ear like a happy little dove? and there was her mother looking benignly at them both.

'If I have got to take you, I suppose I must,' he said. 'Oh, Dollie, my darling, how happy you have made me !' he added a moment afterwards. Happy!—he was absurdly, childishly happy. Dollie made him ask her pardon for daring to think of such cruelty as to give her up, and then she was very penitent because she had been cross with him, and she said so many nice things to him, and he had so much to say in return that it was nearly luncheon-time before the reconciliation was quite complete.

Thereafter, when Grey was in a mischievous mood, and wanted to tease his wife, he always declared Dollie had proposed to him. 'Nothing of the kind,' Dollie would answer with a toss of her little head, 'but I was not going to be thrown aside in that unceremonious fashion ;' but she always added in a contrite tone, 'But I ought not to have called you a coward, Grey.'

CHAPTER XLVI

AND so the golden ball had rolled to Dorothy Maynard's feet.

The little Cinderella of Abercrombie Road was transformed into the young Princess. The fairy godmother had come to her in the guise of a smiling young woman who pressed upon her the pumpkin coach and rich apparel, and all the good things of this life, literally forcing them into her unwilling hands.

Of course Princess Dorothy was dazed at first ; but not overmuch—she was too wise and loving a little soul for that.

When the first shock of her surprise was over it was wonderful how little she cared about it all. Grey was her one thought. If Grey were pleased everything was right.

As for Grey, when his brief sulkiness vanished—melted utterly by Dollie's sweetness — he soon found himself master of the whole situation.

The mother and daughter were utterly dependent on him. Dollie seemed to have no ideas of her own by the way she referred everything to Grey's judgment.

' I think we must do so and so. I think it will be right to follow out such and such a course,' Grey would say. Dollie acquiesced as a matter of course. Grey was master of Crome long before he married Dollie. His hand moved the secret springs that guided the whole household. As for Mary, she turned mischievous and provoking from the moment of her abdication. ' Why do you ask me ?

Go to Miss Maynard; she is the mistress here,' she would say to the bewildered servants; and then her laughing eyes sought Bertie. No one would give an order. Dollie was far too absent to think of such a thing. It was Grey to whom Pratt finally brought his grievances, and from whom he derived the strongest consolation.

'Things will go more smoothly after October,' Grey would say, stroking his dark moustache complacently. 'Just at present things are a little at sixes and sevens, but they will right themselves after a time.'

'We shall be all the better when we have got a master as well as a mistress,' observed Pratt to his wife, for he had a great respect for Mr. Lyndhurst's judgment. 'And what can you expect from a parcel of girls but fair words and chancey ways,' as he often observed.

Mr. St. John was also pleased with Grey's quiet tact and management. There was a soberness and gravity about him that he thought very suitable in his position.

One evening Grey had come up to the Rectory, and Bertie was with him.

Maurice had been talking over the conditions of the will.

'Do you think Mrs. Reid had any suspicion of your liking for Miss Maynard?' he asked, with an inquisitive glance at the young man.

Grey coloured a little, but he answered frankly—

'I cannot help thinking in my own mind that she was perfectly cognisant of it from the beginning. She was very shrewd and observant—wonderfully so. I saw her eyes on us once when I was looking at Dollie. It was love at first sight, you know,' continued Grey, with a conscious laugh. 'Under these circumstances a man is not always master of his own looks.'

'Certainly not,' returned Maurice, with a smile; 'and I am of your opinion that she foresaw exactly how things would end. If she could not secure the mistress she wanted for Crome she was determined to have a master to her liking. After all, things have turned out for the best.

Miss Maynard will enjoy her position far.more than Mary, who was never cut out for a fine lady.'

'I am glad you think so,' observed Grey. He quite agreed with Mr. St. John in this. Bertie looked up, but said nothing. He was writing invisible Maries on the table-cloth, and did not seem to take much interest in the conversation.

'The worst part of it seems to me,' continued Maurice after a pause, 'that you are obliged to give up your pro-fession; that is always a disappointment to a man.'

'I felt it so at first,' answered Grey candidly. 'To tell you the truth, I rebelled for a time at the thought of living on my wife's money, but Dollie and I have talked it over. You see the will makes it a condition that she should reside the greater part of the year at Crome. I could hardly live in London and my wife here—the idea would be pre-posterous; and the distance is too great for me to spend a few hours in town daily.'

'Oh, of course, that is not to be thought of for a moment.'

'I think I must try my hand at farming instead. There are two farms vacant, so Mary informed me some time ago.'

'Two? I only know of Highlands. Mary has been trying to find a tenant for it ever since we came here in June.'

'Well, I am thinking of taking that into my own management; Dollie wants me to try. And then there is Annerley, which is twice its size. Poor Mr. Greaves is dead—you knew that surely?'

'Well, now I do remember Colonel Fullerton speaking about Annerley, and saying it would soon be in the market as poor Greaves was dead. He was a bachelor. Yes, I remember all about it now. It is a splendid farm—the land well drained and in good condition, capital stock, and all the latest improvements. There will be quite a competition for it. Why don't you take it into your own hands, Grey?'

'Because Dollie and I think we have found a better

tenant,' returned Grey with a sudden meaning glance at
Maurice.

And then he said to his brother suddenly, 'Bertie, do
you think you can ride over with me before breakfast to-
morrow to Annerley.   I have promised Dollie that we will
look at the house.'

'All right, old fellow,' returned Bertie lazily, not looking
up from his invisible hieroglyphics.   He was bored and
just a trifle sad.   Here was Grey talking about farms, and
making plans for leading the life of a country squire ; while
Bertie was wondering how he could turn his few talents to
account to increase his slender income.

That night as Mary sat quietly enjoying her thoughts in
the moonlight she heard a light tap at her door, and Dollie
came stealing in like a little white ghost.

' My dear Dollie, I thought you were asleep hours ago.'

' Nonsense,' pouted Dollie, ' why should I not be as wide-
awake as other people ? ' and then she continued coaxingly,
' Mary, I do want to speak to you, and I never get a word
with you now—Bertie monopolises you so.'

' Not more than Grey monopolises you,' returned Mary,
smiling.

' Oh, but we have so much to settle,' observed Dollie
rather consequentially.   ' Do you know what we have been
planning to-day ?—that Bertie should have Annerley, and
then there will be no need for you to go and live in pokey
lodgings in London.'

' Bertie have Annerley ! ' and Mary clasped her hands ;
she had never thought of such a thing.

' Well, why not ? ' demanded Dollie in the most matter-
of-fact way. 'Why should we not have him for our tenant if
we like—my husband's brother ? ' and here Dollie blushed
a little in the darkness. ' Grey says he is sure he will make
a capital farmer, he is so fond of an out-of-door life.   As it
is, he and Ralph are always riding about with Sir Charles,
going over his farms and visiting his tenants.   Bertie has
picked up a good deal of knowledge in that way, and if he
only manages to secure a good bailiff, and to work a little
hard at first, Grey thinks he would do very well.'

'It is very kind and thoughtful of Grey,' returned Mary gratefully; and then she went on more eagerly, 'I should be close to Brotherton if we lived at Annerley, and I should not have to leave Maurice and Janet. And oh, Dollie, I did so dread a London life for Bertie. He has always been accustomed to the country, and he would have felt so cooped up and miserable in lodgings.'

'Yes, and the house at Annerley is so nice—at least Diana says so. Grey has not seen it yet; the rooms are low, but so old-fashioned and comfortable : and there is a dear old garden with a yew-tree walk and——'

'Oh, it is too much, too much!' exclaimed Mary in an agitated voice; 'to be near you all, to get rid of this great place, and to have a home like that for myself and Bertie, not to leave poor Brotherton or Maurice;' and then she stopped and said humbly, 'Oh, how good God has been to us all, to you and to me, and to Grey and Bertie!'

'Yes, indeed,' sighed Dollie; and then for a little while the two girls clung together in a silence that said more than words.

The next morning when breakfast was nearly over, the young men came into the room, splashed with their ride— for it was raining heavily—but looking flushed and excited.

Bertie took no notice of his young hostess; he went round to Mary in his impulsive boyish way and seized her hands.

'Oh, Mary, have you heard? Grey says we are to have Annerley; we can be married in October now!' and Bertie's gray eyes were flashing with joy.

'My dear Bertie,' she remonstrated, trying to liberate herself; but Dollie came to her relief by saying in her demure voice—

'So you approve, Bertie? you have consented to be our tenant?' for Dollie always said 'our,' as though Crome belonged to Grey already.

Whereupon Bertie bethought himself of his manners, and this time Dollie's little hands were in the grip of this very unceremonious young man.

'Oh, what a brick Grey was to think of it! and how

good of you, Hebe!' for he always called her Hebe.
'How am I to thank you both?' and Bertie looked so
dangerously demonstrative, that Dollie felt inclined to run
away.

'Nay, it is Dollie who is the fairy godmother,' put in
Grey; 'I am only her humble servant and mouthpiece at
present! There, come and eat your breakfast, my dear
fellow, and if the rain clears, we will drive out the ladies to
have a look at the house.'

The rain did clear, and Mary made a delighted inspection of her future home. Bertie conducted her proudly
through all the rooms, while Grey and Dollie lingered in
the rose-covered porch. It was just what Diana had
described it—a comfortable old-fashioned house with plenty
of low spacious rooms opening out of each other; and a
long sloping garden with a lawn and mulberry-tree, and
long yew-tree walk, shutting out the farm building; but the
garden itself led into an orchard, and beyond that were the
green meadows reaching to Brotherton.

'Oh, Bertie, what a dear home! what a lovely home!'
whispered Mary, when they had completed their inspection.

'And you will like being a farmer's wife?' he asked with
mischievous eyes.

'Like it? oh, it is too much happiness, living here and
being near Maurice!' she answered in a voice that sobered
him, for he said very quietly—

'I mean to make you happy, dear, if working hard and
loving you will do it;' and Mary's smile was sufficient
answer.

Oh, what days those were that followed! Grey had gone
back to London to wind up his affairs, and came down
from Saturday to Monday to report progress and look
after Dollie; and Bertie had taken up his abode at the
'Rising Sun,' and had already become a favourite of Mrs.
Piper's.

Dollie was justifying her name of the fairy godmother.
With her mother and Mrs. St. John's help, she was furnishing Annerley from top to bottom; nay, more, she had
silenced all Mary's remonstrances in another matter. Her

own trousseau, a very gorgeous affair, was supplemented by another as tasteful, though not so costly.

Mary hesitated a little over these lavish gifts, but her good sense and a certain innate generosity overcame her reluctance, and prevented Dollie's feelings from being wounded.

'If I were in her place I should do just the same,' she thought; and she put aside her own scruples, and praised and admired everything to Dollie's infinite content; she even accepted a few simple ornaments that Dollie had put aside for her out of the discarded jewels. It was not that she cared for them for her own sake, but Dollie would be pleased, and Bertie, she knew, loved all such adornments.

Mary was too much in love not to lay aside her own Quaker taste to please Bertie. All her dresses were chosen with reference to his taste; and as he preferred dark rich colours, Mary soon found herself transformed into a very stately-looking dame, with dainty lace ruffles and little finishes that it would never have entered into the mind of Mary St. John to provide for herself.

Oh, what exquisite days they spent! while Dollie was up at Crome, writing to Grey, or busy with all sorts of affairs; while Bertie was nailing up the creeper, and Mary beside him budding roses, or watering her flower-border in the pleasant old garden at Annerley; how Bertie whistled like a blackbird as he fixed up bookshelves in the empty rooms, or daubed himself and Mary with whitewash.

'This is what I call jolly!' he would say, stretching his long arms when he was tired of hammering or pasting. 'I like to think I have put in the first nails; now old Hargraves may do the rest;' for Hargraves was the name of the upholsterer at Canterton to whom Dollie had given the order for furnishing Annerley.

'It looks very nice,' Mary would say, looking up admiringly at Bertie's handiwork. How clever he was, how capable! those big brown hands of his were as deft as a woman's!

'Oh, it is only pretty well,' Bertie would answer disparagingly; 'but it will be nice for you, Mary, to have an

odd man always on the spot;' and then he whistled a few
more bars.

'Oh, by the by, Ralph will be down this evening. That
was a kind thought of Mrs. Hebe, asking them all down to
the wedding. Lady Emily is so pleased.'

'Dear Dollie, she thinks of everybody!' returned Mary in
a low voice. It was only a week to the wedding—the double
wedding. This time next week she would be Bertie's wife.

'I know what you are thinking about,' observed Bertie,
suddenly looking down on her from his long ladder.
'There, I have done enough work now; we will go and
rest in the porch,' and he jumped lightly down to the
ground, and drew her arm through his.

Grey joined his brother at the 'Rising Sun' before many
days were over. The place was quite in a commotion with
the grand event of the double wedding. Diana and Mabel
Ducie and Lettice and Colonel Fullerton's little grand-
daughter Rose were to be the only bridesmaids.

. Dollie had decided that she and Mary were to be dressed
alike. She would not have a fold or flower different, and
Mary yielded to avoid argument; she only stipulated that
her travelling-dress should be dark tweed of a certain colour
that Bertie liked. They were going into Devonshire for a
fortnight while the furniture was placed in Annerley, and
then Bertie would enter upon his duties, with Mr. Greaves's
old foreman to help him.

It was the evening before the wedding. Bertie and
Mary had walked down to Annerley for the last time, and
Lettice and Ralph were with them.

Grey and Dollie had betaken themselves as usual to
the 'peacocks' promenade,' and there they had sat for a
long time looking at the mossy old sun-dial, with Topaz
perched on the top, and Sapphire strutting before them.

'"I watch the hands of Time!" do you remember that
evening, Dollie?'

'Oh yes! and how wretched I felt, and then you came
and found me crying; how happily it has all ended, Grey!
I really do believe Mary loves Annerley twice as much
already as she does Crome.'

'Mary would never have cared for this place as you do,' he replied. 'At the risk of making you vain I must own you will make a much better mistress of Crome than she. I have watched you, Dollie—often when you did not know I was near—and I thought I had never seen a more bewitching little hostess.'

'Did you really, Grey?' cried Dollie, with her eyes sparkling. 'Oh, I am so glad,' with a happy laugh. This was what she wanted—to please and satisfy him in everything; not to be a silly little thing, childish, incapable, and full of whimseys, but a useful loving woman, worthy of being Grey's wife.

Grey's temperate praise would have been largely annotated by others who knew Dollie. Already the neighbourhood was divided on the merits of the two ladies of Crome. A few of the more sober-minded among them—the Vendales and Fullertons, for example, and Emma Ducie—remained loyal to Mary, but the majority were in Dollie's favour.

She was not pretty. No one except Grey ever called her so, but she was so bright, piquante, and taking, she had such winning manners, and with all her animation she had a stateliness in which Mary was wholly deficient. Grey used to call her his little queen in the first days of their married life.

But sweet as Dorothy Maynard could be, Dorothy Lyndhurst was infinitely sweeter, when she laid aside with her girlhood all the whims and caprices that hedged her in like a prickly little wild rose, when love taught her wisdom, and she blossomed into a gracious large-hearted woman, who was her husband's best friend and counsellor.

But Grey's praise was delightful in the ears of the little bride-elect; and meanwhile Bertie was saying to Mary in the old rose-covered porch at Annerley—

'To-morrow at this time we shall be miles away, you and I.'

'Yes,' returned Mary simply, 'but we shall carry the thought of our home with us, just as it looks to-night;' and she looked away dreamily over the meadows where

some red cattle were grouped under the low alders, and
behind which the sun was setting for the last time before
her wedding-day.   Mary's face was grave and peaceful, but
Bertie's gray eyes had an unwonted gleam in them.

'Yes,' he replied eagerly, 'and we shall see ourselves
sitting in the porch hand-in-hand as we are doing now;
and there is the white gate towards which I shall ride on
my fine new horse—oh, how good it was of Sir Charles to
give it to me!—evening after evening, and you will be
there in your broad-brimmed straw hat to open it for me
and to pet Ruby; and Ruby will get sugar; and what shall
I get, Mary?' and as she blushed and smiled a glow of
feeling crossed his face, and he looked at the setting sun,
and at the quiet figure beside him.   'To-morrow,' he said
softly, 'we begin our new life together.'   And then he held
out his hand to her, 'Come, Mary,' he said, 'Ralph and
Lettice will be tired of waiting for us,' and then they went
down the garden-path and out into the dewy meadows.

Years rolled on over Crome and Annerley, and over the
Rectory where Maurice and Janet still lived.

Mrs. Champneys had died, and her husband had never
returned to take up his delegated duties.   Maurice remained curate in charge for several years until the old
Rector died, and the Bishop offered him the living.

Mr. St. John had long been known for a zealous hard-
working clergyman.   Brotherton was a model village now,
and had its schools and its chapel of ease where Maurice
preached and ministered, and Josiah Culpepper had only
one follower—a deaf old woman, who protested she could
hear him better than 't'otherer parson, for Josiah's a
rare screamer, and powerful mighty preacher, with a deal of
voice and understanding in him,' as old Sallie Hodges
would say.

Maurice found plenty of work with his outlying villages,
and he was well content to spend his life within sight of
his children's graves.   He knew it would have broken
Janet's heart to leave them.   Janet was his helpmate now—
not even Mary was more zealous or hardworking than she.

A great joy had come to Janet. A year after Bee's death she had laid a boy — the much-coveted son — in Maurice's arms.

'Take him,' she whispered. 'This must be our Samuel — our thank-offering,' and Maurice understood her.

They called him Stephen at his baptism. 'For,' said Maurice, as he saw his wife's happy tears fall on the infant's face, 'I trust he will be another Stephen in faith and good works.'

And by and by they had a second son, whom Maurice called Edgar, after a young brother of his who had died.

Janet's health failed somewhat after little Edgar's birth; but for some years she did not become a permanent invalid. As the lads grew into fine handsome fellows — their father's delight and pride — her strength waned, and her sufferings became more severe.

But no one heard a complaint from her lips, not even her husband, who often marvelled over her exceeding patience; but it was only Lettice who really guessed what she endured.

Lettice never married, though she grew into a fair sweet-looking woman. First her father and brothers needed her, and then her ailing mother, and somehow Lettice never thought of herself.

'Father will want me more by and by,' she used to say to herself, for Stephen says he will be a missionary, and there is no knowing what Edgar will do, and poor mother —— ' but here Lettice stopped and sighed.

'Maurice, do you remember what you asked me once,' Janet said to him one evening when he had come in to sit beside her — 'before Steevie was born, if I could be patient and wait a little before I went to the children? I do not think I shall have to wait long now.'

No, he knew that, he told her. The time must soon come when they must be parted, but not for long, oh, not for long. For he knew — this gray-haired priest — that his work had been heavy, and had worn him as though by the weight of years. He had toiled early and late in His Master's vineyard, and the summons to come home, and

rest might be near at any time.   What matter how soon,
he thought.   His day was ending; the night with its
welcome repose would shortly come.   One day upon the
golden harvest-floor the weary servant would come rejoicing,
bringing his sheaves with him.

THE END

J. D. & Co.

Printed by R. & R. CLARK, *Edinburgh.*